"You're a lawyer, huh?" asked the small-town police chief.

"Well, Counselor, whose battle are you here to win?"

Anne's mouth tightened. But then, one hardly expected the police to look kindly on defense attorneys. And most times the feeling was mutual.

"I'm representing myself." She glanced down at eight-month-old Emilie, who banged her rattle on the stroller tray. "And my daughter. I'm here because…" How could she say this?

She forced the words out. "Because I believe you are Emilie's biological father."

Chief Mitch Donovan stared at her, shifted the stare to the baby, then back to her. If his eyes had softened slightly before, when they assessed Emilie, that softness turned to granite now when his gaze met hers.

"Lady, you're joking. I've never seen you before in my life."

A FATHER IN THE MAKING

Marta Perry

&

Deb Kastner

Previously published as *Desperately Seeking Dad*
and *The Marine's Baby*

H HARLEQUIN SUMMER READS

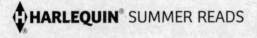 **HARLEQUIN®** SUMMER READS

ISBN-13: 978-1-335-45517-8

A Father in the Making

Copyright © 2021 by Harlequin Books S.A.

Recycling programs for this product may not exist in your area.

Desperately Seeking Dad
First published in 2000. This edition published in 2021.
Copyright © 2000 by Martha Johnson

The Marine's Baby
First published in 2010. This edition published in 2021.
Copyright © 2010 by Debra Kastner

This edition published by arrangement with Harlequin Books S.A.

For questions and comments about the quality of this book, please contact us at CustomerService@Harlequin.com.

Harlequin Enterprises ULC
22 Adelaide St. West, 40th Floor
Toronto, Ontario M5H 4E3, Canada
www.Harlequin.com

Printed in U.S.A.

CONTENTS

A lifetime spent in rural Pennsylvania and her Pennsylvania Dutch heritage led **Marta Perry** to write about the Plain People who add so much richness to her home state. Marta has seen over seventy of her books published, with over seven million books in print. She and her husband live in a beautiful central Pennsylvania valley noted for its farms and orchards. When she's not writing, she's reading, traveling, baking or enjoying her six beautiful grandchildren.

Books by Marta Perry

Brides of Lost Creek

Second Chance Amish Bride
The Wedding Quilt Bride
The Promised Amish Bride
The Amish Widow's Heart
A Secret Amish Crush

An Amish Family Christmas
"Heart of Christmas"
Amish Christmas Blessings
"The Midwife's Christmas Surprise"

Visit the Author Profile page at
Harlequin.com for more titles.

DESPERATELY SEEKING DAD

Marta Perry

In loving memory of my parents-in-law, Harry and Greta Johnson.

And, as always, for Brian.

Trust in the Lord with all your heart and lean not on your own understanding; in all your ways acknowledge Him, and He will direct your paths.

—*Proverbs* 3:5–6

Chapter 1

"I believe you're my baby's father." Anne Morden tried saying it aloud as she drove down the winding street of the small mountain town. The words sounded just as bad as she'd thought they would. There was absolutely no good way to announce a fact like that to a man she'd never met.

In her mind and heart, Emilie was already her child, even though the adoption wasn't yet final—even though the father hadn't yet relinquished his rights.

He would. Fear closed around her heart. He had to. Because if he didn't, she might lose the baby she loved as her own.

The soft sound of a rattle drew her gaze to the rear-view mirror. Emilie, safe in her car seat, shook the pink plastic lamb with one chubby fist, then stuck it in her mouth. At eight months, Emilie put everything in her mouth.

"It'll be all right, sweetheart. I promise."

Emilie's round blue eyes got a little rounder, and her face crinkled into a smile at the sound of Anne's voice… the voice of the only mother the baby had ever known.

Fear prickled along her nerves. She had to protect Emilie, had to make sure the adoption went through as planned so the baby would truly be hers. And confronting the man she believed to be Emilie's biological father was the only way to do that. But where were the right words?

Anne spotted the faded red brick building ahead on the right, its black-and-white sign identifying it as the police station. Her heart clenched. She'd face Police Chief Mitch Donovan in a matter of minutes, and she still didn't know what she'd say.

Help me, Father. Please. For Emilie's sake, let me find a way to do this.

A parking spot waited for her in front of the station. She couldn't drive around for a few more minutes. Now, before she lost her nerve, she had to go inside, confront the man, and get his signature on a parental rights termination.

For Emilie. Emilie was her child, and nobody, including the unknown Mitch Donovan, was going to take her away.

Parking the car, getting the stroller out, buttoning Emilie's jacket against the cool, sunny March day— none of that took long enough. With another silent, incoherent prayer, Anne pulled open the door and pushed the stroller inside.

Bedford Creek didn't boast much in the way of a

police station—just a row of chairs, a crowded bulletin board and one desk. A small town like this, tucked safely away in the Pennsylvania mountains, probably didn't need more. She'd driven only three hours from Philadelphia, but Bedford Creek seemed light-years from the city, trapped in its isolated valley.

"Help you?" The woman behind the desk had dangling earrings that jangled as she spun toward Anne. Her penciled eyebrows shot upward, as if she were expecting an emergency.

"I'd like to see Chief Donovan, please." Her voice didn't betray her nervousness, at least she didn't think so.

That was one of the first things she'd learned as an attorney—never let her apprehension show, not if she wanted to win. And this was far more important than any case she'd ever defended.

The woman studied her for a moment, then nodded. "Chief!" she shouted. "Somebody to see you!"

Apparently the police station didn't rely on such high-tech devices as phones. The door to the inner office started to move. Anne braced herself. In a moment she'd—

The street door flew open, hitting the wall. An elderly man surged in from outside, white hair standing on end as if he'd just run his fingers through it. He was breathing hard, and his face was an alarming shade of red. He propelled a dirty-faced boy into the room with a hand on the child's jacket collar.

The man emerging from the chief's office sent her a quick look, seemed to decide her business wasn't urgent, and focused on the pair who'd stormed in.

"Warren, what's going on?" His voice was a baritone rumble, filled with authority.

"This kid." The man shook the boy by his collar. "I caught him stealing from me again, Chief. Not one measly candy bar, no. He had a whole fist full of them."

Maybe she'd been wrong about the amount of crime in Bedford Creek. She was going to see Mitch Donovan in action before she even confronted him.

She looked at him, assessing the opposition as she would in a courtroom. Big, that was her first thought. The police uniform strained across broad shoulders. He had to be over six feet tall, with not an ounce of fat on him. If she'd expected the stereotypical small-town cop with his stomach hanging over his belt, she was wrong.

"So you decided to perform a citizen's arrest, did you, Warren?" The chief concentrated on the mismatched pair.

She couldn't tell whether or not amusement lurked in his dark-brown eyes. He had the kind of strong, impassive face that didn't give much away.

"Not so old, after all, am I?" The elderly man gave his captive another little shake. "I caught you, all right."

"Take it easy." Donovan pulled the boy away. "You'll rattle the kid's brains."

The boy glared at the cop defiantly, eyes dark as two pieces of anthracite in his thin face, black hair that needed a trim falling on his forehead. He couldn't be more than ten or eleven, and he didn't appear to be easily intimidated. She wasn't sure she could have mustered a look like that—not with more than six feet of muscle looming over her.

"Okay, Davey, what's the story? You steal from Mr. Van Dyke?" His tone said there wasn't much doubt in his mind.

"Not me. Must have been somebody else."

The boy would have been better off to curb his smart remarks, but she'd defended enough juveniles to know he probably wouldn't.

"Empty your pockets," Donovan barked.

Davey held the defiant pose for another moment. Then he shrugged, reached into his jacket pockets and pulled them inside out. Five candy bars tumbled to the floor.

"You know what that is, kid? That's evidence."

"It's just a couple lousy candy bars."

"And I've got a couple lousy cells in the back. You want to see inside one of them?"

The kid wilted. "I don't…"

"Excuse me." Little as she wanted to become involved in this, she couldn't let it pass without saying something. Her training wouldn't let her. "The child's a minor. You shouldn't even be talking to him without a parent or legal representation here."

His piercing gaze focused on her, and she had to stiffen her spine to keep from wilting herself.

"That right, Counselor?"

He was quicker than she might have expected, realizing from those few words that she was an attorney.

"That's right." She glared at him, but the look seemed to have as much impact as a flake of snow on a boulder.

"If she says—" Davey caught on fast.

"Forget it." Donovan planted his forefinger against the boy's chest. "You're dealing with me, and if I hear another complaint against you, you'll wish you'd never been born. Stay out of Mr. Van Dyke's store until he tells you otherwise." He gestured toward the door. "Now get out."

The boy blinked. His first two steps were a swagger. Then he broke and ran, the door slamming behind him as he pelted up the sidewalk.

Anne took a breath and tried to force taut muscles to relax. At least now she didn't have to deal with Donovan over his treatment of the boy. Her own business with him was difficult enough.

The elderly man gathered the candy bars from the floor, grumbling a little. "Kids. At least when you were his age, you only tried it once."

A muscle twitched in Donovan's jaw. Maybe he'd rather not have heard his juvenile crime mentioned, at least not with her standing there.

"You tripped me with a broom before I got to the door, as I recall. You slowing down, Warren?"

The old man shrugged. "Still give a kid a run for his money, I guess." He shoved the candy bars into his pockets. "I'm going to the café for a cup of coffee, now that I've done your work for you." He waved toward the dispatcher, then strolled out.

Donovan turned, studying her for a long, uncomfortable moment. Her cheeks warmed under his scrutiny. He gestured toward his office. "Come in, Counselor, and tell me what I can do for you."

This was it, then. She pushed the stroller through the door, heart thumping. This was it.

The swivel chair creaked as he sat down and waved her to the visitor's seat. Behind the battered oak desk, an American flag dwarfed the spare, small office. Some sort of military crest hung next to it. Donovan was ex-military, of course. Anne might have guessed it from his manner.

Maybe she should have remained standing. She always thought better on her feet, and she was going to need every edge she could get, dealing with this guy.

Anne leaned back, trying for a confidence she didn't feel, and resisted the urge to clench her hands. *Be calm, be poised. Check out the opposition, then act.*

Mitch Donovan had that look she always thought of as the "cop look"—wary, tough, alert. Probably even in repose his stony face wouldn't relax. He could as easily be an Old West gunfighter, sitting with his back to the wall, ready to fly into action at the slightest provocation.

She took a deep breath. He was waiting for her to begin, but not the slightest movement of a muscle in his impassive face betrayed any hint of impatience. This was probably a man who'd buried his emotions so deep that a dynamite blast wouldn't make them surface.

"I realize I have no standing here, Chief Donovan, but you shouldn't have questioned the child without his parents." That wasn't what she'd intended to say, but it spilled out more easily than her real concern.

"I wasn't questioning, Counselor. I was intimidating." His lips quirked a little. "Who knows if it'll do any good."

"Intimidating." There were a lot of things she could say to that, including the fact that he certainly was. "Please don't call me 'Counselor.'"

His brows lifted a fraction. "But I don't know your name."

Intimidating, indeed. She was handling this worse than an Assistant District Attorney newly hatched from law school.

"Anne Morden. I used to be with the Public Defender's Office in Philadelphia." She could hardly avoid identifying herself, but some instinct made her want to keep him from knowing where to find her—to find Emilie.

He nodded, but his face gave no clue as to his thoughts. Strength showed in the straight planes and square chin. His hair, worn in an aggressively military cut, was as dark as those chocolate eyes. Even the blue police uniform looked military on him, all sharp creases and crisp lines.

"A Philadelphia lawyer. Around here they say if you want to win, you hire a Philadelphia lawyer." His gaze seemed to sharpen. "So whose battle are you here to win, Ms. Morden? Not Davey Flagler's."

"Davey? No." The boy had been only a preliminary skirmish; they both knew it. For an instant she was tempted to say she represented someone else, but knew that would never work. The plain truth was her only weapon.

"Well, Counselor?"

Her mouth tightened at the implied insult in his use of the title. But one hardly expected police to look kindly on defense attorneys—and most times the feeling was mutual.

"I'm not representing anyone but myself." She glanced down at Emilie, who banged her rattle on the stroller tray. "And my daughter. I'm here because—" The words stuck in her throat. How could she say this? But she had to.

With a sense that she'd passed the point of no return, she forced the words out. "Because I believe you are Emilie's biological father."

Impassive or not, there was no mistaking the expression that crossed his face as her words penetrated— sheer stupefaction.

Donovan stared at her, shifted the stare to the baby, then back to her. If his eyes had softened slightly when they assessed Emilie, that softness turned to granite when his gaze met hers.

"Lady, you're plain crazy. I've never seen you before in my life."

For an instant Anne was speechless. Then she felt her cheeks color. He thought she meant they...

"No! I mean, I know you haven't." She took a deep breath, willing herself to be calm. If she behaved this way in court, all her clients would be in prison.

His eyes narrowed, fine lines fanning out from them. "Then what do you mean?" The question shot across the desk, and his very stillness spoke of anger raging underneath iron control.

"Emilie..."

As if hearing her name, Emilie chose that moment to burst into wails. She stiffened, thrusting herself backward in the stroller.

Anne bent over her. "Hush, sweetheart." She lifted the baby, standing to hold her on one hip. "There, it's all right." She bounced her gently. "Don't cry."

The wail turned to a whimper, and Anne dropped a kiss on Emilie's fine, silky hair. Maybe she shouldn't have brought the baby with her, but she couldn't bear the thought of being away from her in this crisis.

The whimpers eased, and Emilie thrust her fingers into her mouth. Anne looked at the man on the other side of the desk, searching vainly for any resemblance to her daughter.

"I didn't put that well." She cradled the baby against her. "I'm not Emilie's birth mother. I'm her foster mother. I'm trying to adopt her."

Donovan shot out of the chair, as if he couldn't be still any longer. He leaned forward, hands planted on the desk.

"Why did you come in here with an accusation like that? What proof do you have?"

"I have the birth mother's statement."

That had to rock him, yet his expression didn't change. "Where is she? Let her make her accusations to my face."

"She can't." Anne's arms tightened protectively around the baby, knowing this was the weakest link in her case, the point at which she was most vulnerable. And Donovan was definitely a man who'd zero in on any vulnerability. "She's dead."

Mitch stared at the woman for a long moment, anger simmering behind the impassive mask he kept in place by sheer force of will. What game was this woman playing? Was this some kind of setup?

"What do you want?"

The abrupt question seemed to throw her. She cradled the baby against her body as if she needed to protect it.

From him. The realization pierced his anger. Protecting was his job, had been since the moment he put on a shield. Assist, protect, defend—the military police code. Nobody needed protecting from him, not unless they'd broken the law.

"You admit it, then? That you're Emilie's father?"

He leaned toward her, resisting the urge to charge around the desk. It was better, much better, to keep the barricade be- tween them.

"I'm not admitting a thing. I want to know what brought you here. Or who."

Something that might have been hope died in her deep-blue eyes. "I told you. The baby's mother said you were the father."

"You also told me she's dead. That makes it pretty convenient to come here with this trumped-up claim."

"Trumped up?" Anger crackled around her. "I certainly didn't make this up. Why would I?"

"You tell me." It was astonishing that his voice was so calm, given the way his mind darted this way and that, trying to make sense of this.

One thing he was sure of—the baby wasn't his. His jaw tightened until it felt about to break. He'd decided a long time ago he wasn't cut out for fatherhood, and he didn't take chances.

"That's ridiculous." Even her hair seemed to spark with anger, as if touching it might shock him. "I came here because I know you're Emilie's father."

His life practically flashed before his eyes as she repeated those words. Everything he'd worked for, the respect he'd enjoyed in the two years since his return—all of it would vanish when her accusation exploded. If the story got out, it wouldn't matter that it wasn't true. By the time it had spread up one side of Main Street and down the other, all the denials in the world wouldn't make it go away.

Those Donovans have always been trouble, that's what people would say. *The apple doesn't fall far from the tree.*

"You're wrong," he said flatly. "I don't know who that child's parents are, but you're not going to get anything out of claiming I'm her father except to cause me a lot of grief."

The idea startled her—he could see it in her eyes.

"I didn't come here to create a scandal." She stroked the baby's back, her mouth suddenly vulnerable as she looked at the child.

"Good." He almost believed she meant it, and the thought cut through his anger to some rational part of his mind. He had to start thinking, not reacting. He went around the desk and leaned against it, trying for an ease he didn't feel. "Then why did you come?"

She thought he was capitulating, he could tell. A smile lit her face that almost took his breath away. A man would do a lot for a smile like that.

"All I want is your signature on a parental rights termination so the adoption can go through. Once I have that, Emilie and I will walk out of your life for good."

"That's all?"

She nodded. "You'll never see us again."

"And if I don't sign?"

Her arms tightened around the baby. "I've taken care of Emilie since the day she was born. Her mother wanted me to adopt her. Why would you want to stand in the way?"

They were right where they'd started, and she wouldn't like his answer.

"I don't." He leaned forward, bridged the gap between them and touched the baby's cheek. It earned him a smile. "She's a cute kid. But she's not mine."

She turned away abruptly, bending to slide the baby into the stroller. Emilie fussed for an instant, until Anne put a stuffed toy in front of her.

When she straightened, her eyes were chips of blue ice. "I'm not trying to trap you into anything."

"I'd like to believe that, but it doesn't change anything. I'm still not her father."

She gave an impatient shrug. "I've told you the mother named you."

"You haven't even told me who she is. Or how you fit into this story." He was finally starting to think like a cop. It was about time. "Look." He tried to find the words that would gain him some cooperation. "I believe I'm not this child's father. You believe I am. Seems to me, two reasonable adults can sit down and get everything out in the open. How do you expect me to react when an accusation like this comes out of nowhere?"

He could see her assess his words from every angle.

"All right," she said finally. "You know what my interest is. I want to adopt Emilie."

There had to be a lot more to the story than that, but he'd settle for the bare bones at the moment. "And the mother? Who was she? What happened to her?"

He gripped the edge of the desk behind him. He probably shouldn't fire questions at her, but he couldn't help it.

She frowned. Maybe she was editing her words. "Her mother's name was Tina Mallory. Now do you remember her?"

The name landed unpleasantly between them. *Tina Mallory.* He wanted to be able to say he'd never heard of her, but he couldn't, because the name echoed with some faint familiarity. He'd heard it before, but where? And how much of his sense of recognition did Anne Morden guess?

"How am I supposed to have known her?"

"She lived here in Bedford Creek at one time."

In Bedford Creek. If she'd lived here, why didn't he remember her? "I'm afraid it still doesn't ring any bells."

That was only half-right. It rang a bell; he just didn't know why.

"Doesn't the police chief know everyone in a town this small?" Her eyebrows arched.

Before he could come up with an answer, the telephone rang, and seconds later Wanda Clay bellowed, "Chief! Call for you."

Anne's silky black hair brushed her shoulders as she glanced toward the door.

He reached for the phone. "Excuse me. I have to do the job the town pays me for."

He picked up the receiver, turned away from her. It was a much-needed respite. He let Mrs. Bennett's complaint about her neighbors drift through his mind. He didn't need to listen, often as he'd heard the same story. What he did need to do was think. He had to find some way to put off Anne Morden until he figured out who Tina Mallory was.

"We'll take care of it, Mrs. Bennett, I promise." A few more soothing phrases, and he hung up.

Anne looked as if she wanted to tap her foot with impatience. "Now can we discuss this?"

The phone rang again, giving him the perfect excuse. "Not without interruption, as you can see. Where are you staying?"

She stiffened. "I hadn't intended to be here that long. Why can't we finish this now?"

"Because I have a job to do." His mind twisted around obstacles. He'd also better run a check on Anne Morden before he did another thing. He at least had to make sure she was who she claimed to be. "How about getting together this evening?"

"This evening?" She made it sound like an eternity.

"It's a three-hour drive back to Philadelphia, and Emilie's tired already."

He was tempted to say *Take it or leave it,* but now was not the time for ultimatums. It might come to that, but not if he could make her see she was wrong.

"Look, this is too important to rush. Why don't you plan to stay over?"

"I'd like to get home tonight."

Her tone had softened a little. At least she was considering his suggestion.

"Isn't this more important?" He pushed the advantage.

She looked at the baby, then back at him, and nodded slowly. "It's worth staying, if I can get this cleared up once and for all."

Mitch took a piece of notepaper from the desk and scribbled an address on it. "The Willows is a bed-and-breakfast. Kate Cavendish will take good care of you."

He considered it a minor triumph when she accepted the paper.

"All right." Maybe she'd anticipated all along that this wouldn't be settled in a hurry. "If that's what it takes, Emilie and I will stay over. When can I expect to see you?"

He glanced at his watch, reviewing all he'd need to accomplish. "Say between six and seven?"

She nodded hesitantly, as if wary of agreeing to anything he said. "I'll see you then."

He didn't breathe until she and the baby were gone. Then it felt as if he hadn't breathed the whole time she'd been there. Well, the news she'd brought would rattle anyone.

Just how much stock could he put in what Anne Morden said? He leaned back in his chair, considering.

It didn't take much effort to picture her sitting across from him. Cool composure—that was the first thing he'd noticed about her. She'd reminded him of every smart, savvy attorney he'd ever locked horns with, except that she was beautiful. Hair as silky and black as a ripple of satin, skin like creamy porcelain, eyes blue as a mountain lake.

Beautiful. Also way out of his class, with her designer clothes and superior air.

Well, beautiful or not, Ms. Anne Morden had to be checked out. He hoped he could find some ammunition with which to defend himself, before she blew his life apart.

He reached for the phone.

Chapter 2

Anne put a light blanket over Emilie, who slept soundly in the crib Mrs. Cavendish had installed in the bedroom of the suite. Nothing, it seemed, was too much trouble for a friend of Chief Donovan's. No one else was staying at the bed-and-breakfast now, and Mrs. Cavendish—Kate, she'd insisted Anne call her—had given them a bedroom with an adjoining sitting room on the second floor of the rambling Victorian house.

The rooms were country quaint, furnished with mismatched antiques that looked as if they'd always sat just where they did now. The quilt on the brass bed appeared to be handmade, and dried flowers filled the pottery basin on the oak washstand. A ghost of last summer's fragrance wafted from them.

She would have enjoyed the place in any other circumstances; it might have been a welcome retreat. But not when her baby's future was at stake.

She had to get herself under control before her next unsettling meeting with Mitch Donovan. This afternoon—well, this afternoon she could have done better, couldn't she?

Her stomach still clenched with tension when she pictured Donovan's frowning face. She still felt the power with which he'd rejected her words.

She shouldn't have been surprised. A man in his position had a lot to lose. The chief of police in a small town couldn't afford a scandal.

The sitting room window overlooked the street, which wound its way uphill from the river in a series of jogs. Bedford Creek was dwarfed by the mountain ridges that hemmed it in. What did people in this village think of their police chief? And what would they think of him if they knew he'd had an affair with a young girl, leaving her pregnant?

They might close ranks against the stranger who brought such an accusation. A chill shivered down her spine.

If Mitch Donovan persisted in his denials, what option did she have? Making the whole business public would only hurt all three of them. But if she didn't get his signature on the document, she'd live in constant fear.

What was she going to do? Panic shot through her. She pressed her hands against the wide windowsill, trying to force the fear down.

Turn to the Lord, child. She could practically hear Helen's warm, rich voice say the words, and her fear ebbed a little at the thought of her friend.

Helen Wells had introduced her to the Lord, just as simply as if she were introducing one friend to another. Until Anne walked into the Faith House shelter Helen ran, looking for a client who'd missed a hearing, religion had been nothing but form. It had been a ritual her parents had insisted on twice a year—the times when everyone went to the appropriate church, wearing the appropriate clothing.

They'd have found nothing appropriate about Faith House or its director, Helen Wells—the tall, elegant woman's embracing warmth for everyone who crossed her threshold was outside their experience. But Anne had found a friend there, and a faith she'd never expected to encounter. Helen's wisdom had sustained her faith through the difficult season of her husband's death.

Not that she was under any illusion her faith was mature. *God's not finished with you yet,* Helen would say, wrapping Anne in the same warm embrace she extended to every lost soul and runaway kid who wandered into her shelter. *The good Lord has plenty for you to learn, girl. But you have to listen.*

God could help in this situation with Donovan. She had to believe that, somehow.

But maybe believing it would be easier if she had the kind of faith Helen did.

I'm trying, Lord. You know I'm trying.

A police car came slowly down the street and pulled to the curb in front of the bed-and-breakfast. She let the curtain fall behind her, her heart giving an awkward *thump.* Mitch Donovan was here.

In a moment she heard footsteps in the hall beneath, heard Kate greeting him—fondly, it seemed. Well, of course. Bedford Creek was his home. Anne was the stranger here, and she had to remember that.

By the time he knocked, Anne had donned her calm, professional manner. But after she opened the door, her coolness began to unravel. He still wore the uniform that seemed almost a part of him, and his dark gaze was intent and determined.

"Chief Donovan. Come in."

He nodded, moving through the doorway as assuredly as if he were walking into his office. The small room suddenly filled with his masculine presence.

It's the uniform, she told herself, fingers tightening on the brass knob as she closed the door. That official uniform would rattle anyone, especially combined with the sheer rock-solid nature of the man wearing it.

"Getting settled?" His firm mouth actually curved in a smile. "I see Kate gave you her best room."

Apparently he hoped to get this meeting off to a more pleasant start than the last one. Well, that was what she wanted, too. *You need his cooperation,* she reminded herself. *For Emilie's sake.*

"Any friend of Mitch's deserves the nicest one—I think that's what she said." Anne couldn't help it if her tone sounded a bit dry.

He walked to the window, glanced out at the street below, then turned back to her. "Kate said you took a walk around town."

The small talk was probably as much an effort for him as for her. She longed to burst into the crucial questions, but held them back.

Cooperate, remember? That's how to get what you want.

"I stopped by the pharmacy to pick up some extra

diapers for the baby. The pharmacist already knew I'd been to see you." That had astonished her. "Your dispatcher must work fast."

The source of the information had to be the dispatcher. Mitch Donovan certainly wouldn't advertise her presence.

He grimaced. "Wanda loves to spread news. And it is a small town, except during tourist season."

"Tourist season?"

He gestured out the window, and she moved a little reluctantly to stand next to him.

"Take a look at those mountains. Our only claim to fame."

The sun slipped behind a thickly forested ridge, painting the sky with red. The village seemed wedged into the narrow valley, as if forced to climb the slope from the river because it couldn't spread out. The river glinted at the valley floor, reflecting the last of the light.

"It is beautiful."

"Plenty of people are willing to pay for this view, and the Chamber of Commerce is happy to let them."

"I guess that explains the number of bed-and-breakfasts. And the shops." She had noticed the assortment of small stores that lined the main street—candles, pottery, stained glass. "Bedford Creek must have an artistic population."

"Don't let any of the old-timers hear you say that." The tiny lines at the corners of his eyes crinkled as his face relaxed in the first genuine smile she'd seen. "They leave such things to outsiders."

"Outsiders." That seemed to echo what she'd been thinking. "You mean people like me?"

He shook his head. "They make a distinction between outsiders and visitors. Outsiders are people like the candle-makers and potters who want to turn the place into an artists' colony. The old guard understands that, whether they approve or not. But visiting lawyers—visiting lawyers must be here for a reason."

"So that's why everyone I passed looked twice."

He shrugged. "In the off-season, strangers are always news. Especially a woman and baby who come to call on the bachelor police chief." His mouth twisted a little wryly on the words.

She'd clearly underestimated the power of the grapevine in a small town. But his apparent concern about rumors might work to her advantage.

"No one will know why I'm here from me. I promise."

She almost put her hand out, as if to shake on it, and then changed her mind. She didn't want friendship from the man, just cooperation. Just his signature, that was all.

"Thanks."

He took a step closer…close enough that she could feel his warmth and smell the faint, musky aroma of shaving lotion. Her pulse thumped, startling her, and she took an impulsive step back, trying to deny the warmth that swept over her.

She must be crazy. He was tough, arrogant, controlling—everything she most disliked in a man. Even if she had been remotely interested in a relationship—which she wasn't—it wouldn't be with someone like him.

But her breathing had quickened, and his dark eyes were intent on hers, as if seeing something he hadn't noticed before. She felt heat flood her cheeks.

Business, she reminded herself. She'd better get down to business. It was the only thing they had in common.

"Have you thought about signing the papers?" She knew in an instant she shouldn't have blurted it out, but her carefully prepared speech had deserted her. In her plans for this meeting, she hadn't considered that she might be rattled at being alone with him.

Whatever friendliness had been in his eyes vanished. "I'd like to talk about this." His uncompromising tone told her the situation wasn't going to turn suddenly easy. "About the woman, Tina."

"Do you remember her now?" She didn't mean the words to sound sarcastic, but they probably did. She bit her lip. There was just no good way to discuss this.

"No." Luckily he seemed to take the question at face value. "Do you know when she was here?"

"Emilie was born in June. Tina said she'd been here the previous summer and stayed through the fall." He could count the months as easily as she could.

He frowned. "Tourist season. They come right through the autumn colors. That means there are plenty of transient workers in town. People who show up in late spring, get jobs, then leave again the end of October." He shook his head. "Impossible to remember them all or keep track of them while they're here."

She'd left her bag on the pie-crust table. She flipped it open and took out the photograph she'd brought. A wave of sadness flooded her as she looked at the young face.

"This was Tina." She held it out to him.

He took the photo and stood frowning down at it, straight brows drawn over his eyes. She should be watching for a spark of recognition, she thought, instead of noticing how his uniform shirt fit his broad shoulders, not a wrinkle marring its perfection. The crease in his navy trousers looked sharp enough to cut paper, and his shoes shone as if they'd been polished moments before.

He looked up finally, his gaze finding hers without the antagonism she half expected. "How did you meet her?"

She bit back a sharp response. "Isn't it more pertinent to ask how *you* met her?"

His mouth hardened in an already hard face. "All right. I recognize her now that I've seen the picture. But I never knew her name. And I certainly didn't have an affair with her."

That was progress, of a sort. If she could manage not to sound as if she judged him, maybe he'd move toward being honest with her.

She tried to keep her tone neutral. "How did you know her?"

"She worked at the café that summer." He frowned, as if remembering. "I eat a lot of meals there, so she waited on me. Chatted, the way waitresses do with regulars. But I didn't run into her anywhere else."

His dark gaze met hers, challenging her to argue. "Your turn. How did you get to know her?"

"She answered an ad I'd put on the bulletin board at the corner market. She wanted to rent a room in my house."

His eyebrows went up at that. "Sorry, Counselor, but you don't look as if you need to take in boarders."

"I didn't do it for the money." She clipped off the words. Her instincts warned her not to give too much away to this man, but if she wanted his cooperation she'd have to appear willing to answer his questions. "My husband had died a few months earlier, and I'd taken a leave from my job. I'd been rattling around in a place too big for one person. The roomer was just going to be temporary, until I found a buyer for the house."

"How long ago was that?" It was a cop's question, snapped at her as if she were a suspect.

"A little over a year." She tried not to let his manner rattle her. "I knew she was pregnant, of course, but I didn't know she had a heart condition. I'm not sure even she knew at first. The doctors said she never should have gotten pregnant."

"What about her family?"

"She said she didn't have anyone." Tina had seemed just as lonely as Anne had been. Maybe that was what had drawn them together. "We became friends. And then when she had to be hospitalized—well, I guess I felt responsible for her. She didn't have anyone else. When Emilie was born, Tina's condition worsened. I took charge of the baby. Tina never came home from the hospital."

His strong face was guarded. "Is that when she supposedly told you about me?"

She nodded. "She talked about the time she spent in Bedford Creek, about the man she loved, the man who fathered Emilie."

He was so perfectly still that he might have been a statue, except for the tiny muscle that pulsed at his temple. "And if I tell you it was a mistake—that she couldn't have meant me…?"

"Look, I'm not here to prosecute you." Why couldn't he see that? "I'm not judging you. I just want your signature on the papers. That's all."

"You didn't answer me." He took a step closer, and

she could feel the intensity under his iron exterior. "What if I tell you it was a mistake?"

It was all slipping away, getting out of her control. "How could it be a mistake? Everything she said fits you, no one else."

He seized on that. "Fits me? I thought you said she named me."

She took a deep breath, trying to stay in control of the situation. "While she was ill, she talked a lot about… about the man she fell in love with. About the town. Then, when we knew she wasn't going to get better, we made plans for Emilie's adoption." She looked at him, willing him to understand. "I've been taking care of Emilie practically since the day she was born. I love her. Tina knew that. She knew I needed the father's permission, too, but she never said the name until the end."

She shivered a little, recalling the scene. Tina, slipping in and out of consciousness, finally saying the name *Mitch Donovan*. "Why would she lie?"

"I don't know." His mouth clamped firmly on the words. "I'm sorry, sorry about all of it. But I'm not the father of her baby."

She glared at him, wanting to shake the truth out of him. But it was no use. It would be about as effective as shaking a rock.

"You don't believe me." He made it a simple statement of fact.

"No." There seemed little point in saying anything else.

Mitch's jaw clamped painfully tight. This woman was so sure she was right that it would take a bulldozer to move her. Somehow he had to crack open that closed mind of hers enough for her to admit doubt.

"Isn't it possible you misunderstood?" He struggled, trying to come up with a theory to explain the unexplainable. "If she was as sick as you say, maybe her mind wandered."

For the first time some of the certainty faded in her eyes. She stared beyond him, as if focusing on something painful in the past.

"I don't think so." Her gaze met his, troubled, as if she were trying to be fair. "We'd been talking about the adoption. Certainly she knew what I was asking her."

"Look, I don't have an explanation for this." He spread his hands wide. "All I can say is what I've already told you. I knew the girl slightly, and she was here at the right time. I don't know how to prove a negative, but I never had an affair with her, and I did not father her child."

Something hardened inside him as he said the words. He didn't have casual affairs—not that it was any of Anne Morden's business. And he certainly wasn't cut out for fatherhood. If there was anything his relationship with his own father had taught him, it was that the Donovan men didn't make decent fathers. The whole town knew that.

"If you were to sign the parental rights termination…" she began.

He lifted an eyebrow. "Is that really what you want, Counselor? You want me to lie?"

Her soft mouth could look uncommonly stubborn. "Would it be a lie?"

"Yes." That much he knew. And he could only see one way to prove it in the face of Anne's persistence and the mother's dying statement. "I suggest we put it to the test. A blood test."

That must have occurred to her. It was the obvious solution. And her quick nod told him she'd thought of it.

"Fine. Is there a lab in town?"

"Not here." He didn't even need to consider that. "We can't have it done in Bedford Creek." He hoped he didn't sound as horrified at the thought as he felt.

"Why not?" The suspicion was back in her eyes.

"You've obviously never lived in a small town. If the three of us show up at the clinic for a paternity test, the town will know about it before the needle hits my skin."

"That bad?" She almost managed a smile.

"Believe me, it's that bad. Rebecca Forrester, the doctor's assistant, wouldn't say a word. But the receptionist talks as much as my dispatcher."

"The nearest town where they have the facilities—"

"I'd rather go to Philadelphia, if you don't mind." She shouldn't. After all, that was her home turf.

"That's fine with me, but isn't it a little out of the way for you?"

"Far enough that I won't be worried about running into anyone who'll carry the news back to Bedford Creek." It was a small world, all right, but surely not that small. "I have a friend who's on the staff of a city hospital. He can make sure we have it done quickly. And discreetly." Though what Brett would say to him at this request, he didn't want to imagine.

"This friend of yours—" she began.

"Brett's a good physician. He wouldn't jeopardize his career by tinkering with test results."

She seemed to look at it from every angle before she nodded. "All right. Tomorrow?"

"Tomorrow, it is."

He forced his muscles to relax. Tomorrow, if luck was with him, a simple screening would prove he couldn't possibly be the child's father. Anne Morden would take her baby and walk back out of his life as quickly as she'd walked in.

He should be feeling relief. He definitely shouldn't be feeling regret at the thought of never seeing her again.

Chapter 3

Anne made the turn from the Schulkyll Expressway toward center city and glanced across at her passenger. Mitch stared straight ahead, hands flexed on his knees. He wore khaki slacks and a button-down shirt today, his leather jacket thrown into the back seat, but even those clothes had a military aura.

Nothing in his posture indicated any uncertainty about her driving, but she was nevertheless sure that he'd rather be behind the wheel.

Well, that was too bad. Riding to Philadelphia together had been his idea, after all. He'd said his car was in the shop, and if she thought he wanted to drive the police car on an errand like this, she'd better think again. He'd ride down with her and get a rental car for the return.

The trip had been accomplished mostly in silence, except for the occasional chirps from Emilie in her car seat. Mitch probably had no desire to chat, anyway, and her thoughts had twisted all the way down the turnpike.

Was she doing the right thing? A blood test was the obvious solution, of course, and she'd recommended it often enough to clients. She just hadn't anticipated the need in this situation. She'd assumed a man in Mitch's position, faced with the results of a casual fling, would be only too happy to sign the papers and put his mistake behind him.

But it hadn't worked out that way, and his willingness to undergo the blood test lent credence to his denials. She was almost tempted to believe him.

What was she thinking? He had to be Emilie's father, didn't he? Tina would certainly know, and Tina had said so.

They passed a sign directing them to the hospital, and her nerves tightened. Maybe she shouldn't have agreed to let Mitch make the arrangements, but it sounded sensible, the way he had put it. They could be assured speed and secrecy through his connection.

"I hope your friend is ready for us." She glanced at her watch. Dr. Brett Elliot had given them an afternoon appointment, and they should be right on time.

"He'll be there." Mitch's granite expression cracked in a reminiscent smile. "In high school Brett was always the one with the late assignment and the joke that made the teacher laugh so she didn't penalize him. But medical school reformed him. You'd hardly guess he was once the class clown."

Somehow the title didn't sound very reassuring. She glanced sideways at Mitch, registering again his size and strength. "Let me guess. You must have been the class's star athlete."

He shrugged. "Something like that, I guess."

The hospital parking garage loomed on her right. Anne pulled in, the sandwich she'd had for lunch turning into a lead ball in her stomach. In an hour or two, she might know for sure about Emilie's father.

Mitch's friend had said he'd be waiting at the lab desk. Actually, he seemed to be leaning on it. Unruly hair the color of antique gold tumbled into his eyes as he laughed down at the woman behind the desk. So this was the boy who'd charmed everyone—all grown up and still doing it, apparently.

"Mitch!" He crossed the room in a few long strides and pumped Mitch's hand. "Good to see you, guy. It's been too long."

Brett's face, open and smiling, contrasted with Mitch's closed, reserved look, but nothing could disguise the affection between them. Mitch clapped him on the shoulder before turning to Anne and introducing her.

Brett gave her the same warm grin he'd been giving the woman at the desk, but she thought she read wariness in his green eyes. Then he turned to Emilie, and all reservation vanished.

"Hey, there, pretty girl. What's your name?"

"This is Emilie."

"What a little sweetheart." He tickled Emilie's chin, and even the eight-month-old baby responded to him with a shy smile and a tilt of her head.

Brett gestured toward the orange vinyl chairs lining the empty waiting room. "Since we've got the place to ourselves, let's have a chat about what we're going to do."

The woman behind the desk muttered an excuse and disappeared into the adjoining room. Anne took a seat, Emilie on her lap, and vague misgivings floated through her mind. *These are Mitch's arrangements,* she cautioned herself. *This is Mitch's friend.*

Brett pulled his chair around to face them. "The first step is to do a preliminary screening of blood type and Rh factors. We'll be able to give you those results right away."

"They're not definitive in establishing paternity." She didn't mean to sound critical, but she'd handled enough cases to know it usually went farther than that.

"Not entirely." Brett didn't seem put off by her lawyer-like response. "But there are some combinations that can exclude the possibility of paternity, and that's what we look for first."

Another objection stirred in Anne's mind. "Don't you need the mother's blood type to do that?"

"Yes, well, actually I got the information from the hospital where Emilie was born."

He exchanged a quick glance with Mitch. Obviously they'd arranged that when they talked, too.

"My military records show my blood type." Mitch frowned. "We could have gotten them."

"This is faster than waiting for the military to send something," Brett said, before Anne could voice an objection. "And in a legal matter, we can't just rely on your word."

Mitch's mouth tightened, but he nodded.

"Okay, so if the screening rules Mitch out," the doctor continued, "we stop there. If it doesn't, that still means he's one of maybe a million people who could be the father. So we go to DNA testing at that point. It takes longer, but it'll establish paternity beyond any doubt."

Emilie stirred restlessly on Anne's lap, as if to remind her she'd had a long, upsetting couple of days. Anne stroked her head. "I understand."

"Let's get on with it." Mitch seemed ready for action, and she half expected him to push up his sleeve on the spot.

"Fine." Brett started toward the laboratory door.

Ready or not. Anne picked up Emilie and followed him, suddenly breathless. She'd know something, maybe soon.

Mitch's stony expression didn't change in the least when the technician plunged a needle into his hard-muscled arm. Emilie wasn't so stoic. She stiffened, head thumping hard against Anne's chest, and let out an anguished wail that tore into Anne's heart.

"Hey, little girl." Mitch's voice was astonishingly gentle. One large hand wrapped around the baby's flailing foot. "It'll be over in a second, honest."

When the needle was gone, Emilie's sobs subsided, but Anne didn't have any illusions. The baby was overtired and overstimulated, and she desperately needed to have her dinner and go to sleep. That wouldn't hurt her mother any, either.

"It's all right, darling." She stroked Emilie's fine blond hair. "We'll go home soon."

Brett nodded. "This won't take long. Make yourselves comfortable in the waiting room, and I'll bring you some coffee."

A few minutes later they were back in the same chairs they'd occupied earlier. Anne tried to balance a wiggling Emilie while digging for a bottle of juice in the diaper bag. The juice remained elusive.

"Here, let me hold her." Before she could object, Mitch took the baby from her. He bounced Emilie on his knees, rumpling the knife-sharp crease, his strong hands supporting the baby's back.

The ache between Anne's shoulder blades eased. She watched Mitch with the baby, realizing the ache had just shifted location to her heart. If Mitch was Emilie's father...

She bent over the diaper bag to hide the tears that clouded her eyes. Ridiculous to feel them. Nothing had changed. She blinked rapidly and fished the juice bottle out.

"I'll take her now." She flipped the cap off and dropped it in the bag.

Mitch shook his head and reached for the bottle. "Give yourself a break for a few minutes. I can manage this."

She leaned back, watching as he shifted Emilie's position and plopped the nipple into her mouth.

"You didn't learn that in...the Army, was it?"

He nodded. "Military Police. Matter of fact, I did. A couple of my buddies had families."

She thought she heard a note of censure in his voice. "You have something against that?"

His eyes met hers, startled, and then he shrugged. "Up to them. I just never figured family mixed very well with military police work."

Emilie snuggled against him, fingers curling and uncurling on the bottle, eyes beginning to droop.

"I see you hung around enough to learn how to give a bottle."

His face relaxed in a smile. The effect was startling, warming his whole countenance and demanding an answering smile she couldn't suppress.

"Not too difficult. Besides, I could always give the babies back if they got fussy."

"Of course."

Something hardened in her at the words. The three of them might look, to the casual observer, like a family. That observer couldn't begin to guess how skewed that impression was.

Emilie had fallen asleep in Mitch's arms by the time Brett pushed through the door, a clipboard in his hand. Anne inhaled sharply and saw Mitch's already erect posture stiffen even more.

"Well?" Mitch's voice rasped. "What's the verdict?"

Brett's green eyes were troubled. "Skipping all the technical details, the bottom line is the tests don't exclude you, Mitch. Your blood type means you could possibly be the father."

"Me and a million other guys," he snapped.

Anne's mouth tightened. He'd obviously been hoping against hope he hadn't been caught. Maybe now he'd give up this pose of innocence and sign the papers. But she had to show him she'd keep pressing.

"About the DNA test—" she pinned Brett with her gaze "—I'd like it sent to McKay Labs. I've dealt with them before. And I want a copy of the results sent directly to me."

Brett blinked. "That'll need Mitch's permission."

"You've got it." Mitch moved, and Emilie woke. Her whimper quickly turned into a full-fledged cry.

Brett looked ready to escape. "Expect the results in three to four weeks, then."

Anne nodded goodbye, trying to reach for the diaper bag and her crying child at the same time. "Let me have her."

Mitch handed over the baby.

"There, sweetheart, it's all right." She rocked the baby against her, but Emilie was beyond comforting. She reared back in Anne's arms, wails increasing.

Mitch picked up the diaper bag. "You can't drive home alone with her in that state." He took her arm. "Come on. I'll drive you and then call a cab."

She wanted to protest, but Emilie's sobs shattered her will. She nodded, letting him guide her from the room.

The baby's wails seemed to fry Mitch's brain as he followed Anne's directions through the city streets to a high-rise apartment building. He needed to think this whole thing through, but thought proved impossible at the moment. Who would imagine one small baby could make that much noise?

He took a deep breath as the cry reached a decibel level that had to be against the law inside a small car. Okay, he could handle this. It was no worse than artillery fire, was it?

Besides, it would soon be over. He'd deposit them at Anne's and call a cab. He'd be back in Bedford Creek in a few hours, and the only contact he'd have with Anne Morden and her baby would be when the DNA test came back, proving he hadn't fathered this child.

A padded, mirrored elevator whooshed them swiftly to the tenth floor. He took the baby, wincing at her cries, while Anne unlocked the door. He wanted only to hand her back and get out of there.

She scooped the baby into her arms as the door swung open, and her eyes met his. "This may not be the best time, but I think we should talk the situation over, if you don't mind waiting while I get the baby settled." She managed a half smile. "It won't take as long as you might think. She's so exhausted, she's going to crash as soon as she's been fed."

He pushed down the desire to flee, nodded, and followed her into the apartment. Anne disappeared into the back with the baby, and he sank onto the couch, wondering when the ringing in his ears would stop.

Anne had sold the house she'd talked about and moved here with the baby. He'd found that out in the quick background check he'd run. He glanced around. Expensively casual—that was the only way to describe her apartment. Chintz couches, a soft plush carpet, a wall of books on built-in shelves with what was probably a state-of-the-art entertainment center discreetly hidden behind closed doors—all said money. Assistant public defenders didn't make enough to support this life-style, but there was wealth in her family. This woman was really out of his league.

No question of that, anyway. All she wanted from him was his signature on the parental rights termination—not friendship, certainly nothing more.

Sometime in the last twenty-four hours he'd given up any thought that Anne was somehow attempting to frame him. No, all she wanted was to safeguard her child.

Unfortunately the one thing she wanted, he couldn't give her. Someone else had dated the unfortunate Tina; someone else had fathered her child. But who? And why on earth had the girl said his name? The answers, if they could be found at all, must lie in Bedford Creek.

The baby's cries from the back of the apartment ceased abruptly. Anne must have put some food in Emilie's mouth.

He got up, paced to the window, then paced back. What did Anne want to talk to him about? What was there left to say?

He sat back down on the couch, sinking into its comfortable depths, and reached automatically for the book on the lamp table. A Bible. It nestled into his hand, and he flipped it open to the dedication page. *To my new sister in Christ from Helen.* The date was only two years ago.

Anne came back into the room, her step light and quick. She glanced questioningly at the Bible in his hand, and he closed it and put it back where he'd found it.

"She settled down, did she?"

"Out like a light."

Anne sat in the chair across from him. Her dark hair curled around a face that was lightly flushed, probably from bending over the crib.

"You're probably as beat as she is by this time." She'd put in a couple of high-stress days, driving all the way with a baby, and on a mission like this.

"I could sleep a day or two. But Emilie won't let me."

She leaned forward and her hair brushed her shoulders, moving like a living thing. He had an insane desire to reach out, let it curl around his fingers, use it to draw her close to him.

Whoa, back off. Of all the inappropriate things he could be feeling right now, that was probably the worst.

"You wanted to talk."

"Yes." She nailed him with those deep blue eyes. "I hoped that you might be ready to sign the papers now."

He should have seen it coming. She still wanted what she'd wanted all along, and the inconclusive blood test results had just given her another bit of leverage. But it wasn't going to work.

"I know you don't believe this, but I never went out with Tina Mallory. I did not father her child." He took a breath, hoping he sounded calm.

She raised her chin stubbornly. "Then how do you explain Tina's words?"

"I can't. But there has to be an explanation somewhere. Someone in Bedford Creek must remember Tina, must know who she dated that summer. So while we're waiting for the DNA results, I'll do a little quiet investigating."

Her hands twisted involuntarily, as if she were pushing his words away. He couldn't blame her. She had what must seem to her to be incontrovertible proof of his guilt. All he could do was continue to protest his innocence.

"Bottom line is, I'm not going to sign anything that says I'm that child's parent. I can't, because it's not true. In three or four weeks, you'll know that as well as I do. Maybe by then I'll be able to point you in the right direction."

"I don't want my private business splashed all over Bedford Creek."

"Believe me, it's in my interest to keep it quiet even more than it is yours. I'll be discreet. But I'm going to start looking at this problem like a cop."

Her eyebrows went up at that. "Funny, I thought you always had."

He reminded himself that cops and defense attorneys went together like cats and dogs. "Look, Counselor, I am what I am." Her sarcasm had effectively doused that spurt of longing to hold her, which was just as well. He stood, picking up his jacket. "I'll be on my way now. I don't suppose we'll see each other again."

"I'm afraid you're wrong about that." She stood, too, her gaze locked on his.

He gave an exasperated sigh. "You're assuming that in three or four weeks you'll have proof I fathered Emilie. I know you're wrong."

"Actually, that isn't what I was thinking." She took an audible breath, as if building up to saying something she knew he wasn't going to like. "Emilie and I aren't staying here. We're going back to Bedford Creek until the results come in."

"What?" He could only stare at her. "Why? Why on earth would you want to do that?"

"You're right about one thing—the answers have to be in Bedford Creek. That's where Tina became pregnant. That's where the truth is. I can't just sit here and wonder for the next month. I need to find out, no matter what."

"After the results come—" he began.

She was already shaking her head. "I'm supposed to have a hearing on the adoption in a little over a month. Before then I have to resolve this, once and for all. And that means I'm coming to Bedford Creek."

He lifted an eyebrow skeptically. "Don't you mean you want to keep an eye on me?"

A faint flush warmed her smooth skin. "Let's say I have a high respect for the power of a police uniform. I don't want to see it used against me."

He fought down the urge to defend himself. If a man found it necessary to defend his honor, it must be in question. He took a careful step back.

"No point in my telling you not to worry about that, is there?"

She shook her head. "I won't interfere. You can pretend I'm not even there."

"Now that I can't do." He smiled grimly at her perplexed look. "You're forgetting—people in Bedford Creek already know you and Emilie came to see me. They're probably speculating right this minute about where we are today. You can't come back and pretend we don't know each other, not in a small town."

"I'll say I'm there on vacation. You told me Bedford Creek is a tourist town. My presence doesn't have to have anything to do with you."

Obviously she hadn't thought this far ahead. "Nobody would believe that. If you come back, we'll have to keep up the illusion of friendship. And if we're both going to be looking into what happened when Tina lived there, we'd better figure out a way to cooperate on this, or at least not step on each other's toes."

He could see just how unpalatable she found that, and at some level it grated on his pride. He wasn't that hard to take, was he? It wasn't as if he were asking her to pretend a romantic interest in him.

Her eyes met his, and he could read the determination there. "I suppose you're right. You know a lot more about your town than I do. But I'm still coming. So that means we're in this together, for as long as it takes."

Chapter 4

"Now let me help you with that." Kate Cavendish took the bundle of diapers from Anne's arms before she could object. "Believe me, I remember how much you need to bring when you're traveling with a baby."

"I can manage…"

But Kate was already hustling up the front steps to The Willows, white curls glistening in the late winter sunshine. She propped the door open with an iron door-stop in the shape of a cat, then hurried inside. Anne lifted Emilie from the car seat.

It was silly, she supposed, to be made uncomfortable by so much open friendliness, but she just wasn't used to it. She could only hope Kate's enthusiastic welcome wasn't because the woman thought Anne was here to see Mitch.

That was ridiculous. It wasn't as if they'd returned together. She'd taken two days to organize this trip.

Surely she could take a brief vacation in Bedford Creek without the whole town jumping to conclusions about why she was here.

Kate was probably just delighted to have paying guests at this time of the year. No matter how many tourists might show up in the summer, early March was clearly a quiet time in Bedford Creek. She glanced up at the mountain ridge that cut off the sky. It was sere and brown, its leafless trees defining its bones. She shivered a little.

"Here we go, sweetheart," she said to Emilie. "We'll just pop you in the crib while Mommy unloads the car, all right?"

Emilie wiggled, her arms flailing in the pink snowsuit. After three hours in the car, she was only too ready to practice her new crawling skills. She wouldn't be pleased at the crib, no matter how enticing Anne made it sound.

As they reached the center hall of the Victorian, Kate hurried down the winding staircase. The colors of the stained-glass window on the landing tinged her hair, and a smile lit her bright-blue eyes at the sight of the baby.

"Oh, let me take her, please. I'd just love to hold her." Kate held out her hands.

Emilie leaned her head against Anne's shoulder for a moment, considering, and then smiled, her chubby hands opening toward the woman. Emilie had apparently decided anyone who looked like Mrs. Santa Claus had to be a friend.

"You little sweetheart." Kate settled the baby on her hip with the ease of long practice. "We're going to be great friends while you're here, I can just tell."

"Thank you, Kate." Anne touched Emilie's cheek

lightly. "I appreciate the help. It will just take me a few minutes to unload."

"Take your time." Kate carried the baby toward the wide archway into the front parlor. "We'll get acquainted. I'm surprised Mitch isn't here to get you settled. He's always so helpful to his friends."

Was that a question in Kate's voice? Maybe this was her chance to refute any rumors the woman had heard. Or started, for that matter. She moved to the archway.

"Mitch and I aren't that close. He probably didn't even know when we were arriving."

"Oh, I'm sure he did." Kate turned from the breakfront cabinet, where she was showing Emilie a collection of china birds. "He keeps track of things. And when his old Army friend's widow comes to visit…well, you can just be sure he'd keep track of that." Kate's round cheeks, like two red apples, plumped in a smile. "It's so nice that you could keep in touch."

"Old Army friend…how did you—" *Leap to that conclusion*—that was what she was thinking, but it hardly seemed polite to say so. She'd mentioned that she was a widow when she'd checked in the first time. Kate seemed to have embroidered the rest.

"Wanda had all sorts of ideas about why you were here." Kate tickled Emilie's chin. "I told her, 'Count on it, that'll be why. Mitch's friends from the service have dropped by four or five times since he's been back in Bedford Creek. That's why Anne and her baby are here, too.'"

Mitch clearly knew his town a lot better than Anne did. She owed him an apology for thinking he was wrong about the stir her presence would create. As he'd said, she needed a reason to be here.

Anne opened her mouth and closed it again. What exactly could she say? Wanda, the dispatcher, had probably floated some much more colorful theories about Anne's visit. If Anne denied Kate's story, she'd just fuel the curiosity. She certainly wasn't going to lie about it, but maybe the safest thing was to say nothing and let them think what they wanted.

"I'm sure Mitch is busy." She settled on noncommittal. "I probably won't see much of him while we're here."

Kate swung around again, eyebrows going up in surprise. "Not see much of him? Well, of course you will. After all, his house is right across the street."

"Right—" She stopped. Anything she said now, she'd probably regret. Instead she headed back to the car for the next load, fuming.

So Mitch lived right across the street, did he? He might have mentioned that little fact about The Willows at some point in their discussion. He hadn't wanted her to come back to Bedford Creek at all; that had been clear. He certainly didn't want her to join in his investigation. But apparently he felt that if she did come, she should be under his eye.

Well, they'd get a few things straight as soon as possible. She was used to doing things on her own, and that wasn't about to change now—

It looked as if she'd have a chance to tell him so in the immediate future, because his police cruiser was pulling up directly across from The Willows.

Mitch got out. He closed the door, hesitated a moment, and then headed straight for her.

"Anne. I see you arrived safely. Any problems?"

"Not at all." She tried for a cool politeness. It would help, she thought, if she didn't experience that jolt of awareness every time she saw his tall figure. "We just got in a few minutes ago."

"I'll take that." He reached for the suitcase she'd begun to pull from the trunk, but she tightened her grip.

"I can handle it."

"I'm sure you can." His hand closed on the bag, his fingers brushing hers. "But why should you?"

"Because I don't need any help." Mitch Donovan had to be the only person in her life with the ability to make her sound like a petulant child.

They stood staring at each other, the bag trapped between them. Then his lips twitched slightly. "Something tells me that's your favorite saying."

"There's nothing wrong with being independent." She'd had to be, even when she was a child, even when she'd been married. She didn't know any other way to behave.

You can't do it all yourself, child. Helen's voice echoed in her mind. *Sometimes you have to let go and let God help.*

"You can be independent and still let me carry your bag upstairs."

She held on for another moment, then released the handle. With a half smile, he hoisted the bag, then grabbed a second one with his other hand.

Typical cop, she thought, following with an armload of her own. Give him an inch and he'd take a mile.

Unloading the car took only a few minutes with Mitch helping. She glanced around the same sitting room they'd had before, amazed as always at the amount of gear required by one small baby. Mitch set the stroller behind a bentwood coat rack.

"Looks like that's it."

She nodded. Maybe this was the chance she needed to set some ground rules for this visit. He had to understand that she wasn't going to be a passive bystander to any investigation he planned.

"We need to talk. Have you found out anything more about Tina's stay here?"

His eyebrows lifted. "It's only been a day."

"I don't have much time, if you'll recall. The hearing is in less than a month, and the results—"

The sentence came to an abrupt halt when Kate, holding the baby, stuck her head in the door. "Getting settled?"

Anne managed a nod, her heart thumping. In another instant she'd have said something about DNA testing, and Kate would have heard. She'd have to be more careful.

Mitch gestured toward the stroller. "Why don't we take Emilie out for a walk? I'm sure she's tired of being cooped up in the car."

Now that was exactly what she didn't want: to have the whole town see them together and speculate about them. "I don't think so. I need to put things away."

But Kate was already handing the baby to Mitch. "Good idea." She beamed. "This little one could use some fresh air, and the sunshine won't last that much longer. I'll help you put things away later, if you want."

Mitch bounced Emilie, who responded with a delighted squeal. She patted his face with her open palms. He looked at Anne, eyebrows raised, and she knew exactly what he was thinking. If she wanted to talk to him, they might have more privacy on a walk.

With a strong sense of having been outmaneuvered, Anne reached for the stroller.

When they reached the sidewalk in front of the

house, Mitch bent to slide Emilie into her seat. His big hands cradled her, protecting her head as she wiggled. Anne's heart gave an unexpected lurch at the sight. His gentleness dissolved some of the irritation she'd been holding on to, and she tried to retrieve it.

"I understand you live right across the street." *And you should have mentioned that.*

Mitch straightened, nodding. "I bought the house a year ago." He shrugged. "Got tired of living in rented places. I wanted something of my own, where I could decide on the color of the walls and pound a nail in if I wanted to."

The cottage, with its peaked roof and shutters, pristine front door and neatly trimmed hedges, proclaimed its owner's pride.

"It's charming." The house was an unexpected insight into the man. She'd have expected him to live in a furnished apartment, something closer to spartan barracks. "Convenient to the station, too, I guess."

"Just a couple of blocks." He shrugged. "But nothing in Bedford Creek is very far away, as long as you don't mind walking uphill." He smiled. "Or down."

He held the gate open as Anne pushed the stroller through it to the street.

"You might have mentioned this was your neighborhood when you suggested The Willows."

He paused, looking down at her with a quizzical expression. "Does that make a difference?"

"It certainly adds to the impression I'm here to see you." She felt herself blush.

"Believe me, nothing I did or didn't do would change that idea." His hand closed over hers on the stroller handle. "Why don't you let me push?"

She'd put mittens on Emilie, and maybe she should have done the same for herself. If she had, she wouldn't have to feel the warmth and strength of his hand over hers. And Anne wouldn't be struggling with the ripple of that warmth traveling right to her heart.

"Fine." She snatched her hand away. "As long as you push it by the café where Tina worked. I want to see the place for myself."

His answer would tell her whether he was ready to accept her role in finding out the truth about Tina, whatever it was. This would certainly be easier if she didn't have to fight him every step of the way.

But unfortunately, even that wouldn't eliminate the problem that became clearer each time she was with Mitch Donovan. She was ridiculously—and unsuitably—attracted to the man who might be Emilie's father, and who might have the power to take Emilie away.

So Anne wasn't giving up on her determination to play detective, Mitch thought. It would have been too much to hope she might, but somehow he had to convince her. Because if he had a civilian meddling in this situation, he could forget any hope of keeping things quiet while he found out the truth about Tina Mallory and her baby.

"I'll take you to the café." He tried to keep reluctance from showing in his voice. "I'll even buy you a cup of coffee there, if you want."

She glanced up at him as they walked along the street. "Do I sense a 'but' coming?"

He shrugged. "But Cassie Worth, the owner, isn't the most forthcoming person in the world, especially with strangers. I haven't had a chance to sound her out yet. Maybe you'd better let me see what I can find out first."

"Give me a little credit. I didn't intend to cross-examine her."

"Like birds don't intend to fly?"

Her lips twitched in a smile he suspected was involuntary. "Meaning I can't help being an attorney any more than you can help being a cop?"

"Something like that." He eased the stroller over a patch of ice on the sidewalk. He frowned, glancing up at the storefront of Clinton's Candles. Clinton would have to be reminded to keep his walk clear.

"How will I find out anything if I don't ask?"

"If you start asking a lot of questions, it'll get around. Make people curious—more curious than they already are."

They walked in silence for a few minutes, as she apparently considered that.

"I'll be discreet," she said finally. "That's the best I can do."

He glanced at her. Silky hair brushed the collar of her black leather jacket as she moved. There was nothing remotely discreet about the presence of such a beautiful stranger in Bedford Creek, especially one accompanied by a baby. It probably wouldn't do any good to tell her that, but he had to try. Maybe a blunt reminder would get through.

"I have a lot to lose if you're not."

She looked up at him. He seemed to feel her intense blue gaze penetrate the barriers he kept around him.

"I don't see…" She shook her head. "They're your people. Seems to me they'd take your word over a stranger's, if it came to that."

The apple doesn't fall far from the tree. The refrain he'd heard too often in his childhood echoed in his mind, but he wasn't about to share it with Anne. Would anyone, other than Brett and Alex, his closest friends, take his side? He didn't care to put it to the test.

"I thought we agreed neither of us wanted this to become public knowledge."

She glanced at the baby, and her mouth softened. "I don't relish publicity any more than you do. But I have to find out about Tina." She looked back up at him, and he could read the fear in her eyes. "If you're telling me the truth, then I don't have much time."

"I know."

He felt the clock ticking, too. It must be much worse for Anne, with three to four weeks to get back the DNA test results he knew would prove him innocent. And about the same time until her hearing. No wonder she wanted to launch into an investigation.

His steps slowed. "We'll find out. I don't expect you to trust me on this, but I'm telling you the truth. We'll find out."

She nodded, and he thought he saw a sheen of tears in her eyes. "Yes." She cleared her throat. "The café… is it near here?"

"Right across the street." He gestured toward the Bluebird Café. "Let me buy you that cup of coffee."

The baby seemed to enjoy bouncing down over the curb and across the street. She pounded on the stroller tray with both tiny fists.

The Bluebird Café, its façade painted a bright blue to match its name, was one of a series of shops that staggered down either side of Main Street. They were like so many dominoes, looking ready to tumble to the valley floor, but they'd stood where they were for a hundred years or so.

A bit different from Anne's usual setting, he knew, a vision of that luxury high-rise flitting through his mind. What did she think of Bedford Creek in comparison? Of him?

Whoa, back up and erase that. It didn't matter what Anne thought of him. Not as long as, in the end, she accepted the fact that he wasn't Emilie's father.

Anne held open the frosted glass door, its placard advertising Cassie's chicken-and-dumpling soup. He lifted the stroller up the two steps from the street and pushed it inside, not wasting time looking up for either admiration or approval in those sapphire eyes.

"Not especially crowded," Anne observed, unzipping Emilie's snowsuit.

"Empty, as a matter of fact. It's too late for lunch and too early for supper." He gestured. "So you have your choice of seating."

She picked a booth halfway back, and by the time they were settled, Cassie had appeared from the kitchen.

"Afternoon, Chief." She twitched her bluebird-trimmed apron and shot Anne a suspicious glance. "What can I get you?"

"Coffee?" He raised his eyebrows at Anne, and she nodded. "Two coffees."

"That's it?" Cassie made it sound like a personal affront that they didn't order anything else.

Again he looked at Anne, and she shook her head. "I had lunch on the way." She gave Cassie a hundred-watt smile. "Another time I'll try your chicken-and-dumpling soup."

That smile would have had him picking himself up off the floor, Mitch thought. Cassie just jerked her head in a nod, but her usual grim expression seemed to soften slightly as she plodded back toward the kitchen.

"Does she give all her customers such a warm welcome?"

He leaned against the blue padded seat. "I told you she wouldn't be very forthcoming."

"A clam is more forthcoming." She took an animal cracker from her bag and handed it to Emilie. The baby pounded it once on the stroller tray and then stuffed it into her mouth. "Why did she open a restaurant, of all things, if she didn't want to be around people?"

He shrugged. "Not that many ways to make a living in Bedford Creek. You either work at the furniture factory or you make money off tourists. And Cassie is a good cook. You'd better come back for that chicken-and-dumpling soup."

"I guess I may as well sample the local cuisine while I'm here."

"And chat with her about Tina while you're at it?" That was obviously in her mind. "Maybe you should let me bring the subject up."

She pierced him with an intent look. "Would you, if I didn't push? Or would you ignore it?"

"I said I'd work on it, and I will." He couldn't keep the irritation from his voice. Persistence was a good quality, but he didn't appreciate having it turned on him. "I've already started a couple of lines of inquiry."

She looked as if she'd like to believe him. "What did you find out?"

The *clink* of coffee mugs announced Cassie's return, and Mitch shot Anne a warning glance. Cassie might not be the yakker Wanda was, but he still didn't want her knowing his business.

Cassie slapped down the mugs, more bluebirds fluttering on the white china. She took a step back, then looked at Anne.

"Fresh apple dumplings tomorrow. Get here early if you want it."

He suspected laughter hovered on Anne's lips, but she didn't let it out. "Thanks, I'll remember."

When Cassie was safely back in the kitchen, he shook his head in mock amazement. "Apple dumplings. Believe it or not, you've made an impression. Cassie doesn't offer her apple dumplings to just anyone."

Amusement lit Anne's eyes. "Dumpling soup and apple dumplings? I'd look like a dumpling if I ate like that."

He let his glance take in her slim figure, sleek in dark slacks and a sapphire sweater that matched her eyes. "You don't look as if you need to worry."

She couldn't meet his eyes. "I didn't know investigating was so calorie-intensive."

"Maybe you ought to leave it to the pros. I can tackle the apple dumplings for you."

She shook her head, smiling but stubborn. "What were you going to tell me before Cassie came back out?"

Right. The message was clear: he'd better keep his mind on business.

"I did some preliminary checking on Tina Mallory. She lived in town for six months, worked for Cassie from June to October. Once the tourist season ended, Cassie let her go. Far as I can tell, she left sometime the following month."

"Why Philadelphia, I wonder? She never told me that."

So, he could tell her something she didn't know about her friend. "Turns out she lived awhile in Philadelphia. I'd guess when she realized she was pregnant, she wanted to go somewhere familiar."

"Familiar? Do you mean she still had friends or family there?"

Fear probably put the sharp edge in Anne's voice. Maybe it hadn't occurred to her that Tina might have family. Family that could possibly have a claim to Emilie. He shook his head quickly.

"Not that I can tell. Apparently it was always just her and her mother—no father in evidence. And her mother died about four years ago." He curled his fingers around the warm mug. "She'd apparently lost touch with any friends she once had. But there certainly had to be more job opportunities in Philadelphia than anywhere around here."

"That makes sense. I just wonder why she never told me she'd lived there. In fact, I'm sure she said she was from Los Angeles."

"Sounds as if Tina was a little careless with the truth at times."

She gave him a level look, one that said she knew just what he meant. "She was young," she said finally. "She tried to make herself interesting. But that doesn't mean I should discount everything she said."

He'd better not let himself enjoy the way Anne's eyes lit up when she smiled, he thought. Or try to figure out a way to prolong moments when they laughed together across the table as if they were friends.

They weren't friends, and Anne obviously intended that they never would be.

Chapter 5

By the next morning, Anne had nearly succeeded in convincing herself she'd imagined that unsuitable attraction to Mitch. It must be a product of emotional stress. She'd ignore the feelings—she'd always been good at that, thanks to her parents' example.

She maneuvered Emilie's stroller over the curb. One thing she knew about parenting without a doubt: Emilie wouldn't grow up in the kind of emotional desert she had. If she and Terry had had children… But she'd finally realized her husband had no desire for a family. In marrying him, she'd just put herself in another emotionally barren situation.

No, not for Emilie. She bent to tuck the snowsuit hood more closely around the baby's ears, since the weather had turned cooler. Emilie would have love overflowing from her mother. If…

The Bluebird Café, she hoped, might provide some answers. At least today she wouldn't have Mitch sitting across from her when she dropped Tina's name into the conversation. If Cassie did know whom Tina had dated, and if that person was Mitch, she might not want to say anything in front of him.

The hardware store carried a display of window boxes and planting tools. Anne hurried past. Not even the most rabid gardener would be buying window boxes today, she thought. But it was easy to imagine the narrow wooden houses, tucked along the steep hillside, decked out with flowers in every window. Bedford Creek would look like a village in the Swiss Alps.

She pulled the café door open, to be greeted by a wave of warm air scented with apples and cinnamon, and accented with chatter. It wasn't noon yet, but the Bluebird was crowded already. It was obviously the place to be when Cassie made her famous apple dumplings.

She glanced around, aware of the flurry of curious looks sent her way. The only empty table, a small one set for two, was in the front window. She maneuvered the stroller to it. Bringing up Tina's name in a casual way wouldn't be easy with the number of people in the café. She would have to linger over her lunch, hoping to outlast most of them.

"Hi. Can I help you?" The waitress was younger than Cassie, with a name tag showing her name: Heather.

Anne felt a spurt of optimism. This girl, close in age to Tina, might remember more about Tina than Cassie did, assuming she'd worked at the café then.

"I'll have the chicken-and-dumpling soup." She put down the plastic-coated menu and smiled at the girl, whose spiky hair and multiple mismatched earrings had to be a fashion statement in a small town. "I've heard it's your specialty."

"You bet." Heather's hazel eyes ticked off every detail of Anne's slacks, cashmere sweater and gold jewelry. "Cassie's famous for it. Anything for the baby?"

"No, that's it."

She'd wait until the girl came back with her food to build on the conversation. Maybe by then she'd have lost the feeling everyone in the place was listening to her.

She bent to pull a jar of baby peaches from the diaper bag. As she straightened, the door swung open again and Mitch walked in.

Her cheeks were warm because she'd been bending over, that was all. She concentrated on Emilie, aware of Mitch's voice as he exchanged greetings with what sounded like everyone in the place. With any luck, he'd be joining one of them for lunch.

Apparently luck didn't have anything to do with it. Mitch made his way, unhurriedly, to her table. The chair scraped, and he sat down across from her as if they'd had a lunch date.

"Somehow I thought I'd find you here." He bent to greet Emilie, who responded with a crow of delight when he tickled her.

"Probably because I mentioned yesterday I wanted to come back for the chicken-dumpling soup." *And a private conversation with Cassie.*

His smile told her he knew exactly what she was thinking. "Good day for it." He waved across the room to Heather. "Another bowl of the chicken soup here, Heather."

The girl nodded. "You bet, Chief."

"You guessed—" At his warning glance she lowered her voice. "You guessed I wanted to talk with Cassie myself. I'd rather do it in private."

"You mean without me around." His face kept its relaxed expression, probably for the benefit of anyone who might be watching, but his eyes turned to stone. "I have an interest in this, remember?"

"I remember." She could so easily see his side of it. If he was innocent, naturally he'd want to protect himself by knowing anything she found out. Unfortunately, if he was guilty, the same thing applied.

"Then you can understand why I'm here." His square jaw seemed carved from granite.

"All right." She didn't have much choice. She needed his cooperation, whether she liked it or not. "Let me bring it up."

"Go ahead. But don't be surprised if she can't tell you much. If you haven't been here during tourist season, you can't imagine how crazy it is."

The soup arrived in huge, steaming pottery bowls. Heather put down a basket of freshly baked rolls nestled in a blue-checked napkin. She looked from Anne to Mitch.

"Anything else I can get you? Chief, don't you want a sandwich with that? Cassie made pulled pork barbecue."

"I'm saving room for a dumpling. You've got one back there with my name on it, haven't you?"

"Sure thing." Heather smiled, touching one earring with a plum-colored nail.

Anne could so easily imagine Mitch having this conversation with Tina. Could imagine this sort of encounter, day after day, leading to an invitation, then to an involvement he might later regret.

"Sounds as if you've been waiting on the chief for a long time." That probably wasn't the most tactful way into what she wanted to ask, but she couldn't think of a better one.

Heather shrugged. "Almost a year I've been working here. You get to know the regulars, believe me." The girl frowned at the sound of a persistent bell from the kitchen, then spun away, bluebird-trimmed apron rustling.

"I could have told you Heather didn't work here when Tina did."

"I'd rather find out for myself."

He shrugged. "I figured." He dipped the spoon into his soup.

"Attorneys prefer to ask the questions." She took a spoonful, and rich chicken flavor exploded in her mouth, chasing away the chill. "It's in my blood, I'm afraid."

"A whole family of lawyers?" He sounded as if that were the worst fate he could imagine.

"Just my father. He has a corporate practice in Hartford."

"Your mother's not a lawyer, too?"

She tried to imagine her mother doing anything so mundane, and failed. "My mother's social life keeps her occupied. And I don't have any brothers or sisters." The last thing she wanted to discuss right now was her parents. Their reaction to Emilie had been predictable, but it had still hurt. "What about you? Big family?"

She'd thought the expression in his eyes chilly before; now it had frozen. "One brother. My mother died when I was in high school. My father was long gone by then."

"I'm sorry." She suspected pain moved behind the mask he wore, but he'd never show it, not to her, probably not to anyone. "That must have made you and your brother very close."

He shrugged. "Link works heavy construction, mostly out west. He hasn't been back to Bedford Creek in a couple of years."

Anne's heart constricted. Loneliness. She recognized the symptoms. He probably wouldn't believe her if she said she knew how he felt. He probably wouldn't believe having wealthy parents who'd stayed married to each other didn't guarantee a happy family life. Didn't guarantee you wouldn't marry someone just like them. She felt the familiar regret that her marriage hadn't been… more, somehow. Deeper.

By the time their apple dumplings arrived, most of the crowd had filtered out of the café. Anne took one look at the immense dumpling, served in its own small iron skillet, and swallowed hard.

Her face must have given her away, because Mitch chuckled. "Somebody should have warned you, I guess. But you have to make a stab at it, because Cassie will be out to see how you like it."

"That's more dessert than I eat in a month."

Mitch plunged his fork into flaky pastry, and apple syrup spurted out, mixing with the mound of whipped cream. "Live dangerously. It's worth it."

The first taste melted in her mouth. By the time Cassie appeared, ready to accept applause, Anne had made a respectable dent in the dumpling.

"Wonderful, absolutely wonderful." She leaned back in her chair. "I couldn't eat another bite."

Cassie's thin lips creased in what might have been a smile. "I'll wrap it up for you. You can finish it later."

There was nothing to do but smile and nod. "I'll do that. It was just as good as I'd heard it was."

Cassie smoothed her apron. "You hear that from Mitch?"

"It might have been Mitch who told me. Or it might have been a friend of mine who used to work here. Maybe you remember her. Tina Mallory?"

Cassie frowned. "Little bit of a thing? Big blue eyes?"

"Yes, that's Tina." She held her breath. Was she about to find out something?

"Let's see…it wasn't this past season. One before, I guess. Good waitress. What's she up to now?"

"I'm afraid she passed away a few months ago."

"A kid like that?" Cassie shook her head. "You just never know, do you? I'm sorry to hear it."

"I'd hoped to meet her friends while I'm here in Bedford Creek. Do you know of anyone she was especially close to…a boyfriend, maybe?"

The woman sniffed. "Got enough to do without keeping track of the summer help's boyfriends, believe me. Can't recall anybody offhand. She came in, did her job, got along with the customers. None of my business who she hung out with after work."

Anne's hope shriveled with each word. It looked as if this would be a dead end, like so much about Tina. "If you think of anyone, would you let me know?"

"If I do."

Cassie's tone said she doubted it. Apparently Tina had passed through Cassie's life without leaving a trace.

She picked up the dumpling pans. "I'll put this in a box for you."

When she'd gone, Anne met Mitch's gaze. His look was unexpectedly sympathetic.

"Sorry. I know you hoped she'd remember something."

"It's a small town. I thought everyone knew everything in a small town."

"They do, believe me." There was an edge to Mitch's words. "But that's only regarding the other locals. When the town is flooded with tourists and summer help, you might not notice your best friend on the street."

She still found that hard to picture, but apparently it was true. If so, the chances of finding anyone who remembered anything about Tina had diminished.

"You think I ought to give up." That was what he had in mind; she was sure of it.

He shrugged. "I think you ought to leave it to me. But I suspect you're not going to."

"If you—" She stopped, realizing Cassie had emerged from the kitchen with the leftover dumpling.

"There you go." Cassie deposited the package in front of her, patting it as if it were a pet. "And I thought of something. About that friend of yours."

Anne struggled to keep the eagerness from her voice. "Did you remember someone who knew her?"

"In a manner of speaking. Seems to me she roomed with another one of the summer waitresses—girl named Marcy Brown."

"Is she here?"

Cassie shook her head almost before the words were out of her mouth. "Summer help, that's all she was. Went off at the end of the season. None of those girls stick around once the season's over. No jobs for them."

Anne tried to swallow her disappointment. "Do you know where she went from here?"

"Seems to me she was headed someplace warm for the winter. Key West, I think it was." Cassie's expression showed disapproval. "Those kids…they just flit from place to place. I might have an address for her, if I had to send her last check, but she's probably long gone by now."

"I'd like to have it just the same, if you can find it."

The woman nodded. "See what I can do, when I have the time." She frowned. "There was one other thing."

"What's that?"

"Seems to me both those girls got into that singles group Pastor Richie had at Grace Church. Maybe someone there kept up with her."

"Thank you." She was past worrying about what Cassie thought of her interest. "I appreciate it."

It was something. Not much, but a little something that just might lead somewhere.

And as for the frown in Mitch's brown eyes…well, it wasn't unexpected, was it. She'd just have to live with his disapproval, because it probably wouldn't change.

So, it looked as if he'd been wrong about how helpful Cassie might be. But then, Mitch had been wrong about a lot of things since the moment Anne walked into his life.

Those blue eyes of hers were intent on her prize. This lead to Tina's friend would encourage her. If he didn't get control of her search, she'd be chasing it all over Bedford Creek. And sooner or later someone would find out why.

"I suppose you want to rush off to Pastor Richie right now."

"Maybe not this precise moment. But it is a lead to Tina's roommate."

"That was eighteen months ago. The chance that Pastor Richie knows where to find this Marcy Brown isn't very great."

"I have to try."

A stubborn look firmed her mouth, and he suppressed the urge to smooth it away with his finger. That would really be counterproductive.

"Look, I know Simon Richie. Why don't you let me talk to him?"

"How do you know him?"

She'd probably think this coincidence suspicious, but it couldn't be helped. "Because I go to Grace Church."

Her eyebrows lifted. "Did you also belong to the singles group?"

"No." People went to that, for the most part, because they wanted a social life. He didn't, so he didn't attend. "But I know Simon Richie pretty well. The questions would come better from me."

"I'd rather ask him myself."

Somehow this sounded familiar. If Anne Morden ever depended on anybody but herself, he had yet to see it.

"Look, if you go walking into Simon's office asking about this girl, it's going to make people wonder."

"I don't see why. I'll just say I'm a friend of a friend."

She clearly still didn't see the rampant curiosity with which people in town surveyed her every move.

"Let me find a less obvious way of going about it."

She seemed to be weighing that, and for a moment he thought she'd agree.

"Grace Church…isn't that where Kate belongs?"

He nodded.

"Kate's invited me to go to a church potluck supper with her tonight. I'm sure I'll have a chance to meet your Pastor Richie. I can bring up the subject casually."

He pictured her mentioning it in front of several of the most notorious gossips in town. She was determined, so there was only one thing he could do.

"Fine." He smiled. "I'll pick you up at ten to six, then."

Her eyes narrowed. "What do you mean?"

"Didn't Kate tell you? We often go to the church suppers together." *Sometimes, anyway.*

He was doing what he had to. If he expected to stay in control of this situation, he needed to keep tabs on Anne.

Unfortunately, he had a strong suspicion he had another motivation.

"Well, don't you look nice." Kate turned from the kitchen stove to assess Anne and Emilie. "Both of you."

Anne brushed one hand down the soft wool of her emerald skirt. It matched the green of Emilie's jumper, so she'd decided to wear it. "Is it too dressy?"

Kate shook her head. "You look as pretty as a picture. I'm sure Mitch will say the same."

Oh, dear. There it was again: Kate's insistence on pairing the two of them up like bookends.

When she'd returned to the house earlier and told Kate they were going to the potluck, the elderly woman had been delighted. Anne had tried to dissuade Kate's all-too-obvious matchmaking, to no avail.

Well, what should she say? That Mitch wouldn't care how she looked? That the only reason he'd decided to take them to the potluck was to keep her from blurting out something indiscreet to Pastor Richie? It was only too obvious that that was behind his sudden desire to go with them.

There wasn't a thing she could do about Kate's misapprehension, so she might just as well change the subject. "Are you sure I can't fix something? Or stop at the bakery and buy a cake?"

"Goodness, no. There'll be more food than we can eat in a week, as it is. Everyone brings way too much stuff to these suppers."

Anne had to smile. Kate's righteous assertion was undercut by the fact that she'd prepared an enormous chicken-and-broccoli casserole, and even now was putting a pumpkin pie into her picnic basket.

"You don't think you're taking quite a bit yourself?"

"This little thing? Why, Mitch will probably eat half my casserole himself. That boy does love home cooking…probably because his mother never had time to cook much for them." Kate's eyes were filled with sympathy. "You do know about Mitch's family, don't you?"

"I know his mother died when he was in high school." She held Emilie a little closer.

"Well, his father had left before that. Poor woman worked to take care of those two boys. I'm sure no one could blame her if she wasn't there to cook supper every night. Or if she went out now and then, just to cheer herself up." Kate yanked open a drawer, muttering to herself about potholders.

Reading between the lines, it sounded as if Mitch had pretty much raised himself. Probably that, along with the military, had made him the person he was.

And what kind of person was that? Anne stared out

the window above the sink, where dusk had begun to close in on Kate's terraced hillside garden. A man who'd buried his emotions—that's what she'd thought the first time she'd seen him, and nothing had changed her mind about that. A man who had to be in control, whatever the situation.

That might make him a good cop. But it wasn't a quality, given her strong independent streak, that she'd ever found appealing in a man. Besides, she wasn't interested. In future, her family would consist of Emilie and her, that was all.

She'd told herself she could ignore the attraction she felt for Mitch. Unfortunately, it didn't seem to be working. That attraction kept popping to the surface every time they were together.

Well, if she couldn't ignore it, she could at least control it. She'd remind herself twenty times a day, if she had to, that he wasn't the kind of man for her, even without the complication of Emilie's parentage.

The doorbell rang. Kate, her hands full of casserole, nodded toward the front hallway. "Would you mind getting that, dear? It'll be Mitch, I'm sure."

"Of course." Carrying Emilie, she walked down the hall. This was a good chance to test her resolution. She swung open the door.

"Come in, please. Kate's almost ready."

Mitch stepped into the hallway, seeming to fill it. "Hey, there, Miss Emilie, are you ready to go to church?"

Emilie bounced and held out her arms to him.

"Let me take her."

Anne started to turn away just as he reached for the baby, and his hands clasped her arms instead. For a moment they stood touching, the baby between them.

Mitch's large hands tightened, their warmth penetrating the soft wool of her sweater. They were so close that she could see the network of lines at the corners of his eyes, the sweep of his dark lashes, a tiny scar at the corner of his mouth. Those chocolate eyes fixed on hers, and she could hear his breathing quicken. She had to fight the urge to step forward, right into his arms.

She took a deep breath, released Emilie to him, and stepped back. "I'll just get our coats." Astonishing, that her voice could sound so calm.

Obviously reminding herself twenty times a day wasn't going to be enough.

Chapter 6

It was a good thing Anne had pulled away when she did, Mitch decided as he drove them to the church. A very good thing. Because if she hadn't, he just might have kissed her.

Disaster—that's what it would have been, plain and simple. The woman already suspected him of seducing a young girl and leaving her pregnant. What would she think of him if he tried to kiss her?

He pulled into the church parking lot and found a space. He'd better get his head on straight where Anne was concerned. The best way to deal with his inappropriate feelings was to solve Anne's problem for her so she could leave, as soon as possible. And the next step in doing that was to get the information from Pastor Richie himself, and do it without arousing anyone's suspicions.

"Looks like a good turnout." He held open the door to the church's fellowship hall.

"Goodness, half the town must be here." Kate bustled in, depositing her picnic basket on the nearest table. "Now, Mitch, why don't you get one of the high chairs for Emilie before they're all gone. I'll find us a nice place and introduce Anne around."

A warning bell went off in his brain as he went reluctantly in search of a high chair. Who did Kate have in mind for Anne to meet? He could think of at least a half-dozen gossips of both sexes he'd just as soon she avoided.

He'd have to keep an eye on her while looking for a chance to talk to Simon Richie before she did. Right at this moment, he could use a little help.

And there it was. With a sense of relief, he spotted Alex Caine's tall, lean figure. Alex, like Brett, was a friend he could count on. He'd help keep Anne out of trouble.

He deposited the high chair, muttered an excuse to Anne, who seemed to be avoiding his eyes, and worked his way through the crowd to Alex.

"Alex. I'm glad to see you."

His friend, leaning on the stick he sometimes used since surviving a plane crash a year ago, gave him a sardonic look. "Don't you mean you're surprised to see me?"

He grinned. "That, too." Another legacy of the accident seemed to be that Alex didn't socialize much.

"I decided this was my best chance to see your Ms. Morden. And baby."

"Not my Ms. Morden." *And not my baby.* But he didn't need to say that to Alex. He'd said it once, and it was a measure of their friendship that Alex accepted his denial without question.

Alex's gaze rested on Anne. "Kate seems to have adopted her already. Are you sure it was a good idea to bring her and the baby here?"

"Kate invited them. And once Anne found out Simon Richie might have some information on the girl's roommate, there was no stopping her from coming."

Alex took a step or two toward the wall, so they were safely out of the flow of traffic and of earshot. "Have you remembered anything else about the girl—Tina, was it?"

"Tina." He gave a frustrated shake of his head. "What's to remember? I barely knew her. She was a nice kid who poured my morning coffee, that's it. I can't figure why she'd lie about something like this."

"I'd hate to believe you're never going to know the reason."

He could see Alex's mind ticking over possibilities. Even back in high school, Alex had always been the one with the analytical approach to everything. Where Brett had relied on charm and Mitch on strength, Alex had been the thinker of the team.

"The roommate's the best bet, I suppose," Alex said. "If anyone knows who the girl dated, she would."

Mitch frowned, watching Anne settle Emilie in the high chair. "It just keeps eating at me. Why me? Why did she give my name?"

Alex was silent for a long moment, so long that Mitch turned to look at him. He encountered a searching gaze. "Have you thought about Link?"

Mitch's stomach twisted at the name. *Link.* His brother. "Yes." He bit off the word. "Of course I have. I know what you're thinking. Using my name would be just the sort of sick joke he'd find funny. But you're forgetting, the girl knew me. Besides, he wasn't in Bedford Creek then."

"You sure?"

"I'm sure." Link had a tendency to show up on Mitch's doorstep whenever he was broke or in trouble. "We had a fight the last time he was here, that previous spring. A bad one. I told him I was done bailing him out. He hasn't been back since." He managed a half smile. "I'd like to believe that means he's gotten his act together, but I doubt it."

"People change."

"Not Link." *Not our father.*

Alex shrugged. "I'll take your word for it. Look, they're starting to get the food ready. You need my help with something before I round up my son for dinner?"

"Just keep an eye on Anne. I want to see Simon alone before she has a chance to collar him. But I don't want her getting the third degree from any of our local busybodies."

"And you expect me to prevent that?" Alex lifted an eyebrow. "You're underestimating them."

"But I'm not overestimating you." Mitch grinned. "You know they're intimidated by the Caine name. And you can flatten anybody with that superior look of yours. Just use it."

Simon Richie charged into the hall then, filled with an energy that never ceased to amaze Mitch. Simon had to be close to sixty, but nothing slowed him down when it came to taking care of his flock. If either Tina or her roommate had left an address, Simon would find it.

"I'm going to try and catch him after he says the blessing," Mitch said. "Remember, keep your eye on Anne."

Alex sketched him a mock salute. "Will do."

He bowed his head and tried to concentrate on the words of the prayer. Simon had an informal way of addressing God that made Him sound like a personal friend Simon was inviting to share their meal. It always made him vaguely uncomfortable. Mitch believed, of course. But Simon seemed to have found a closeness that had always eluded Mitch.

The prayer over, a wave of people swept toward the long serving table. Anne still stood at her chair, eyes closed in prayer for another moment. The sight seemed to clutch his heart. What prayer kept her so still, so focused?

Anne gripped the plate Kate had given her and edged closer to the serving table. Kate had insisted on watching Emilie so she could go first, since Mitch seemed to have disappeared. She'd noticed him talking to a man Kate said was Alex Caine, owner of Bedford Creek's only industry. The next time she looked, he was gone.

Not that she cared. The memory of that moment in Kate's front hall made her uncomfortable. She hadn't come to this dinner to be with Mitch.

"I don't think we've met." The woman in front of her smiled a welcome. "Let me introduce you to some of these hungry people."

By the time she'd reached the end of the buffet table, half-a-dozen names buzzed in her mind and way too much food had found its way onto her plate. She'd begun to feel that all she'd done since arriving in Bedford Creek was eat.

"I'm finished." She deposited her plate across from

Kate, next to the high chair Mitch had put at the end of the table. "You go on now, Kate."

Kate rose and looked around the crowded room with a frown. "I don't know where Mitch is. He'd better get back here before the food's gone."

"I don't think there's any danger of that." And she'd probably have a more placid meal if he weren't sitting next to her, drawing her awareness with every breath.

She'd just given Emilie a biscuit to chew on when she became conscious of someone standing across from her. She looked up to meet an intent stare.

The older woman's narrow face formed a brief smile. "You'll be Kate's new guest."

Anne nodded. "Anne Morden. This is Emilie."

"I'm Enid Lawrence." The woman's gaze swerved, sharply curious, to the baby and back again. "Tell me, what brings you to Bedford Creek?"

Anne should have been better prepared for a direct question, she thought. As she groped for an answer, someone intervened.

"Excuse me, Enid." It was the man she'd seen Mitch talking with earlier. "I think your daughter is trying to get your attention." He diverted the woman smoothly away from the table, taking the chair she'd been blocking. "I'll keep Anne company until Kate gets back."

Enid Lawrence frowned. For a moment Anne thought she'd argue, but then she nodded, giving Anne a frosted look. "We'll talk later." It almost sounded like a threat.

She moved away, and Anne assessed Mitch's friend, Alex Caine. He was tall, nearly as tall as Mitch, but not as broadly built. His lean, aristocratic face was handsome, but marred by a scar that ran along one cheek.

He had the inward look Anne had seen before in people who lived with pain.

"Alex Caine." He held out his hand. "Sorry if I interrupted, but Enid can be overwhelming at times. "Curiosity' is her middle name."

She lifted her eyebrows. "Did Mitch suggest I needed protecting?"

She caught a flash of surprise mixed with amusement in his dark eyes. "You caught us, I'm afraid. Mitch thought you might prefer not to explain why you're here too many times tonight."

Now it was her turn to be surprised. "Mitch told you?" She'd have expected him to guard that information more carefully.

"Mitch and I go back a long way. He doesn't keep many secrets from me. Or from Brett."

"I see."

He frowned. "I'm not sure you do. I know Mitch as well as I know anyone. He tells me he didn't—" He stopped, probably reminded of the number of people in the room. "Let's just say I'd trust him with my life." Some emotion she couldn't identify flickered in his eyes. "In fact, I already have."

A dozen questions bubbled to her tongue, but she didn't have a chance to ask any of them. Kate came back, and in the flurry as she settled, Alex excused himself. The next instant, someone slid into the chair next to her. She didn't need to look to know it was Mitch. That aura of solid strength touched her senses.

He brushed her sleeve. She looked, startled, to find he was handing her a slip of paper.

"What's this?" She started to unfold it, but his hand closed over hers.

"It's that information you wanted—"

His fingers tightened a little, and her skin seemed to tingle from their pressure.

"—the latest address and phone number Pastor Richie could find. I had him jot it down for you."

She looked at the address, somewhere in Florida, written in an unfamiliar hand on church stationery. She folded the paper and slipped it in her bag.

"I didn't expect you to do that. Thank you."

"My pleasure." A smile tugged at his mouth. "No ulterior motives, I promise you. I just thought it would cause less comment if I asked. I hope you find her."

Perhaps he didn't expect her to believe that, but it sounded genuine. He'd given the information to her, rather than following up on it himself. Almost as if they could trust each other.

Careful, her lawyer's mind cautioned. *Look at all the evidence, then make a decision.*

She'd like, just this once, to rely on her instinct, the instinct that said he was telling the truth. That he could be trusted.

Unfortunately she couldn't. Not with Emilie's future at stake.

Anne rolled the stroller through the police station doorway, the memory of the last time she'd done that flickering through her mind. Only a few days ago, but it seemed like a lifetime. Odd, that she'd begun to feel at home in Bedford Creek so quickly, almost as if it had been waiting for her.

"Ms. Morden!" Wanda exclaimed. "Look who's here, Chief."

Mitch stood in the doorway to his office, ushering

someone inside. He swung around at Wanda's words. Anne wasn't mistaking the warmth in his eyes at the sight of her, was she?

"Anne. I hoped I'd see you today." He sent a glance toward his office. "Trouble is, I have someone here right now. Can you wait?"

Aware of Wanda's sharp eyes dissecting every gesture, Anne nodded. "Actually, I have a couple of errands to run. Why don't I come back in, say, half an hour."

"Sounds good." He reached past her to hold the door for the stroller, and his hand brushed her shoulder. "I'll see you then."

She pushed the stroller up the sidewalk, still feeling that casual touch. When the number Pastor Richie had passed on proved no longer valid, directory assistance and even the pastor had been unable to help her further. She had no choice but to ask Mitch for his help in tracking down Marcy Brown. But now she wondered if she'd made the right decision in bringing this to him. Everything Mitch had done was consistent with his being an honorable man who was telling her the truth. But could she rely on him to trace Tina's roommate?

The street staggered its way up the hill, and by the time she reached the pharmacy she was winded. She purchased shampoo and a teething ring, then glanced at her watch as she went out the door. Another fifteen minutes before Mitch expected her.

Someone had placed a bright yellow bench outside the pharmacy, probably for the convenience of all those tourists everyone assured her showed up in the summer. She sat down, positioning the stroller so the baby was out of the wind. The weak sunshine touched her cheeks, a promise of summer to come. A fat robin, back from his trip south, perched on the edge of a sidewalk planter and cocked his head.

A shadow fell across her. "Ms. Morden."

She looked up at the woman who'd introduced herself at the church supper the night before—the woman Alex had seemed determined to help her avoid. Her mind scrambled briefly, then came up with a name.

"Mrs. Lawrence. It's nice to see you again." Or was it? Alex had steered the woman off, implying she was a gossip, and that avid look in her eyes seemed to confirm it.

"I hoped I'd run into you." The woman perched on the bench next to her, tucking her brown wool coat around her legs. "We didn't have a chance to get acquainted last night. I'm Enid."

"I met so many people last night. Your congregation is so friendly to a stranger. It made me feel at home."

"You're from Philadelphia." The woman made it a statement, as if docketing facts. "Kate told me that. But she didn't say why you're here."

Anne edged an inch farther from that blatant curiosity. "Didn't she?"

Enid Lawrence shook her head with an affronted look, as if she had a right to every morsel of knowledge she could collect. "She didn't. It's not to see Chief Donovan, I hope?"

Anne weighed the probable results of outright rudeness in deterring the woman and decided even that wouldn't work. "Not exactly," she evaded. "Bedford Creek is so charming. I understand you have quite a lot of visitors."

"Tourists." She sniffed. "But I'm glad you're not here to see that Mitch Donovan."

The venom in the woman's voice startled her. Everyone she'd met thus far seemed devoted to Mitch. Enid Lawrence seemed to be the exception.

Enid apparently took silence for interest. "He's not really one of us, you know."

"One of us?" She'd certainly had the impression Mitch had grown up in Bedford Creek. What was the woman driving at?

"He's a Donovan." Enid sniffed again. "Everyone in town knows what the Donovans are like. Worthless, the lot of them. The father would steal anything that wasn't nailed down, and those boys were just as bad. Carousing, getting into one scrape after another. Troublemakers, both of them. As for the mother and her drinking..."

The venom had spilled out so quickly that Anne hadn't had time to react. Suddenly revulsion ripped through her with an almost physical shudder. She got up quickly. "I'm afraid I have to go."

Enid frowned. "I'm just telling you because you're a newcomer. I wouldn't want you to be taken in."

"I don't care to discuss Chief Donovan with you." Her anger surprised her. Shouldn't she be taking the opportunity to find out anything she could about Mitch? Instead, she felt the need to defend him.

The woman rose, bringing her eyes to a level with Anne's. "Fine, if that's all the thanks I get for taking an interest. Mitch Donovan wouldn't even be here if Alex Caine didn't owe him something."

Anne managed to get the stroller out from beside the bench, her hands shaking a little. "Excuse me, please."

She swung the stroller around and set off downhill, heels clicking in her rush to get away from the woman.

No wonder Alex Caine had intervened last night. The woman was absolutely poisonous.

Her words trickled through Anne's mind. Mitch was not trustworthy—that was the gist of it. The woman was convinced Mitch was no good, apparently because of his father's reputation.

Unfair, her instincts shouted. That was unfair. The woman had no right blackening Mitch's reputation because of what his father had done.

But she'd also talked about trouble Mitch and his brother had gotten into, had implied that made him not trustworthy. Trusting him was what she was about to do. And it was something she didn't do easily.

Her impetuous charge down the hill had already brought her to the police station. If she saw Mitch while Enid Lawrence's bitter words echoed in her ears… Fair or not, she just couldn't do it. She'd have to go back to the house and think this over.

"Anne." Mitch opened the door and held it for her. "I've been watching for you. Come in."

She could feel herself flushing. "It was nothing important. I don't need to bother you now."

His brown eyes seemed to frost over. He stepped onto the walk and closed the door. "Don't you mean you've just had an interesting discussion with Enid Lawrence?"

She felt as guilty as if she'd sought out the woman. "How did you know she was talking to me?"

He jerked his head toward the bench outside the pharmacy. "I was watching for you to come back. I saw your little chat."

"I certainly didn't instigate it."

"You didn't avoid it, either." His jaw looked tight.

Her faint feelings of guilt changed to anger. "I

walked away from her, in case you didn't notice. I'm not interested in gossip, even if—"

"Even if it supports the things you'd like to believe about me?"

His expression froze as a passerby eyed them. She seized a chance to gain control.

"I didn't go looking for the woman." She lowered her voice. "I'm not soliciting gossip about you, if that's what you think."

That probably was exactly how it looked, and there wasn't a thing she could do about it.

Or maybe there was.

The words pressed on her lips, wanted to be said. She could take the woman seriously or not. If she didn't, there was an easy way to prove it, by asking for his help.

She took a deep breath. "Now can we forget Enid Lawrence?" She wasn't sure she could, but she wanted to try. "I need your help. I want you to help me find Marcy Brown."

A few minutes later they walked back toward the house together, in tacit agreement that the subject was better discussed away from the station.

Anne looked carefully at her feelings. Could she forget Enid's poisoned words?

"Worried about it?"

She glanced up at Mitch, startled and guilty, then realized he was talking about the roommate, not about what Enid had said.

"No, not worried, exactly." She could hardly tell him she was trying to sort out her opinion of him. "Concerned about the time element, I suppose. How will you try to find Marcy?"

"Plenty of ways to track people down." He frowned.

"The trouble is, this isn't a police case. It limits what I can do."

That hadn't occurred to her. "What *can* you do?" She hoped her question didn't sound as sharp to him as it did to her. If he couldn't or wouldn't use police resources, what good had it done to ask him?

"Believe me, if people knew how easy it is to get information on them, they'd be shocked. I can follow up on her social security number and credit reports, for a start."

"That should lead somewhere, surely. It's not as if the woman is trying to hide from us. She doesn't know we're looking for her."

"We'll find her." He slowed while she eased the stroller over a bump in the walk. "I just hope she knows something useful."

"Girlfriends do talk to each other."

He nodded. "That's about what Alex said. He thinks Tina had to have confided in someone, and who better than her roommate."

"I hope we're both right." She stuffed her hands in her jacket pockets. "He surprised me last night. When I realized you'd told him, I mean."

"We don't keep many secrets from each other."

It was much the same thing Alex had said. "He told me he'd trusted you with his life." She hadn't intended to say that, and knew it sounded like prying.

"Ancient history."

Enid had implied Alex's friendship was somehow owed to Mitch, and the thought left an acrid taste in her mouth. She didn't want to think that about either of them. She wanted to believe they were who they seemed to be.

"Is it something you can talk about?"

His gaze rested on her face for a long moment, then he shrugged. "If you want to hear it. It's not a big secret. Just some trouble we got into when—"

He stopped abruptly, then swung away from her. "Just a second."

Before she could say a word, he'd vaulted over the picket fence in front of the house they were passing. He plunged into the shrubbery by the porch and emerged a second later with a wriggling captive. Davey Flagler.

Apparently Mitch's police instincts never shut off. That was something important to remember as she tried to understand him. He was always a cop.

Chapter 7

Great. As if things weren't already bad enough, now Davey had to act up again. Mitch tightened his grip on the boy, who wiggled like a fish on a hook.

He couldn't kid himself. Anne's opinion of him had probably taken a nosedive after her little chat with Enid Lawrence, and no wonder. He could just imagine what Enid had to say about him and his family.

Davey was going to make matters worse. Anne would go into her defense attorney mode; she wouldn't be able to stop herself. And they'd be adversaries again, armed with their own visions of what was right.

Well, it couldn't be helped. He had a job to do, and he was going to do it, regardless of what Anne thought of him.

"Trespassing, Davey?" He eyed the culprit. "You

wouldn't have been thinking about that package on Mrs. Jefferson's porch, now would you?"

"I don't know what you're talking about." Sullen black eyes stared up at him. "You're crazy."

Over the boy's head he caught the flicker of surprise that crossed Anne's face. She hadn't noticed the package, any more than she'd noticed the kid. Being a cop had heightened his ability to register what other people didn't.

"Crazy?" He glared at Davey. "I'd be crazy to take your word for anything. Go ahead, tell me what you were doing in Mrs. Jefferson's yard."

"I wasn't after any package." Davey nearly spat the words at him. "I thought I heard a cat."

He could almost see the wheels turning in Davey's brain as he tried to come up with a plausible story. At least the kid wasn't an accomplished liar—yet.

"It looked like it was hurt." Davey put on a righteous expression that wouldn't have convinced the most gullible person in the world. "I was just trying to help. You always think I'm doing something wrong."

"That's because you usually are." Anger surged, and he shoved it down. A cop had no right to feel anger. That wasn't part of his job. Mitch didn't know why Davey set off a firestorm within him every time he dealt with the kid, but he had to stay detached.

"The boy didn't actually take anything, as far as I can tell."

Anne's intervention didn't do a thing to douse his anger. "Only because I grabbed him first," he said, tightening his grip as Davey wiggled again. "Guess I'll have to speak to the delivery man about leaving things on porches. Looks like that's just too much temptation."

"You're declaring him guilty without any evidence at all." Anne's eyes shot angry sparks. "You don't know what was in his mind."

"Just stay out of it, Counselor. I don't need advice on how to do my job."

"Maybe you do. You can't accuse someone of something that hasn't been done yet."

"Look, this isn't the big city." Anne would never understand what things were like in a small town. Or why.

"Believe me, I'm only too aware of that. You wouldn't get away with this there—not without someone filing a complaint, anyway."

He counted to ten. It didn't help. "A cop in a small town is different. People expect us to anticipate trouble, and most times we can. And they expect us to prevent it, not wait around until it happens."

He had a sudden mental image of himself explaining, talking too much in front of the kid, and knew it was because he wanted Anne to think well of him. And that was probably an impossible goal.

"You can't—" she began.

"Yes, I can."

He turned to the still squirming boy. He had to concentrate on his job, not on what Anne thought of him.

"I want to see you and your father at the station tomorrow, right after school."

"But my dad might have to work. Or maybe—"

"No excuses, just be there. Because if you're not, I'll come after you. Got it?"

Davey's mouth set, and he nodded.

Mitch released his grip. Davey didn't bother trying to act macho. He just ran.

Mitch watched him go, then turned back to Anne, knowing he'd see condemnation in her eyes.

"I suppose you're proud of yourself, bullying a boy like that."

"What do you know about 'a boy like that'?" His anger flared again, startling him.

"I know anyone would respond better to kindness than to threats."

"Kindness!" She didn't understand. She never would. "Let me tell you what it's going to take for Davey Flagler to turn into a decent citizen instead of winding up in big trouble. He's going to have to work harder, perform better, be smarter than anyone else, because he's starting a lot of steps behind. And he won't do that if people make excuses for him."

Anne looked at him for a long moment, blue eyes blazing in a white face. "Are you talking about Davey Flagler? Or are you talking about yourself?"

She didn't wait for an answer. She walked away quickly, head high, pushing the stroller toward Kate's place and leaving Mitch fuming.

Hours later Anne slowed as she approached the front porch of Mitch's house. She stopped just beyond the pool of light from the street lamp. When she'd told Kate she needed to talk to Mitch, Kate had been only too eager to watch Emilie for her.

The windows of his small house glowed with a warm yellow light. She shivered, huddling a little deeper into her jacket. The temperature had dropped like a stone the moment the sun went down, and the stars were crystalline in a black sky.

She couldn't stand out here in the dark and the cold.

She might as well march right up to the door and get this over with.

Her cheeks went hot in spite of the cold air. She couldn't believe she'd spoken to Mitch the way she had. Even if she had been right, they didn't have the kind of relationship that allowed her to say something so personal.

Lord, I'm sorry. I let my temper get the better of me again. I acted as if I knew what was right for everyone.

Confessing her mistake was one step in the right direction. Now she had to tell Mitch. She bit her lip. She had to tell him, because that was the right thing to do. It was also the only way to get things back on an even keel between them. That was all she wanted.

She went quickly up the steps and rang the bell.

Mitch opened the door, a dark bulk against the light behind him in the hallway. She couldn't make out his expression, which might be just as well.

"Anne. I'm surprised to see you."

He said the words in such a neutral tone that she didn't know what to make of his mood. "I came over to apologize." It was better just to blurt it out. "I said things I shouldn't have this afternoon, and I wouldn't want you to…"

The sentence died out. The problem was that she really did think she knew why he reacted to Davey as he did. She just didn't have the right to say so.

"Forget it." He stepped back, opening the door wider. "Come in. You don't have to stand out there in the cold."

"I shouldn't. I left Emilie with Kate, and I wouldn't want to impose." And going into his house felt like stepping too far into his life.

He moved under the light. "I'll bet Kate is having

the time of her life. If you come back too soon, she'll be disappointed." He gestured. "Come in, please. We can't talk with you hovering on the doorstep."

He was probably right about Kate. She stepped into the tiny hallway, and he closed the door behind her.

"In here." He ushered her through an archway on the right. "Make yourself comfortable. I have coffee brewing."

Before she could protest, he'd vanished through the door at the back of the hall. She shrugged, turned to the archway, and stopped in surprise. Whatever she'd expected of Mitch's house, it wasn't this.

Pale yellow walls and warm wooden wainscoting set off a living room that might have appeared in a country living magazine. The room was brightened with chintz; braided rugs accented the wide-paneled wooden floors. A fire burned cheerfully in the brick fireplace. It certainly didn't look like any bachelor's apartment she'd ever imagined.

She crossed slowly to the fireplace. It took a moment to realize what was missing. There were no family pictures. Mitch had a family-oriented room without any hint of family. In fact, only one photo graced the mantel. She moved closer, holding out her hands to the blaze, and looked at it.

Mitch, Brett and Alex. She should have expected that. They couldn't have been much more than high school age in the picture, but she recognized each of them at first glance. The photo had been taken outdoors, with the three of them lined up on a log.

"Looking at the three monkeys?" China mugs rattled on a tray as Mitch came in with the coffee. He put the tray on the coffee table and came to stand next to her.

Too close, that was all she could think. He stood too close for her peace of mind. He was dressed as casually as she'd ever seen him, in jeans and a cream sweater that made his skin glow. She couldn't breathe without inhaling the faint musky scent of his after-shave lotion.

She forced herself to concentrate on his words. "Why three monkeys? You mean like 'hear no evil'?"

"Something like that. It's what Brett always calls that picture."

Something almost sad touched his eyes as he looked at it, and she found herself wanting to know why. "You were pretty young there, weren't you?"

"Teenagers." He shrugged. "Thought we had the world by the tail, like most kids that age."

He gestured toward the couch, and she sat, then wished she'd taken the chair instead. He left a foot between them when he sat beside her, but it was still too close.

Businesslike, she reminded herself. *You want to get things back on a nice, businesslike basis.*

Then he smiled at her over his coffee mug, and her heart thumped out of rhythm. They were alone together. Maybe she should have brought the baby, as a sort of buffer between her and Mitch.

"I really am sorry." She hurried into speech, because it seemed safer than sitting in silence.

"Forget it."

"Have you?"

"No," he replied.

She met his gaze, startled, and he gave her a rueful smile.

"I decided I'd better not forget it, because I think you're right."

That smile was doing such odd things to her that she wasn't sure she could say anything intelligible. Luckily, he didn't seem to expect anything.

"I've been sitting here going over it. Trying to be angry." He frowned into the flames. "Instead, I kept seeing Davey's face, thinking about his family. Wondering if you're right about me." He shrugged. "It would account for a lot."

"Your family…" She stopped, remembering the unpleasant things Enid had said about his family. About him.

His face seemed to freeze. "I could never count on my family for anything."

"I'm sorry." It seemed to be all she could say.

He reached forward, picking up a poker to shove a log into place. The flames leaped, casting flickering shadows on the strong planes of his face.

"When I look at Davey, I guess I see the kid I was. Running the streets with no one who cared enough to make me behave myself."

Maybe it was safer to keep the focus on Davey, instead of on Mitch. "Does Davey have anyone?" she asked.

"Just his father." His expression eased slightly. He'd probably much rather talk about Davey than himself. He leaned elbows on his knees, letting the poker dangle. "Ed Flagler doesn't mistreat the boy, as far as we can tell. He just doesn't pay attention to him. Davey's headed for trouble if something doesn't change."

Obviously she'd been wrong. He did care what happened to the boy.

"You're planning to talk to the father. Do you think you can get through to him? Make him see the damage he's doing to his son?"

"It's worth a try." His mouth tightened into a grim, painful line. "At least he's still there. That counts for something."

Pain gripped her heart suddenly, but it wasn't for Davey. It was for Mitch. He betrayed so clearly the lonely boy he'd been. Maybe he still hadn't admitted to himself how much his father's leaving had hurt him.

This house—she glanced at the room with new eyes. Mitch hadn't just bought a place because he was tired of renting. He'd created a home here—the home he'd never had before.

She cleared her throat, trying to suppress the tears that choked her. "If talking to the father doesn't do any good, what will you do about Davey?"

"Guess I can't just throw him in a cell." He sent a sideways glance at her. "Some smart lawyer would probably get after me if I did that."

"Probably," she agreed.

"So I'm going to put him to work."

"Work? Isn't he kind of young for that?"

He shrugged. "Never too early to learn the value of work, especially for a kid like Davey. I figure I'll offer to pay him for doing some odd jobs around the station, maybe even around here. That might make him see he doesn't have to steal if he wants something."

He understood the child better than she'd thought. He was going to a lot of trouble for Davey.

"Better watch out. He might start looking up to you."

His mouth quirked. "That'll be the day. Far as he's concerned, I'm the enemy."

"It's pretty obvious the boy needs a role model. Maybe he's found one."

Some emotion she couldn't identify shadowed his

eyes. "I'm not setting myself up to be a substitute father. With the example my father set for me, I don't know how."

There wasn't anything she could say to that, was there? But it was pretty clear that her goal of getting things back to a businesslike basis between them was doomed to failure.

The pain in her heart for the lonely boy who lurked inside him told her she'd already started to care too much.

What was the matter with him? He was saying things he'd never said to a living soul. Not even to Alex, though Alex probably guessed most of it. Somehow in a few short days, Anne Morden had managed to touch a part of him he'd closed off a long time ago.

She looked as if she didn't know what to say. *Change the subject,* that was what he had to do. Get off the painful topic that touched too close to his heart.

He nodded toward the mantel photo of himself with Brett and Alex. "That picture was actually taken on the trip I started to tell you about today."

"Trip? Oh, you mean the incident Alex mentioned."

"Our adventure." He felt his voice get lighter as he steered away from the painful subject of fatherhood.

"I'm almost afraid to ask what kind of adventure, especially since Alex seems to think you saved his life."

He shook his head. "Alex exaggerated. If anything, he saved my life. Or maybe we all saved each other's lives."

Anne picked up her coffee mug and leaned back. The plain gold band she wore on her right hand winked in the firelight. "That sounds like a story."

Probably she was as glad as he was to get off painful subjects. "Our senior camping trip. The three of us were assigned to work together. We were orienteering—you know, finding our way in the woods with just a map and a compass."

"I know. Believe it or not, I went to summer camp once upon a time. I can even build a campfire."

"You get the idea, then. We were supposed to find our way to a meeting point. Trouble was, nobody'd counted on Brett losing the map. Or on a torrential rainstorm. The three of us ended up trapped in a quarry with the water rising." Amazing that he could smile about it now. "It was like every bad disaster movie you ever saw."

"It doesn't sound like much fun to me. How can you joke about it?"

"You know what teenage boys are like. We thought we were indestructible. Right up until the moment we realized we might not get out."

He'd been making light of it, but all of a sudden the memory got a little too real. He felt the cold rain pelting his face, felt the wind threatening to rip his slicker from his back. Felt his hands slipping from cold wet rock.

"What did you do?"

"First we blamed each other. Then we fought about how we were going to get out."

"That sounds predictable."

"That almost got Alex killed."

In an instant he was back in the quarry, grasping Alex's hand as the water pulled at him. His hand slipping, muscles screaming...

"What happened?"

"Brett and I managed to get him onto a rock." They'd huddled, drenched, clinging to each other, sensing death was only a misstep away. "That got us smart in a hurry. We prayed. And we realized working together was the only way we'd ever get out."

He'd never forget the next few hours. They'd struggled up the rock face, helping each other, goading each other on. They'd finally reached the top, exhausted but alive.

"No wonder you've stayed close all this time. It changed your lives."

She was too perceptive. She saw right through him, saw the things he didn't say.

"I guess it did." His voice had gone husky, and he cleared his throat. "Before that, I figured people were right about me, so what was the use of trying? Afterward…well, it seemed that if God bothered to pull me out of that quarry, He expected something from me."

"That's when you went into the military?"

He nodded. "Nobody needed me here." She probably knew he was thinking of his family, disintegrated completely by that time, thanks to his father.

She reached toward him, as if to offer comfort. But when her hand touched his, something far more vivid than comfort flashed between them.

Firelight reflected in the eyes that met his—wide, aware.

He shouldn't. But he couldn't help it. He leaned forward until his lips met hers.

The kiss was tentative at first, and then he felt her breath catch. Her lips softened against his. He drew her closer, inhaling the warm sweet scent of her. He didn't want this to end.

Her hands pushed against his chest, and he released her instantly.

She drew back, cheeks flushing, eyes not quite meeting his. "I think I'd better go." She shot off the couch.

Choking down his disappointment, he nodded.

He could try to pretend it hadn't happened, but that wouldn't work. He'd blown it. This time he'd really blown it. He'd given in to the need to hold her, and now she'd never want him near her again.

Chapter 8

Mitch shoved his desk chair away from the computer hard enough to hit the wall. Why wasn't he finding anything on the elusive Marcy Brown? It was as if the woman had vanished off the face of the earth.

Wanda would probably do this search better than he could, but he wasn't about to involve her in it. No, he'd just have to struggle on and hope he didn't drive himself crazy before he came up with something.

He couldn't kid himself that his current state of frustration had much to do with his lack of success. The problem gnawing his gut and tangling his nerves was a lot more personal than that: Anne, and last night's kiss.

How had he let himself do that? In fact, how had he let the entire situation happen? He'd told Anne things about himself that he'd never told anyone else, and what he hadn't told her she'd guessed. And then he'd capped his indiscretion by kissing the one woman in the world he should have had sense enough to keep his hands off.

The trouble was, he'd let himself become attracted to Anne. He frowned at the chair where she'd sat that first day, when she'd dropped her bombshell into his life. She'd been an unwelcome intrusion, maybe even a threat. Now...

Now she'd become important to him. But even if it hadn't been for the complication of Emilie's parentage, she was out of his league. And even if none of that existed, there would still be an impenetrable barrier between them. All she wanted was a family, and that was the one thing he'd decided a long time ago that he'd never have.

His fists clenched on the arms of the chair. *The apple doesn't fall far from the tree. Those Donovans are all alike.* You hear that often enough when you are a kid, you get the message. He wouldn't risk being the kind of father his had been.

He reached toward the keyboard. *Find Marcy Brown.* That was the only useful thing he could do.

The telephone rang. He frowned, snatching it up. Hadn't he told Wanda not to disturb him?

"Mitch, Wanda said you were busy, so don't you go blaming her." Kate sounded more flustered than usual. "I just had to talk to you, and I've got to leave in a few minutes."

"Leave? Where are you going?" Kate never left the bed-and-breakfast when she had a guest. It was unheard of.

"My sister's had a bad fall, maybe broken her hip." Kate's voice trembled on the verge of tears. "I just don't know, at her age, what we'll do if it's broken." She took an audible breath. "I've got to go, right now."

"Of course you do," he soothed. "I'm sure Anne won't mind moving to another bed-and-breakfast, under the circumstances."

"Well, we've got that taken care of. Anne says she'd rather stay here, since she's got the baby settled and all. There's plenty of food in the kitchen, and she says they'll be just fine."

"Then you don't have to worry, do you? You just get on to your sister's and call if there's anything you need."

"That's just it. I need your help."

"You've got it." Kate surely knew by now that she could count on him.

"I want you to look in on Anne and the baby. Promise me, now."

"I'm sure Anne…"

Doesn't want me looking in on her. That's what he wanted to say, but he couldn't.

"Please." Worry laced Kate's voice. "Anne didn't feel well when she came in last night, I could tell. I want you to check on them."

If Anne hadn't felt well, it was probably because of what had happened between them, but he could hardly say that to Kate.

"All right. I promise I'll look in on Anne and the baby."

And somehow or other I'll keep my hands off her and my feelings in check.

"Are you sure you're going to be all right?" Kate hovered at the door, car keys in hand, a worried expression on her face.

"We'll be fine," Anne said for what seemed the tenth time. Kate's worries about her sister were undoubtedly spilling over onto everyone else. She balanced Emilie on one hip and gave Kate a reassuring smile. "We're used to being by ourselves, don't forget."

"You've been looking a little pale since last night." Kate frowned. "Are you sure…"

"I'm fine." *Except for a monster of a headache and the feeling I've made a complete fool of myself.* "You go on. And if there's anything else you want me to do here, just call and let me know."

Kate nodded, finally edging her way out the door. "Mitch will be by to see if you need anything. He promised."

She felt the smile stiffen on her face. "He doesn't have to do that."

"I'll feel better if he does." Kate turned, waved bye-bye to Emilie, and started down the steps. Apparently the thought that Mitch was in charge gave her enough confidence to leave.

Anne closed the door and leaned against it. The last thing she needed or wanted was to have Mitch checking up on her. After last night's fiasco, she didn't know how she'd manage to look him in the eye.

What had gotten into her? She'd practically invited him to kiss her. And when he had, she'd bolted like a scared rabbit.

She hadn't been prepared for the devastating effect of his lips on hers—that was the truth of the matter. She'd been involved in the closeness of the moment, responding to his openness with her. She'd told herself they were becoming friends. The next moment they'd touched, and she'd known this was something much more powerful than simple friendship.

She rubbed her temples wearily. Maybe if she could get rid of this headache, she could think about the whole subject rationally. Her cheeks felt hot, and her ability to reason seemed to have vanished. Emilie's teething had given her a restless night and too much wakeful time remembering that moment in Mitch's arms.

"How about a nap?" She stroked the baby's cheek. "Okay? Emilie will take a nap and Mommy will, too. Then we'll both feel better."

And then maybe she could get her composure back in place before she saw Mitch again.

It was nearly suppertime, and none of those things had happened. Emilie fussed, chewing restlessly on a teething biscuit, then throwing it on the floor. The fourth time Anne picked it up, she decided her head would probably explode if she bent over one more time.

You couldn't get sick if you were a single parent. She'd come to that realization at some point in the last few months. You just couldn't, not unless you had a reliable baby-sitter on tap. At home in Philadelphia there were a half-a-dozen people she could call.

But she wasn't at home, and the only person she knew well enough to call in Bedford Creek was the one person she definitely would not call.

She bounced the wailing baby on her hip and started down the stairs. She'd better get the teething ring she'd put in the refrigerator to chill. Maybe that would soothe Emilie.

A wave of dizziness hit her halfway down. She sat abruptly, clutching Emilie, and leaned her head against the rail.

"It's all right." She patted Emilie, wishing someone would say that to her. "It's going to be all right. We're fine."

The knock on the door sounded far away, too far

away for her to do anything about it. Maybe whoever it was would just go away.

Thirty seconds later the door clicked open. Mitch appeared in the hallway. "Anne?" He looked, then took the steps two at a time and knelt beside her. "What is it? What's wrong?"

"Nothing." She made a valiant effort to straighten up. "I'm fine."

"Funny, you don't look fine. Your cheeks are beet red, and your eyes are glazed."

"Thanks," she muttered. She should have been offended, but it took too much effort.

He put his hand on her forehead. His palm felt so cool. She just wanted him to leave it there until the throbbing in her temples went away.

"You're running a fever." He touched Emilie's cheek. "What about the baby? Is she sick, too?"

She struggled to concentrate. Okay, she was sick. No wonder she felt so bad. "Just teething, I think."

"Come here, little girl." He lifted Emilie from her arms. "Are you feeling cranky? Let's give Mommy a rest."

To her astonishment, Emilie's wails ceased. The silence was welcoming.

"Thank you." She forced herself to focus. "If you could just bring me her teething ring and a bottle, maybe I can get her settled."

"Settled? You don't look capable of picking up a marshmallow, let alone a baby." His arm went around her. "Come on. I'll help you to bed."

She couldn't resist leaning against that strong arm, even though she knew she shouldn't. "I'm fine, really I am."

"I know." He sounded amused. "You can do it yourself. But this time you can't, literally."

He stood, taking her with him, apparently not having a problem carrying the baby and lugging her, too. She forced herself to put one foot in front of the other, aware Mitch was almost carrying her.

When they reached the suite, he plopped Emilie in her playpen, to which she immediately objected. Anne winced at her cries and reached for her.

"No, you don't." Mitch steered her toward the bedroom. "The last thing that baby needs is to get whatever bug you have. Do you want me to call a doctor for you?"

She shook her head, the movement making her wince again. "It's probably just the twenty-four-hour virus Kate says has been going around. I'll be fine, honestly."

"After you get some rest." He half carried her to the bed and sat her down. "Don't worry. I'll take care of Emilie."

She wanted to object, but the bed felt so good after a mostly sleepless night. She slid down bonelessly, her head coming to rest on the cool, smooth pillow.

"Just a little nap," she murmured. "Then I'll be fine."

"I'll bring you some water." Mitch pulled up the quilt and tucked it around her gently. Her eyes closed. She thought she felt his fingers touch her cheek, and then she heard him move away.

Just a short nap, that was all she needed. She slid rapidly toward sleep. Just a short nap.

The baby was still crying. Well, one thing at a time. Mitch crossed to the playpen and picked up Emilie. This time no magic happened—she continued to wail, although the volume decreased.

"Okay, little girl, it's okay." He bounced her on his hip the way he'd seen Anne do when she fussed.

"Everything's going to be all right. Mitch will take care of you."

Yeah, right. It was one thing to give a baby a bottle and then hand it back when it cried. Taking complete care of one was something else entirely.

Emilie seemed a little calmer when he talked, so he did his thinking out loud. "I guess I could call somebody else to help. Wanda, maybe."

It seemed to be working. The baby's sobs quieted to whimpers, and she looked up into his face.

"But do I really want to do that? Open us up to her curiosity? No, I don't think so."

Besides, he'd told Anne he'd take care of them.

"So I guess you're stuck with me." He smiled at Emilie. She smiled back, and he felt as if he'd struck gold. "Let's get some water for your mommy, and we'll look for that teething ring she mentioned."

He tickled Emilie, getting a belly laugh that startled and amused him, then headed for the kitchen.

It was harder than it looked to manipulate a glass of ice water, a bottle of aspirin and a baby. He didn't want to put her down, because she might start crying again. He had an uneasy suspicion that if she did, he wouldn't find it so easy to stop her.

"Okay." He stuffed the aspirin bottle in his back pocket and set the water pitcher back in the refrigerator with his free hand. "Let's get this up to Mommy. Maybe I'll have to ask her where the teething thing is."

He started to close the door, then realized that pink, gel-filled donut looked out of place in Kate's refrigerator. "Hey, is this yours?" He held it out to Emilie, who grabbed it and stuffed it in her mouth. "I guess so."

He picked up the glass. "One more time up the stairs, okay?"

Emilie seemed content to be put in her playpen now that she had the teething ring to chew on, so he deposited her and tiptoed into the bedroom.

Anne lay on her side, one hand under the pillow. Her black hair tumbled about her face, curling damply on her neck. He brushed it back, resisting the urge to let his fingers linger against her soft cheek.

"Anne." He hated to disturb her, but she probably should take something for the fever.

She stirred, and her eyes opened, focusing on him.

"I brought you some aspirin and a glass of water."

She nodded, propping herself on one elbow long enough to down the tablets with a thirsty gulp of water. "Emilie…"

"Emilie's fine. I found the teething ring, but you'd better tell me what to feed her and when."

"I'll get up." She started to push the quilt aside, and he tucked it back over her firmly.

"No, you're not getting up. I can feed Emilie. Just tell me what I need to know."

She sank back on the pillow, apparently realizing she wasn't going anywhere very soon. "The baby food's down on the kitchen counter. Give her—" she frowned, as if trying to concentrate "—give her something with meat and a fruit. That'll be fine for now."

Her eyes drifted closed.

Which fruit? he wanted to ask. *What about a bottle?*

But already she'd slid into sleep, her breath soft and even, her lashes dark against pale skin. She looked vulnerable, and he had a ridiculous urge to protect her. He shook his head. In such a short time she'd touched some tender place in his soul, and he wasn't sure how he was going to get her back out again.

Mitch went quietly back out to the living room of the suite and looked down at Emilie, who was gnawing on the teething ring. "Well, I guess it's just you and me, kid. Tell you what, you cooperate, and we'll get along just fine."

Supper, he decided. Feed her, and then she'd go to sleep, right? He carried her down to the kitchen.

Luckily, Kate had already set up a high chair. Unluckily, Emilie didn't seem to want to go into it. She stiffened her legs, lunging backward in his arms.

"Come on, sweetheart. A little cooperation here."

Emilie didn't agree. Trying to put her in the high chair was like trying to fold an iron bar.

He'd seen Anne put some small crackers on the tray when they'd been in the café. Maybe that would work. He gazed around the kitchen, looking for inspiration. He found a small box of crackers stacked with the jars of baby food. Quickly he shook a few onto the tray.

"Look, Emilie. You like these."

She stopped in mid-cry at the sight.

Holding his breath, he slid her into the high chair. She snatched one of the crackers and stuffed it in her mouth.

"Okay, one problem solved." He fastened the strap around her waist, then turned to the array of baby food on the counter. "Let's see what looks good."

Actually, as far as he was concerned, none of it looked good. He reminded himself that he wasn't eight months old. Maybe to Emilie this stuff looked like filet mignon.

He heated up the chicken-and-rice mixture.

"Here we go, Emilie." He shoveled a spoonful of chicken into her mouth.

She smiled, and most of the chicken spilled right

back out of her mouth, landing down the front of her ruffled pink outfit.

Half an hour later Emilie was liberally sprinkled with chicken, rice and pears, to say nothing of the cracker crumbs. Also well adorned were Mitch's shirt, the high chair and the floor. The way things had gone, it wouldn't surprise him if some of the chicken had found its way into the house next door.

"Maybe we're done." He lifted her cautiously from the chair, holding her at arm's length, a new admiration for Anne filling him. She did this every day, and she didn't have anyone to spell her.

"Okay, let's get you cleaned up." He glanced at his shirt. "Me, too."

He carried her upstairs and eased open the door to the bedroom. Anne slept, still curled on her side. He tiptoed to the bed and touched her forehead. Her skin seemed a little cooler than it had earlier, unless he was imagining things.

Okay, he could do this. He carried Emilie into the bathroom. He looked at the tub, then shook his head. No way. Emilie would do with a sponge bath tonight.

By the time they were finished, Emilie was clean and he was wet. He bundled her into a sleeper and carried her out to the playpen. She settled without a murmur.

He stretched out on the couch, wedging one of the small pillows under his head. He closed his eyes. Peace, heavenly peace...

Sometime later a piercing wail split the air. He catapulted off the couch, heart pounding. Emilie. He reached her in a second, bent to scoop her up.

"Hey, it's okay. Don't cry."

The wail went up in volume and in pitch. Anne would never be able to sleep through this, would she?

But apparently she could.

"Shh, Emilie, it's all right. Don't cry, okay?" He felt like crying himself. If there was a more helpless sensation in the world than this, he didn't know what it was.

"It's all right. Honest." He bounced her, walking across to the windows, then back.

Strangely enough, that seemed to soothe her. The wails decreased. He settled her against his chest and turned to walk the length of the room again. Maybe he could walk her back to sleep, then get some rest himself.

That was only half right. Emilie dozed against his chest, her head nestled into the curve of his neck. But the instant he tried to put her down, her eyes popped open and the wail started again.

Okay, that wouldn't work. Looked like he'd have to keep walking.

This wasn't so bad, was it? He circled the room for the twentieth time or so. He'd walked guard duty longer than this and been more tired. He could do it. It might not be the way he'd pick to spend this evening, but he could do it.

His father's face flickered briefly in his mind, and he banished it instantly. He didn't think about Ken Donovan, not anymore.

But his father wouldn't have put in a night like this— not in a million years.

Chapter 9

Anne came awake slowly, pushing herself upward from fathoms-deep sleep. Something was wrong, and for a moment she couldn't think what it was. Then she realized it was the first morning in months Emilie hadn't wakened her.

She shot upright in the bed, then grabbed her head. The headache had disappeared, replaced by the sensation that her head was about to drift off into space. Slowly, cautiously, she swung her feet over the side of the bed.

Mitch had been here, hadn't he? Or had she dreamed it? No, of course she hadn't. Mitch hurrying in the door, helping her up to bed, saying he'd take care of Emilie.

The crib was empty. Where was Emilie?

She forced herself to her feet and stumbled to the door, yanked it open. Emilie—

Mitch lay on the floor, sleeping. He cradled Emilie between his arms. She slept, too, her head pillowed on Mitch's chest. His strong hands held her firmly even in sleep.

She could fall in love with this man.

The realization hit her like a kick to the heart, followed immediately by a wave of panic. What was she thinking? She didn't intend to fall in love with anyone, certainly not with Mitch.

She tiptoed across the rug and reached for Emilie. Her touch was so gentle that the baby didn't wake, but Mitch's arms tightened instantly. His eyes flickered open, warming when he saw her. He smiled.

Her breath seemed to stop. She wanted to reach out to him, to touch the firm lines of his face, to wipe away all the reserve that hid his feelings. She wanted…

She took a step back. This was dangerous. She couldn't let herself feel this way.

"Good morning. Feeling better?" Mitch shifted position, and Emilie woke. She cooed, patting Mitch with both small hands.

"I'm fine. Really." Anne reached for the baby. "Let me take her. Goodness, I never expected you to stay all night. You should have wakened me."

He grinned. "That would have taken an earthquake. Besides, we got along fine." He stood, still holding the baby. "I'm not sure you should be up yet. You look a little dizzy."

"I just need a shower to clear my head. Then I'll be okay. Really, you don't have to do anything else. I'm sure it's time for you to get ready for work." And the sooner he was out of here, the sooner her breathing would return to normal.

He glanced at his watch. "It's early yet. Suppose I take Emilie downstairs and start some breakfast while you get that shower. Then we'll see how you feel."

Anne would have argued, but he was already out the door with Emilie. Short of chasing him down the stairs, there wasn't much she could do. And a shower might clear her head and help her get rid of thoughts about Mitch that didn't go anywhere.

Standing under the hot spray helped her body, but it didn't seem to be doing much for the rest of her. Her heart and mind still felt jumbled with confused feelings. She couldn't—shouldn't—feel anything for Mitch under these difficult circumstances.

She tilted her head back, letting the water run down her face. After Terry's death, she'd made a deliberate decision that she'd never marry again. Maybe she wasn't cut out for marriage; maybe she just didn't have the capacity for closeness that it required.

It might be different with someone like Mitch. The thought slipped into her mind and refused to be dislodged.

By the time she dried her hair and pulled on a sweater and slacks the light-headedness had eased. She certainly wouldn't be running any marathons today, but she could take care of Emilie. Mitch was probably itching to get out of here.

The picture that met her eyes when she entered the kitchen didn't suggest any desire on Mitch's part to run out the door. He was spooning cereal into Emilie's mouth, sipping at a mug of coffee between bites. Both of them seemed perfectly content. Mitch looked too casually attractive with a slight stubble of beard darkening his face.

"You didn't need to do that. I can feed her."

"Hey, I'm just getting good at this." He caught a bubble of cereal that spilled out of Emilie's mouth when she smiled. "And this time I remembered the bib."

The coffee's aroma lured her to the counter, where she poured a steaming mug. "You tried to feed her without a bib? That must have been messy." She should have told him that when she'd explained about the food, but her mind had been so foggy, it was a wonder she'd said anything coherent at all.

"Messy isn't the word for it. We both needed a complete washup afterward, to say nothing of the kitchen."

Guilt flooded her. Emilie was her responsibility, not his. "You should have wakened me."

"Really?" He lifted an eyebrow, and amusement flickered in those chocolate-brown eyes. "If Emilie's screaming didn't wake you up, I don't think I could have."

"I'm so sorry." Embarrassment heated her cheeks. "I never should have…"

"What? Gotten sick? Give yourself a break, Anne. You're not some kind of superwoman."

"I know, but I still feel guilty leaving Emilie to you when she's teething and miserable."

He paused, spoon half in Emilie's mouth, looking at the baby intently. "If that clink I just heard means anything, the teething problem might be solved for the moment."

"Really?" She hurried around the table and bent over Emilie. "Let Mommy see, sweetheart." She rubbed Emilie's gum, feeling the sharp edge of a tooth. "Look at that! Emilie got a new tooth."

Mitch's smile took in both of them. "Good going, Emilie."

The baby cooed. The image of the three of them, smiling at each other, seemed to solidify in Anne's mind. It might almost be the picture of…a family.

She blinked rapidly. She shouldn't think things like that. "I can finish feeding her."

"No, you can sit down and eat something, so you won't almost pass out on me again. How about some cereal? An egg?"

Actually, she did feel a bit hollow inside. "Maybe a piece of toast."

Mitch reached out to put two slices of bread in the toaster. "Will you please sit down? You're making me nervous."

"I didn't really pass out." Her memory of those moments on the stairs was a little fuzzy, but she was sure of that. She sank into the chair he pushed out for her. "I'm grateful you came in just then. I'm not sure what we'd have done without your help."

"Kate made me promise to check on you two. I guess she knew what she was doing." He scooped the last spoonful of cereal from the bowl and offered it to Emilie, but she turned her head away.

"Better stop there," Anne advised, grinning. "Her next move will be to swat the spoon, and you'll be coping with flying cereal."

"You're the mommy. I guess you know best." He set the bowl on the table. "Anything else I should give her?"

"Let her work on that bottle of juice." He'd turned her thanks away so easily that she felt compelled to say something more. "I want you to know how much I appreciate your help. Getting sick is a big problem when you're a single parent. You don't have anyone to spell you."

He nodded. "Believe me, sometime in the wee hours I got the picture. Parents should come in sets, if possible." His smile turned into a searching look. "I guess you and your husband must really have wanted a family."

It was a natural assumption. She was tempted to let it stand, but that seemed wrong.

"I don't think having a family was ever part of Terry's idea of marriage. He saw us as the classic yuppie couple—two jobs, no kids." Her mouth twisted a little. "He never seemed to want more than that. Two busy professionals with no time for kids and not much time for each other."

She hadn't intended to say that much, and surprise at her candor mingled with embarrassment.

His hand covered hers for a brief moment, sending a flood of warmth along her skin. "I guess that's why you feel the way you do about Emilie."

"She means everything to me." She blinked back the tears that suddenly filled her eyes.

Emilie, apparently feeling she'd been out of the conversation long enough, pounded her bottle on the tray. "Ma, ma, ma, ma, ma!"

"The experts say that's babbling, but I think it's 'Mama.'" Anne covered her ears in mock dismay at the onslaught of noise. "Oh, Emilie, stop."

Mitch caught the flailing bottle, closing his large hand around Emilie's small one. "Hey, little one, enough."

Emilie fastened her wide blue gaze on him. "Da, da, da, da, da!" she shouted.

Anne didn't know which of them was the more embarrassed. Mitch's cheeks reddened beneath his tanned skin and hers felt as if they were on fire.

"It's just nonsense syllables," she said quickly. "She doesn't know what they mean." Embarrassment made her rush to fill the silence with words. "Not that you wouldn't—I mean, I'm sure you'd make a great father." The words slipped out before she had time to think that they might not be wise.

His face tightened until it resembled the mask he'd put on against her that first afternoon in his office.

"I guess that's something I'll never know. I decided a long time ago I wasn't cut out for fatherhood."

She must have murmured something, but she wasn't sure what. She was glad she hadn't believed in that image she'd had of the three of them as a family. For a lot of reasons, it was clearly impossible.

Mitch's office was his refuge. Trouble was, it didn't seem to keep out thoughts of Anne.

Her vulnerability. Her strength. Her determination to take care of the child she saw as hers.

He'd tried to tell himself that last night was nothing—or at least, the sort of thing he'd do for anyone. But he couldn't. It was just too tempting. He'd been part of their lives last night, hers and Emilie's. He'd been important to them in a personal way—not as a cop, but as a husband, a father, would be.

One night. He shoved his chair away from the desk. It had only been a few short hours. Maybe he'd held up to that, but in the long run, there were no guarantees he wouldn't turn out to be just like his father. He wouldn't wish that on any kid.

The sound of raised voices in the outer office interrupted the uncomfortable thoughts. He opened the door to find Wanda and Davey glaring at each other, toe to toe.

Wanda turned the glare on Mitch. "You were the one who hired this twerp. Are you going to let him get away with this?"

He suppressed a sigh. "Maybe I could tell you, if I knew what he'd done."

Wanda flung out her hand toward the big front window. "I told him to wash the window. Did he do it? No! He messed around and let the cleaner dry on the window, and now it looks worse than it did before. He ought to be paying me if I have to clean up after him."

"You're not going to clean up after him."

"Go ahead, take her side. I figured you would." Davey threw down the roll of paper towels. "I'm getting out of here."

Mitch grabbed the kid. The look in the boy's eyes was familiar. He knew what that feeling was, because he'd been there himself. It was wanting someone to care whether he'd done something right or not, and being afraid of that wanting.

"Davey's going to do it again, and this time he'll get it right. That's what I'm paying him for."

"What if I don't want your stupid old job?"

This was familiar, too. He knew what it was like to want to bite someone for taking an interest.

"You don't have a choice, remember? Your father and I agreed you'd work for me, and I'd forget the little incident with the package." Anne would probably call it blackmail, but if it worked, it was worth it.

"All right, all right!" Davey snatched up the roll of

towels. "I'll do your stupid windows, but then I gotta get home for supper."

"If he's going to do that window, you can stay right here and watch him." Wanda planted her hands on her hips. "Baby-sitting isn't in my job description."

"Baby-sitting! Who you calling a baby?"

Mitch gestured Wanda toward her desk and turned Davey to the window. He wasn't going to give up on the kid, not this easily.

But what had happened to the quiet life he'd had before Anne walked into it?

The late afternoon sun warmed the air enough to flirt with spring as Anne pushed the stroller up Main Street. Getting out for a while was a good idea. She'd hung around the house until she'd begun to drive herself crazy.

Thinking about Mitch too much, remembering those moments in the kitchen this morning—she couldn't dwell on it. There wasn't anything between them and there never would be, because he was determined to avoid the very thing that had become the most important in the world to her.

So she wasn't going to think about it anymore. She and Emilie would enjoy the sunshine, she'd pick up a few things at the grocery store, and they'd have a cozy supper, just the two of them. They didn't need anyone else.

"Ms. Morden! How nice to see you out and about. I heard you were sick."

Pastor Richie hurried down the sidewalk, beaming at her.

"I'm fine now, thank you." And how on earth had

he heard about it so quickly? "Just one of those twenty-four-hour viruses, I guess."

He shook his head. "Nasty things going around." He bent to pat Emilie's cheek. "This beautiful little one didn't get anything, I hope."

"Nothing but a brand-new tooth." She couldn't help sounding like a proud mama some of the time.

"Well, isn't that nice." His round, cherubic face grew a bit serious. "Have you had any luck with your efforts to find that young lady you were looking for?"

"No, not yet. Mitch is checking out some leads."

"I looked back over the roster of the singles group for that time, and it jogged my memory. Ellie Wayne was a member then, and I believe those girls hit it off. She might have stayed in touch."

Anne's pulse jumped a notch at the possibility. "Is this Ellie Wayne still in town?"

"Goodness, yes. She runs the gift shop just the other side of the police station. Would you like me to ask her about the girl?"

"Thanks, but I'll do it." She couldn't help the size of her smile, which probably betrayed the fact that her interest was far from casual. "That's so nice of you. Thank you."

"My pleasure." He beamed at them both impartially. "Will I see you in church this Sunday?"

"Yes, of course. We're looking forward to worshiping with you. I hope the baby's not a problem."

He patted Emilie's cheek again. "How could she possibly be a problem? We have a nursery, but if you feel more comfortable keeping her with you, that's fine."

How much was she giving away to his wise eyes? He seemed to guess or to know more than she'd said.

"Thank you. We'll see you Sunday, then."

A lead, at last, she thought, pushing the stroller forward with renewed energy. And it was one she could follow up herself. She didn't need to involve Mitch at all, which was probably for the best.

She walked on down the street. Many of the shops were closed, probably until spring. She looked up at the mountain ridge. The faintest greenish haze seemed to cover it—not spring, but maybe a hint of it.

The bell over the gift shop door tinkled as she lifted the stroller up the step from the street. The mingled aroma of herbs, dried flowers and candles swept over her.

"Help you?" The woman behind the counter wore her thick dark hair in twin braids that swung almost to her waist. She had a strong, intelligent face, innocent of makeup, and a welcoming smile.

"Just looking."

Anne lifted the baby into her arms. Trying to push the stroller along the narrow, crowded aisles would be a recipe for disaster.

"Are you interested in something special?"

She glanced around. It would probably be diplomatic to buy something. "I'd like a dried-flower arrangement. Something with mauve and blue in it."

"This way." The woman came out from behind the counter. "You're Chief Donovan's friend, aren't you? Staying at The Willows?"

She couldn't get away from the mention of him, not in this town. She nodded. "Anne Morden."

"Ellie Wayne." She touched Emilie's hand. "What a beautiful baby."

"I think Pastor Richie mentioned your name to me.

We were talking about a…well, a friend of a friend who used to be in the singles group with you. Marcy Brown. Do you remember her?"

Ellie nodded, her eyes assessing Anne.

"I just wondered if you happened to have her current address."

"Why do you want it?" Ellie's question was blunt.

"We had a mutual friend who passed away a few months ago. I wanted to let her know." And ask her some questions, too.

"I'm sorry." Ellie's eyes darkened with sympathy. "I have an address from a Christmas card, if that'll do you any good. I think she was moving, but her mail might still be forwarded. So I guess a letter could reach her."

"I'd really appreciate it." A few-months'-old address was better than nothing.

"I'll get it for you."

As the woman moved away, the bell on the door jingled.

Anne turned. Mitch stood in the doorway, and her heart was suddenly thumping loud enough for her to hear.

Chapter 10

What exactly is Anne up to now? Mitch had glimpsed her from the window where he was supervising Davey's reluctant cleaning. He'd expected her to turn into the station and had been ridiculously disappointed when she'd gone past. And somewhat surprised when she'd walked into the gift shop.

Her slightly guilty expression told him she was doing something she thought he'd disapprove of—some sleuthing, in other words. If she had some reason to believe Ellie knew something, he wanted in on it.

"I'm helping a customer. I'll be with you in a moment." Ellie gave him a wary look. He didn't think she disliked him; the uniform raised that response in people sometimes. Ellie was generous with others, cautious with him.

"I know." He responded with a bland smile. He

turned to Anne. "I'm surprised to see you out already. You must be feeling better."

"Yes, I'm fine." That faint flush in her cheeks probably wasn't from the fever. She was embarrassed at being caught.

"Excuse me, Chief." Ellie brushed past him to lift down a dried-flower wreath, which she held out to Anne. "What about this one?"

Anne touched it gently. "It's beautiful. Did you make all these yourself?"

Ellie smiled at the praise. "And the baskets. Some of the pieces are on consignment from local artists."

Anne had managed to get more out of Ellie in two minutes than Mitch had in two years, he thought. But he didn't think she had come in here just because she liked Ellie's crafts.

"I'll take this one. And I'd love to have that address, if you don't mind writing it down for me."

Ellie glanced from her to Mitch, then nodded. "It'll be in my files in the office. I'll get it."

When she'd disappeared, he lifted an eyebrow at Anne. "Address?"

"It seems she received a Christmas card from Marcy Brown."

"She just happened to volunteer that information?"

"No, of course not. I asked her."

He suppressed a flicker of irritation. "I thought we agreed you wouldn't go around town asking questions of everyone you meet."

"I didn't do any such thing." Her eyes snapped. "I happened to run into Pastor Richie, and he suggested I talk with Ellie. Apparently she and Marcy struck up a friendship in the singles group, and he thought they might have been in touch."

Mitch winced. Looked as if he owed her an apology. Again. "Guess I shouldn't have jumped to conclusions."

"No, you shouldn't have." She sounded as if she wanted to hold on to her annoyance a bit longer. "And how did you know I was here?"

He gestured toward the station next door. "I was standing at the window, supervising."

"Supervising what?"

"Davey's window washing."

He liked the way her face softened at the boy's name. It would be nice to imagine that it did so at the mention of his name, but he doubted it.

"He's been testing the limits to our arrangement, and Wanda refuses to have anything to do with this project."

She actually smiled. Apparently he was forgiven. "You'll do a better job of it, anyway."

"I doubt it, but it's nice of you to say so."

They were standing close together, so close that he could smell the faint, flowery scent she wore. He had to fight the urge to step even closer.

She looked up at him, and her blue eyes seemed to darken. "I'm sure—"

Ellie bustled in from the storeroom or wherever she'd been, her gaze darting from one to the other of them. "Found it." She waved a slip of paper at Anne.

Anne turned to her with what Mitch suspected was relief. "Thank you. I really appreciate this."

The woman shrugged. "No problem. I'll box up the wreath for you."

Ellie busied herself at the far end of the counter, and an uneasy silence grew between him and Anne. What was she thinking? Was she remembering the moment when they'd kissed? Or was she wishing he'd leave her alone?

Anne glanced up at him. "I wouldn't want to keep you from your work."

That seemed to answer the question. He shrugged. "Yeah, I'd better get back to the station. I'll see you to-morrow."

"You will?" She looked startled and not entirely pleased at the thought.

Well, she'd just have to lump it. "I promised Kate a while ago I'd paint the sunroom for her. Davey and I are going to work on it tomorrow, since it's Saturday."

"I see." She managed a smile, but it didn't look par-ticularly genuine. "I'll see you tomorrow, then."

"One more bite, sweetie." Anne spooned cereal into Emilie's mouth as morning sunlight streamed through the kitchen windows. "We need to get you dressed, be-cause Mitch is coming."

Emilie smiled, cereal dribbling onto her chin, just as if she remembered who Mitch was and looked for-ward to seeing him.

"There. All done." She wiped away the cereal and put the bowl in the sink. Whether or not either of them wanted to see Mitch was beside the point, anyway. He was com-ing, and she couldn't do anything about it but try and handle his presence better than she had the day before.

That encounter in Ellie's store had been a miserable display. She'd let her confused feelings for Mitch make her uncomfortable and awkward in his presence.

She had to cope with the attraction she felt for him, and she had to do it now. She couldn't go on this way.

Emilie banged on the high chair tray with both fists,

as if in emphasis, and Anne lifted her out. She smoothed the fine, silky hair off the baby's forehead.

Maybe the most important question to ask was whether she still believed him to be Emilie's father. She tried to look at it as an attorney, instead of seeing it personally, but she couldn't separate the two.

Anne had grown to know him too well during her time in Bedford Creek. She'd seen the man behind the uniform and the shield, and she liked what she saw.

Integrity. That was the word for it. Every moment she spent with him made her more convinced he was a man of integrity. Every moment lessened her conviction that he was Emilie's father.

She put her cheek against Emilie's soft one. If her father wasn't Mitch, who was it? Time was ticking away, and she didn't seem to be getting anywhere. Was she letting her tangled feelings for Mitch distract her from what was really important here?

Well, if so, that was coming to an end. Regardless of what she might feel for him, the truth was that there would never be anything between them. Everything else aside, Mitch's attitude toward having children made it impossible.

Being Emilie's mother was a full-time job, and giving Emilie the warm, close family relationship Anne had never had herself would fill the empty spaces in her heart. She didn't need or want anything more.

A clatter on the front porch told her the workmen had arrived. Ignoring the way her heart lurched, she went to open the door with Emilie in her arms.

"Good morning." She caught Emilie as the baby made a lunge for Mitch. "I see you're ready to work." She was going to be pleasant, she told herself. She would act as if none of the events of the last few days had happened.

Mitch had a stepladder balanced on one broad shoulder, and he carried two cans of paint in the other hand. His faded jeans had definitely seen better days, as had the T-shirt that stretched across his chest, showing every muscle.

"We'll have the sunroom looking brand-new before you know it." A smile warmed his face, erasing the remnant of annoyance over their last meeting.

A tingle ran along her nerve endings. Her heart didn't seem to have listened to the lecture she'd just given.

She focused on Davey with a welcoming smile. The boy carried a bucket filled with painting gear and wore a disgusted expression. Obviously, this wasn't his idea of the way to spend a Saturday.

She waved toward the sunroom that adjoined Kate's kitchen. "I'll leave you to it. I'll be upstairs getting Emilie dressed if you need anything."

He nodded. "Come on, Davey. This way."

The boy trudged after him down the hall as if headed to his own execution. Suppressing a smile, Anne started up the stairs. Mitch had his work cut out for him in more than painting.

Half an hour later, Anne admitted the truth. She was delaying returning downstairs, delaying seeing Mitch again; she didn't want to put her resolution to the test. But it was time for that to stop. She picked up Emilie and headed downstairs.

"Goodness, you two are fast." They'd already stacked the furniture in the middle of the room and covered it with a drop cloth.

Mitch looked up from opening a can of paint. "I'm

paying this guy by the hour, so I've got to get my money's worth."

"Looks as if you're doing that."

Anne realized Davey's gaze was directed at the baby with a mix of curiosity and trepidation. She smiled at him. "This is Emilie."

He jerked a nod in response, then came closer. "She's pretty little, isn't she?"

"She's almost nine months old." She bounced the baby. "This is Davey, sweetheart."

He took another step closer. "Can she say my name?"

"Probably not. She doesn't say much yet." She tried not to think about the moment when Emilie had looked at Mitch and said "Da-da."

"I never been this close to a baby before." Tentatively, Davey held out one rather dirty hand toward Emilie.

With a happy gurgle, Emilie lunged forward and latched her fist around his finger, smiling.

"Looks as if she likes you," Anne said.

Davey looked at the tiny hand, then up at Anne. "She does, doesn't she."

A smile spread across his face, changing him from the sullen, angry delinquent into a little boy who liked being liked.

That smile… Her heart warmed at the sight. Somehow seeing a smile like that from the boy made Mitch's efforts seem worthwhile.

"I'm sure she does." She glanced at Mitch. Had he seen what she had?

His gaze met hers and he nodded slightly, as if they shared a secret. The intimacy of his look closed around her heart.

She cleared her throat. "I'll put Emilie in the playpen

here in the kitchen. That way she can watch you paint without smelling the fumes. They wouldn't be good for her."

Davey nodded gravely, as if storing that information for possible future use. He detached his finger carefully.

"You watch," he said. "You're going to see some good painting."

He returned to the sunroom with determination. Whether it would last or not she couldn't guess, but it was nice to see.

She plopped Emilie into the playpen, sliding it over so the baby had a view of the sunroom. Emilie seemed to enjoy the unusual activity. She clutched the playpen's mesh and watched every movement with wide blue eyes.

Mitch paused, roller in hand. "Have you heard anything from Kate yet?"

She'd nearly forgotten. "She called last night. It looks as if her sister didn't break her hip, after all. She's badly bruised, so Kate plans to stay and take care of her a bit longer, but she sounded very relieved."

"I'll bet. Kate loves her independence, and I gather the sister can be pretty bossy at times. Kate will be glad when she can get home again."

"She asked about you." Actually, Kate had asked if Mitch was taking good care of her. "I told her you'd be coming to paint today. She kept saying you didn't need to do it and she could manage herself."

He grinned. "That's Kate. She's always doing kind things for other people, then is surprised when they want to do something for her."

Was that behind Mitch's friendship with his elderly neighbor? Maybe Kate had been kind to him at a time when he needed kindness.

"She's a good friend," Anne said.

He nodded, smoothing the roller along the wall in a swath of pale yellow. "The first year I came back, she invited me to spend Christmas with her. Alex and his son had gone away, and I didn't have anyone else. She made it sound as if I did her the favor."

Anne leaned against the door frame. "I'm sure she enjoyed it as much as you did."

"She didn't eat as much." He paused, a reminiscent look in his eyes. "She kept saying she loved to see people eat what she'd prepared, so I made her happy."

"Turkey and all the trimmings?"

"What else would you have for Christmas?"

"Hamburger and fries." The words were out before she knew it.

Mitch stared. "Why on earth would your folks serve that?"

It was clearly not the mental image he had of her family life. She shrugged. "They didn't. They'd gone away for the holidays… Gstaad for skiing, I think. The housekeeper didn't want to fix a big dinner just for the two of us, so we hit the burger hut instead."

"Sounds like some of the Christmases I remember as a kid. I always figured other people got the magazine-picture type of Christmas dinner, with the whole family around the table and the father carving a turkey." His voice betrayed the longing he'd probably felt as a child for that kind of Christmas.

Her heart clenched. She knew something about lonely holidays. "My ideal of Christmas was always the one in *Little Women,* where they all sacrificed to give to others and didn't need anything but each other to be happy." She'd reread that story every year at Christmastime.

"I remember it." His eyes met hers. "I'm sorry."

She knew he wasn't talking about Louisa May Alcott.

She bent over the playpen to hand Emilie a toy. "Actually my happiest Christmases have been the last few, once I figured out what it was we were celebrating."

"I wanted a bike for Christmas." Davey's voice startled her. She'd nearly forgotten the boy was there. "I asked for one last year, but my dad didn't have the money for it." He sat back on his heels. "It wasn't his fault, you know."

"I'm sure it wasn't," she said gently. Her heart hurt for him. "Maybe you'll be able to make enough money to buy a bike yourself."

Davey shot a glance at Mitch, then stared at the paintbrush in his hand. "Maybe." He didn't sound very optimistic.

Mitch reached over and touched the boy's shoulder lightly. Davey let the hand stay there for a moment, then pulled back.

Mitch looked at Anne, his smile a little crooked, and she knew he was as touched by the boy as she was. The sudden rapport, the sense of knowing what he was thinking—where had that come from? And what was she going to do about it?

"I'll start some lunch." She escaped to the other end of the kitchen, pulling open the refrigerator door to cool her face.

She'd never intended to let her guard down, never intended to see so deeply into someone's heart. She leaned her head against the edge of the refrigerator door. She and Mitch had begun to open up to each other in a way she hadn't expected. Now that he'd come so far into her life, how was she ever going to get him out again?

* * *

Anne pulled the mail from the box and checked it quickly. All for Kate. There was nothing that could be a response to the letter she'd sent to Marcy Brown's last known address.

Shivering a little in the cold wind, she closed the mailbox and hurried back inside. Emilie was napping, and the house was too quiet. She stacked the mail on Kate's hall table. Something to do, she thought. She desperately needed something constructive to do.

Maybe Mitch's inquiries had gotten somewhere. But then, he'd have been in touch immediately.

She'd avoided him for the last few days. Maybe he'd been avoiding her, too, and for pretty much the same reason. After all, they both knew there couldn't be anything between them. The kind of closeness they'd experienced on Saturday could only be bittersweet in light of that. It was safer not to see much of each other, safer not to take the chance of wanting something she couldn't have.

She glanced at the phone. She'd called Helen in Philadelphia yesterday. Helen was the only one of her friends who knew the whole story, and so the only one she could talk to about it.

But Helen had been involved in dealing with a runaway in crisis, and Anne hadn't wanted to tie her up with her worries. So she'd just asked Helen to keep on praying about the situation.

"Always, child." Helen's voice was as warm as her heart. "You know I'm always praying for you and that dear baby God has given you. Trust Him."

Anne was trying so hard to trust.

If only she could think of something useful she could do. She'd tried Cassie again, but the woman hadn't remembered anything more. Then Anne had gotten a list from the pastor of everyone in the singles group. But no one seemed able to help. It was as if poor Tina hadn't made any impression at all in Bedford Creek. And Marcy Brown had disappeared, leaving no trace but a single Christmas card.

She walked restlessly back through the house to the kitchen and picked up the teakettle—

She stood still, kettle in hand, staring out the back window. Why was the shed door standing ajar?

She blinked, leaning a little closer to the window. Mitch had put the stepladder away in there on Saturday; she'd watched him do it. She'd seen him close and latch the door. Now it stood partially open.

Her heart began to thump. She should call the police, she should—

Now, wait a minute. The rational side of her brain kicked in. It was the middle of the afternoon. She was in Bedford Creek, not the big city. Why was she letting her imagination run away with her?

She grabbed her jacket from the hall closet and slipped out the back door. It would only take a moment to check. Probably the wind had blown the door open. Or maybe the latch had broken.

She crossed the wet grass, caught the door and pulled it wide, letting light flood the interior. It showed her the ladder, the lawn mower, the folding chair, an old croquet set.

And Davey Flagler, curled up under a wicker table, sound asleep.

"Davey?"

He woke instantly at the sound of her voice, and sat up so fast that his head brushed the table.

"Are you all right? What are you doing here?"

He slid out from under the table, face sullen. "Just sleeping, okay with you?"

"Seems like a cold place to sleep." Carefully, she thought. She had to handle him carefully. Whatever was wrong, she wouldn't get it by pushing. "Why don't you come in the house where it's warm?"

"Nah." He grabbed a small backpack he'd been using as a pillow. "Guess I'll get going now."

Anne didn't move from the doorway when he approached, and he glared up at her. "You going to let me out, or what?"

"Tell me what's going on, Davey." She gave him a level look. "You obviously should be in class, and here you are sleeping in Kate's shed. Is something wrong at school?"

He stared another moment, then his gaze slid away. His thin shoulders shrugged. "School's okay."

"Something wrong at home, then?" The little she knew about his family situation flashed through her mind.

"Look, I don't have to tell you anything. You're not my boss."

"No, but I'd like to be your friend. Come on, Davey. Tell me what's wrong. I won't tell anyone else, unless you say it's okay."

"Promise?" His tone was skeptical.

"I promise."

He stared down at the ground, his face troubled as he tried to put on a brave front. "We got evicted, that's what. Guess my dad was late with the rent again. Landlord threw us out."

His father must have been very late, if the landlord

had gotten far enough in the legal process to evict them. She longed to touch the boy, but he was like a porcupine with all its quills standing on end.

"Is your dad out looking for another place?"

He shook his head.

"Then where is he?"

Davey didn't say anything, and a suspicion grew in her mind.

"Davey, you can trust me. Where's your father?"

He hesitated a moment longer. Then he looked up, and she thought she read fear behind the defiance in his eyes.

"He's gone, all right? He's gone, but he'll be back. I know he'll come back for me."

Oh, Lord, tell me what to do. My heart is breaking for this poor child, and I don't know how to help him.

Slowly, very slowly, she reached out to touch his shoulder. "Davey, I think you need some help with this one. You can't hide out in Kate's shed forever, you know."

"I don't want help!" He jerked away, fear leaping in his eyes. "You tell anyone, they'll maybe put me away."

"Nobody's going to put you away. I'm a lawyer, remember? I won't let them, okay?"

He studied her face for a moment, as if assessing the chance she was telling him the truth. Finally he nodded.

"Okay."

She let out the breath she'd been holding. "Maybe we ought to go down to the police station and—"

He went back a step, shaking his head. "No! I don't want to go there."

"What if Mitch comes here to talk to you? That's all—just talk."

His mouth set, and he stared down at his shoes. "All

right," he said finally. "Long as all he wants to do is talk. He starts thinking about anything else, I'm outta here."

Luckily, Emilie was awake when they got into the house. Davey, fascinated, played with her, while Anne called Mitch and explained quickly.

He didn't bother asking for details or second-guessing her actions. "I'll be right there."

By the time Mitch arrived, they were all in the kitchen having a snack. Emilie gnawed on a biscuit while Davey wolfed down one sandwich after another.

"Hey, Davey." Mitch moved into the room easily, his voice low. He seemed to know without asking how skittish the boy was.

Davey eyed him suspiciously over the top of his grilled-cheese sandwich. "You can't put me away. Anne already told me, and she's a lawyer. You can't put me away."

Mitch sank into a chair, reaching out to filch a quarter of a sandwich from Davey's plate. "Who said anything about putting you away?"

"Well, I'm just telling you." Some of the tension seemed to go out of him.

"You do need a place to stay, Davey," she pointed out. "You can't live in the shed."

"I can take care of myself. I'm almost eleven. I don't need anybody."

"You're not going to be put away, and you're not going to live in the shed." Mitch's voice was firm. "Way I see it, you just need a place to stay until your dad comes back. So, I figure the best thing is for you to move in with me."

Chapter 11

For an instant after the words were out of his mouth, Mitch couldn't believe he'd said them. What did he know about taking care of a kid, especially one with Davey's problems?

"Do you mean that?" Anne's gaze held his, warning him, maybe, that it was a bad thing to say if he didn't.

"I mean it." It felt right to him. The problem would probably be convincing the kid that it was right.

He glanced at Davey, who was looking at him with a startled, disbelieving expression. Was there a little hope in that look? He wasn't sure.

But he was sure of one thing. He'd begun to take some pride in the way the boy was shaping up, and he didn't intend to give up on him now.

Anne rested her hand lightly on Davey's shoulder. "Seems like a really good idea to me."

It was nice to see the approval in her eyes, but he wasn't doing it for that. He just couldn't let the kid slip through the cracks the way he almost had.

"What do you say, Davey? You willing to stay with me for a while?"

Davey stared at the tabletop, as if fascinated by it. "You don't need to. I'll be okay."

"Davey…" Carefully, now. He didn't want to scare the kid. "I know you're used to being pretty independent. But the law says you can't live on your own yet. So you've got to stay with someone. You have any relatives you'd rather be with?"

The boy shrugged. "Just my dad."

It had a familiar, lonely sound that reverberated in Mitch's heart. He didn't want to have to call Child Services on the kid. He wanted to work this out, somehow.

"Well, then, what do you say? I'm not that hard to get along with."

Davey stared at his hands. "Okay. I guess so." He looked up. "Just 'til my dad gets back. He'll come back for me."

"Sure he will." Mitch wouldn't dream of challenging the defiant note in the kid's voice. He'd have a look for Davey's father himself, but from what he'd seen, maybe the kid would be better off without him.

He wasn't about to sign on for the long haul, but he could do this much.

He could practically hear Anne's sigh of relief.

"You'll need to get approval as an emergency foster home from Child Services," she said. She was thinking like an attorney again. "I've been through that with Emilie, so I can help you out."

"Sounds good. I know the caseworkers. I don't think

they'll raise any objections to Davey staying with me for the time being."

He'd always believed God had pulled him out of that quarry all those years ago for a reason. Maybe this was it.

Anne stood at the front window the next morning, watching as Davey, schoolbooks in hand, trudged down the street toward the school. She'd found it surprising how quickly and smoothly the question of Davey's custody had been settled. Maybe it was because Bedford Creek was a small town, or maybe because Mitch was the police chief. Nobody made waves about the situation.

He was now waiting in the doorway, maybe to be sure Davey headed in the right direction. Then Mitch went back inside, and the door closed. Apparently, he wasn't headed to work yet.

Anne stared thoughtfully at the house. If Mitch weren't at the office, he wouldn't see her heading into Ellie's gift shop. She bit her lip, torn by conflicting arguments.

So far she had nothing, absolutely nothing, to present at the adoption hearing about Emilie's father. Mitch's search had come up empty; everything Anne tried was a dead end.

But Ellie—Ellie might have had more to say if Mitch hadn't walked in on them. Anne could go back to see her. She could even bring up Tina's name and see if the woman remembered anything about her that might be a lead.

Ellie was too bright to interpret a second visit as

something casual. She'd know this was important to Anne. She'd be curious; she might talk about it.

But the clock was ticking. Maybe the time had passed for the caution she'd agreed to when she'd come to Bedford Creek. If there was the faintest possibility Ellie had answers, Anne had to go after them.

Kate, who'd returned the previous evening, leaped at the chance to watch Emilie when Anne said she wanted to go out. Anne hurried to the car. It would be faster to drive, with less chance of running into Mitch coming or going and forcing her to explain why she was talking to Ellie again.

A parking space in front of the shop, no other customers... She couldn't imagine why Ellie bothered to open until tourist season, but she was grateful for it.

Ellie raised her eyebrows when she walked up to the counter. "Are you interested in another wreath?"

"Not exactly." How much did Ellie guess of her motives? "We didn't really have a chance to finish our conversation the other day."

Ellie shrugged, dark eyes wary. "We were interrupted, remember?"

"Yes, well, I thought we might talk about it a little more." The woman was so cautious, it was difficult to read her.

Ellie stared at her for a long moment, then leaned against the counter. "Did you have any luck with the address I gave you?"

"Marcy had moved, and there wasn't a phone listing for her. I sent a letter, hoping it would be forwarded, but I haven't heard anything yet." And maybe she never would.

"What else do you want? I don't know any other way

to find Marcy. She's not good about keeping in touch, and we weren't best friends or anything."

"I wondered…" This was the tricky part, and there didn't seem to be any casual way to bring it up. "I wondered if you remembered another friend of hers—Tina Mallory."

Ellie stared at her, eyes unreadable. Then she shrugged again. "I remember her. I never knew her very well, though. Are you trying to find her, too?"

Obviously she found Anne's interest suspicious, to say the least. "No. Tina was the mutual friend I mentioned. The one who died a few months ago."

"That young girl?" Ellie's reaction was much the same as Cassie's had been. "That's hard to believe. What happened to her?"

"She had a heart problem that had never been diagnosed." Anne felt as if she were using Tina's death to gain the woman's cooperation. "I know she and Marcy were good friends, and I thought Marcy ought to be told, but I haven't been able to locate her."

Ellie shook her head. "Wish I could help, but I don't know any other way to find her."

"Maybe you remember other friends Tina made when she lived here." Surely she remembered something helpful. "I'd like to get in touch with them, too."

"I can't think of any." Ellie frowned. "She was a dreamy kid, kept pretty much to herself. I never got to know her very well."

"What about boyfriends?" The opportunity was slipping through her fingers, dissolving away into mist like every other lead to Emilie's father.

"Boyfriends?" Ellie looked at her with an expression Anne couldn't interpret.

"Yes, boyfriends." Maybe she didn't sound as pushy as she feared she did. "She was a young girl. She must have gone out with someone while she was here."

"Funny you should ask me about that." Ellie picked up one of the dried-flower arrangements on the counter, tweaking it as if to keep her hands busy.

"What's funny about it?"

"Funny because you're such good friends with Mitch Donovan."

"What do you mean?" A heavy weight seemed to press down on her, as if she knew the answer before the woman spoke.

Ellie twisted a flower into place, then looked at her. "I thought he was the man Tina dated."

Pain ricocheted through her. It carried a clear message. She'd gotten far too involved with Mitch Donovan—been far too willing to believe him.

She cleared her throat, trying not to let her voice or her face express any emotion at all. "What makes you think that?"

Ellie frowned, dark braids flapping as she shook her head. "Not sure, really."

Anne had to have more than this. "Did you see them together?"

"No…no, I don't believe I ever did. Unless maybe it was at the café. Tina worked there, you know."

"Yes, I know. But you must have some reason for thinking they went out besides seeing Tina wait on him."

Or did she? Anne wondered. Sometimes body language between two people told you all you needed to know about their relationship. Her stomach knotted at the thought.

"Maybe it was something Tina said. Or Marcy said."

Her face brightened. "Yes, that's it. It was something Marcy said."

Anne's heart pounded loudly enough for her to hear, but she'd keep her voice level in spite of it. "What did Marcy say?"

"Well, I don't remember exactly."

She gripped the counter, holding back the need to shake the truth out of the woman. "What *do* you remember?"

"Seems to me…" She paused, head cocked as if listening to voices in the past. "I know what it was. Marcy said Tina was crazy about the chief. "Head over heels in love with him"—that's what she said."

Head over heels in love. Anne wanted to grapple with Ellie's revelation, to assess it the way she would any piece of evidence in a case, but she couldn't seem to make her mind work that way. Ellie's words had blown a gigantic hole through her heart.

This is crazy. How could her instincts possibly be so far off the mark? She thought she knew Mitch. How could the person who helped her when she was sick, who took in young Davey, possibly have been lying to her all along?

She couldn't reconcile the two images of Mitch. They just didn't fit.

She'd begun to trust him. That was what drove the hurt deep into her heart. She didn't rely on people easily, thanks to her parents' example, but she'd begun to count on Mitch. How could she possibly be so wrong?

There was only one thing to do, one way to cope with this. She'd have to confront Mitch and find out the truth, Anne decided as she left Ellie's shop and got into her car.

* * *

But her courage left her when she reached Mitch's house. What was she going to say? How could she believe him?

She had to confront him with it, that was all. Nothing would be more unfair than to condemn him on the basis of a rumor. No matter how difficult, she had to face him. She rang the bell.

She had rung it a second time before she heard answering footsteps in the hall beyond.

"All right, all right." The masculine grumble sounded annoyed. "I'm coming." The door swung open.

"Anne." A quick smile lit his eyes. "Come in." He gestured with the hand that didn't hold the overflowing laundry basket. "I'm getting caught up on a few things before I go to the station."

She followed him into the hallway.

"We picked up Davey's clothes last night. Poor kid doesn't have much, and what he does have needed to be washed." He set the basket down. "I thought I'd…"

He stopped suddenly, his dark brown eyes focusing on her face. He went still, his gaze probing as if he could see into her heart.

"What is it? What's wrong?"

"I… " She opened her mouth, then closed it again. This was so difficult. The home he'd created surrounded her, warm and welcoming. It didn't seem the right place for the accusation she had to make. And she couldn't fool herself, any more than she could fool him. It *was* an accusation.

"Tell me." He reached toward her, but stopped before his fingers touched her arm.

Maybe she was putting out warning signals, she thought.

"What's going on?" he pressed.

"I talked to Ellie this morning." *Just get it out, any way you can.* "I asked her about Tina. She remembered something."

His face stiffened. "It can't have been anything good."

"Why do you say that?"

"Because you look ready for a fight, Counselor."

If he wanted the facts, he was going to get them. "Ellie remembered Marcy talking about Tina. And you."

"There was no Tina and me." He narrowed his eyes. "No matter what Ellie says."

"Ellie wasn't making any accusations." Her voice grew stronger as the woman's words rang in her mind. "She was just repeating what Marcy said."

"And that was...?"

"That Tina was crazy about you. "Head over heels in love"—that's what she said."

He looked...astonished. That was the only word for it. "Ellie said that? I knew she didn't like me, but I didn't think she'd make up something about me."

"She wasn't. At least, I don't think she was doing anything other than repeating what Marcy had said to her."

"Hearsay, Counselor?"

She stiffened. "We're not in a court of law. I'm trying to find the truth. The two things don't always go together."

"No, I guess not." He took a step toward her. "But I thought we were beginning to trust each other."

She winced at the pain in his voice. That had to be genuine, didn't it?

"I just… I just don't know."

"We're back at the same old impasse then, aren't we." His mouth hardened. "All I can say is that I barely knew the girl. If she had feelings for me, I wasn't aware of it. I certainly never dated her."

"Then why?" Her voice threatened to break. "Why would she say those things?"

She flung out her hands, and the question seemed to vibrate in the air between them.

"I don't know." His voice was heavy, final. "I guess there's nothing else to say."

She swallowed hard. "I guess there isn't. When the DNA results come—"

"When the DNA results come, you'll know I'm telling the truth. I wish you could trust me until then, but it's pretty clear you can't."

Everything in her cried out to believe him. But she couldn't. She could only shake her head and walk away.

Mitch tried to ignore the emotions that surged through him. It didn't work. They pounded at him. Anger, pain, disappointment. He'd thought… *What* had he thought? That she'd begun to care for him? That she returned the caring he'd tried so hard not to admit?

He couldn't deny it now. He looked bleakly at it. He cared for her. And she didn't trust him. That was it, bottom line. She didn't trust him.

Just like his father. Nobody'd trusted Ken Donovan, with good reason. He'd betrayed everyone who'd made that mistake—every friend, every employer. Everyone who'd given him a chance to make something of himself.

And then he'd betrayed his family. To Mitch, looking at that was like looking into a black hole. Worse, it was a hole that threatened to suck him in.

The doorbell rang. Anne? Impossible.

But he crossed the hall in a few long strides, grabbed the knob and flung the door open. And looked into the face of his brother.

"Link."

"Hey, big brother." Link slouched through the door without waiting for an invitation. He dropped an overloaded duffel bag on the floor and turned to Mitch. "Don't look so glad to see me."

In spite of everything that experience had taught him to expect from Link, he couldn't help a surge of affection. Link, looking at him with that boyish grin, hair falling in his eyes, was for a moment the little brother he'd tried to teach and protect.

He held out his hand. "It's been a long time."

Link gripped his hand briefly. "Can't say it looks like much has changed in Bedford Creek while I've been gone."

"Don't suppose it has." Be careful. He couldn't let Link in on the biggest change in Bedford Creek. The one in the house right across the street. Link wouldn't be any support. In fact, he'd probably enjoy seeing Mitch embarrassed.

"Small town attitudes, small town minds." The familiar mocking note came into Link's voice. "How do you stand it?"

"I'm happy here. Some people wouldn't be." He snapped the words.

"Happy? How can you be happy knowing everyone in this town is looking down at you?"

"Nobody looks down at me." His temper flared. That was Link, pushing the familiar buttons. "Not anymore."

"Yeah, right." Contempt saturated the words. "You're the police chief now. That just means they'll use you to clean up their messes. But don't make the mistake of thinking they have any respect for you."

"You'd know a lot about that, wouldn't you? You don't have any respect for anyone or anything."

They were back to the old arguments, the ones they never seemed to get past.

Link shrugged. "I just look at the world a little differently from the way you do. Realistically. Nobody's going to give you a break, so don't expect it, and you won't be disappointed."

Like Anne, who didn't trust him, Mitch thought. He stared bleakly at his brother, wondering how, in a few short moments, Link had managed to zero in on his pain.

Chapter 12

Anne looked out the front window the next morning for what must have been the twentieth time. The police car still sat in the driveway, so Mitch hadn't left yet. Also for the twentieth time, she longed to run across the street, to tell him she believed in him. DNA results or not, she believed in him.

But she couldn't do it. Each time she thought she was ready to take that step, something held her back.

When she thought of the pain in Mitch's eyes the day before, she wanted to do whatever it would take to wipe it away.

Then the doubts crept in, poisoning her thoughts. What if she was wrong? What if Ellie's presumption was true? What if Mitch really had been the man in Tina's life?

Why can't I know, Lord? Why can't I know the truth, and then I could trust him?

No calmness came to still the tumult inside her. No answer presented itself, fully formed, in her mind. She didn't know, she just didn't know.

She heard the steps creak outside and turned back to the window in time to see the mail carrier going down. Kate was busy in the back of the house; Emilie safely napping upstairs. She might as well bring the mail in.

Anne carried a fat bundle inside and began to sort it on the hall table. Most of it was for Kate, of course, but—

She stared at the envelope with McKay Laboratories on the return address, and her heart started to hammer uncomfortably.

It was here. The DNA report was here, a week earlier than she'd hoped. When she'd called the lab to give them her address in Bedford Creek, she'd been told they were backed up with tests.

"Anne? Is something wrong?"

She'd been so preoccupied that she hadn't heard Kate come in from the kitchen. The elderly woman was drying her hands on a tea towel, looking curiously at her.

"No, no, nothing." Her face must betray that as a lie. "I'm fine. Excuse me."

Clutching the envelope, she hurried up the stairs. Kate would think her rude, but she just couldn't help it. She had to get away from the woman's curious eyes while she held Emilie's fate in her hands.

She slipped into the sitting room quietly and sank into the nearest chair. It was here, and now that it was, she could hardly bear to open it. She wanted to know; she was afraid to know.

Help me, Lord. Please help me. I'm afraid.

Suddenly the conviction she'd been seeking filled

her, taking her breath away. The certainty pooled inside her, deep and sure. It wasn't Mitch. Whoever it was, it wasn't Mitch.

She opened the envelope and pulled out the results. They confirmed what she already knew. Mitch Donovan hadn't fathered Tina's child.

Thank you, Lord. Thank you.

She had to tell him. She folded the envelope and stuck it in her pocket. She had to tell him, now.

Kate stood in the hallway, glancing through a catalog. She looked up as Anne came down the stairs.

"I don't know why they keep sending me these things. I never order anything from them." Her gaze was keen on Anne's face, but clearly she wouldn't intrude.

Anne swallowed hard. She'd like to confide in Kate, but she couldn't. "I need to speak to Mitch for a moment, and Emilie's napping. Would you mind…?"

"Of course not." Kate's response was immediate. "You go on. Take as long as you want."

She'd reached Mitch's door before the thought occurred to her that he might be angry. He might well say, "I told you so."

Well, he deserved to be able to say it, and she had to give him that chance. She knocked at the door.

Mitch pulled it open, his gaze both surprised and wary when he saw her. "Anne."

"May I come in?"

"Of course." He stepped back, his expression giving nothing away.

She walked in, trying to find the right words. Funny, she'd felt just that way the first time she'd seen him. Apprehensive, tense, struggling to find the right words. Maybe there weren't any.

She swung toward him and held out the envelope. He took it automatically, staring from it to her with a frowning intensity.

"It came." She took a breath. "I want you to know this. I don't see any reason why you should believe it, but it's true. Before I opened the envelope, I knew what it would say. I knew it wasn't you."

He flicked at the opened envelope flap with his finger. "I see you still had to look."

All right, she deserved that. "Yes, I guess I did."

He nodded, his face expressionless. Then he handed the envelope back.

"Aren't you going to look at it?"

He lifted an eyebrow. "Why? I know what it says."

She turned away from that searching gaze. "I wish…" Her cheeks grew warm. "I wish things could have been different. I'm sorry I put you through this. Maybe I never should have come to Bedford Creek."

He took a step closer, not touching her, but close enough that she could feel the heat of his body. "If you'd never come, I'd never have met you."

She tried to smile. "I would think you'd consider that an advantage."

He shook his head. "I'll trade the suspicion for the chance to know you any day of the week."

For a moment her eyes met his. The barriers he usually put up were gone, and she seemed able to see right into his soul. To see the integrity. He wasn't a man who hid his weaknesses behind a façade. The only thing hiding behind his mask was strength.

He reached out to touch her cheek. His palm was warm and strong against her skin. The feel of him seemed to spread out from his fingers, coursing along her nerve endings, warming her all the way through.

"Mitch." She barely breathed his name.

He slid his hand down her neck, leaving longing in its wake. He grasped her shoulder and drew her toward him.

It was all right now. He hadn't been involved with Tina; he wasn't lying to her. She could trust him. She could let herself care about him. She leaned toward him, expecting to feel his lips on hers.

Instead he held her close, his cheek against hers.

"Will you tell me something?" His voice was soft, a whisper in her ear.

"Tell you what?" How she could think clearly enough to tell him anything, she couldn't imagine. Her mind seemed totally involved in the feel of his cheek was against hers, how strong his muscles were under her hand, how the two of them fit together perfectly.

"Tell me why it's so hard for you to trust."

The words brought her back...back to a world where explanations had to be made, where people had a right to know things, no matter how painful.

She met his eyes. "Are you sure you want to know?"

Mitch watched the play of emotion on her face. She'd come so far into his life in such a short time and now he couldn't imagine doing without her.

"I think I already know some of this. It has to do with your parents, doesn't it?"

He could feel the resistance in her. She didn't want to tell him this. The muscles in her neck worked, as if she had swallowed something unpalatable.

"Poor little rich girl." Her voice mocked herself. "That's what it sounds like, so I don't talk about it."

"You can talk about it to me." He led her to the sofa, sat down next to her. "I want to understand." He managed a smile. "After all, you know the worst about me, don't you?"

She stared down at her hands, still resisting, still holding back. Then she looked up at him, her eyes defiant. "My parents never hit me. They never mistreated me. I had everything I needed."

He rested his hand on the nape of her neck, feeling the tension there. "You couldn't have had everything you needed, or you wouldn't feel the way you do."

Anne stiffened. "There's nothing wrong with the way I feel. I just…"

"You just can't rely on anyone."

"Well, maybe I can't. Maybe people aren't very reliable."

"Some aren't." He met her look steadily. "But some are."

"I guess I have trouble telling the difference. After all, I was married to someone who recreated the same pattern. That wasn't smart, was it?"

Her anger was still there, but he recognized it for the defense it was. If they were ever going to get past this, he had to get her to level with him.

"I think I can almost fill in the blanks." It could be that throwing it right at her was the only way. "Your parents provided you with every material thing you needed. They just neglected the little things—love, attention, support."

"They probably thought they were doing the right

things for me. I should have been stronger. I should have been able…"

"What? To tell them how to be parents?" Anger licked along his veins, at two selfish people he'd never known. "They had a beautiful child, and they never bothered to let her know just how precious she was."

"You don't know that."

She tried to smile, but it was a pitiful effort that wrung his heart. He could feel the pride that had kept her silent slipping away.

"I used to think maybe I wasn't pretty enough, or special enough, or what they wanted." She shook her head. "I used to think if only I'd been a boy, it would have been different. My father always wanted a son."

He slid his hand comfortingly down the long sweet curve of her back. "Used to think?"

She glanced at him, and he saw the tears that sparkled on the verge of spilling over. "Then I met my friend, Helen. And through Helen, I found out I had another Friend. One who considered me precious, even if my parents hadn't."

He nodded. "I thought it was something like that. When I saw the dedication in your Bible."

Her blinding smile broke through the tears that had gathered. "First it was Helen, introducing me to the Lord. And then God brought me Emilie. Once I had a child, I realized how wrong they'd been. Emilie opened me up to a whole new dimension in my life. I could never ignore her the way they ignored me."

The smile hurt his heart. He wanted her to smile that way for him. To light up because he was part of her life, too.

"She means everything to you."

"She means——" Her voice choked a little. "If I have Emilie to love, none of the rest of it matters. If I don't…"

She stopped, and he saw the pain that filled her eyes. Pain and fear.

"What if I lose her? What if I go into that hearing with nothing, and the court decides to put her into a foster home? It could happen. I've seen it happen."

"It's not going to happen. Not to you and Emilie."

He wanted to wipe the fear away, banish it for good. Why couldn't he do that one thing for her? *Assist, protect, defend.* He wasn't doing a very good job of any of those for Anne.

"You don't know that." Her hands clenched. "No one knows."

"Don't." He drew her close against him, wanting only to comfort her. "Don't torture yourself like this."

"I can't help it." She turned her face into his chest, and he felt her ragged breath on his skin through the thin cotton of his shirt.

"It's going to be all right." He cradled her face between his palms so he could see her eyes, will her to believe him. "You've got to hold on to that."

Her gaze locked with his, and as her eyes darkened, all the breath seemed to go out of him. Her lips were a scant inch from his, and he longed to close the gap, to taste her mouth, wrap his arms around her and not let go. But how could he? What she needed from him was comfort now.

Then she lifted her mouth to his, and all his rational thought exploded into fragments. He drew her closer, the blood pounding through his veins. Her mouth was warm and sweet, and the two of them fit together as if they'd been made for each other.

This was right. It had to be.

"Well, well—"

The voice was like a splash of icy water in Mitch's face.

"—looks like my big brother has company."

Mitch let her go so suddenly that for an instant Anne was totally disoriented. She had to force herself out of a world that had included no one but her and Mitch. Someone else had come in. What was a stranger doing in Mitch's house?

Except that it wasn't a stranger. Mitch had said his name. *Link.* This had to be the brother—the one Mitch didn't want to talk about.

"Mitch, aren't you going to introduce me to your friend?" He crossed toward them from the hall, his walk an easy slouch as different as possible from Mitch's military bearing.

Mitch didn't speak, and his silence made her nervous. She held out her hand.

"I'm Anne Morden." She bit back any further explanation. To say anything more would show her embarrassment, would imply she had some reason to feel embarrassed.

Link took her hand, holding it a bit longer than was necessary. "Link Donovan. Mitch's little brother."

He was slighter than Mitch, not quite as tall or as broad. But the same dark-brown hair fell on his forehead, longer and more unruly than Mitch's military cut, and the same chocolate-brown eyes assessed her.

"Link is here for a visit. A brief one." Mitch seemed to make an effort to rouse himself from his silence.

"He works out west."

"Sometimes." Link eyed him. "Sometimes my travels bring me back to Pennsylvania, and good old Bedford Creek. My big brother would rather I stayed out west."

"I didn't say that." Mitch grated the words.

Anne looked at him. Mitch had the closed, barricaded look he'd worn the first time she met him. She thought she sensed anger seething underneath, but he obviously didn't intend to let it out.

"Close enough." Link shrugged. "But here I am back again, like the proverbial bad penny. And Mitch still wishes I'd go away."

That was clearly an appropriate time for Mitch to protest that he didn't want to be rid of his brother, Anne thought. But he didn't. He just gave Link that daunting stare.

She, at least, would have found it daunting. But Link seemed unaffected.

He shrugged. "Well, guess I'll let you get back to… whatever it was you were doing."

He sauntered back out again, and in a moment she heard the front door slam.

She'd opened her mouth to say some conventional words, but Link had gotten out the door before she could muster them.

Mitch shot off the couch. He strode to the window and looked out, as if assuring himself that Link was gone. "Sorry. Link just showed up yesterday. He does that."

"Not very often, it seems." She tread warily, not sure of his feelings.

"It's been two years," Mitch said. "I could see your

mind working when you looked at him. You were won-dering if he could be Emilie's father."

"I suppose I was." That should hardly surprise him, under the circumstances. "I wonder that about every man I meet in Bedford Creek."

"You don't need to wonder about Link." His voice was harsh. "I know exactly when he was here last. Two years ago next month, right at Easter. Wanting me to bail him out of trouble again, like he always does."

His anger seemed all out of proportion, and she felt her way, unsure what was driving it. Or what she could do to defuse it.

"And did you help him?"

Mitch's frown darkened. "I lent him money again. Although I don't think *lend* is the right word, since he's never repaid a cent. And then I told him it was the last time. That he'd better find someone else to get him out of trouble, because I wouldn't do it again."

Thoughts tumbled through her mind, most of which were probably better not expressed. "I see." But she didn't.

"I never figured I'd say that about my own brother. When we were kids, I used to think we'd always be best friends."

He went silent, and she tried to find the words that would get him talking again.

"I always dreamed of having a brother or sister," she began. "I imagined it would be the best thing, to have someone to share things with."

"There wasn't much to share at our house." His mouth became a thin line. "Except maybe a slap or two when our father had had too much to drink."

"You tried to protect your brother." She knew that much without asking. It was in his nature.

"I tried. But Link figured out early how to talk his way out of trouble. And he did it even if that meant he blamed me."

Anne could sense the pain he'd felt at his brother's betrayal. "Mitch, you can't still hold him responsible for that. Any kid would—"

He swung toward her. "I don't blame him for that." The words shot toward her, loud in the quiet room. "I blame him because he's turned out just like our father. I can't understand that, and I don't think I ever will."

The pain came through in his words so clearly that it pierced her heart. She suddenly saw a younger Mitch, trying to protect his brother and having that protection thrown back in his face.

"No." She said it softly. "I guess I wouldn't, either."

For a moment he didn't respond. Then his head jerked in the briefest of nods.

Let me in. Please don't shut me out. "Have you been in touch with him at all since that last time?"

"No. I didn't expect to hear from him. He'd stay away until he thought I had time to get over it. Until he thought he could hit me up for money again."

"Maybe he's changed. Maybe he's done some growing up since then."

He shook his head. "Look, there's no point in rehashing this. Link is the way he is, and I don't figure I'm ever going to change him. I'm just sorry he came in when he did."

"Because we were kissing?" She smiled, inviting him to see the humor in it. "That's not so bad, is it?"

"You don't understand." His face refused to relax. "Link would like nothing better than to embarrass me."

She raised her eyebrows. "Why is it embarrassing to be caught kissing someone? You're not hiding a wife in the closet, are you?"

He shook his head stubbornly. "It's not funny. You don't know what he's like."

"I know what you're like." She closed the space between them, putting her hand on his arm. It was like a bar of iron. "Link doesn't matter to me, except for the way he affects you."

"I shouldn't have kissed you, knowing he could walk in at any minute. I should have had more sense."

Her patience abruptly ran out. She was trying to be reasonable, trying to be on his side, and he just wouldn't let her. "If that's the way you feel about it, maybe you shouldn't have kissed me at all." She snatched her jacket from the chair. "I think I'd better go."

He didn't try to stop her.

Chapter 13

"Finish up that homework before you watch television." Mitch leaned over the history book and notebook Davey had spread out on the kitchen table. "Mrs. Prentice said you're behind in your assignments."

Davey gave him a rebellious look. He picked up the yellow pencil with an elaborate sigh.

At least there was one person in his life who wasn't arguing with him. Mitch picked up the dish towel and started drying the silverware from dinner. Davey might be unhappy about having someone keep an eye on him while he did homework, but maybe at some level he understood Mitch was doing it because he cared. Mitch hoped so, anyway.

Understanding didn't extend to other people in his life. Anne didn't understand why he felt the way he did about his brother. As for Link... Who knew what

Link understood? How to get his own way—that was all that had ever mattered to him. He didn't care about anything else.

He tossed a handful of spoons into the drawer. Link's return had upset too much. He should be with Anne right now, helping her, mapping out a plan for the adoption hearing. Instead she was so angry she'd probably slam the door in his face if he went over there.

He couldn't blame her for that. He hadn't intended it, but to her it had probably sounded as if he were ashamed of kissing her. Of caring about her.

I didn't mean it. He tried saying the words in his mind, tried imagining what her response would be.

Nothing encouraging appeared. Instead, he could only see her face the way it had looked earlier—angry, hurt, disappointed.

"You two look busy." Link's tone made it clear he didn't mean that as a compliment.

Mitch turned toward the doorway. Link's hair was wet from the shower, his shirt and pants freshly pressed.

"Going somewhere?"

"You're not wishing me gone, are you, big brother?"

Aware of Davey's dark eyes watching them, Mitch shook his head. "I already said you were welcome." *As long as you don't cause trouble.* "I just wondered where you were off to."

Link swung a leather jacket around his shoulders. "Going to meet up with some of the guys. It'll be just like old times."

"Not too much like old times, I hope." Link had run with a rough crowd in high school, and Mitch had no desire to have to arrest his own brother.

"You never did think much of my friends." A defensive note crept into Link's voice.

Mitch gave him a level look. "I think of them as little as possible. You'd be better off if you did the same."

"Hey, you've got your friends, and I've got mine. Can't say I ever cared for yours, but maybe your taste is improving. Your Anne's a cut above most of the local talent. You seeing her tonight?"

He should be. "No."

"Too bad." Link didn't sound sorry. "Maybe you scared her off. Maybe she'd like to try out a different Donovan brother."

The plate he was holding clattered into the dish drainer, and Mitch took a step toward his brother. "You leave her out of this, you hear?"

Link lifted a mocking eyebrow. "Little bit of a sore spot there? Hey, don't worry. She's not my type, anyway." He turned away. "Expect me when you see me."

Mitch counted to ten, then made it twenty. Nobody could make him madder than Link could. Maybe that was because nobody knew his trigger spots quite so well. Or enjoyed pushing them quite as much.

He turned back to the table, to discover Davey was gone. The history book still lay there, and the notebook was pristine. If any homework had been done, there was no sign of it.

Fuming, he went in search of the boy. He found him in the living room, parked in front of the television. Mitch snapped off the set in the middle of a car chase, earning a glare from Davey.

"Hey! I was watching that."

"How about your homework?"

"Done." Davey's tone was airy. "All done."

Mitch held out the text and notebook. "Show me. You were supposed to write the answers to ten questions. Show me."

"Listen, I know all that stuff. I don't need to write it down."

"If you knew all that stuff, you wouldn't be getting a *D* in history."

"It's dumb, anyway." Davey glared at him. "I'll bet you never did your homework. I'll bet your brother never did. So why do I have to?"

"Because I said so!" There were a lot better reasons than that, but at the moment his fuse was so short that he couldn't think of any. He tossed the book at Davey. "Get up to your room, and don't come out until the work is finished. And don't count on watching TV again any time soon."

"You're not my boss!" Davey let the book fall to the floor. "I don't have to do what you say. When my father comes back—"

"If your father comes back, you can argue with him. Until then, you'll live by my rules." He scooped the book off the floor and shoved it into Davey's hands. "Now go upstairs and get started."

Davey glared at him for another moment. Then he turned and stamped up the stairs, each footstep making its own protest. The door to his bedroom slammed shut.

Mitch held on to the conviction that he was right for about another minute-and-a-half. Then his anger cooled and the truth seeped in. He'd just blown up at Davey because he was angry with Link. To say nothing of being angry with himself.

Oh, he was right: the kid had to do his homework. But Mitch was the grown-up in the equation. He shouldn't have lost his temper. He certainly shouldn't have said anything about Davey's father.

He glanced uncertainly toward the stairs. Should he go up and apologize? Or say something about the boy's father? But the man seemed to have done an excellent job of disappearing.

He could have stood some impartial advice. If he hadn't made Anne thoroughly disgusted with him, he could have asked her. She and Davey seemed to have connected. But that door was closed until he managed to make amends.

Maybe the best thing was to leave the kid alone for a bit. He glanced at his watch. He'd give Davey an hour, then see how he was getting along. If he hadn't done the questions by then, maybe he could use some help. Then they could have a snack and watch something on television together, the way he'd always imagined families did.

Mitch sat down with the newspaper and tried to concentrate on the printed words. Unfortunately, too many things kept intruding. Was he doing the right thing for Davey? What was he going to do about Link? And most of all, how could he make things right with Anne?

Her face seemed to form against the black-and-white page, angry and hurt. The two of them had been closer than they'd ever been this afternoon. They'd reached a new level of understanding and trust, quite apart from the kiss that had shaken him as he'd never been shaken in his life.

And then it had all fallen apart.

Finally he put the paper down and looked at his watch: forty-five minutes. Good enough. He'd go fix things with Davey. It would be practice for trying to fix things with Anne.

He went up the steps quickly, forming the words in his mind. No indication that he was backing down on the homework issue, just a friendly offer to help—that was the right tone to take.

He tapped lightly on the door, then opened it. "Davey?"

He was talking to an empty room. The history book lay on the crumpled bed, and the window stood open to the cold night air. Davey was gone.

Anne put a light blanket over Emilie, tucking it around the sleeping baby. Emilie sprawled on her back, rosy face turned slightly to the side, hands outstretched. The pose spoke of perfect trust, perfect confidence. In Emilie's view of the world, everything was secure.

A lump formed in Anne's throat. Emilie didn't know it, but things weren't as secure as all that. Anne was the only person standing between her and an uncertain future. She'd never before felt so alone.

For a few brief moments that afternoon she'd begun to think life didn't have to be this way. She'd started to believe she really could have the kind of relationship she'd always thought was a mirage—one based on trust and openness. Something very good had begun between her and Mitch.

And then Mitch let his feelings about his brother spoil everything. Why couldn't he talk to her about it? He'd been so determined to hold everything inside, so irrationally angry. She didn't understand, and she probably never would.

The doorbell rang, suddenly and persistently, breaking the stillness in the old house. Startled, she closed the door to the bedroom gently, then went out into the hallway. She leaned over the stairs. What on earth was going on?

She saw Kate hurry toward the door. If something was wrong, she shouldn't let Kate face it alone. She started down the steps as the older woman unlocked the door and pulled it open.

Mitch erupted into the hallway. "Have you seen Davey?"

"No, not today." Kate ushered Mitch in and closed the door. "Why?"

Heart pounding, Anne hurried down the rest of the stairs. Mitch wouldn't look like that unless something had happened.

"Mitch?"

He looked over Kate's head toward Anne. "It's Davey. He's run away."

She barely registered Kate's exclamations of dismay. She was too occupied with the message Mitch's dark eyes were sending her.

Help. For the first time in their relationship, he wanted—needed—her help.

"What can we do?" Knowing why the boy had run could wait. Finding him—that was the important thing.

"I thought maybe he'd come over here." He glanced at Kate.

"We haven't seen hide nor hair of him." Kate clasped her hands in front of her. "Poor child. It's getting cold out, too. He shouldn't be out there in the cold and the dark. If he goes into the woods—"

"What do you want us to do?" she asked again. Mitch needed their help, not Kate's woeful predictions.

He shook his head. "Not much you can do if he hasn't come here. I'll get some people together and start a search."

"Maybe he'll come back on his own. Once he cools off, I mean."

"I did that a time or two." A muscle twitched in Mitch's jaw. "But I was a teenager then, not a ten-year-old. And it's supposed to drop below freezing tonight. I don't think it's safe to wait."

"No." She shivered, thinking of the lonely mountainous woods that surrounded Bedford Creek. "Let me get a coat. I'll help look."

"You don't know the area well enough." His rejection seemed automatic, but she wasn't going to be left behind to worry.

"I'm another pair of eyes. I can go with someone who does know." *Like you.*

Mitch gave a curt nod, obviously too intent on the search to argue.

"I'll watch the baby." Kate seemed glad to have something constructive to do. "I'll put the outside lights on, so he'll know someone's home if he wants to come here. And I'll start the prayer chain, if that's all right with you."

Mitch nodded. He looked at Anne. "Ready?"

"Right away." She grabbed her jacket from the coat tree.

"Let's get down to the station. I'll call the search team out from there."

She hurried after him down the steps, his anxiety palpable, pulling her along. *Hurry, hurry.* The cold wind, whistling down the mountain, made her thrust her hands into her pockets.

"He'll be all right." She said it to Mitch's back. "We'll find him."

He yanked open the cruiser door, and she slid into the passenger seat. When he got in beside her, his face was taut in the glare that spilled from the dome light.

"I hope so. Looks like I was the wrong choice for the boy."

She shook her head. "If you made a mistake, you can fix it. The important thing now is to find him."

For a moment longer he stared at her. Then he nodded, and his usual stoic mask seemed to fall into place.

"Right." He clasped her hand for an instant. "Thanks."

He started the police car, and it lurched forward.

She peered out the side window as the car spun around the corner. Dark, too dark to see much. She leaned her forehead against the window, hoping against hope that Davey would spring suddenly into view, safe and sound.

But he didn't.

Please, Lord. She stared out into the darkness. *Please, Lord. Be with us and guide our search. And be with that poor lost child.*

She hugged herself, shaking a little. A lost child. At the moment it seemed they were all lost children, in one way or another.

"Shall we have a moment of prayer before we start?" Pastor Richie stepped to the front of the group of searchers who'd gathered at the station.

Anne could sense the urgency seething in Mitch, but he nodded. She clasped her hands in prayer. They needed all the help they could get. Twenty searchers, armed with powerful flashlights, looked like a lot, especially when coupled with those who were already cruising the streets in cars. But it probably wasn't enough—not when they were looking for one small boy in the dark.

Pastor Richie lifted his hands. "Loving Father, we come to You in desperate need. One of Your children is lost. Guide our search, that we may restore him to safety. We know You're watching each of us as a loving father tends his children. We put our search in Your strong hands. In Christ's name we pray, Amen."

Please, Lord.

She saw Mitch's hands flex, as if he were trying to relieve the tension. Again she felt the urgency that drove him.

"Okay," he said. "You have your assignments. Everybody know what to do?"

She nodded with the rest. It had already been decided she'd go with Mitch, giving him another pair of eyes to search the blocks around his house.

"All right. Let's go find him."

The crowd scattered quickly.

Mitch slid into the car and turned the key in the ignition before she even got the door closed. "I don't think he'll have gone far."

The streetlights they passed first illuminated his face, then cast it in shadow.

She clasped her hands. "What if he has some destination in mind?"

He sent her a sharp glance. "What do you mean? What destination?"

She didn't want to say this, but she had to. "Maybe he wants to find his father."

"He's said he doesn't know where he is. Anyway…" His voice trailed off.

She thought she could fill in the blanks. Mitch wouldn't have gone after his own father, or at least that's what he told himself now. So he didn't want to believe it of Davey, either.

Help him, Lord, please. This is really hurting him. It reminds him too much of his own past.

Mitch pulled to the curb at the end of the block and grabbed a flashlight. "Look, we've got to make some assumptions to go on. I don't think he's on a wild-goose chase after his dad, but if he is, the team checking the road out of town should spot him. Meanwhile, we've got to get on with the search."

"I know." She slid out, grabbing her own flashlight and zipping her jacket against the cold. "I wasn't trying to second-guess you."

He nodded. "Second-guess away, if you want. I know you care about him."

"Yes." *And about you.* But that was something she'd probably never have a chance to say.

Mitch swept his light in a wide circle, illuminating shrubs, trees, barren flower beds. "Let's start with the front. Check under every hedge."

She nodded and followed him into the yard, whispering a silent prayer.

They worked their way through one yard, then a second. Mitch was an organized, meticulous searcher, leaving nothing to chance. For the most part they worked in silence, occasionally consulting in low voices.

Three houses later she paused after checking under a lilac bush and watched Mitch swing a beam of light through low-hanging branches. "You act as if you've done this a lot. Conducted a search, I mean."

He bent to direct his light under a porch. "Often enough. We have a pretty well-organized search-and-rescue routine. It's a lot more difficult when someone's lost in the woods."

He straightened, looking up, and she followed the direction of his gaze. The bulk of the mountain was black against a paler black sky, looming over the town in an almost menacing way.

She shivered a little. Maybe people who lived here all the time got used to the mountain's presence. She hadn't, yet. Often it seemed protective, but tonight she was aware of its dangers.

"Davey wouldn't go up there. Would he?"

The beam of the flashlight showed her the tight line of his mouth. "I don't think so. I hope not."

"Please, Father." The prayer came out almost involuntarily. "Please be with that child."

"You sound like Simon Richie. I'm sure he's praying and searching at the same time."

The strained note in his voice caught her by surprise. "Aren't you?"

He shrugged. "I guess I figure God wants me to get on with my job, not go running to Him every time things get tough."

She checked a row of trash cans. Nothing. "Don't you think the Father wants to hear from His children when they're in trouble?"

Mitch swung his light toward her, maybe in surprise. For a moment he didn't say anything. Then, his voice harsh, he said, "I don't know. I don't have much experience with a good father."

The undertone of bitterness in his voice startled her. She kept forgetting, God forgive her. She kept forgetting how complicated his feelings were toward his own father. If that had spilled over into his relationship with his Heavenly Father, it wasn't surprising.

Be careful, she warned herself. *Don't make things worse.*

"I know what you mean." She tried to keep it light. "If I believed God was a father like mine, I'd never be able to pray at all."

He stopped, the flashlight motionless in his hand. Had she gone too far?

Then he nodded. "Maybe you've got something there." His hand closed over hers warmly. "Let's search and pray."

An hour later they'd completed their grid as best they could. Looked like he'd been wrong about where the kid was likely to be found, Mitch thought. Where *was* he?

He slid into the cruiser next to Anne. She was shivering a little, and he started the heater before flipping the radio switch.

"Wanda. Got anything?"

"Nothing, Chief, sorry. Most teams have finished their first grid and gone on to their second." Wanda sounded briskly efficient. "You have anything?"

"Nada." His jaw clenched. Where was the kid? "I'll check in again in an hour."

Anne stirred beside him, leaning forward to look down the empty street. "Every house has its porch light on."

He nodded. "Word's spread. People want Davey to know he could walk up to any door in town right now."

"I didn't—" Anne's voice sounded choked. "I hope he sees. And understands."

"Yeah. Me, too."

Davey, where are you? Where did you run to?

Where would he run? Mitch tried to look at it rationally. If he were the kid, where might he go?

Home? But Davey didn't have a home, not anymore. Flagler had never bothered to provide his son with even minimum security.

Some people thought they didn't have homeless people in Bedford Creek. He knew better. Maybe they didn't have people sleeping on the streets, but there were those who didn't have a safe place to live.

Home. The word kept coming to him, refusing to go away. *Home.*

Are you trying to tell me something, Lord?

He glanced at Anne. That was the kind of conversation she probably had with God all the time. He hadn't realized, until tonight, that it was lacking in his own life. Or why.

He started the engine, and Anne looked at him.

"Where do we go next?"

He shrugged. "Maybe I'm wrong, but I've got a feeling. Let's go down to River Street and have a look at the place where Davey used to live."

A few minutes later they pulled up in front of a dilapidated house. It was dark and appeared empty. Still, something inside Mitch kept driving him. He had to check it out.

He approached the front door and tried it, sensing Anne coming up behind him and looking over his shoulder. A brand-new padlock glinted in the light from his flash. Looked like the landlord hadn't been taking any chances. But there might be another way in, a way a kid would know.

"I'll check the back. Why don't you stay here?"

She nodded, rubbing her arms against the chill, and he stepped off the creaky porch.

He prowled around the house, checking windows. The side door, too, bore a shiny new padlock. No sign anyone could have gotten in, not even a skinny kid.

He stopped at the back of the house, shining his light along the black windows. Nothing. This had turned into been a wild-goose chase. He'd better get back to his assigned grid and stop following hunches. One of the other searchers would cruise this neighborhood, anyway.

As he turned, his light flickered across the dirt-bare space stretching between the house and the river. He stopped. The light touched a decrepit building sagging into itself at the edge of the river.

Check it. The voice in his mind was insistent. *Check it.*

He stalked toward the building—little more than a shed, really. There were plenty of other places that would be warmer and drier for a kid out in the night.

Still, something drove Mitch. He had to look. He grabbed the sagging door. It stuck tight, and for a moment he thought it was locked.

He rattled it, putting his shoulder into it. The door popped open.

He took a step forward, flashing the beam of light around the interior. Nothing. Some battered boxes, a stack of lumber on one side, broken glass littering the floor.

"Davey!" His voice echoed in the cold darkness. Futile. The kid wasn't here.

He turned away, stepping through the open doorway. Then just as he started to shut the door, something creaked behind him. He froze.

His hand tightened on the door frame, and he swung the light toward the lumber pile. There might be—could be—just enough room behind it for one small body.

"Davey?" He reached the stack, moved to the side of it and peered along the wall. "Davey? You there?"

"Go away!" The boy's voice was shrill. "Go away! I hate you!"

Chapter 14

"Davey, listen to me."

Behind him, Mitch could hear Anne's running feet. She must have heard. He held out a warning hand. No use spooking the boy by having too many people around. From the corner of his eye he saw her stop.

"No!" A scrabbling noise accented Davey's answer. The kid was trying to get around him to the door.

"Come on, Davey, I just want to talk."

This time Davey didn't bother with a verbal answer. He just spurted past.

Mitch grabbed, caught the sleeve of a windbreaker, and pulled the boy toward him. He wrapped both arms around the kid, trying to still his frantic struggles.

"Let me go! I don't wanna be with you. Let me go!"

"Davey—" Mitch clamped his arms tighter "—you have to let me talk to you. To tell you I'm sorry."

The slightest pause in the boy's flailing encouraged him to continue. "Listen, I was wrong. I was mad about something else, and I snapped at you instead." *Just like my father used to do.* The lump in his throat threatened to choke him. "I was wrong."

"Yeah, you were." Davey sounded angry, but he stopped struggling. "That stupid history—"

"Hey, I wasn't wrong about that. You still have to do your homework." He eased the pressure of his grip. He could sense Anne moving closer, but kept his focus on Davey. "That's part of the bargain. But I should have helped you, not yelled at you."

"Yeah." The boy's voice was muffled. "I thought maybe you…"

He put his hand gently on the kid's head. "What did you think?"

"I figured you were going to tell me to get out." The words came out defiantly, but Mitch could hear the fear underneath. "So I just figured I'd go before you got around to it."

Pain was an icy hand around his heart. *Lord, give me the right words. Please.* It was the kind of prayer he'd never felt comfortable with, but it came out so naturally now, warming him.

"Hey, we have a deal, remember? I don't go back on a deal." He held the boy a little away from him, so he could see his face in the dim light. "You're going to stay with me until your dad comes back. Right?"

Davey nodded, then looked down at his toes. "What if I do something you don't like?"

"Then I might yell. But I wouldn't tell you to go. No way." That was what he'd always wanted, but never had—the assurance that someone was there, whatever he did, no matter what. Just always there. "You've got my word on it."

Holding his breath, he released the boy. "We okay now?"

Davey peered up at him. Apparently whatever he saw satisfied him. He nodded.

Some of the tension slipped away. "All right. Let's get you home."

"Okay."

Davey took a step away. Then he stopped, waiting while Mitch shut the rickety door. He fell into step beside him as they walked to the patrol car.

Anne's gaze met Mitch's as she joined them. Her eyes were bright with tears. She touched Davey lightly on the shoulder. "Hi, Davey. I'm glad you're okay."

Davey nodded. Then he slid into the cruiser. Anne brushed a tear away with the back of her hand and followed him.

Thank you, Lord. He got in and picked up the mike to let Wanda know to end the search. *Thank you.*

Davey fidgeted.

"Mitch?"

"Yeah?" He glanced at the boy.

"People were looking for me?"

"You bet people were looking for you. What'd you think, we'd just let you go?" Mitch gestured down the street, where every porch light was on. "See those lights? They're for you. Because people heard you were out there and wanted you to know it was okay to come to them."

He could see the muscles in Davey's throat work. "You sure?" The kid's voice wavered.

"I'm sure."

With a little sigh, Davey leaned back against the seat, hands relaxing.

Mitch saw Anne surreptitiously wipe away another tear.

Davey would still be a handful; he was sure of that. But if this night had convinced the kid that people cared what happened to him, they'd come a long way.

Anne climbed a little stiffly from the car when they pulled up in front of Mitch's. They'd stopped at the burger hut for sandwiches, and Davey had wolfed down two. Now he looked so tired he could hardly hold his eyes open, and she was in about the same shape.

"I'll say good night now."

Mitch caught her arm. "Come in for a minute." His smile flickered.

She wanted to stay. She wanted to go. Finally she nodded.

As soon as they got inside and he'd disappeared up the stairs with Davey, she had second thoughts. What was the point of this? They'd said everything there was to say that afternoon, and still Mitch had shut her out. He had been ashamed or embarrassed about kissing her. Could she believe any of that had changed, just because they'd come together over Davey's crisis?

She picked up her jacket, then tossed it over the back of the chair. She wouldn't be a coward about this. If Mitch wanted to talk, they'd talk.

She was sitting in the living room, leafing through a copy of a police magazine, when he came back downstairs. He'd shed his jacket, and the sleeves of his flannel shirt were rolled back, as if he'd been helping Davey get washed up. He glanced at the magazine in her hands.

"Getting up to date on the latest weapon regs?"

She shook her head, let the magazine drop onto the end table. "How is he?"

"Okay." Mitch sank to the couch next to her and leaned back, closing his eyes. The lines of strain were obvious on his face. It had been a difficult night for all of them—Mitch, Davey, the searchers who'd looked and prayed.

"Thank heaven you thought of looking there."

Mitch sat up. "Thank heaven is right. Something led us straight to him."

Yes. Something… Someone…had. "A lot of people were praying."

"I know." His face relaxed a little. "Thanks for your help tonight. That's what I wanted to say." His hand closed over hers. "Thank you. For everything."

"You're welcome. You and Davey both."

"I don't want to let him down."

Was that what was eating at him? Doubts over his ability to care for Davey? "You won't."

He shrugged. "Donovans don't have a very good record." His tone was light, but she knew him well enough to hear the pain under the words. "My dad left. My mother escaped into a bottle. Link turns tail at the sight of responsibility."

Her heart hurt for him. He was so sure, so in control on the outside. But inside he measured himself by his family. That was obviously behind his determination not to have a family of his own. The fear he'd turn out just like his own father.

"Maybe…" She went slowly, trying to find the right words. "Maybe you inherited everyone's share of responsibility. Assist, protect, defend. Like that crest in your office."

His smile flickered. "Military Police. I adopted that motto when I went in. They're good rules. They let you know what's expected of you."

She could see so clearly the boy he must have been, trying to make up for a bad start by finding something solid to hang on to. "We all need that."

"I need something else, too." His eyes darkened. "I need to say how sorry I am. About today."

The quarrel seemed to have taken place an eternity ago. "It's all right."

"No, it's not." He smiled wryly. "You got to see the worst aspect of having a brother. He knows me better than anyone, so he can push all my buttons. I was wrong to let that come between us."

His fingers moved softly against her wrist, tracing circles on the delicate skin. Each touch seemed to go right to her heart.

"Yes." Her breath caught on the word. "You were wrong."

His dark brown gaze was intent on her face. "Will you let me make up for it?"

Some faint warning voice told her she was getting in too deep, in danger of being swept away, like that story he'd told her.

She could retreat to safer ground. Go back to being the person who'd decided against having a man in her life. It would be safer, but it wouldn't be better.

She touched his cheek, feeling warm skin, the faint prickle of beard. He put his hand over hers, pressing her palm against his skin.

Her heart was so full that it stole the words. But

she knew she loved him. She'd seen it coming, tried to avoid it, but nothing had done any good. She loved him.

Mitch drew her into his arms. She could feel the steady beat of his heart as she wrapped her arms around him. Her own heart threatened to overflow. She held him tightly. They had both come home at last.

Mitch lingered at the kitchen table over a second cup of coffee the next morning. Davey had gone off to school a little heavy-eyed, grumbling a bit, but he'd gone. At least he'd seemed confident Mitch would be there when he came home.

He lifted the cup to his lips, smiling. Funny thing, how he'd found himself smiling at odd moments ever since last night. Ever since he'd held Anne in his arms and dared to think about having a family.

Given the way Anne felt about Emilie, given the family wars she'd been through herself, she wouldn't trust a new relationship easily. But she'd taken the first painful steps from behind her safety barricades, and so had he.

Noise in the hallway wiped the smile from his face. It was stupid of him to tense at the very sound of his brother's footsteps.

If just knowing Anne could bring him this far from the person he'd been, he ought to be able to get through one breakfast conversation with his brother without snapping. He could try, anyway.

Link wandered through the doorway, spotted the coffeepot and made straight for it. He didn't glance at Mitch until he'd taken several long gulps from his mug.

Maybe it was up to Mitch to get the conversational ball rolling. "How did your reunion go?" At least he hadn't heard any damage reports, so it couldn't have been too wild a time.

An expression of disgust crossed Link's face. "You wouldn't believe it. The old gang is going domestic. Getting married, buying houses, having kids… I thought I was in an old television rerun."

Mitch grinned. "Wedding bells are breaking up the old gang, huh?"

"That might be okay for them." Link responded with an answering grin that reminded Mitch of the little brother who'd once looked up to him. "But it's definitely not in my plans."

"What are your plans?"

Link shrugged. "The company wanted to send me to Anchorage on a project, but I turned it down." He shook his head. "Not for me. A two-year commitment, responsibility of crew chief…definitely not for me."

That was Link all over: running from any hint of something settled. "A little responsibility isn't a bad thing," Mitch said. He tried to keep the words light, but he could tell from the tightening of Link's expression that he didn't succeed.

"This town is getting to you, big brother. Be responsible, settle down, act just like everybody else and maybe they'll like you. Maybe they'll forget what you came from."

His hand tightened on the coffee cup. "That's not what's important to me."

"Sure it is." Link slammed his mug down on the table. "You think I don't know? I watched you at that fall festival when the mayor called you up on stage, said what a great job you'd done. You were eating it up. You'd have licked his boots for that praise."

Link's words moved slowly through his mind. The foliage festival Link meant wasn't the most recent one. It was the one before.

His heart turned to lead. It was the one that was held when Tina Mallory was in town, when Link wasn't supposed to have been anywhere near Bedford Creek.

He looked at his brother. "That was the festival before last. I thought you weren't here then."

He could see the wheels turning in Link's mind, see him backpedaling. See him deciding it didn't matter.

"Yeah, so? That was after you'd told me never to darken your door again. I didn't bother to tell you I was in town. Place was so crowded with tourists, you'd never have noticed unless I'd walked right up to you. I wanted to see my buddies."

"And who else did you see?" The words tasted like ashes in his mouth.

"What do you mean?"

"I mean Tina Mallory." He could see it, rolling inexorably toward him. Link and Tina Mallory. Emilie. He almost didn't need to ask. He knew the truth, bone deep, and it was crushing him.

"Tina?" Link shrugged, turning away, not meeting his eyes. "Don't know her."

"You did." Mitch stood, feeling as if he forced his way upward against a huge weight. He pressed his fists against the table. "You knew her. You went out with her. You left her pregnant."

"Pregnant?" Link's face lost its color. "What are you talking about?"

"Tina Mallory. Cute little kid who worked at the café. A little kid you got pregnant." He hammered the words at his brother. "She's dead now, if you care."

"No!"

He could see Link's mind working feverishly, trying to find an excuse, an evasion. He felt suddenly very tired, as if the past had rolled over him and flattened him, and he'd never be right again.

"Don't bother to deny it. I can see the truth in your face."

A hunted look flickered in Link's eyes. "All right, I dated her a couple times. We got close. But I didn't know anything about a baby. I went back to the job. Tried to call her maybe a couple months later, but she'd left town. I never heard from her again. She never told me anything about any baby."

Given Link's history, the words rang true, but it didn't seem to make much difference whether his brother had known about the baby or not. He could only think it was the end of everything.

"It wasn't my fault!" Link slammed his fist down on the table. "I know what you're thinking, but it wasn't just me. It was her, too."

"She was a kid."

"She was old enough to know what she was doing. And if you think you're going to tangle me up in this, you're wrong." He thrust away from the table and reached the back door almost before he finished speaking.

"Wait a minute." Mitch reached toward him. "We have to talk about this. For once in your life you have to face your responsibility."

"*You* talk about it, big brother. I'm getting out of here." He flung open the door before Mitch could get around the table, then looked back over his shoulder. "And think about this, while you're at it. The only reason she even went out with me was because I was your brother."

That stopped Mitch in his tracks. "What are you talking about?"

"That's right." The old mocking, defiant Link was back. "She went out with me because she had a crush on you, and you never gave her the time of day."

He slammed out.

Mitch stared at the door, pain wrapping around his heart. It looked as if he and Link, between them, had just proved that everything people had ever said about the Donovans was true.

That was what Anne would think. *Anne.* A fresh spasm of pain hit him.

He had to tell her, even though it might mean the end of everything between them.

There was only one thing he could do before he faced Anne with the truth. He'd catch up with Link and make him agree to sign the papers before he disappeared again. At least he could spare Anne that much pain.

She'd take the baby… *His niece.* An even stronger pain slammed his heart, shattering it. She'd take Emilie and the papers, and leave. He'd never see them again.

He wasn't sure how he'd go about living with that.

Chapter 15

"There we go, sweetheart." Anne snapped Emilie's romper. "All clean and dry and happy."

Emilie waved both arms, seeming ready to launch herself into space from her diaper change. Anne lifted her, planting a kiss on the soft round cheek.

"That's my girl. We'll just go downstairs and maybe…"

Maybe they'd look out the window and see Mitch? That was what she was thinking; she couldn't deny it.

Happiness seemed to bubble up inside her. Last night had been frightening, but it had been good, too. Thanks to Davey, she and Mitch had found their way past some of the barriers between them.

Arms snug around Emilie, she started down the steps. For the last eight months, she'd believed having Emilie in her life was all she'd ever need to be happy.

Now…now she was looking beyond just herself and Emilie, to the possibility of a real family.

Even a month ago she wouldn't have thought it possible. But she'd already trusted Mitch more than she'd ever trusted anyone in her life. Maybe she really could take that next step, a step toward the kind of emotional intimacy she'd never imagined having. If she and Mitch could reach that, they'd share the kind of love she'd never believed would be hers.

The telephone rang in the hall below, and Kate rushed in from the kitchen to snatch it up, smiling at Anne and Emilie as they came down the stairs.

"Good afternoon. The Willows."

She listened for a moment, then held the receiver out to Anne.

"It's for you. Let me take that sweet child while you're talking."

Anne exchanged Emilie for the telephone. Kate, cooing to the baby, walked back toward the kitchen.

Anne lifted the receiver. Mitch? There was no reason to think he'd call this afternoon, but even so her heart beat a little faster. "Hello?"

"This is Marcy Brown." The girl's voice was hesitant. "You wrote me about Tina?"

Her stomach turned over, and she gripped the receiver. Marcy Brown, at last. "I'm so glad you called. And sorry I had to break such bad news to you. The thing is, Marcy, I need to find the baby's birth father in order to finalize the adoption. I'm hoping you can tell me something about him."

Silence seemed to press along the connection.

"I—I don't…well, didn't Tina tell you who it was?"

Careful, careful. "Tina mentioned one name. Mitch

Donovan. But I know he's not the father, and I can't begin to guess why Tina would lie about it."

Marcy's sigh came over the line clearly. "She said that, did she? I told her not to, but she wouldn't listen."

"You know, then." The blood seemed to be pounding in her ears. "You know who Emilie's father is. You know why she named Mitch."

"Yeah, well, that part's nuts, but Tina went off the deep end sometimes. Thing was, she really liked the chief, always talked about how nice he was to her and what a great guy he was. I think maybe when she realized the other guy was gone and wasn't coming back, she sort of pretended. You know, pretended that Mitch Donovan was the one, so everything would be all right. She didn't mean any harm by it... At any rate, it was Link Donovan. You know who I mean? The chief's brother."

The hallway did a slow spin around her, and she sank down abruptly on the bench. "How... But how can that be? I thought he wasn't even in Bedford Creek when Tina was here." That was what Mitch had said. He wouldn't lie to her.

"He was there—"

Anne could almost hear the shrug.

"—just for a couple weeks in the fall. It seems to me I did hear him say he didn't want his brother to know he was in town. Like they'd had some big fight or something."

The certainty settled on her like a weight. Mitch had mentioned the quarrel. Probably he'd never suspected Link was back in Bedford Creek at the crucial time.

"You're sure?"

"Oh, yeah. He was the only guy she went out with,

and I think she just went with him because he sort of reminded her of the chief."

"I understand." She did. Tina, reaching out for love, had snatched at whatever was offered. But it hadn't been love.

A few more exchanges, a promise to send a photo of Emilie, and Anne put down the receiver. She knew now. She had the information she'd come to Bedford Creek to find.

And after asking Kate to watch Emilie, she headed out to find Mitch.

Ten minutes later, she stopped on the sidewalk outside the police station, stomach knotting. This would be difficult, so much more difficult than that first day, and she'd thought nothing could be worse than that.

Help me, Lord. Help me find the words. This news is going to hurt Mitch so much. I don't want to cause him pain, but he has to know.

She took a deep breath and opened the door.

Wanda looked up at her entrance, smiled, and waved her toward the inner office door.

Anne tapped, then opened the door. Mitch stood at the desk, head bent, just hanging up the phone. Her heart gave a little jump at the sight of him. For an instant thoughts of her reason for being there slipped away, and she was back in his arms again the night before, knowing she loved him.

No. She couldn't let herself think about that, not now. Not when she had to tell him something that would hurt him so badly.

"Anne."

She half expected him to round the desk toward her, but he didn't. "I have some news," she said, then stopped. This was so difficult, but she had to do it. She'd tried handling everything on her own, and it hadn't worked. Surely she and Mitch had come far enough to deal with this together.

"What is it?" He did come around the desk then, reaching toward her as if expecting the worst.

"Marcy Brown called." There wasn't any way to say this but to get it out. "She knew about Tina's pregnancy. Knew who the father was." She swallowed hard. "She even knew why Tina named you."

He didn't say anything, just stared at her from under lowered brows, his face expressionless. The mask was back in full force, as if he needed its protection.

"She said…" She took a steadying breath. "She said it was Link."

There, it was out. Mitch would be shocked, denying it, but…

But he wasn't. He just stood there, looking at her, and she read the knowledge in his face.

"You already knew." The words were out before she thought about them. He *knew*.

Pain gripped her. All this time she'd been desperate to find the truth, all this time…

"How could you do this?" The blood pounded in her head. Later she'd need to weep, but not now. Now she had to react to this betrayal.

"Anne, it's not what you think."

"You knew how important this is. How could you lie to me?" Maybe she wouldn't be able to hold back the tears until later. They stung her eyes, salty and bitter.

"I didn't!"

Her heart turned to stone. "You knew. You didn't tell me. What is that but a lie?"

He reached out to her, as if to touch her, and she recoiled. He let his hand drop, eyes darkening.

"I didn't know, not until today. You can't believe I've been lying to you all along—"

"When today?" It was like being back in a courtroom, but she'd never tried a case that held so much personal anguish for her.

He stiffened. "This morning. Link told me the truth this morning."

"And you kept it from me." Her head throbbed. "How long were you going to keep it from me, Mitch? Until after he was gone again? Until he wasn't here in Bedford Creek to embarrass you?"

"No! That's not why I didn't tell you. Anne, you have to believe me. I only wanted—"

She shook her head. "You're wrong. I don't have to believe you." She could barely breathe against the heartache. "I was wrong ever to trust you. It's a mistake I won't make again."

Mitch stared at the door that had closed behind Anne—that closed on any chance he might have to make things right.

He could go after her, but what would he say? *I was wrong?* She knew that already, and nothing he could say would make it any different.

He'd ruined everything with his black stubbornness. If he'd gone to her with the truth right away, maybe there would have been some small chance to make things right. Now there was none.

He'd told himself he was trying to spare her, to delay telling her until he could find Link and try to repair the damage. But maybe she was right. Maybe he was really trying to spare himself.

He hadn't fixed anything. He'd lost his brother and he'd lost Anne, and this was one thing he couldn't blame on his father. This one was all his fault.

One way or another, he had to find Link. Getting Link to cooperate wouldn't change things between himself and Anne. How could it? But at least it would make things right for her and Emilie. That was all he could expect.

Getting Link's signature was the only thing left Mitch could do for Anne, and he wasn't going to fail.

But two hours later the possibility of failure loomed a lot larger. He drove down River Street one more time. He'd tried every friend of Link's he could remember, tried every place his brother might be staying. He met nothing but blank looks. No one had seen his brother since the day before.

He seemed to be out of options. His stomach twisted. He'd have to see Anne, let her know what he was trying to do. She wouldn't want to see him, but he had to tell her he wouldn't give up until he had Link ready to sign.

He stopped in front of Kate's place, took the steps two at a time. He rapped on the door.

Kate swung it open and looked at him, her gaze a little startled. "Mitch. Is something wrong?"

"I need to see Anne. Will you let her know I'm here?"

But Kate was shaking her head. "I can't do that."

"What do you mean?" He could sense bad news coming, see it in the way her gaze slid away from his.

"Anne's gone." Kate gave a helpless little gesture. "I couldn't talk her out of it. She took the baby and went back to Philadelphia."

* * *

The road snaked ahead of Anne, glistening a little in the gray afternoon light. The cold, light rain slicked the pavement, and she slowed as she started up the steep hill. Maybe if she kept her mind on the road conditions, she could keep the pain at bay a little longer.

It didn't seem to be working. Her breath caught on a little sob.

Mitch, how could you do this? How could you betray me this way?

Emilie wiggled in her car seat, just beginning to fuss. She hadn't been happy to be packed up so abruptly. And Kate… Kate hadn't understood at all, but Anne hadn't been able to explain her sudden need to leave.

She still couldn't, not even to herself. She'd just known she had to get away from Bedford Creek, away from Mitch.

"Hush, Emilie. It'll be all right. We'll be home soon."

That was what she needed to hear someone say to her. *It will be all right.* But there was no one to do that.

Why, Lord? she prayed bleakly. *Why did You let me begin to trust, begin to care, only to face betrayal?*

She could have handled the fact that Link was Emilie's father. She could even understand Tina's convoluted reasoning in naming Mitch as the father.

Tina had thought Mitch was everything Link wasn't—solid, responsible, trustworthy. She'd probably thought she could count on Mitch to do the right thing.

Anger pulsed through her; she tightened her grip on the wheel. She'd thought that, too. And they'd both been wrong. He'd chosen to protect his brother instead of her and Emilie.

What would Link do? Her throat tightened. She

should have stayed, tried to see him, tried to get his signature on the forms. That was why she'd come to Bedford Creek in the first place.

But she wasn't the person she'd been then. That Anne Morden would have put on her lawyer's armor and faced down both the Donovan brothers. Now she'd started to care too much, and she couldn't do it, not without letting Mitch see exactly how much he'd hurt her.

So she'd go home. She'd go back to Philadelphia, hire a private investigator, put the whole thing in professional hands.

Emilie's cry went up an octave, and Anne winced. She turned her head to take a look, and felt the car swerve. Her fingers tightened on the wheel. She must be more tired than she'd thought. She couldn't—

The car swerved again, sliding across the road, and she fought the steering wheel. It wasn't her—it was the rain. She touched the brake, barely tapping it. If she could just get onto the gravel berm, they'd be all right.

The car swung across the road, out of control. Her stomach turned over. She clenched the wheel, jerking it, but it was no good—she'd lost control entirely. They careened sideways, nothing between them and the steep drop-off but a narrow gravel stretch and a ditch.

She couldn't stop. Her mind flashed ahead to an image of her car sliding off the mountain, tumbling down the steep slope, plunging into the trees below.

Help us, Father! Help us!

Seconds became an eternity…spinning trees, whirling lights, frantic prayers. And then the car slid gently to rest against the opposite bank.

The sobs she heard were hers. Emilie's crying had

stopped, maybe out of her amazement at the ride. Anne twisted in the seat, touching the baby with frantic hands.

"Are you all right? Emilie, are you okay?"

Emilie batted at her hands, then stretched, twisting irritably in the car seat.

She was all right. Anne leaned her forehead against the seat back. The baby was all right. They were both all right, no thanks to her.

"Thank you, Lord." She patted Emilie, then wiped away the hot tears that spilled down her cheeks. "Thank you."

I wasn't in control. But You were.

She turned, leaning back in the seat, relief flooding her. God had been in control. Even though she hadn't trusted, even though she'd been trying to do it all herself, God had been in control.

"I haven't been trusting You, have I?"

Helen would probably smile at the question. Wise Helen had seen what Anne needed. Believing wasn't enough. She had to trust, too.

She brushed her hair back from her forehead. "I'll try, Lord. I'll try."

She couldn't have a relationship with God unless she could trust. She couldn't have a relationship with another person unless she could trust.

She looked back over the last twenty-four hours. She'd told herself she loved Mitch, but she hadn't trusted him enough to give him a chance to explain. Maybe things could never be right between them; maybe there were too many barriers. But whatever happened, she couldn't run away. She had to give him a chance.

Something else was crystal clear in her mind. Unless Mitch could open up, unless he could find a way to deal with the family problems that haunted him, they didn't stand a chance.

Her heart turned to lead. Dealing with that pain might be more than Mitch was able to do. But she'd learned something in these difficult weeks. Having a relationship built on trust, based on openness, really was possible.

She'd never believed that before, but now she knew it. And she couldn't settle for less.

Slowly, carefully, she put the car in gear and started back toward Bedford Creek.

Chapter 16

"Look, just stay by the phone for me, okay?" Mitch frowned at Wanda. "I've asked half the town to call me if they spot Link. Someone's bound to see him."

"All right, all right." Wanda dropped the purse she'd picked up, preparing to going home. "But you owe me for this one."

He owed a lot of people—Anne most of all. But she was gone. He looked bleakly down the years he would be missing her. Why couldn't she have given him a few minutes' grace? That was all he'd wanted. Now—

He heard the door, spun around, and his breath caught in his throat. Anne stood there, holding the baby. He'd never seen a sweeter sight in his life.

She was pale, and she clutched Emilie too tightly. The baby wiggled restlessly.

"What's wrong?" He took a step toward her, battling

pain, grief, regret. Something was wrong besides the obvious, but whatever it was, she probably wouldn't accept help from him. The only thing he had left to offer her was Link's signature on that form.

She shook her head. "Nothing. We're all right. We just... I decided we needed to come back."

"I'm glad you did." Easy, don't push. "I'm trying to find Link, so I can—"

The telephone rang, and he nearly leaped across the desk. Wanda said a few words, then hung up and turned to him. He could read the message on her face. Someone had spotted Link.

"Behind Grace Church. His truck's parked there."

Adrenaline pumped through his veins. Something positive to do, thank heaven. He turned to Anne.

"You wait here with Wanda. I'll find Link and bring him back."

But she was already shaking her head. "We'll go with you."

The last thing he wanted was Anne observing an ugly scene. "That's not a good idea. I'll do better with him alone."

"I'm going." Her mouth set stubbornly, she turned toward the door.

"Anne..."

Frustrated, he shook his head. He didn't want her there when he confronted his brother. But it didn't look as if he had a choice.

If he'd picked the worst place in the world to confront his brother, this would be it, Mitch thought as he pulled up to Grace Church Cemetery. His throat tightened. Link was on one knee in front of a double headstone, carefully clearing away the dried leaves that littered it. He looked very young, kneeling there in the brown grass in front of their parents' graves.

Mitch and Anne's footsteps grated on a patch of gravel. Link swung around, his face hardening when he saw them. "What are you doing here?"

"Looking for you." Mitch stared down at his parents' headstone. "Guess I should have thought sooner to look here."

"Why would you?" Link stood, fists clenching. "Not a place you spend much time, is it?"

"I guess not." He stared down at the epitaph. At his father's name. His father hadn't come back until it was too late to say the things that needed to be said between them. Maybe he could keep from making the same mistake with Link. "Look, we need to talk."

Link shrugged, his face cold. "I've got nothing to say."

"Fine, just listen, then." He couldn't let himself think about Anne, standing so silently beside him.

"Sorry, don't have time." Link spun, but Mitch grabbed his arm.

"Make time, Link. This is important."

"To you?" His expression made it clear that didn't weigh with him.

"To this baby girl." He jerked his head toward Emilie, his eyes never leaving Link's face. "She deserves a chance in life."

Link's gaze swiveled to Anne and the pink snow-suited bundle she carried. "Tina's baby." Link said it with certainty.

"That's right. How did you know?"

He shrugged. "Wasn't hard to figure out, once I knew

part of it. Why else would Anne and the baby be in Bedford Creek?"

"Listen to me, Link." His throat was so tight that he had to force the words out. "When Tina knew she wasn't going to make it, she wanted Anne to adopt her baby. She wanted to give her a chance at a good future."

"Okay, I'm giving her that chance, too." Link's gaze slid away from the baby. "I'm getting out of here. That's the best thing I can do for her." He nodded toward the headstone. "After all, that's what he did for us. Like father, like son, right? He just should have done it sooner."

The bitterness in his brother's voice seeped into Mitch's heart. He was used to it in himself. He'd never guessed it ran so deeply in Link. He felt a sudden revulsion. It wasn't doing either one of them any good.

"Don't, Link. Don't think that about yourself."

"Why not? It's true, isn't it?"

Conviction pounded through his veins. He knew, now, what he had to do. What they both had to do, if only it wasn't too late.

"What he did doesn't matter anymore. At least, it only matters if we let it." He reached toward his brother. "Don't you see what we're doing? We're still letting him control our lives."

"Not you. Not Mr. Upright Citizen. Your life is as different as it can be from his."

"Don't you get it?" Mitch caught his brother's arm. He had to make him see. "I'm doing everything I can to be different from him. You're doing everything you can to be like him. That means we're both still letting him run our lives."

For a moment Link stared at him, dark eyes unreadable. "Yeah, well, there's not much we can do about that, is there?"

"We can stop." The conviction settled into his soul, so strong he didn't even mind the fact that Anne was hearing all of this. "We can forgive him."

He hadn't known it was true until he'd said it. A sense of release slid through him. All this time, trying to be the opposite of everything his father stood for, he'd still been holding on to his resentment. Letting it control his life.

Link jerked free of him. "I can't!" A shadow crossed his face. "And what difference would it make if I could? He's gone."

"It won't make a difference to him. Just to us."

He put his hand on Link's shoulder, feeling his brother tense at his touch. It drove a knife through his heart. He never should have let things get so bad between them. Link was the only family he had in the world, probably the only family he ever would have.

They stood side by side, looking down at their parents' graves. "Let it go, Link. Let them go."

"Not what you'd call a perfect set of parents, were they?" Bitterness still laced Link's words.

"No, I guess they weren't. But that doesn't mean we have to repeat their mistakes." His hand tightened on his brother's shoulder. "I haven't exactly been a perfect big brother, either. Maybe I can do better, if you give me a shot at it."

Mitch felt the tension begin to seep out of Link. "So…if I were trying to do better than they did…" He choked, but went on. "What would I do about this baby?"

That one Mitch knew the answer to. "Sign the papers so Anne can adopt." He looked at her, seeing the way she cradled the baby close, as if defying anyone to take her away. "Nobody could possibly be a better parent to that little girl than she will be."

Link looked at Anne and the baby, not speaking. Then he let out a long breath. "Okay. Let's do it."

Mitch's eyes stung with unshed tears. He nodded. "Follow us back to the office. We can take care of it there."

A few minutes later Link stood by the desk in Mitch's office. His hands clenched into two tight fists. "I'm ready."

Anne looked shell-shocked, as if she couldn't handle much more. "Are you sure?"

Link took a step forward and touched Emilie's soft curls. An emotion—sadness?—crossed his face. Then he nodded.

"I'm sure. She belongs with the mother who loves her." His voice roughened. "I guess Tina knew that. I won't interfere."

Mitch tried to swallow the lump in his throat. This had been a long time coming, but he finally was getting to see his little brother step up and do the right thing, instead of running away. Maybe there was hope for Link…hope for both of them.

Anne juggled the baby as she fumbled with the catch to her bag.

"Let me take her." Mitch reached out, and Emilie came eagerly into his arms.

For a moment he thought Anne would snatch the baby back, but then she nodded.

Give me a chance, Anne. Give us a chance. He wanted to say it, but he couldn't.

Anne unfolded the paper slowly, then held it out to Link.

He took it to Mitch's desk, leaned over to read it. A muscle worked in his jaw, the only outward sign of his feelings. He reached for a pen and scrawled his signature in a quick slash across the bottom of the page.

Anne's breath escaped in an audible sigh. She had to be thinking that it was over, that Emilie was safe at last.

Link handed the paper to her, and she folded it quickly.

"That's that, then." Link tried to smile, but it didn't quite work. "You don't need to worry I'll cause problems. I won't."

Mitch's heart hurt for Link. His little brother had finally started to grow up, but it was a painful process.

"What are you going to do?"

Link shrugged. "Think I'll take on that job in Alaska I told you about." He aimed a light punch at Mitch's arm. "Who knows? Next time I come back, I might have turned into a responsible citizen. Like my big brother."

"Stranger things have happened."

Link glanced from him to Anne. "Looks to me like you could stand to talk things out."

Mitch, cradling Emilie in his arms, nodded. *If Anne will talk to me, that is.*

Link crossed to the door, then looked at them. "You know, I'm not cut out to be a father." He paused. "But I think I could be a darn good uncle, if the position opens up."

He closed the door before either of them could respond.

Anne looked at her baby...hers now, for good. The three of them were alone here, just as they'd been that first day when she came to break the news to Mitch. Emilie was perfectly happy in Mitch's arms.

"We do need to talk." Mitch's voice was a low rumble.

She nodded. "I guess that's why I came back. I couldn't..."

How could she say it? The words didn't seem to exist to explain the tangled emotions she felt at the sight of him.

Mitch looked at Emilie's face, as if trying to discern some resemblance to his brother. "I really didn't think it could be Link. I was so sure he wasn't in town when Tina was here. Sure that was one thing I couldn't blame on him."

"I know." She hesitated, feeling her way. They had to get this out between them. "But I don't know why you didn't tell me when you found out."

Because you couldn't trust me? Just like I couldn't trust you?

He shook his head. "How can I make you understand? The truth just hit me like a sledgehammer. All I could think was that it proved the Donovans were just as bad as everyone always said."

She saw the anguish in his face as he said the words, and it reached out and gripped her heart, too.

"I wouldn't have thought that. I don't think it now. Link was wrong, but at least he's starting to face up to it."

"Maybe he'd have faced it sooner if I hadn't blown up at him." He touched Emilie's hand, and she latched onto his finger. "Anne, you have to know I never intended to hurt you and Emilie. I just wanted a chance to find Link and clear things up with him before I told you. That's all. I would have told you today." He looked at her, dark eyes intense. "I wish you could believe that."

Her heart started to pound. He wanted to know she trusted him. Was that so much to ask?

"You...you and Link have made a start at working things out." That wasn't what she wanted to say. Why was it so hard to tell him what she felt?

He nodded. "The truth is, I let my feelings about my father color everything else in my life. My relationship with my brother, my career, even my relationship with you. I finally saw I had to forgive him, if I wanted any kind of a future." He looked at her, his dark eyes steady. "What about you, Anne? Are you ready to put the past to rest so we can move on?"

That was the question she'd started to face out on that road. She'd let her relationship with her parents govern her relationship with God, just as Mitch had. She hadn't even recognized she was doing it. It was time for both of them to stop.

She looked at Mitch holding her child, and her heart swelled. "I'd like to try."

The love in his eyes took her breath away. "We've got a few hurdles to get over. But God's not finished with us yet." He took a step toward her. "I love you, Anne. I want to try and make this work. Will you stay? Will you marry me?"

If she didn't take this chance, she knew she'd miss the best God had to offer her. She moved forward, letting Mitch's arms enfold both of them. "We'll stay."

Epilogue

"Da, da, da, da!" Emilie stood in the stroller and banged on the tray.

"All right, Sweetheart." Anne maneuvered the stroller through the summertime crowds on the sidewalk. "We'll go to the station and see Mitch."

The baby plopped back into her seat, apparently satisfied. Emilie hadn't mastered the sound of "Mitch" yet, but that didn't matter. After their wedding this fall, he really would be her daddy.

Anne dodged a tourist with a camera and pushed through the station door. Wanda gave her a welcoming smile.

"Chief!" she shouted. "Anne's here."

Davey dropped the broom he'd been wielding and rushed to Emilie. "Can I take her out of the stroller, please? I want to show Wanda how she can walk."

"Of course." Anne smiled. Emilie held her arms out to the person she considered a big brother, and he lifted her carefully from the stroller.

In the months Davey had been living with Mitch, he'd blossomed. That wary, sullen look was completely gone from his eyes. Neither his father nor any other relative had been located, but Davey's permanent placement with Mitch gave him the security he'd never had before. Perhaps, one day, she and Mitch would be able to adopt him legally, but that wouldn't make him any more their son than he already was.

Trust in the Lord with all your heart. She still had to remind herself of that each day. God would work out what was right for Davey, in His own time.

The office door opened, and Mitch came toward her quickly. "Anne." Love shone in his eyes as he kissed her. The mask he'd once worn was gone now entirely, and his face no longer hid his emotions. His feelings were written plainly for her to read.

His arm still around her, Mitch reached for Davey and Emilie. The baby toddled toward them, clutching Davey's hand, beaming.

Mitch swept Emilie up in his arms, and Anne put her hand on Davey's shoulder, drawing him close.

Family. They were a family. She looked up at Mitch, her heart overflowing with love. She hadn't really known the meaning of the word before. Now, each day, she and Mitch discovered how deep, how blessed their love could be.

She'd come to Bedford Creek to find Emilie's father. God had seen to it that she found so much more.

* * * * *

A *Publishers Weekly* bestselling and award-winning author of over forty novels, with almost two million books in print, **Deb Kastner** enjoys writing contemporary inspirational Western stories set in small communities. Deb lives in beautiful Colorado with her husband, miscreant mutts and curious kitties. She is blessed with three adult daughters and two grandchildren. Her favorite hobby is spoiling her grandchildren, but she also enjoys reading, watching movies, listening to music (The Texas Tenors are her favorite), singing in the church choir and exploring the Rocky Mountains on horseback.

Books by Deb Kastner

Love Inspired

Rocky Mountain Family
The Black Sheep's Salvation
Opening Her Heart

Cowboy Country
Yuletide Baby
The Cowboy's Forever Family
The Cowboy's Surprise Baby
The Cowboy's Twins
Mistletoe Daddy
The Cowboy's Baby Blessing
And Cowboy Makes Three
A Christmas Baby for the Cowboy
Her Forgotten Cowboy

Visit the Author Profile page at
Harlequin.com for more titles.

THE MARINE'S BABY

Deb Kastner

To Katie. You have the kindest heart *ever*, and I have so much to learn from you. I'm so proud of the young woman my "baby" girl has become. I love you more every day.

For by grace you have been saved through faith,
and that not of yourselves;

it is the gift of God, not of works,
lest anyone should boast.

—*Ephesians* 2:8–9

Chapter 1

The baby, sleeping soundly with her tiny thumb pressed in her mouth and her index finger crooked over her button nose, was cooperating beautifully.

The car seat, not so much.

Sergeant First Class Nathan Morningway scowled at the offensive piece of equipment and grunted as he tried the release lever again. At least he *thought* it was the release lever. The directions enclosed in the box had been less than helpful, and he'd chosen to wing it instead. He now wished he'd at least *kept* the useless instructions instead of wadding them up and tossing them in the nearest garbage can.

How hard could this be?

As a marine, he'd taken apart and reassembled countless firearms. He'd defused hundreds of bombs and improvised explosive devices over the years. And he couldn't handle a simple baby seat?

Nate tried the lever once more, and then decided it wasn't worth the effort. He'd just have to figure out how to use the uncooperative piece of equipment after he'd spoken to his brother.

Instead, he unhooked the straps, intending to take baby Gracie out of the car seat and carry her in his arms. The only problem was—and Nate hadn't noticed this until he'd already unbuckled the harness—Gracie's arm was wrapped like a noose around one of the straps, anchored by the thumb she was sucking.

Oh, boy. He really hated to do this, but he didn't see any other way around it. Holding his breath, he gently pulled on Gracie's little fist. She made a small murmur of protest and sucked even harder.

Nate tried again, more firmly this time. Gracie's thumb left her mouth with a pop. The baby's enormous brown eyes opened and blinked back at him. Her chin started quivering, her face scrunched up adorably and a moment later she was howling at the top of her lungs.

Nate grimaced. He still couldn't believe something *that small* could make so much noise. He'd never been around babies before in his entire life.

And now…

Now.

His throat tightened and burned as he fought to suppress the memories. He had to concentrate on other issues right now, the most pressing of which was letting his brother, Vince, know he was back at the lodge. That was enough to worry about all by itself.

"All right, little one," Nate soothed, pulling the pink-clad infant awkwardly to his chest. "I'm here for you. Don't cry, sweetheart."

Nate was surprised when the baby instantly calmed to his voice, curling into his chest and gurgling contentedly. He got a whiff of her soft downy hair and the unique smell of baby shampoo, and his heart flipped right over. Little Gracie had him wrapped around her tiny pinky finger, and there was no denying it.

Gracie wasn't just his responsibility—she was the love of his life. From the moment he'd signed the legal documents that made him not only her godfather, but her legal guardian, Nate had fallen hard for the little one, hook, line and sinker.

Too bad he didn't know the first thing about raising an infant. That would be problematic, but Nate had more immediate concerns—showing up at Morningway Lodge unannounced.

His parents'—his *father's*—dream, and now his brother's ministry, the lodge was an affordable retreat center for families of those recuperating from spinal injuries at the nearby Rocky Mountain Rehabilitation Hospital. The lodge was his family's business, and Nate's worst nightmare.

Or rather, his brother *Vince* was Nate's worst nightmare. He had been in the past, and in all probability, he would be again now.

There was only one way to find out, and Nate had never been a procrastinator.

Kissing his baby girl on her soft cheek, he tucked his palm beneath her head and marched up the stairs onto the pinewood porch of the main lodge. He inhaled deeply of the fragrant wood as he let himself in the front door and moved up to the courtesy desk. It was the scent of home and his childhood.

It felt odd to be back home.

Since no one was manning the desk, Nate shifted Gracie securely into one arm and rang for service. He waited a moment, and then, when no one appeared, he bounced his palm several times on the bell.

"I'm sorry to keep you waiting." A young woman whirled into the office behind the desk, brushing her shoulder-length wavy blond hair from her forehead with the tips of her fingers. "Oh, what a darling little baby girl!"

When the woman met his gaze, Nate's breath stopped short in his throat. She had the most luminous chocolate-brown eyes he'd ever seen, and they were openly friendly.

More than that. Brimming with joy. He thought the look in her eyes exactly matched her spacious, heart-stealing smile.

How could anyone be truly happy working as a clerk at Morningway Lodge? Despite the fact that he was glad to be coming back home at last, Nate couldn't think of anything he'd rather *not* do other than work here. Tucked inside the foothills of the great Rocky Mountains, this place was officially the middle of nowhere.

Nate had always been a social person and loved being part of a crowd. It had been that way since he was a small boy.

He couldn't imagine spending his whole life working in such an isolated area. Coming home to the lodge now was a temporary solution to his immediate problem, until he could work out something more permanent—and more agreeable to his outgoing nature. If it weren't for his father's possibly life-threatening stroke, Nate wouldn't be here at the lodge at all.

Anywhere was better than this.

He glanced down at the baby, who was wiggling in his arms and babbling sweet, nonsense syllables that reminded Nate of the call of a dove. Gracie leaned her whole tiny frame toward the woman behind the desk, her arms outstretched to the lady. To Nate's surprise, the baby was smiling—the first time he could remember seeing Gracie smile since her parents had passed.

He swallowed past the lump in his throat. Gracie certainly never smiled at *him* that way.

Nate wrapped his other arm around the baby and pulled her close to his shoulder, feeling oddly possessive of the still-wiggling infant, who protested audibly at his restrictive action.

The clerk had, perhaps instinctively, reached toward the baby, but when Nate adjusted Gracie onto his shoulder, the woman dropped her arms, choosing instead to reach for a large date book on the counter and flip through the pages to the appropriate date.

"What name is your reservation under?" she queried in a soft, sweet voice that matched her looks exactly.

"I—er—don't have a reservation," Nate stammered, thrown off by her question.

The woman's smile wavered. "Oh, I'm sorry, sir. We don't take walk-ins. Do you have someone staying at the physical rehab center? I can put your name on our waiting list. I know it's around here somewhere." She fumbled around the desk, riffling through piles of papers in search of the elusive file. "I'm sorry if I appear disorganized. I don't usually run the desk."

"That's okay, ma'am. I'm just here to see Vince," Nate informed her. "Could you get him for me?"

"I'm sorry, sir," she apologized again. "Mr. Morningway asked not to be disturbed. Would you like to leave him a message?"

Mr. Morningway?

Nate frowned and shook his head to dislodge the uncomfortable image which had formed there, the caricature melding of his pop's and brother's faces. His brother was getting formal in his *old age,* two years older than Nate's own twenty-eight years.

"He'll want to see me," Nate insisted.

The woman glanced uncertainly over her shoulder toward the back office.

Smiling inwardly, Nate was about to give his name when a harried-looking Vince slipped behind the booth, pushing his rectangular glasses up on his nose and then scrubbing a hand through his already ruffled hair. A surprising thatch of gray fell across his forehead, a shockingly light streak through his otherwise dark brown hair.

"Is there a problem out here?" Vince queried the woman before he spotted Nate.

Nate could tell the very moment his elder brother saw him, as Vince's face creased into a frown, his brow furrowed. Nate smiled, but Vince only grunted and continued to glower.

"Hello, brother," Nate said, ignoring Vince's sour-lipped expression.

"Nate," Vince replied, his blue eyes narrowing and shifting between Nate and little Gracie.

Leaning close to the baby to inhale her sweet, unique and somehow calming scent, Nate fidgeted, waiting for Vince to take the lead. Even after all these years away from the lodge and his brother, Vince somehow unsettled him, which only served to annoy Nate more.

The good son glowering at the black sheep of the family. Nate couldn't help but think this whole idea was a gigantic mistake and wondered for the hundredth time why he had decided to come.

"What are you doing here?" Vince asked after a long pause. His voice was a severe monotone that Nate remembered well.

"This is my home, too," Nate reminded him gruffly, though that wasn't completely true.

Morningway Lodge *had* been his childhood home, but he'd been gone for nearly ten years now. And here he stood, lingering at the front desk like a regular patron. It was hardly the same thing.

"*Your* home?" the woman standing next to Vince echoed, her voice laced with surprise. "You never told me you had a brother, Vince."

"This *was* your home, Nate," Vince said, glancing between Nate and the woman at his side and shrugging apologetically to her before turning his gaze back on Nate. "You left, remember?"

Nate did remember. And he hadn't regretted it for a single moment. He had his reasons for leaving, and Vince of all people knew what they were.

"Jessica, this is my brother, Nate. Nate, Jessica," Vince offered curtly, almost as an afterthought.

Nate nodded at Jessica, wishing the woman wasn't present to hear this interchange between him and his brother. It was humiliating.

Grasping in desperation, Nate switched tactics. He didn't want to argue with Vince, especially in front of a woman who was nothing more than a stranger to him. "Don't you want to meet your new niece?"

Vince's expression instantly went from angry to astonished, his eyes widening to enormous proportions as he looked at the baby with new eyes. His mouth opened and closed several times without sound.

"My what?" Vince squeaked, his voice a good octave over its usual deep tone.

Nate chuckled. He hadn't planned to spring this news on his brother in quite this way, but it was worth it just to see the look on his face. "Your niece. Vince, this is Gracie."

"I didn't know you had a child," Vince grated, but he reached out a tentative finger, which Gracie promptly clasped and pulled toward her mouth. Vince smiled at the baby.

"She's not mine," Nate amended. "I mean, she's mine. But she's not *mine*."

Vince's eyebrow shot up in surprise. He reached for Gracie, softly cooing to her. Nate was surprised at how easily and naturally Vince held little Gracie. Nate always felt like a big, uncoordinated gorilla with the baby in his arms.

He shrugged as emotion welled in his throat. Explaining the situation to Vince was going to be the most difficult part of an entirely excruciating exchange.

"Hi there," Vince said, directing his words to the baby. "I'm your uncle Vince. I'm afraid your daddy didn't tell me anything about you."

Daddy. Nate wasn't sure he was ready for that word yet—or if he ever would be.

"Like I said, she's not mine. She is my friend Ezra's daughter. Ezra was my battle buddy in the marines—

and my best friend. He had my back in Iraq. I would be dead a dozen times over if it wasn't for him."

Nate paused when his voice cracked. Shaking his head, he cleared his throat and tried again. "When Gracie was born, Ezra and his wife, Tamyra, asked me to be Gracie's godfather. Two weeks ago, Ezra and Tamyra were involved in a fatal car accident. Tamyra died on the scene. Ezra was in critical condition for twenty-four hours before he passed."

Vince frowned, his blue eyes surprisingly empathetic. "I'm sorry to hear it."

When Nate didn't immediately continue his story, Vince pinched his lips together for a moment, debating, Nate thought, on whether or not to ask the question that was obviously plaguing him. "I still don't understand. Why do *you* have Gracie?"

"I was at Ezra's side when he passed on," Nate explained tightly, absently brushing Gracie's dark, curly hair back from her forehead. He felt the need to touch the baby even as Vince continued to hold her. "Ezra was an only child, as was Tamyra. He…" he swallowed hard "…asked me to raise her."

Vince whistled low and shook his head.

"Wow. That's quite a story." He kissed Gracie's forehead. "But I have to ask—why didn't you just tell him you wouldn't do it? I'm sure you'll agree you aren't exactly father material, Nate."

The woman laid a hand on Vince's forearm as if to restrain him. Her gaze darted to Nate before she flashed Vince a cautionary warning glance.

A nice gesture, Nate thought sardonically, but decades too late.

He glared at Vince. Nate privately agreed with his

brother's assessment of his character, but he still didn't like it that Vince had voiced his opinion aloud, especially with a beautiful, smiling stranger present.

Besides, the man Nate was now didn't even remotely resemble the boy who'd run off and joined the U.S. Marines ten years ago. It took him a moment to collect his thoughts enough to voice them.

He could argue, but really, what was the point? Vince wasn't going to change his mind.

"Be that as it may," Nate growled at last, "it was Ezra's dying wish that I take Gracie's guardianship. They even wrote me into their will. To be honest, I'm not sure there were any other living relatives who could take Gracie. The bottom line is that I made Ezra a promise, and I'm not going to go back on it."

Vince scoffed and shook his head again. "That would be a first."

"Vince," Nate warned with a hiss, his eyes narrowing. "Lay off."

How dare his brother question his honor? Nate was a marine now. Or at least he had been. He'd been honorably discharged at the end of his last tour of duty in order to take care of Gracie. It had been his own decision. The life of a military single father wasn't what he wanted for the baby girl.

Besides, he didn't know how he would be able to properly care for Gracie if he was gone all the time. He finally had the time and opportunity to return to his childhood home and see his ailing father, and at the time, it had seemed the right thing to do.

Now he doubted his own wisdom.

His father no doubt expected the worst from him,

and would not care one way or the other whether Nate showed up. Why was he trying so hard?

Because, he mentally amended, answering his own question, it was the right thing to do. And Nate respected himself, even if his family didn't extend him the same courtesy.

Nate eyed Jessica's hand, which was still on Vince's forearm. Maybe the best thing to do was just change the subject.

"Did you get married and forget to send me the invitation?"

Jessica colored brightly and withdrew her hand from Vince's arm as if she'd touched a burning stove top. Nate couldn't help but chuckle at the mortified expression on her face.

Vince just rolled his eyes and snorted.

"Hardly. When would I have had time to get married? I can't even make time to date. You left me to take care of everything around here, remember? I didn't have the luxury of doing whatever I wanted with my life the way you did, bro. I still don't." Bitterness rolled off of every syllable.

Nate clenched his fist. So Vince viewed him as a problem already, did he? Why was Nate surprised? He surreptitiously glanced at his watch. He had only been here for five minutes.

Vince hadn't changed one bit since Nate had left all those years ago.

Nothing had changed.

Chapter 2

Nate wanted to punch the sneer right off his brother's face, but he restrained himself, with effort. Maybe later, when Jessica wasn't there to watch.

Vince smiled at Jessica and shrugged an unspoken apology to her, and then slipped the suddenly fussy baby into her arms.

Nate would normally have felt a bit uncomfortable with a stranger holding the baby, but he observed the natural way the woman cuddled Gracie to her shoulder and wished he had some of whatever instinct it was that made some people so easy around babies.

The woman closed her eyes and tucked her chin close to Gracie's curly head. Jessica smiled, and then frowned, and then smiled again.

What was up with that?

"Jessica runs the day care center down the road,"

Vince explained with a wave of his hand, as if he were brushing off the question Nate hadn't even thought to ask. "You'll no doubt need some assistance with Gracie here, and no one knows children better than Jessica Sabin."

Nate opened his mouth to argue and then closed it again. His gaze slid back to the pretty blond-haired woman at Vince's side, who was now cuddling baby Gracie in the curve of her arm and murmuring in pleasant undertones. Nate was hesitant to admit Vince might be right, but the way the pretty woman immediately calmed the fussy baby did much to persuade him.

There was no denying it. He *did* need help with Gracie. That was a fact.

"Thanks," he said at last, casting Jess half a grin. "I appreciate the offer."

Vince nodded, looking pleased with himself. "Do you want me to go get Pop? I'm sure he'll want to know you're home. And I know he'll want to meet the baby."

Nate shook his head fiercely. He knew he had to face his father sooner or later, but he was definitely leaning toward *later*. He was under enough stress without confronting Pop.

"No. I don't want him to know I'm here, Vince. At least, not yet."

When Nate saw his father again, he wanted it to be on his own terms. In his own good time.

He leveled his gaze on his brother. "Promise me you won't say anything to him."

Vince arched his eyebrow and shrugged. "Whatever floats your boat. I won't say anything. But you need to go see him. When you're ready."

Nate scowled at his brother. All his life, Vince had

ordered him around. Why had he expected things to be different now?

He sighed inwardly. He hadn't really expected change, and that saddened him more than anything.

"Where are you staying, again?" Vince asked in what Nate thought was an overt attempt to steer the subject to more neutral ground.

Nate shrugged and grimaced.

"I didn't say," he murmured. "Here at the lodge, I hope. Unless, of course, that's an inconvenience to you."

Nate thought the look on Vince's face was clear affirmation that Nate was, in fact, a considerable inconvenience to his elder brother, but Vince's soft words belied his expression. "As you pointed out, this is your home. You are always welcome here. Your old cabin is still waiting for you."

Vince hadn't rented out Nate's old cabin?

That came as an overwhelming surprise to him. Desperate to affirm his independence, Nate had moved into his own cabin and away from the family quarters in the lodge on his sixteenth birthday. He'd selfishly not cared how his family felt about it. Yet Vince had kept the cabin intact and waiting for him, at his own loss, for Nate knew Vince could have been cashing in by renting the cabin out to guests.

Yet he hadn't. Why?

He shook his head. Not wanting to think too much on what that might mean, he turned his attention to the smiling woman by Vince's side.

"Jess," Nate offered, nodding his head toward the woman and reaching his hands out for Gracie. He suddenly and inexplicably wanted the infant back in his arms, even if it felt awkward, and probably looked worse. "I can take the baby now."

"It's Jessica," she corrected, only briefly glancing at Nate before her gaze returned to the baby, whom she didn't immediately relinquish. "What can I do to help?"

"Not a thing, ma'am," Nate snapped impatiently, then winced at his own harsh tone. With Vince glowering at him, he felt as if he was on trial, and all because, as Vince had said, Nate wasn't exactly *daddy material*.

But he would learn to be. And quickly. He was nothing if not determined.

"Sorry," he apologized gruffly, but that didn't stop him from scooping Gracie back into his arms. He kissed the baby's soft cheek, wishing she would smile at him as she did at Jess.

It didn't seem fair to Nate that Gracie started squirming and protesting the moment she was back in his arms, squawking and reaching out for a woman she had only just met, rather than wanting to be in her own guardian's arms.

Not that Nate could blame her.

Jess shrugged. "No problem."

"Thank you, anyway," he continued, trying to take the edge off his earlier tone, "but I'm sure Gracie and I will get along just fine on our own, at least for right now. We'll see how it goes."

Vince barked out a laugh and shook his head in disbelief.

"Oh, right, little brother. You have been taking care of babies all your life."

"Well, no, but…"

"You *do* know she needs a diaper change?" Jess asked, arching one golden eyebrow and grinning wryly.

Nate might have taken offense, but her large brown eyes radiated kindness.

"I—er, well of course I know," Nate said, patting Gracie on her plump behind.

In truth, he hadn't noticed until Jess brought it to his attention. What Nate knew about babies could fit onto the head of a pin.

That was one problem he was going to have to fix, and fast.

"Would you like me to change her for you?" Jess asked with a polite smile. Her gaze was steeped in amusement, but Nate couldn't argue. A rough-cut marine holding a tiny baby girl had to look fairly humorous to anyone's eyes, especially to this day care director, who no doubt took care of babies every day.

He shook his head before he could think better of it. "I've got it. Thanks."

"You're sure?" Jess queried.

Nate shook his head again. "I'll just go over—" He hesitated, looking around the lodge's day room. No thought presented itself that would reasonably complete his sentence, so he let it dangle as awkwardly as the baby squirming in his arms.

"The sofa, perhaps?" she suggested. This time Nate was certain he heard a little teasing in her tone, not that he could blame her.

"Right. The couch." He moved toward the sofa as he spoke, not wanting to make eye contact with either Jess or Vince.

"Do you have a changing pad?" Jess asked from directly behind his left shoulder.

Nate couldn't remember what he had in the diaper bag, but by the weight of it, he was positive he'd packed everything, including the kitchen sink. He'd certainly cleaned out the infant shelves of the baby store where he'd stopped to pick up necessary baby items on his trip to Colorado.

Settling himself on the couch, Nate propped Gracie on his knee and reached for the diaper bag.

Changing pad. Changing pad.

What did a changing pad look like?

Chuckling, Jess seated herself next to Nate. "Here you go," she said, pointing to a folded piece of vinyl.

When Nate didn't move fast enough, Jess snatched up the changing pad and unfolded it on the surface of the couch, then gently removed Gracie from Nate's arm and arranged her on the surface.

"Diaper?" she queried, lifting an open palm.

Nate knew what *that* was, anyway. He handed her a fresh diaper and the box of wipes he'd purchased.

He belatedly realized he was allowing the woman to take over, but he brushed it off, knowing it would be useful to watch an expert change Gracie's diaper for once, and certainly the baby would appreciate it. His own attempts to change the infant during the drive to Colorado were questionable at best, to which Gracie's current saggy baggies attested.

And he hadn't even known about the changing pad. He'd just changed her on a blanket.

Jess had Gracie's diaper off in moments, despite how the baby girl wiggled and kicked. Her soft, sweet voice affected Nate more than he cared to admit, so it wasn't any surprise to him that Gracie responded with happy smiles and coos.

He just wished the baby girl would respond to *him* that way.

* * *

"Oh, you poor little thing," Jessica told the wriggling infant, before glancing back at Nate. He might be considered handsome in a rough-cut sort of way, with his military-short light brown hair and gold-flecked eyes, but he obviously knew nothing about taking care of a baby.

"What?" Nate queried. Jessica thought he sounded slightly defensive, and that, for some reason, embarrassed her. She felt her face warm under his intense gaze, hating that she was so easily ruffled.

"Gracie has a diaper rash." She tried not to make it sound like an accusation, but thought it probably sounded like one, regardless. Her face went from warm to burning hot, and she was concerned that her countenance would reflect how she was feeling inside. She had to be as red as a cherry.

Pursing her lips, she deliberately softened her next words. "Do you have any ointment?"

"Ointment," Nate repeated, digging haplessly through the diaper bag. "What exactly am I looking for?"

"A tube, like toothpaste," Jessica said with a laugh. Now that she wasn't the only one flustered, she could relax about it.

Nate continued his search, but to no avail. After a moment he gave up rummaging and shrugged at her.

"I don't think I have any," he admitted wryly. He flashed Jessica a rueful grin. "I'm afraid I'm not as armed and organized as I need to be. I didn't know what Gracie would need, so I thought I bought a little bit of everything I could find. Obviously I missed something."

"Babies require a lot of gear," Jessica informed him,

efficiently wrapping Gracie in a clean diaper with the ease of experience. "I'd be happy to go into Boulder with you tomorrow to help you stock up on basic supplies."

Nate flashed her a lopsided smile. He *was* a handsome man, she thought again. If she were looking for that sort of thing.

Which she definitely wasn't.

She wasn't looking for any kind of man at all—now or ever. Military men included, even if they looked ridiculously heartwarming and adorable as they toted around cute little baby girls.

Especially if they toted around cute little baby girls. Even the thought choked her up emotionally, and she was immediately on the defensive.

"In the meantime," she suggested, refusing to dwell on the past and reluctantly turning her mind back to the problem at hand, "we need to do something for Gracie's rash. I think I have some petroleum jelly back at my cabin. That will do in a pinch."

"Petroleum jelly? I would never have thought of that," he admitted with a low whistle and a shake of his head. "I'm definitely a newbie."

He laughed, obviously comfortable enough with himself to smile at his own weaknesses. Jessica admired that, and wished her own personality was more like that. "And there are no doubt many things I haven't thought of, where a baby is concerned. Like what I'm going to do with her while I am out looking for a job, for starters."

"We have an opening at the day care," Jessica replied, jumping in more quickly than she should have. She had her reasons for being hesitant, yet her mouth opened before her brain had a chance to get in edgewise. But as it was too late to take back the words, she continued.

"I'd be happy to care for Gracie on weekdays if you want to drop her by."

Nate smiled again, at once both a charming and disarming gesture. "I'll do that."

No, no, no, no, no! the voice inside of her railed.

Not now.

Not *this* baby, who reminded her all too much of a similar tiny, smiling infant; one little baby she would never forget.

She had come to Morningway Lodge in part to escape from her memories, not indulge them with someone else's baby. And though she'd cared for several infants since taking the position here, none had affected her the way Gracie had, from the first moment Jessica had seen her.

The memories were still far too painfully fresh and easily goaded to the forefront of her mind. Her own sweet baby, Elizabeth, had had big brown eyes and curly black hair, as well. Maybe that was it.

Maybe it was that the children in her day care, who belonged to the families who resided at Morningway Lodge while their loved ones recuperated at the nearby physical rehabilitation hospital, never stayed around for more than a few months.

It was safe, relatively, not to get emotionally involved. But Nate—and Gracie—were Morningways. They could be around forever.

By offering to help Nate Morningway, she realized with a sharp stab of pain to her heart, she had potentially just become her own worst enemy.

Chapter 3

Nate never appeared.

Jessica stared out the large bay window overlooking the front side of the day care and sighed. Absently she noted the long shadows of the pine trees that signaled that the sun would soon be setting.

Friday afternoon, and not a word from Nate, other than the time he'd called—at the last minute—and canceled their trip to the baby store in Boulder. In the week since, he'd not once brought Gracie by the day care. In point of fact, Jessica hadn't seen Nate—or Gracie—at all. Not even in passing.

She didn't know why it bothered her, but it did nonetheless.

Actually, she knew *exactly* why it bothered her.

Gracie.

That little baby girl had captured Jessica's heart the

moment Nate had walked into the lodge with her in his arms. What a sweetheart.

Melancholy drifted over her like a black storm cloud and burst into rain, flooding through her heart and leaving her limbs weak.

Jessica couldn't deny the fact that Gracie reminded her of Elizabeth. There wasn't a single day that went by that Jessica didn't think of Elizabeth and weep, not in two years. Every single day and night since eight-month-old Elizabeth's unexpected death from SIDS, Jessica's arms and heart had painfully ached for the child.

That was why, she supposed, that as much as it had hurt, holding Gracie had been such a blessing. Babies were God's special gift, even those that only stayed on this earth a short while.

And there was just *something* about Gracie, something special that set her apart. Something that felt different than her experiences with the other babies she'd cared for since she'd taken the position as director of the day care at Morningway Lodge nearly a year earlier.

Why hadn't Nate brought Gracie by?

For better—or more likely for worse—Jessica had looked forward to interacting with the sweet baby girl every day at the day care.

Well, she realized as she finished putting toys back in the bin and surveying the empty toddler room at the day care, there was one way to find out. She would swing by Nate's cabin on her way home from work and find out what was keeping the man. And if she got to spend a little time with Gracie, that was a plus.

After locking up, she headed straight to Nate's cabin, walking quickly and with purpose. She didn't want to give herself time to talk herself out of it, and maybe never see the baby again.

Gah! she thought as she finally stood on the doorstep of Nate's cabin. This was awkward, especially for a self-proclaimed introvert like Jessica.

She could definitely be accused of being a worrywort. But a busybody? Not so much.

Given the pros and cons of her current actions, the list was hardly equal. There were more than enough reasons for her to turn herself around right now and walk away. No harm done, right?

With a quiet murmur and a shake of her head, Jessica raised her hand and knocked on the screen door. Gracie might need her, she reminded herself.

The baby *probably* needed her, with only an inexperienced and obviously proud-to-a-fault marine taking care of her.

The door behind the screen was open. When no one immediately answered her knock, Jessica cupped her hand to her forehead to block the glare of the evening sunshine and peered inside.

"Hello? Mr. Morningway?" she called softly, her heart loudly humming in her ears. "It's Jessica Sabin from the day care."

"Door is open, Jess," called Nate's coarse, disembodied voice. "In the kitchen. And please. It's Nate. Mr. Morningway is my pop—or my brother."

Jessica let herself in, fighting herself every step of the way. This was so far out of her comfort zone it wasn't even funny, but she wouldn't let that stop her. It wasn't the first time, and she was certain it wouldn't be the last, though it didn't help that Nate was such an incredibly handsome man.

Okay, that was enough of that kind of thinking. She was going to talk herself out of this yet.

"Ay-uh, ay-uh, ay-uh," Gracie screeched when Jessica entered the kitchen. She banged her fists repeatedly on the tray in a staccato rhythm.

The baby was seated in her high chair and facing the door. Nate sat with his back to Jessica, an infant spoon in one hand and a jar of pureed carrots in the other. He didn't look around when she entered the kitchen, his gaze solely focused on his infant ward.

"One more bite," he coaxed, holding the spoon to Gracie's tiny mouth. "Come on now, girl. Open wide and say ah."

"Ah, ah," Gracie complied, giving Jessica a wide, toothless grin. She flapped her arms wildly and banged her little fists on the high chair with excited abandon. Jessica had never felt so welcome as she did from the baby's innocent greeting.

"Well, she's glad to see *you,*" Nate commented, sounding at once amused and annoyed. Taking advantage of Gracie's open mouth, he slipped a spoonful of carrots between her lips.

"Ah-bbbb," said baby Gracie.

"Ack!" exclaimed Nate as Gracie's enthusiastic raspberry covered his olive-green T-shirt with orange spots.

Jessica couldn't help the laughter that bubbled from her chest.

"Sure, sure. Feel free to laugh." Nate shot Jessica a faux glare across his shoulder, his features crinkled in distaste but a wry, self-deprecating grin on his lips that belied his tone.

Jessica clapped a hand over her mouth, but not before another giggle escaped.

"I'm sorry," she apologized, her shoulders heaving from the hopeless effort of restraining her laughter. "It's just that you look so—"

"Foolish?" he offered, joining his own laughter with hers.

She was going to say *cute,* she realized, feeling a blush rise to her cheeks. And just how would that have sounded?

To cover her own embarrassment, Jessica reached for the baby wipes on the table and methodically scrubbed Gracie's face and hands before lifting the infant from the chair and into her arms.

"Feeding this baby is *way* harder than it looks," Nate observed wryly. "I'd rather face an IED."

"IED?" Jessica queried. Leaning in close to Gracie's cheek, Jessica inhaled deeply. She could never quite get enough of the just-bathed lotion smell that was distinctive to babies.

"Improvised explosive device," Nate clarified. "A homemade bomb."

"You defused bombs in the marines?"

"That was my specialty. I suspect it doesn't translate well into civilian life, though. One thing I know for certain—my training is of absolutely no use in learning to take care of Gracie."

Jessica chuckled softly. "No, I don't suppose it is. I'll pray for you, though."

"I—er—just let me go change my shirt real quick," Nate said before beelining it straight out of the kitchen. "I'll only be a moment," he tossed over his shoulder as he went.

Jessica didn't miss Nate's discomfort at her mention of prayer, but her faith was an intricate part of who she was. God had pulled her out of the mire of her own desperation, and she couldn't help but be vocal about her love for Christ now.

She wondered about Nate's faith—or lack thereof. His brother, Vince, was a committed Christian.

None of your business, she reminded herself once again, frowning.

Still, she didn't mind the opportunity to regain her equilibrium that Nate's quick exit had afforded her. She was grateful for a moment to step back and catch her breath, emotionally speaking.

She could be in deep water here. Mentally, she acknowledged her physical attraction to Nate and recognized it for what it was, and then determined within herself to let it go.

As long as she didn't dwell on it, there was no harm, no foul, she told herself resolutely. There was *no way* she was going to submit herself to heartbreak again in this lifetime.

Anyway, the only reason that Nate appeared so adorable to Jessica was his association with baby Gracie. Or at least that was what she was going to keep telling herself. Over and over again, if necessary.

Jessica turned her attention to Gracie, noting that she wasn't the only one to appear flushed—Gracie's cheeks were a rosy red. Alarms blared in Jessica's head and her heartbeat picked up tempo as she pressed the back side of her fingers to the baby's warm face.

"Nate?" she called hesitantly.

"Yep?" he replied from just behind her.

She whirled around, her gaze reaching only to the middle of Nate's well-built chest. His height unnerved her all the more. She tilted her head up to make eye contact with him.

"Do you have a thermometer?" she queried, patting Gracie gently on the back to reassure herself as much as the baby.

"I think I do," Nate said, and then frowned. "Why? Is Gracie sick?"

Jessica shook her head and tried to smile reassuringly. "She feels a little warm, but I'm sure it's nothing to worry about."

"Should I call the doctor?"

"No," she assured him, keeping her voice calm and level. "Babies often run mild fevers when they are teething. That's probably all it is."

One corner of Nate's mouth tipped up in a half grin and he shook his hand in mock pain. "She's teething, all right. For a little nipper with bare gums, she sure can pack a punch. And I noticed she's been drooling a lot more these past couple of days."

"Sounds normal," Jessica agreed, fighting the stinging lump of emotion growing in her throat. Her own baby, Elizabeth, had only just cut her first two bottom teeth when—

"Here we go," Nate said, fishing a digital thermometer out of the diaper bag. "How do you keep this thing in her mouth?"

Jessica chuckled despite herself. "That would be an interesting trick. I'd like to see you try."

She winked. "Actually, we're going to put it under her arm."

With that, Jessica sat in the chair Nate had abandoned and gently placed the thermometer under the baby's shoulder. Gracie squirmed and verbally protested at being held so snugly, but Jessica held her tight and kept her amused by babbling baby talk at her, repeating whatever random sounds Gracie made.

"I'm glad that's you and not me," Nate said, sitting down next to Jessica and running a palm over Gracie's downy hair. "She's already mad enough at me as it is, for trying to slip her some carrots."

"Fruit is much sweeter and tastier than vegetables," Jessica agreed, smiling at Nate. "As a baby *or* as an adult."

Nate laughed. "Don't let Gracie hear you say that, or I'll never be able to feed her anything more than peaches and bananas."

"It'll get easier," Jessica assured him. "It just takes time and patience."

"And a lot of T-shirts."

Jessica chuckled. Nate had changed one olive-colored T-shirt for another. She wondered if the marine had any other color in his wardrobe.

The thermometer beeped and, unconsciously holding her breath, Jessica peered at the results. Nate leaned forward to look with her.

"Ninety-nine-point-four," Jessica read aloud. "Just remember, when you take a baby's temperature under her arm, you need to add a degree, so that makes it one-hundred-point-four."

"Then she does have a fever," Nate said in alarm, his brow furrowed.

"Only a mild one. She's probably teething, as I mentioned earlier. But you should keep an eye on her, just in case."

"I will," Nate vowed.

"Which, as it happens, brings me to the reason I stopped by in the first place."

Nate arched an eyebrow as Jessica slid Gracie from her arms to his.

"I was under the impression you were going to make use of the day care while you were out job hunting. I started to worry when you never showed."

"Oh, that." Nate shrugged and kissed a wiggling Gracie on the forehead before lowering her into the playpen in the corner of the kitchen, where it was visible not only in the kitchen, but from the living room, as well. "Yes, well, I've had a change of heart."

"How is that?" Jessica was surprised at how her emotions plummeted at Nate's words. She told herself repeatedly that it was none of her business what Nate did with Gracie. While that was probably true, she still cared—maybe too much.

"I decided not to look for a job right away," Nate explained. "I put away most of the money I made when I was in the marines, so I have enough to live off—for now, anyway. I'm not sure if I'm going to be staying around long enough to make it worthwhile for me to pursue anything permanent."

"I see," Jessica said, though she didn't. And she wasn't about to analyze the way her heart dropped at Nate's indication that he wouldn't be around for long.

"Becoming Gracie's guardian is a big adjustment for me. I'm like any parent with an infant, I guess, only I didn't have nine months to prepare for her arrival, so I'm working on a curve."

"I imagine it's a big change for you from being a single man in the military." Jessica paused thoughtfully and then asked the question that was plaguing her. "If you aren't planning to stay at Morningway Lodge, then where will you go?"

Nate snorted. "Anywhere but here."

Jessica wanted to question Nate further about his negative feelings toward the lodge, but she wasn't sure he'd be keen on her poking her nose into his business any more than she already had.

She sighed. "I love it here. It's so quiet and peaceful compared to the ruckus of a big city. You can see and hear God all around you."

Nate stared at Jess, his gaze wide. She spoke so freely about God, as if she was intimately acquainted with Him. It was the way his mother had always spoken of the Almighty, Nate remembered, a feeling of nostalgia washing over him.

But Nate wondered at such naiveté, such sweet and innocent belief as these women shared.

He'd seen the ravages of war firsthand. He knew better than to believe in fairy tales.

He nearly blurted out that he wasn't *looking* for God, but caught himself before he said the words out loud and couldn't take them back.

There was no sense being rude, especially since her faith was clearly very dear to her. He retreated to his usual mode of dealing with issues he didn't really want to address—he clammed up.

Jess didn't appear to notice his sudden silence, and continued thoughtfully.

"Growing up, I lived in Los Angeles. Far too much noise and pollution for me. I'd rather have the clear, beautiful Rocky Mountains any day of the week, thank you very much."

"Is your family still in California?"

She hesitated and her smile faltered, then dropped. Her gaze became distant for a moment, as if she had traveled in her mind to some other time or place; but at length she nodded.

Nate had the impression he'd just intruded where he was not wanted. There was much Jess was not telling him, but he would not presume to pry based on their very short acquaintance. He didn't care for others disrespecting his privacy, and he wasn't going to disrupt her.

He thought the best thing to do would be to change the subject. Baby Gracie's soft babbling had turned to crying, so he reached into the playpen and plucked her into his arms. She quieted at his touch, but her eyelids were heavy and drooping.

"Gracie needs a nap," he commented, bouncing the little girl on his shoulder to soothe her as he crooned. "Don't you, sweetie pie?"

"Looks like," Jess agreed.

"She won't go down unless I rock her," Nate said, nodding his head toward the small living room, where an old wooden rocking chair stood in one corner.

"May I?" Jess asked softly.

"Be my guest." Nate handed Gracie off to Jess, who seated herself in the rocker and began to hum a quiet lullaby.

Even after a week with the baby, Nate still wasn't comfortable when Gracie was fussy. He marveled at how quickly Gracie settled down in Jess's arms. The woman was a natural with children.

He leaned his shoulder on the door frame separating the kitchen from the living area and folded his arms across his chest. There was something just *right* in the way Jess held the baby, he observed; even Gracie instinctively reacted to it.

Nate smiled at the pretty picture Jess and the baby made. Like a little family, almost. Ezra would have been glad to see it, he thought with a mixture of joyfulness and sorrow.

"You'll be a wonderful mother to your own child someday," he murmured.

It was the highest compliment Nate could think to give her, so he was stunned at her reaction.

She turned eight shades of rose before her face bled to a deathly white.

"Are you okay?" he asked when she shot to her feet, swaying precariously. Her grip on Gracie was firm, but he could see that she was shaking.

"I—I'm sorry," she stammered, thrusting the baby at him. "I have to go. Now."

With Gracie wiggling and kicking in his arms, Nate watched helplessly as Jess bolted out the front door and up the path leading away from his cabin. She was running—literally running—away.

He shook his head, bemused. What had he said that had set her off that way? And more to the point, he thought perplexedly, how was he going to fix it?

Jessica's cabin was only a few doors down from Nate's, though it was a steady, uphill climb. She walked—nearly ran—the distance in half the time it usually would have taken her.

By the time she entered the emotional haven of her own small cabin, her chest was heaving and she was gasping for air. Her heart was racing so quickly she could hear it pounding in her ears, but it wasn't only—

or even mostly—the physical exertion causing the excruciating pain in her chest.

She was embarrassed and shamed by her actions with Nate, running out on him as she had, without a single word of explanation.

It was just that Nate's off-the-cuff comment had hit her right between the eyes. He couldn't possibly have known what he was saying, and he had most certainly meant his observation as a compliment.

Jessica hadn't been prepared for the maelstrom of emotions that barraged her when she once again held baby Gracie in her arms. The scene had somehow transformed into something pseudo-intimate—*domestic*—between the three of them.

Nate. Jessica. Gracie.

A home and a family had once been the greatest desire of Jessica's heart. But she'd already gone that route, and with devastating results. If she was now alone in the world, it was because she wanted it that way.

As much as she loved being around the baby—or more accurately *because* she loved being around the baby—it would be better for all concerned if she altogether avoided Gracie and her handsome marine guardian.

If she was not careful, her heart would be shattered again, perhaps this time beyond repair.

No, Jessica thought, not even consciously aware she was clenching her fists. She couldn't—*wouldn't*—let it happen again.

Chapter 4

After Nate put Gracie down for a nap, he slung a dish towel over his shoulder and filled the kitchen sink with hot, soapy water.

That was another thing about caring for an infant—the amount of dishes and laundry increased exponentially with the addition of just that one tiny baby girl. He had always had simple needs. This was *way* out of his realm of experience.

Nate set to work scrubbing out baby bottles and bowls of caked-on baby cereal, but his mind was quick to wander back to earlier that afternoon, and the bizarre way Jess had acted.

What was with the woman, anyway?

Nate had noticed her odd behavior from the first time they'd met—the on-again, off-again, hot/cold way Jess acted whenever she was around him. Or perhaps more to the point, when she was around Gracie.

The worst part, though, and the thing, if he was being honest with himself, that stymied Nate the most, wasn't Jessica's unfathomable actions at all. He might not yet understand it, but he could explain it away fairly simply. There must be a reasonable, rational explanation for whatever it was that was bothering her, and eventually, he would figure out what that reason was.

But at the moment, he was dwelling on something else entirely—that flash of time frozen in his mind when the three of them were together in the living room. Jessica's presence had formed it into a homey, domestic atmosphere unlike anything Nate had ever experienced before.

Well, maybe that description was pushing it. His cabin was no more than bachelor's quarters littered with a brand-new smattering of baby items. Not exactly what anyone would describe as *homey*.

But it wasn't so much how the situation had looked. It was how it had felt.

And Nate really liked that feeling.

He realized he was daydreaming and snorted at his own silly behavior.

What was he thinking?

He used the dish towel to scrub his face and force his mind back to the present. His cheeks carried a week's growth of beard on them—because, for the first time in ten years, he could go without shaving.

He shook his head. He'd been alone for far too long to be conjuring up fantasy families in his mind, where none existed in reality.

Still, the idea of a family wasn't completely without merit.

Tamyra, Nate remembered, had rounded out Ezra, taken the rough edges off the heretofore certified bachelor. After the wedding, Ezra had been the happiest Nate had ever seen him. And then baby Gracie had come along and added exponentially to their love. She had, Nate realized, completed the picture.

He recalled being a little envious of his best friend. True love made life worth living, Ezra had told him a dozen times. But Nate'd had his work and his wanderlust, and that had been enough.

At the time.

Now everything was different. Not just in his circumstances, either. His heart felt as altered as the difference between a Colorado blizzard and a California summer. His priorities had shifted from thinking only of himself to having someone else as the center of his existence.

He had a baby to consider now—a little girl who deserved to be raised in a family with both a father and a mother.

Someone like Jess, he realized. A woman who was sweet and caring and who knew how to care for an infant; who would love Gracie the way Nate loved Gracie.

As if on cue, the baby made an enormous pterodactyl scream from the playpen, startling Nate and setting his hair on end. He dashed to the playpen and scooped Gracie into his arms.

Gracie was hot to the touch. He didn't need the thermometer to tell she was burning up with fever. Panic immediately coursed through him, stinging his limbs like an explosion of white-hot nails in an IED.

Snatching the thermometer from the tabletop, Nate rushed to the rocker and took a seat. He attempted to mimic what Jess had done, placing the tip of the thermometer under the baby's arm, but it was a lot more difficult than it looked, even if Gracie wasn't fighting him the way she had with Jess.

She *wasn't* fighting him, but was staring up at him with her big brown eyes as if pleading with him to make her all better.

He didn't know how.

She was frighteningly lethargic.

He checked the thermometer, and another surge of panic coursed through him.

Gracie was running a fever of one hundred and four degrees.

The sound of her cell phone ringing startled Jessica from her sleep. She groaned loudly. She'd nodded off in her easy chair and now her shoulders were stiff and she had a kink in her neck.

Stretching her head from side to side to work loose her muscles, she reached for her purse, which she'd haphazardly tossed on the coffee table earlier. Groggily she dug for the still-pealing phone.

"Hello?" she said, her voice still a little slurred as she wiped the sleep from her eyes with the palms of her hands.

It wasn't surprising that she'd fallen into a deep, dreamless slumber—ever since she was a child, sleep had been her defense mechanism against stress. Her mind and body simply shut down, giving her the rest needed to face her trials afresh.

"Jess?" The one word was laced with so much fear and alarm that Jessica was instantly alert.

"Nate? What's wrong?"

"It's Gracie." Nate's anxious, labored breathing set Jessica right on edge, and she gripped the phone more tightly within her grasp. "She spiked a high fever. I don't know what to do."

"Oh, no!" Jessica inhaled sharply, her whole heart and soul immediately appealing to the Heavenly Father to protect the sweet little baby girl. She tried to quell the rising alarm in her head with little success. "How high?"

"One hundred and four degrees. Jess, what should I do?"

"I'm on my way over," she asserted, trying to keep her voice calm and reassuring despite the way her heart was pounding in her head. Adrenaline coursed sharply through her veins, making her tingly and light-headed.

Whatever promises she had made herself earlier about not seeing Nate or the baby again flew right out the window as if they had never been.

They needed her now.

There was no question that she would be there for them, at whatever cost to her own heart.

She was already reaching for her coat and sliding her feet into her old hiking boots. Her thumb was poised over the phone's exit button when Nate spoke again, his voice rushed.

"I...I phoned you because...because I didn't know who else to call," he stammered.

It occurred to Jessica that the obvious choice would be Vince, who was family. Wouldn't that have made the most sense? Why hadn't Nate called him?

But now was not the time for such questions. She

rapidly ticked down the list of vital issues, forcing her mind to concentrate on priority.

"Does she have any other symptoms? A sneeze? A cough?"

"She's pulling on her ear and crying," Nate choked out. "Does that mean anything?"

"Okay, listen, Nate," Jessica said, an instinctive sense of God's strength and peace enveloping her as she took control of the situation. "You need to get her temperature down."

"How do I do that?" he asked, his voice tight. "I just gave her some more medicine, but it will take some time to see any effect. What else can I do?"

Jessica heard Gracie pealing in distress, and her heart turned over.

"Hush, baby girl," Nate crooned. "Uncle Nate's trying to help you, honey. Jess?" he queried uncertainly. "What do I do?"

"Fill the sink with lukewarm water. You need to give her a sponge bath," Jessica directed. "That's going to be the fastest and most effective way to bring down her temperature."

"She's so tiny." Nate's taut voice cracked with emotion.

"And she's not going to be happy about that bath. It's hard to be a parent at times like this."

Jessica realized Nate had referred to himself as Gracie's godfather, but they both knew he was acting in a much greater capacity. "You have to do what is best for Gracie even if it appears to be hurting her."

"I'll do what I have to do," he vowed solemnly, "as long as she gets better."

"She will."

Gracie howled again, her little voice hoarse from screaming.

"I have to go," Nate said.

"Of course. Gracie needs your full attention, which you can't give her while you're still speaking on the phone with me."

"Yeah," he agreed. "But, Jess?"

"Yes?"

"Hurry."

His one word sent a shiver down her spine. "I'm heading out the door right now.

"And, Nate?"

"Hmm?"

"I'm praying for you guys."

She heard the hesitation, and the way Nate quietly cleared his throat. She was on the verge of apologizing when he broke into her thoughts.

"I…" Once again he hesitated. "Well, anyway, thank you. For Gracie, I mean."

"Don't give it another thought," she assured him. "Just get her bathed."

"I'm already on it," he promised.

And she was already out the door.

During the whole ten minutes it took her to rush to Nate's cabin, Jessica petitioned God for Gracie's health and safety. She more than most knew the singular pain of losing an infant. She would never wish that kind of agony on anyone, most especially the kind of man who would put his own life on hold in order to care for a baby who was not his own flesh and blood.

Jessica prayed for Nate as well, that God would give

him comfort and peace. Based on what she knew of Nate, she suspected he was not a Christian.

But hadn't God reached Jessica through just such a tragedy? She prayed it would not take that kind of pain and anguish for Nate to find God.

She briefly considered phoning Vince to let him know what was happening with baby Gracie, but she hesitated, and with good reason. Nate had made a pretty clear statement when he'd called Jessica and not Vince; and from their earlier conversations, it was clear to Jessica that there were definite issues between the two brothers.

Yet tension or no tension, Vince was Nate's brother, his family, and Jessica thought he ought to know what was happening with Gracie. She had been acquainted with Vince a good deal longer than Nate, and she had no doubt that Vince would want to be updated.

But in the end, she decided against calling Vince and simply focused on getting to Nate's cabin as quickly as possible. Whatever the situation was between Nate and his brother, she had to respect his wishes, even if they'd never been spoken aloud.

Even though it was a downhill hike, it felt like forever before she reached Nate's cabin. Several times she thought she should have driven, but she'd been certain she could arrive at the cabin just as quickly on foot. Walking, she could hike straight there. The road was winding and out of the way.

Finally, she broke through the tree line and spied the cabin in front of her. The front door was open, so she let herself in, not wanting to disturb Gracie on the off chance she was sleeping.

She blinked rapidly as her vision slowly adjusted to

the darkness of the cabin after having been out in the bright sunshine. Simultaneously, she took in a number of things.

Gracie was sound asleep in her playpen, her chubby legs curled under her. Her arm was wrapped around an enormous, well-worn stuffed orange-and-white-striped fish and her little thumb was tucked in her mouth. Jessica noted with thankfulness that the baby appeared to be resting peacefully, her tiny chest rising and falling in a deep, reassuring rhythm.

Nate was slumped in a wooden chair he'd pulled close to the playpen, his back to the door and his head buried in his hands. Jessica approached him quietly, not wanting to disturb Gracie's slumber.

He jumped, startled, when Jessica laid her hand on his shoulder. She could feel the tension he was carrying in the knotted muscles of his back.

"Hi," Jessica whispered. "I got here as quick as I could. How is she?"

"Jess," Nate groaned as he stood and turned toward her. "Thank you for coming."

A moment later, he swept her into a hug that knocked the wind from her lungs. He clasped her tightly for a few moments. She felt him shudder deeply a moment before he let her go. Concern, compassion and tenderness flooded through her for this man who'd given up so much to take on the care of baby Gracie.

"It's going to be okay," she reassured him when he released her. "*She's* going to be okay. It looks like she is sleeping soundly now, and we can take comfort that God is watching over her."

Jessica wished her words carried more impact, but internally she knew that just because God was in control and, as Jessica had said, was watching over little Gracie, that didn't necessarily mean everything would be all right—at least from her incomplete, staring-into-the-mirror-darkly, human perspective.

God's ways, Jessica had painfully learned, were not always man's ways.

But it didn't hurt to pray.

Nate's face crumpled into dozens of harsh lines, but his gold-flecked eyes held hope. Jessica could see how desperately he wanted to believe her words. His short brown hair was tousled and sticking up every which direction, making him look incongruously and heart-wrenchingly vulnerable next to the muscular strength of the sturdy marine.

"In Isaiah there is a beautiful description of Jesus as the Shepherd over His little lambs," she continued, wanting desperately to comfort Nate. "It goes like this. 'He shall gather the lambs in His arms and carry them in His bosom,'" she quoted softly.

Nate squeezed his eyes shut and Jessica thought the rough-edged marine might be fighting tears.

"I hope so," he said, his voice cracking with emotion. "I really hope so."

Jessica took his hand and led him back to his chair, pushing him gently into his seat before pulling another chair up next to him and seating herself. She reached her arm over the side of the playpen and brushed the backs of her fingers against Gracie's cheek. The baby's skin still felt warm, but not alarmingly so. Jessica was almost certain Gracie's fever was falling.

She sighed in relief. "I think her temperature has gone down some."

Nate swallowed hard and nodded. A muscle twitched

in the corner of his strong jaw. "The poor little thing screamed so hard when I gave her a sponge bath that she wore herself completely out. She fell asleep right afterward. I don't mind telling you, she had me scared there for a while."

Jessica struggled for a moment with her own memories, with the sudden way her own baby had been taken from her. Elizabeth had been healthy and happy when Jessica had put her to bed. The next morning she wasn't breathing.

Just like that.

Jessica struggled to contain her emotions, to pull the painful memories back behind the iron wall of her will so Nate would not be able to see what she was feeling on her face.

This was a different situation. It wasn't Elizabeth all over again. Babies got fevers. That was just how it was. And it wasn't necessarily life-threatening. There was no reason for her to panic.

Nate and Gracie needed her strength and support right now, she reminded herself sharply. Breathing deeply, she clenched her hands together and fought for all she was worth.

Nate's groan interrupted her turmoil thoughts, jarring her back to the present.

"I feel so helpless." Elbows on his knees, Nate clasped his hands together and leaned his scruffy chin on them. "I just wish there was more I could *do*," he admitted roughly.

"There is," Jessica whispered, reaching for Nate's hand. When he glanced up at her, a question in his eyes, she smiled softly. "We can pray."

Nate stared at her for a moment, and then nodded, his jaw tight.

Jessica bowed her head and closed her eyes. "Heavenly Father, we are thankful that Gracie is in Your tender care. Watch over her and keep her safe. Lord, we ask that You restore Gracie to health and give her little body strength to work through this fever.

"And be with Nate, Lord. Give him wisdom and peace. Amen."

Jessica looked up and caught Nate staring at her, wide-eyed. She wondered if he had prayed along with her, or merely watched her as she prayed. She felt a little self-conscious for a moment, then brushed it off.

What mattered was that she *had* prayed. And God was good. She prayed once again, silently, this time, that Nate would be able to see the grace of God.

Chapter 5

Instead of the peace for which Jess had petitioned, Nate was filled with an inexplicable sense of unease. Still seated in a hard-backed kitchen chair placed next to the playpen, his muscles clenched and ached.

Stifling a groan, he lifted his arms over his head and stretched from side to side, working the knots and kinks out of his shoulders. He wasn't the kind of man to just sit around and wait, and every fiber of his being was itching to move.

He'd been sitting still far too long, watching the even rise and fall of baby Gracie's breath as she slept. She hadn't budged in a couple of hours. Nate didn't know whether that was a good thing or a bad thing, but he took encouragement from the fact that Jess no longer hovered over the baby.

In fact, to his surprise, Gracie wasn't the only one sleeping.

Nate's gaze drifted to the sofa—a two-person love seat, really, as that was all that would fit in the confines of the small cabin—where Jess had curled up and nodded off. Her face had softened during sleep, her arm curled around her neck and a lock of her wavy blond hair lightly brushing her cheek.

His brow furrowed when he noticed her lips turning down, as if she were having a bad dream. In the short time Nate had known her, Jess was nearly always smiling. Her radiant grin was the first thing he'd noticed about her, and it bothered him that somehow she'd lost her peace during sleep.

His fingers tingled with the unfathomable urge to brush that lock of hair off her cheek and smooth the frown from her lips.

Nate had told her it was fine for her to leave, now that the crisis with Gracie appeared to have passed, but Jess wouldn't hear of it. Her chin, which gave the point to her heart-shaped face, had jutted out stubbornly at the mere suggestion.

She was the sweetest, kindest woman he'd ever had the pleasure to know; yet it occurred to him that he might like her to have his back in a fight. Her strength of character, which Nate thought made her faith so vibrant, was remarkable.

And, at the moment, much appreciated.

Secretly, Nate had been glad of her stubborn insistence that she stay, though he'd never admit it out loud. Gracie might be out of immediate danger, but her temperature had spiked very quickly before. He didn't want to go through that kind of a scare again.

Ever.

Not alone, at least. With Jess here, circumstances didn't feel quite so black.

He knew he should be taking the lead from Jess and rest while the baby was sleeping, but try as he might, he couldn't shut off his brain. Usually he exercised his way to exhaustion, but that was impossible given the circumstances.

What he wouldn't give for a nice, long, head-clearing run. It sure would beat sitting here over-thinking everything.

But he wasn't about to leave Gracie's side, not for the hour or more it would take him to get in a good workout. All the same, he found he could no longer sit quietly with his thoughts. Maybe a breath of the fresh, cold mountain air would calm his heart, if not clear his head.

He stood quietly, smiled down at Gracie for a moment, and then tossed a blanket over Jess's shoulders. He let himself out the front door, careful not to let the screen door slam on his way out.

With a sigh, he jammed his hands into the front pockets of his jeans and took a cleansing breath of the crisp air. He stepped into the darkness, away from the soft stream of light streaming from the front window of his cabin. The gravel crunched under the soles of his sneakers.

Why was he so uneasy? For sure, part of it was Gracie's illness, but that wasn't all of what was making his gut clench.

"I love that baby girl," he said aloud, his breath frosting in the air. "I'd do anything for her."

Nate scrubbed his fingers into the short ends of his hair as he stopped under the shadow of a pine and looked up at the stars. He'd forgotten how full the night sky appeared here at the lodge.

Whom, he wondered, did he think he was addressing with his rambling thoughts?

God?

That smacked of hypocrisy. He'd never been a praying man.

Not until today, anyway.

Not until Jess had taken his hand and spoken to God so simply and expectantly on his and Gracie's behalf. She had voiced petitions Nate couldn't have even begun to put into words.

But he'd been *thinking* about it, hadn't he?

Or maybe more accurately, he'd been feeling it. He might not ever have considered praying aloud, but that hadn't stopped him from hoping there was a God watching down on Gracie in His mercy.

And God had answered. Hadn't He?

In Nate's initial rush of panic over Gracie's high fever, God had sent Jess. Or rather, she'd come when Nate had called her, but from where he was standing, that was the same thing. And now it appeared Gracie was going to be fine.

Maybe she had never been in any real danger, he supposed. Be that as it may—her fever was down, and she looked to be over the worst of it.

Thank God.

But thanking God didn't seem to be enough. Not to Nate. If he was going to acknowledge God, he ought to be *serving* God. It only made sense, and Nate was nothing if not pragmatic.

"I'll do it," he said aloud into the darkness, adding a clipped nod for good measure.

"Do what?" asked a sleepy-voiced Jess, stepping from the shadows.

Startled, Nate's heart hammered in his chest as he turned to the sound of her voice.

"I thought you were sleeping."

Her hair was mussed from napping, which, Nate thought, was somehow endearing. She had wrapped herself in the blanket he'd covered her with earlier, and he could see her breath on the crisp air.

She arched her eyebrow and pursed her lips, acknowledging that she was completely aware he'd just deliberately dodged her question.

With an unexpected wave of amusement, he realized he was out in the cold weather with nothing heavier than a T-shirt and jeans, and was pacing around speaking out loud to himself.

He must look like a real nutcase.

He felt mirth bubbling up in his throat, and for the first time since the night Ezra had died, he felt the tremendous, ominous weight in his chest lighten and dissipate.

He threw back his head and laughed.

When Nate laughed, his entire countenance changed.

The night was dark, with only a sliver of a moon, but Jessica was close enough to see the feathering of laugh lines around his gleaming golden eyes and the indentation of the adorable little dimple that suddenly appeared in his left cheek.

It was the first time Jessica had seen Nate laugh, and her heart turned right over, even as an answering smile drew the sides of her lips upward.

"You should do that more often," she murmured, stepping closer.

"Do what?" he asked, punctuating his question with another chuckle. "Talk to myself?"

"Laugh," she answered, giggling. "It looks good on you."

"Like a crazy man?"

It occurred to her that Nate *was* acting a little out of the ordinary. It wasn't so much that he was talking to himself—she'd been guilty of an occasional soliloquy when she was the only one in the room—but rather the fact that he was outside in a short-sleeved shirt in weather cold enough to frost his breath.

The thought made her shiver, and she pulled the woolen blanket more closely around her shoulders. Warmth immediately washed over her, and it wasn't just from the blanket. She hadn't covered herself with a blanket when she'd dropped off to sleep on the sofa.

She hadn't meant to sleep at all.

Yet she had.

And sometime after that, Nate had thought to pull a blanket around her.

It had been a long time since anyone had done anything to care for her. She prided herself on her newfound independence, but Nate's thoughtfulness warmed her nonetheless.

"Are you cold?" Nate asked solicitously.

"A little," she admitted. "But not nearly as cold as you must be."

He looked down at his bare arms as if just now realizing he was without a coat, and then he threw back his head and laughed again.

Jessica took a step back. Maybe the man *was* off his rocker.

"Not crazy," he assured her as he turned her by the shoulders and pressed her back toward the warmth of the cabin. "Just punchy, I guess. You'd think I'd be used to sleep deprivation after ten years in the marines, but that doesn't hold a candle next to this—caring for an infant 24/7."

A sudden wave of sadness gripped Jessica's heart, but she pushed it away and forced herself to smile up at the gruff marine who was now holding the cabin door open for her.

"No? Go figure."

Nate followed her inside, shaking his head emphatically as he went.

"Not even close. Frankly, I don't know how parents do it."

Jessica leaned over the playpen to check on Gracie. The baby was awake and had rolled onto her back, staring up at Jessica with her enormous brown eyes and sucking steadily on her thumb.

Jessica smiled down at Gracie, reaching for her just as the baby crinkled up her face and started to wail.

"That's easy," she told Nate as she tucked baby Gracie to her shoulder and patted her back. "It's love. Pure and simple."

His smile never leaving his face, Nate stepped forward and kissed Gracie's cheek. His crisp, musky scent followed his movement, and Jessica couldn't help but inhale deeply, her head reeling.

"And who wouldn't lose their heart to little chubby cheeks like these?" he asked softly.

Gracie reached for Nate, and Jessica handed the baby

off to him, her heart skipping a beat at the sheer delight radiating from Nate's eyes.

"She feels cool," he said, rubbing his cheek against Gracie's. "I think her fever must have broken."

Jessica placed the backs of her fingers against Gracie's forehead and then nodded in agreement. "She's definitely doing better. Why don't you check her temperature with the thermometer and I'll see if I can't rustle her up a bottle."

Nate nodded and took a seat in the rocking chair, propping Gracie on his lap.

"The formula is in the cabinet over the sink, and there's bottled water in the fridge."

Nate already had the thermometer under Gracie's arm and the baby was protesting loudly, so Jessica moved to the kitchen, finding all the equipment just where Nate had indicated. She went to work, quickly mixing the formula in a clean bottle she took from the strainer.

She felt oddly at home puttering around in Nate's kitchen, knowing he and Gracie were waiting for her just around the corner. She surprised herself sometimes. At times painfully shy, she usually had to forcefully put herself out there, but with Nate and Gracie, she felt natural.

Comfortable.

And that thought in itself was enough to make Jessica's emotions immediately swing to the polar opposite, until her nerves were stinging with the urge to flee.

She could not afford to get too *comfortable* with Nate.

He was leaving.

Soon.

He'd said as much, earlier that day. He was only here to see his sick father.

And then...

And then *nothing*.

There was absolutely no sense dwelling on the inevitable.

With a sigh, she placed the bottle in the small microwave on the counter and punched the start button, warming the milk for a few seconds.

Nate had called *her* when Gracie became ill. But then again, she was the resident child-care expert. And even if there was something more to it than that, there *couldn't* be more to it than that.

Jessica knew she had to have a care after her own heart. She wasn't ready for any kind of relationship with a man, especially a man with a baby. She wasn't sure she ever would be.

And how foolish was it to even be considering any of this? There was a baby in the next room howling for her bottle.

"That's a good sign," Jessica commented as she entered the living room and handed Nate the bottle. "Her fussing, I mean. It shows she's feeling better."

Nate chuckled as Gracie rooted for the bottle. "If you say so."

Jessica slid onto the sofa, tucking her legs underneath her. "I do. Gracie obviously caught a touch of something, but I think the worst is behind her."

"Thanks to you."

Jessica shook her head. "You know I can't take the credit. The glory belongs to God."

To her surprise, Nate nodded his agreement.

She smiled. "But I'm glad I could be here for you and Gracie."

"Not as glad as I am."

"Which does raise a question," she continued, knowing she was headed into deep water but unable to stop herself from asking.

"Go ahead," he encouraged when she didn't jump right in with her question. "It's okay."

"If it's none of my business, just tell me it's none of my business."

Nate's jaw tightened almost imperceptibly, but he nodded for her to continue.

"Why didn't you call Vince today?"

The muscles in Nate's neck strained as he swallowed hard and his jaw was equally tight. He didn't immediately answer.

"I've known Vince for almost a year now," she explained. "I think he would have wanted to be there to support you and Gracie."

Nate scowled.

"I know he would," she amended hastily.

"No," he snapped, then shook his head, inhaled and exhaled harshly. "I've had the unfortunate experience of being around Vince a lot longer than you have. Trust me. I know him. He doesn't want anything to do with me. I'd hoped things would change when I came back home, but they didn't."

"But Gracie…"

"I'm not saying Vince has anything against Gracie. It's me he doesn't like. There's a lot of bad blood between the two of us."

Jessica didn't know what to say. She couldn't imagine her employer being painted with the large, harsh strokes Nate was using, but she knew that to Nate at least, that was how Vince appeared.

"I'm sorry," she said, resting her hand on his forearm. "I shouldn't have brought up the subject. I can see it's touchy."

"And I'm sorry I snapped at you," Nate responded, his voice reticent. "You inadvertently touched my hot button and I overreacted."

"I'm sorry," she said again.

"Don't be. My frustration is not with you. I wish there was some way to bridge the gap between my brother and me. For Gracie's sake, if not mine. But honestly, I don't see that happening."

"There must be some way." Jessica didn't have a clue as to what that might be, though, so she clamped her mouth shut.

When would she ever learn to think first and speak later—to mind her own business?

"I'm open to suggestions," he quipped, but he frowned as he said it.

Jessica took the unspoken hint, judging what Nate really meant, and not what he said. "And I am officially butting out and keeping my mouth shut."

They both chuckled, but Jessica felt as if she'd broken the tenuous personal bond which had formed between them, and she wondered how to get it back.

"Too little, too late," she muttered. She hadn't really meant to say the thought aloud, and certainly not loud enough for Nate to overhear her.

"Not at all," he assured her.

She felt her face reddening under his amused gaze, but he winked at her, putting her at ease. His features looked far less strained and his smile was genuine.

If he could let it go, could she do any less?

"Believe me," he continued, "nothing you said is anything I haven't been thinking about since before I set foot back on Morningway grounds."

"I hope…" Jessica started, and then she stammered to a stop. "I'll pray for you."

"Thank you. I need all the help I can get."

Jessica's eyebrows rose. Nate sounded sincere—genuinely earnest. She prayed she wasn't imagining things, that Nate's heart was actually shifting toward an authentic faith in God.

It sure looked that way.

Trauma had that funny effect on people, and she should know. What was the old saying? There were no atheists in foxholes?

"I'm not blaming everything on Vince," he explained, his voice low and gruff as he tenderly gazed down at the baby in his arms. "I believe you when you say Vince is a good person. Ten years can change a man. I'm living proof of that."

He paused and scrubbed a hand down his face. "The truth is, I burned a lot of bridges when I left Morningway Lodge ten years ago.

"I was young and foolish and headstrong. And I had a chip on my shoulder the size of Colorado. The day I turned eighteen, I took off and joined up with the marines. I didn't tell Vince—or my pop—that I was leaving. I just went. I wrote them a letter from boot camp. I suppose, given those circumstances, I can't blame Vince for holding a grudge."

"Oh," Jessica breathed, then clapped a hand over her mouth.

He paused and looked up, his golden gaze warming

hers. His slightly twisted smile was self-deprecating and apologetic.

"So anyway, you can imagine that my pop won't be too happy to see me, either."

"You haven't seen him yet." She hadn't meant to form her thoughts as a statement, but she was belatedly aware it came out sounding that way.

Nate shook his head.

"I might have been wrong about Vince," she said softly. "But I think you should visit your father. He's not feeling well."

Nate shifted Gracie to his shoulder and patted her softly on the back. He stared at Jessica a moment, his brow low over his eyes, and then nodded.

"I know. When I heard about his stroke, I was on my second tour of duty in Iraq, so I couldn't come home to see him. I understand he's gotten worse recently." His voice was laced with regret, and his feelings showed in the way his lips turned down at the corners as he spoke.

"You should go see him," she reiterated, thinking of the last time she'd seen the old man several weeks ago. He hadn't looked well even then. As Nate had said, he had taken a turn for the worse recently and was confined to his room.

"I will. I guess that just goes to show you what a coward I am."

A coward? A man who'd served his country in the war, defusing bombs so his comrades would be safe? A man who had…

"I don't think anyone would call you a coward, Nate," she said softly. "You stepped up and took the guardianship of your best friend's baby. I think that shows great depth of character."

Nate's gold-specked eyes glowed with the compliment. "Thank you. That means a lot, coming from you."

Jessica shuddered inwardly. Nate didn't know what he was saying. She was the biggest coward of all.

"And you're right," he continued. "I do need to see my father. He's the reason I came back to Morningway Lodge in the first place, although I admit I've been a little sidetracked since I've been here. But I will go and see him," he vowed. "And soon."

Chapter 6

Jessica had never been a late sleeper, not even on weekends. And today was no exception.

The past week had flown by, between work and checking on Nate and Gracie every evening. She never stayed long, not wanting to throw the baby off her newly formed routine. Gracie had, Jessica noted, recovered nicely from her fever and was busy trying to learn to crawl around Nate's cabin.

It was Saturday morning, exactly a week after Gracie had spiked her high fever. Jessica was up with the sun, despite having had a deep, dreamless sleep the night before. Though she'd had a full eight hours, she felt as if she'd had no rest at all.

Nate's words to her the week before had echoed through her mind, taunting her incessantly. Though their conversations over the past week hadn't gone beyond remarking about the unusually crisp fall weather and Gracie's happy recuperation, Jessica distinctly felt there was always something unspoken hanging in the air just over their heads.

She had been absolutely sincere when she'd complimented Nate's character. He was the bravest and strongest man she knew.

But it bothered her that her good opinion was obviously so important to him. His warm, golden gaze had said as much as his words, and his words had been shocking enough.

He had somehow erroneously set her on a pedestal, though she couldn't conceive of why.

And he was *wrong*.

So utterly wrong about her.

Sweeping her hair back into a ponytail, she threw on sweatpants and a hoodie and her favorite pair of running shoes and, after stretching, took off jogging down a well-worn path by her cabin.

Her daily morning jog was her quiet time, the time she lifted her burdens to God and found peace and sustenance for the day ahead.

But this morning she found it hard to pray. Her mind was so jumbled she couldn't even put coherent thoughts together, much less lift them to the Lord.

When—and more to the point, *how*—had her life become so complicated?

She had come to Morningway Lodge to retire from the mainstream world, and she had worked hard for the peace and stability she had attained in her life. She held it to her heart and guarded it close.

And then one day a rough-edged marine and his baby girl had arrived at the lodge and had changed everything. That was the *when,* and probably, she thought wryly, the *how,* as well.

She had felt compelled to visit Nate and Gracie every evening after work this week, just to see how the baby was doing, or at least that was what she told herself. Avoiding them wasn't even an option. She had come too far to turn back now.

Truthfully, she didn't even want to try.

Jessica recognized the trust Nate had placed in her by admitting the mistakes he made in his youth. She sensed he wasn't the type of man to give much away, and she felt honored and humbled that he'd chosen to share about his life with her.

She had a lot to learn from Nate—a man who had acknowledged his past and vowed to move forward. Jessica knew herself not to be nearly that strong. She had buried her past rather than acknowledging it.

She winced at the sudden stitch in her side. She'd been running full-force without realizing it. She would have laughed at herself if she could have caught her breath enough to do so. Shaking her head at her own lack of sense, she slowed her pace to a jog and then turned back toward her cabin.

She was hiding the truth. From everyone. She'd buried the past, as much as anyone could who'd been through the type of trauma she'd faced.

Certainly no one at Morningway Lodge knew of her struggles, and that was the way she liked it.

And how she would keep it.

At least for now.

In the meantime, she decided, she would be a friend to Nate. If she was cautious with her heart, there would be no harm done.

She would be careful. Nate had told her he was leaving soon, and all that would be left in his wake would be a few happy memories of the time she had shared with him and Gracie.

It was a little early to call on Jess, but Nate had decided to move forward with his plan to see his father; and to do that, he needed Jess's help.

Gracie was doing fine. Her fever was long gone, and she was back to happily waking at dawn. In the amazing resilient way of small children, the baby had bounced back to good health. Her color was excellent and she was merrily complaining about the pureed squash Nate tried to feed her. It was almost if the previous week's crisis had never happened.

After his own quick breakfast of toast and strong coffee, he bundled Gracie up in a one-piece pink snowsuit with a furry hood that Nate thought made her look like a little Inuit baby. He chuckled as he strapped her into her baby backpack and set off for Jess's cabin.

When he arrived at her cabin, he knocked quietly at first, and then a little louder. Jess didn't answer the door, and he assumed she was still sleeping. It was Saturday, after all.

He turned to go, thinking he would return later, at a more acceptable hour of the morning.

Just as he stepped away from the door, he spotted Jess approaching at a jog, her short blond ponytail swinging behind her. Her cheeks were pink from the cold and exertion, and she was out of breath.

"Nate," she called, coming to a halt before him and leaning her palms against her knees to catch her breath. "What's up? Is Gracie okay?"

Nate grinned and turned to the side, dipping his shoulder so Jess could see the baby bundled on his back. "She's fine. Her fever is gone and she's back to disliking the vegetables I attempted to feed her this morning. Emphasis on *attempted*."

Jess laughed, her light tone echoing in the crisp air. "Babies are amazing, aren't they? They bounce back from sickness so…"

Her sentence came to an abrupt halt just as her face fell. She pinched her lips together tightly and squeezed her eyes shut, but not before Nate had glimpsed the sheer pain and agony in her gaze.

She was hurting.

She didn't say so out loud, but Nate knew it as sure as he knew the beat of his own heart.

Without a second thought, he wrapped his arms around her and pressed her to his chest. She didn't protest, but curled into him as if seeking shelter in his arms.

Emotion welled in his throat. More than anything, he wanted to protect this woman, to defend her against whatever grief was chasing her, to erase the pain in her gaze.

She had been there for him when he needed her. How could he do any less for her?

"Quickly," Jess finished, her voice muffled in the fabric of his brown leather bomber jacket. "Babies heal so quickly."

Jess took a step backward. Nate took the hint and released her, though he kept his hands on her shoulders as he gazed down at her, trying to read her expression.

Her eyes were bright, but her features were calm. There was hardly a trace of distress left over for Nate to see.

What had just happened?

Jess was smiling up at him, and as far as he could tell, it was genuine. Nate admittedly had little experience where women were concerned. Were they all in possession of such quick-changing moods, or was it only Jess who acted that way?

Clueless. He was absolutely at a loss.

"What just happened?" he asked aloud.

"I'm sure I don't know what you mean," she replied with a dismissive wave of her hand; but she couldn't hold his gaze. Her eyes flickered to a spot just over his left shoulder.

Mind your own business.

She didn't have to say the words aloud for the message to come through loud and clear. Nate felt a little rejected by her emotional retreat, as well as experiencing a sharp sense of discouragement that she didn't trust him enough to confide in him.

He'd poured out his heart to her last week, and yet was receiving nothing in return. He knew he hadn't been wrong to trust her, but he wished with all his heart that she could trust him.

Then again, he reminded himself, the bond of friendship they had formed was unusual—and swift—forged on the heels of crisis.

"Okay," he murmured. He tried to shrug, but the backpack weighed his shoulders down.

"Okay," she agreed, taking another step backward and completely out of Nate's reach. "And why are you here, again?"

"Oh, that," Nate said, bemused for a moment as his mind grappled to catch up with her.

Being with Jess really did a number on him. He was

so turned around he had almost forgotten why he'd come in the first place.

Anticipation pulsed through him, followed quickly by a strong case of nerves. "I've been thinking about what you said."

She raised her brow. "What did I say?"

"About visiting my pop," he concluded eagerly. "Gracie is doing so much better this morning that I thought now would be a good time."

"I agree," she said, smiling her encouragement and making Nate's head spin even more.

"I know the day care isn't open today, but I hoped you could watch Gracie for me."

She nodded. "I could do that. But don't you think your father will want to meet his precious new little granddaughter?"

Nate winced, recalling the cool reception Vince had given him on his homecoming. Nate had no reason to believe Pop would be any more responsive.

Then again, Vince *had* been kind to the baby. Maybe Gracie would help break the ice.

No. He couldn't risk it, and he wouldn't use an innocent baby as a shield.

"I don't know how this is going to go down," he explained, his voice gruff. "I've given Pop a lot of reasons to be angry with me. I don't want Gracie caught in the cross fire of my mistakes. I've noticed how she picks up on everyone's emotions, and I don't want to take the risk of upsetting her."

Jess laid a hand on his forearm. "I appreciate how you put Gracie's needs before your own."

Her warm gaze reinforced her words. Nate squared

his shoulders, feeling a good inch taller just because of her radiant smile.

Jess believed in him.

It was a novelty.

Outside of the marines, where he had naturally excelled and had won the respect of all his men, Nate hadn't much experience in being built up. His own family had done nothing over the years but tear him down.

"I'll tell you what," she continued. "How about I run in and change my clothes, and then Gracie and I can accompany you up to the main lodge."

His heart lit up and he knew it must show on his face. "You'd do that for me?"

"Of course." She waved a hand as if brushing the thought away.

He wondered if she had any idea just what a special woman she was.

He wanted to tell her right there on the spot, but he'd never been particularly good with words, and at the moment, he felt more tongue-tied than ever. In the end, he simply nodded.

"I can stay in the dayroom with Gracie while you are visiting with your father," she said, cementing her new plan. "Then, if everything goes well—and I really think it will—Gracie will be right there in the building, making it much more convenient for you to introduce her to her grandfather."

Nate didn't have Jess's faith that his meeting with Pop would go well, and he laid the blame for that squarely on his own shoulders; but he smiled anyway.

How could he not, when Jess had caught him up in the excitement of the moment?

"Thanks," he choked out.

Jess waved him off again. "It's nothing. I'm glad to help."

It wasn't *nothing*.

It was everything. And so, Nate was beginning to realize, was this woman.

With Nate and Gracie waiting just outside her cabin door, Jessica hurried to change from sweatpants into jeans and to quickly run a brush through her hair, which was rather tangled from having been in a ponytail. As she worked, she prayed fervently.

She would have liked to think her motivation was pure and blameless, and not the self-serving petition she knew it to be.

If Nate reconciled with his father—and she had been speaking from her heart when she told Nate she believed that would happen—then maybe Nate would have a reason to stick around Morningway Lodge a little longer. And even though she knew such an occurrence would put her heart at risk much more so than it already was, she couldn't help but wish it to be so.

The day was cool but clear, so she and Nate decided to walk the short distance to the main lodge. Jessica chattered on about inconsequential things as they went, holding up the entire conversation all on her own. Nate made polite one-word responses and little else.

She was a little self-conscious about being the one doing all the talking, but she sensed Nate's mood shifting inward. Every time a period of silence overtook them—meaning Jessica stopped talking for any length of time—the mood between them felt uncomfortable to her and, she thought, to Nate as well.

While he didn't contribute much to the conversation, he clearly appreciated the distraction.

So she kept talking—about the weather, her work at the day care, descriptions of some of the more colorful guests and their children who'd inhabited the lodge over the past year.

It wasn't until they'd entered the main lodge and Nate was fumbling with his backpack that she stopped talking. She steadied the backpack as Nate slipped it in front of him, and then tucked her hands under Gracie's shoulders while he worked the baby's legs loose from the tight material.

She kissed Gracie's soft cheek before tucking her against her hip and flashed Nate her most encouraging smile. "Well, I guess this is it."

Nate's lips pursed for a moment as he swallowed hard and worked his fingers through the short tips of his brown hair. "Yeah. I guess it is."

"Is what?" came Vince's voice from the front desk. Jess hadn't seen Vince standing there when they'd entered; and if the way Nate's shoulders visibly tightened and the slant of his clenched jaw was any indication, neither had he.

Nate didn't answer, and Jessica took her cue from him, remaining silent as Vince approached. Unconsciously, she tightened her hold on Gracie, then purposefully relaxed again, knowing the baby would respond to the cues she was getting from Jessica.

"How's my little niece?" Vince asked in the high-pitched singsong voice men used with children and animals. He reached for Gracie, and when the baby held out her arms to him, Jessica had no choice but to relinquish the baby to him.

"Oh, you are a sweetheart," Vince crooned as Gracie laid her plump little hands on his face. Vince kissed the baby's forehead, and then turned to Nate.

"How's fatherhood treating you? You ready to wave the white flag in surrender yet?"

Jessica thought Vince's tone was teasing, but she didn't miss the way Nate drew himself up, his shoulders tight and his fists clenched against his sides.

"I don't surrender," he informed Vince through gritted teeth, his gaze narrowing. "Not now, and not ever. Just so we're straight."

Vince shrugged as if he didn't care one way or the other, but his gaze became hooded.

Jessica remembered Nate's comment about the bad blood between the two brothers, but all she could see was two grown men acting as mulish and stubborn as a couple of quarrelsome little boys. Each man was clearly taking his cues from the past, when they'd both been hotheaded teenagers.

Didn't they realize they were both grown men now—capable, at least in theory, of talking through their problems as adults?

Jessica's gaze shifted from Vince's closed expression to Nate's open glower.

Obviously not, Jessica thought, pressing her lips together to keep herself from grinning, knowing any humor she found in the situation would only add kindling to an already sparking blaze.

If she didn't step in and stamp out the fire right now, she thought the two men might regress even further—into an all-out brawl.

Men.

She shook her head and stepped between them, stopping just shy of holding her hands palm out to stop them from advancing on each other.

"How would you like to spend some time with your new little niece, Vince?" she asked in a firm but placating tone.

"Well, sure. I'd love to," he said, then frowned. "If Nate doesn't have a problem with it."

Nate glared at him.

"Why do you ask?" Vince queried, blatantly ignoring Nate as his attention shifted to the baby he still held in his arms.

Nate stepped to Jessica's side. "I'm here to see Pop. Jessica is keeping the baby out here for me while I go in to visit."

Jessica let out a breath she hadn't even realized she'd been holding as the tension, while still fairly highstrung between the two men, dissipated enough that she was fairly certain one wouldn't suddenly lunge at the other.

Fairly certain.

"Are you?" Vince asked, his voice cool.

"Unless you have a problem with it," Nate responded, echoing Vince's earlier sentiments.

Vince's eyebrows arched and he shook his head.

"Not at all. About time, if you ask me. I didn't tell Pop you were back home, like you asked. He'll be surprised to see you."

"That's one way to describe it," Nate answered, his voice so low that while Jessica barely heard the statement, she was sure Vince had not.

Slipping her hand into Nate's, she squeezed reassuringly. "Take your time with your father, Nate. I'll stay here with Vince and Gracie. There's no reason to rush."

Nate met her gaze, his eyes at once apologetic and grateful. He clipped a nod.

"I'll be back soon," he said, and then made a smooth, military about-face and strode toward the hallway.

Jessica watched him go, praying once again that Nate wouldn't find things with his father as bad as he imagined them to be. After what she'd just witnessed between Nate and Vince, she was no longer so sure about Nate's reception with his father.

And if things went poorly, she might be saying goodbye to Nate and Gracie much sooner than she would have thought. Her stomach tightened uncomfortably at the same time her throat closed. If Nate and Gracie left Morningway Lodge, would her heart leave with them?

Chapter 7

It didn't take Nate more than a minute to reach the suite of rooms located on the far end of the first-floor hallway. He knew right where they were. These had been his parents' rooms when Nate was growing up, with the boys sharing the room across the hallway. Now it was just Pop alone in the suite. Nate wondered if Vince still occupied the room across the way.

Nate hesitated in front of the door, noting how the glass door at the end of the hallway, which gave clients an easier access to their rooms from outside, was shaking from the breeze. He could feel the chill seeping through the edge of the glass door, and made a mental note of it, thinking it ought to be repaired. Not that it would be easy to mention a suggestion with any negative connotation attached to it to Vince.

Not that Vince would care to listen to any of *his* suggestions. Nate knew he had lost any claim to Morning-way Lodge when he'd entered the military. That was how he wanted it to be, and it was a sure bet Vince didn't want him interfering in any way.

Shaking his head to dislodge the unwelcome thoughts, Nate rapped three times on the door to his father's room. He waited a moment, and then when no one answered, he tried the knob.

It turned. Thinking his father might be resting, he swung the door open on silent hinges and let himself into the room.

The living quarters were much the same as Nate remembered them. Several of his mother's cross-stitched pictures still hung on the walls, and the furniture was the same—two plump old blue fabric easy chairs sat at an angle from an equally worn cream-colored sofa and a knotted pine coffee table that lent the décor a quaint look Nate had always loved. A small dining table and two hard-backed chairs stood in the far corner.

No need for a kitchen, Nate knew, for the chef in the main lodge always brought in meals for them. An open doorway in the middle of the right wall led to the tiny bed and bath.

It was only after he'd taken a moment to draw in his surroundings that Nate noticed his father, tucked into a wheelchair and facing the window. The curtains were open and the sun was streaming down on the old man, giving Nate the peculiar feeling he was looking at someone larger than life.

And that, Nate acknowledged silently, was what his father had always been to him.

Larger than life.

"I told you I wasn't hungry," Jason Morningway bit

out without turning to see who was in the doorway. "Just take it away."

"Pop?" Nate asked hesitantly.

His father jerked, then froze.

"Pop? It's Nate."

"Nate," the old man repeated, wonder in his voice. "My son."

Nate's throat welled with emotion and he tried to swallow it back, but the stinging pressure at his Adam's apple simply wouldn't go away, making it difficult for him to breathe.

Slowly, the old man appeared to regain at least a semblance of use in his upper body, and using his right hand, he put pressure on the switch that turned his chair around. After a moment of adjusting the switch, Jason gazed up at his son.

Nate felt as if he'd been sucker punched in the gut. His breath swept audibly from his lungs.

This was the man who had so completely intimidated Nate as a boy?

Gone was the height and strength Nate remembered. In its place was a tiny, shriveled man confined to a wheelchair, with a flannel blanket tucked around his legs. His gray eyes were filmy and the muscles on the left side of his face drooped slightly.

Nate hadn't realized until that moment how devastating his father's stroke had been. Pop looked eighty, not the sixty-eight years old Nate knew him to be.

"Come here," Jason commanded, and Nate immediately obeyed, for it was the imposing voice that Nate remembered from his youth.

His father stared up at him for a long moment without speaking. Nate noticed the way the old man's shoulders were quivering and thought it might be from strain, so he swiped a hard-backed chair from the dining table and seated himself in front of his father.

He wanted to reach out and touch the old man, if nothing else to reassure himself that the moment was real, but he didn't move a muscle.

His father had never been the touchy type. Nate could count on one hand the number of times Jason Morningway had embraced him as a child.

So he was surprised when his father lifted his frail right arm and clasped Nate on the shoulder. Nate could feel the chill of Jason's hand through his shirt and he shivered unconsciously.

"Nate," the old man said again. "My son."

"I'm here, Pop," Nate said. "I'm here."

Though he knew it wasn't his fault that he couldn't be here when his father had collapsed, that he had been a continent away fighting for his country, he still felt guilty for his absence.

"A marine," Pop said, as if somehow reading Nate's thoughts.

Where Nate had expected anger, he heard pride, and his mind clouded with unexpected sensations.

"Yes, sir. Ten years, now."

The old man wet his dry, split lips with the tip of his tongue and cracked a wavering half smile. "Your mother would have been proud."

Nate's eyes stung with unshed tears. He hadn't cried since he was a small boy, and he wasn't about to do so now, but the pressure behind his eyelids didn't go away even after he blinked repeatedly.

"You've come home," Pop said, as if he'd only now realized the fact. "Why?"

"Yes, well, I don't know, really. And I doubt if I'll be staying."

His father's face fell, and Nate scrambled to bring the tenuous smile back to Pop's lips. Two minutes with his father and he'd already blown it.

"I have a baby," Nate blurted.

At this awkward pronouncement, Pop's gaze narrowed into an expression Nate was more familiar with. This was the father Nate had expected. Perhaps things hadn't changed as much as they had first appeared.

"You got married?" the old man barked. "Vince never said."

"No, sir," Nate answered. He would have continued his explanation, but Pop cut him off.

"I raised you better than that."

So the man still had some fight in him, did he? Somehow, his father's reaction relieved Nate—Pop the way he had been and not as he was now.

"Yes, sir. I know you did. The baby is not my biological child. She was my best friend Ezra's daughter. My battle buddy in Iraq. When he died, I became Gracie's legal guardian."

"Gracie," his father repeated, testing the name on his lips. "Where is she?"

"A close friend of mine is watching her in the dayroom."

"Well, I want to meet my little granddaughter," Pop said, fidgeting with the blanket on his lap. Nate could see the old man only had one good arm to work with. His left arm lay virtually useless by his side. "How about you bring her to me?"

Nate stretched forward to tuck the blanket around his father and felt a shiver rock through the man.

"Are you cold?" Nate asked solicitously. Central heating kept the lodge at a comfortable seventy degrees, but Pop's skin felt cold to the touch.

"I'm always cold," Pop grumbled. "I can't seem to warm up, not even under a dozen blankets. That stroke of mine nearly did me in. Still might," he said with a disgusted grunt.

Nate wanted to cringe at his father's fatalistic statement. He'd told himself over and over throughout the years he'd been gone that he didn't really care about his family, for they never really cared about him.

But that wasn't true. This was his *father*. Nate loved him despite his flaws.

Nate tucked the flannel blanket more tightly around his father's frail shoulders.

"I'll go get Gracie," he said, deciding the best thing to do was get Pop's mind off his ailments. "It'll just be a moment."

Pop grunted again and turned his chair back toward the window. "I'll be here. Got no place else to go."

The defeatist tone to his father's voice saddened Nate. It was as if the man had just given up. He could understand the feeling, even if he didn't agree with it. Pop was confined to a small set of rooms and a wheelchair.

That would take the fight out of most men, Nate thought.

But not his pop.

Pop was a scrapper and always had been. He'd started a business with little more than a wish and a prayer, and had built it up for himself with his own two hands. He'd worked hard over the years to provide for his family.

Only to have it end like this?

Nate vowed to himself it would not be so.

* * *

Jessica looked up just as Nate entered the dayroom. She tried to read his expression as his gaze met hers, wondering how it had gone with his father, but it was hard to tell.

His eyes were wide and his lips pinched. He looked lost, Jessica thought, like a little boy who'd wandered away from his parents in a department store and had looked up only to find the faces of strangers swarming in and out around him.

She was thankful she was the only one there to witness it. Vince had spent a couple of minutes playing with Gracie, and then had excused himself to go back to the office.

"How did it go?" she asked softly.

Nate didn't immediately answer. Instead, with the gold flecks in his eyes shimmering brightly, he reached for Gracie, who flapped her arms and babbled excitedly at his attention.

"Okay, baby girl," he murmured, swinging Gracie in the air and then kissing her chubby cheek. "Your grandfather wants to meet you."

"Oh!" Jessica exclaimed, releasing the breath she'd been holding. "It went well, then?"

Nate's gaze met hers over the top of the baby's head, and he gave a clipped nod. He smiled, but it didn't quite reach his eyes.

Impulsively, she stood and moved to Nate's side, giving him a quick, spontaneous hug.

"Poor Pop," Nate said, shaking his head. "I had no idea the stroke had debilitated him to such a colossal extent."

"You couldn't have known."

Nate snorted. "Maybe deep down I knew, and I just didn't want to face reality."

"You're here now," she gently pointed out, absently stroking his shoulder.

"Well, I'm too little, too late," he snapped derisively.

"Not at all. How can you say that? He was glad to see you, wasn't he?"

Nate's lips twisted as he nodded.

"And if that wasn't enough, I'm sure baby Gracie is going to make his day."

Nate gazed down at Gracie, and then offered his hand to Jessica. "He seemed anxious to meet her."

"Then what are we waiting for?" Jessica asked, pulling him toward the hallway.

Nate didn't say anything, but he allowed her to lead him down the hallway and back to his father's suite of rooms.

"Pop?" he called, entering the room without knocking on the door this time. "I've brought Gracie."

Jessica had seen Jason Morningway off and on at the lodge, though he had been too ill in the past few weeks to make the foray out to the dayroom to interact with others. He looked a bit weaker than she remembered, but the joy shining from his gray eyes was unmistakable.

"My granddaughter," he announced, wheeling his chair forward. "Thank the Good Lord. I didn't think I would live to see the day."

Nate's hand clenched tightly over Jessica's for a moment, and she gave him a reassuring squeeze back before letting go.

Nate crouched before his father and propped Gracie up on his knee, so the old man could see her and interact with her.

"Little darling," Jason crooned, reaching his hand toward Gracie.

The baby wasn't shy with strangers; or maybe, Jessica thought, Gracie instinctively knew that Jason Morningway was family. Gracie clasped her little fist over her grandfather's index finger and babbled happily at him.

"She's quite a talker," Jason said with a gruff laugh. "How old is she?"

"Six and a half months," Nate answered with a tentative smile. "And she's already more than a handful, let me tell you."

"As were you," his father countered, a faraway look reaching his eyes. "Even before you were born, you were always on the move. I remember your mother saying she thought you were going to be a circus acrobat. And then as a toddler, we couldn't keep you still for more than a minute. You'd climb on bookshelves, throw your ball through a window. One time you hid in the middle of an apparel rack at a department store and your mother couldn't find you. You scared the wits out of her that day."

Nate flashed Jessica a wide, surprised gaze. Did Jason remember that Gracie was not Nate's biological child? He spoke as if the fact had slipped his mind.

Jessica shook her head briefly. There was no sense pressing the issue with Jason, who would probably forget again the moment they left the room. Strokes could play havoc on the mind.

Besides, Jessica thought, in all the ways that mattered, Nate *was* Gracie's father. There was far more than genetics involved here.

Jason seemed to notice the silent exchange between Nate and Jessica, for his gaze focused on Jessica and the side of his mouth that worked correctly crooked up into a half smile.

"And who is this lovely creature?"

Nate rocked back on his heels, pressing Gracie close to his chest. "I'm sorry, Pop. I thought you already knew her. This is my…" he hesitated "…friend. Jessica Sabin."

Jessica noticed his hesitation and wondered if he'd been about to say something different, but she didn't have time to dwell on it.

"I'm the day care director, Mr. Morningway. I've been here at the lodge for about a year now. We've met before, at a couple of social events."

Jason frowned, the right side of his face crinkling to match the left. "I'm sorry. I don't remember."

"Think nothing of it," Jessica gently assured him. "There are so many people coming and going in and out of Morningway Lodge at any given time, you would be hard-pressed to remember names and faces. After a while, it all becomes a big blur. I can't remember names to save my life—except, of course, for the kids I work with." She chuckled.

Jason settled back in his wheelchair, looking at ease once more. As Nate stood, he flashed Jessica a grateful smile and reached for her hand.

"Jess has been a godsend," he remarked. "She has really helped me out with Gracie. I would have been lost without her. She's the resident expert where babies are concerned."

Jessica shrugged off the compliment, uncomfortable

with the way both Nate and his father were beaming at her, as if she were someone special.

Jason's gaze dropped to where Nate's and Jessica's hands were joined, and he smiled crookedly again. "Such a lovely little family you have there, son."

Jason's innocent comment sent such an intense bolt of shock through Jessica that she quivered as if she'd just been struck by lightning. She immediately snatched her hand away from Nate's, feeling almost singed by the contact of his fingers.

She expected the surprise in Nate's gaze as his eyes met hers, but not the golden glimmer that spoke of something else entirely.

Feeling branded by a look that surpassed even the touch of his hand, she quickly turned away, only to meet another familiar pair of eyes as she spotted Vince in the doorway behind them.

Vince was leaning against the doorjamb, his arms crossed in front of him. For the briefest moment, Jessica glimpsed such a look of pain and betrayal that she winced inwardly.

Then, just as quickly, Vince's gaze became hooded under lowered brows. Cold, hard anger jetted from his eyes, replacing any other emotions Jessica had seen just a moment before; so swiftly, in fact, that she wondered if she'd seen anything else at all.

"Right, Pop," Vince growled. "What we have here is the perfect little family. Isn't that just so sweet to see? How incredibly happy you must be that your prodigal son has returned."

Still glowering, Vince turned on his heels and swiftly stalked away before anyone could offer a reply to his harsh words.

Jessica whirled around, wondering how to diffuse the situation. Not surprisingly, Nate was glowering at the now-empty doorway, and Jason's expression was a mask of confusion, followed by a mixture of acknowledgment and regret.

"Your brother is not happy." Though Jason was stating the obvious, both Nate and Jessica stared at him as if he'd just made some spectacular revelation.

"No kidding," Nate groaned. "I'm sorry, Pop. I never should have come back here. I'm just making things worse for everybody."

"No." Jason's one-word response was clear and shrill and brooked no argument. The foggy look that usually clouded his eyes had dissipated completely and he was looking at Nate with cool lucidity.

Nate's eyebrows rose and his jaw dropped. Jessica thought her expression might mirror Nate's, and she pinched her lips together to make sure her mouth was still firmly closed.

"This is your home," Jason continued. "You belong here. Gracie belongs here."

Privately, Jessica agreed with Jason's assessment, but she knew it would take much more than a few simple words to convince Nate.

"But Vince—" Nate started to argue, and then was cut off by his father's harsh look.

"Vince has not been happy for a very long time. Far before you came back home. I know you think you're the cause of all his troubles, but you aren't. Vince has many things to work through, but it will go better for him if he has his brother's support."

"I don't know, Pop."

Jason jerked his head to one side. "I raised two very stubborn sons."

Jessica pinched her lips again, this time to keep from smiling. She definitely agreed with Jason's opinion of the relationship between Nate and Vince. She had never met two more willful men.

Nate frowned and shrugged, but didn't offer any further comment.

Jason smiled, looking as if he'd won a battle. "Good, then," he said, as if punctuating the conversation. "Now let me see my little granddaughter."

Chapter 8

It wasn't any real surprise to Nate that Jess had bowed out as soon as they'd left the main lodge. He didn't know whether to be distressed or relieved. Clearly she didn't want to talk about what had happened between Nate and his father—and most especially Vince—and Nate couldn't say that he blamed her.

He bundled Gracie back up in her snowsuit and plopped her into the backpack before swinging it on his back and adjusting the shoulder straps.

"Ready to go, little lady?" he asked the squirming baby.

Gracie patted him on the head, which he took as her version of "Let's go!"

Nate realized he had inadvertently thrust Jess right into the middle of a family squabble. In all fairness, she *had* known Vince longer than she'd known Nate. Not to mention the fact that Vince was Jess's employer. It wouldn't be right of Nate to make her choose between the two of them.

He was certain she'd had no idea what she was getting into when she'd offered her support to him today. *He* hadn't known it would go down like this.

His father, at times lucid and at others frighteningly befuddled.

Vince barging in on their reunion and disrupting what would otherwise have been a tender moment.

Pop commenting on what a sweet little family Nate and Jess and Gracie made. Right out of left field, but dead on the money, Nate thought.

At least on his and Gracie's side of things, it certainly was. The more time he spent with Jess, the more time he wanted to spend with her. Although if he were honest, the look of utter shock and surprise on Jess's face when Pop had made his pronouncement about their *little family* led Nate to believe Jess hadn't thought about it as much as he had—if at all.

Was she just being friendly to a hopeless-case marine and his baby? If the current he felt running so strongly between them ran no deeper than that on her side, how was he going to turn the stakes in his favor?

It was more frightening to Nate to face rejection from Jess than to face danger or pain.

The question now was definitely *how,* not *if.* Jess had become too much an ingrained part of his and Gracie's life for Nate to even consider not pursuing a relationship with her. He'd never experienced the kinds of heartfelt sensations he did when he was around Jess. That had to count for something.

He stepped out of the lodge and absently noted that the weather was now cloudy and overcast, kind of like his mood right now, he thought. But he suddenly had to thrust those thoughts aside as he was confronted with a more immediate problem.

Rather than hide out in his office as Nate would have expected his brother to do, Vince was at the side of the lodge, measuring and cutting long sections of two-by-fours, a baseball cap turned backward on his head and a pencil tucked behind his ear.

Nate's first thought was to turn another direction, but it was already too late for that. There was no avoiding Vince now.

Vince, obviously spying Nate, had pulled himself to his full height and allowed the tape measure he was using to snap shut, echoing in the air. He stared at Nate as if he thought him from another planet.

With a sigh, and an immediate, involuntary tightening of his shoulder muscles, Nate trod up to Vince and slid to a stop in the gravel. Vince glared at him, and Nate scowled back.

"What is your problem, man?" he demanded, tightening his hold on the straps of the backpack cutting fiercely into his shoulders.

As soon as the words were out of his mouth, Nate wished them back, but the damage was already done. Vince's brow dropped so low Nate could barely see his blue eyes sparking with anger, and Vince clenched and unclenched his fists as if he was internally fighting the urge to strike out.

Bring it on, Nate thought. This was a long time in coming.

As an angry haze swept over him, he forced himself to take a mental step backward. This wasn't the way to solve their problems.

He was annoyed that his father's reception had been so much warmer than Vince's, but now he'd made it twenty times worse for himself with his big mouth. His father had been right to call him stubborn. He was that, and a dozen other bad qualities, all wrapped up in a big, oafish military frame.

Would he ever take a clue from Jess and learn to control himself?

"Sorry," he apologized hastily. "I didn't mean that the way it sounded."

Vince's scowl darkened even further. "I know exactly what you meant. Don't try to sidestep the issue and take it back now."

"Look, I said I was sorry," Nate said again, holding his hands out in a conciliatory manner. "What can I do to make it up to you?"

"Ha!" Vince snorted. "What do you think? You're about ten years too late asking that question, little brother."

What, Nate wondered, was *that* statement supposed to mean?

Ten years ago, Vince hadn't wanted anything to do with him. He was nothing more than a roadblock to Vince's ambitions. Because Nate had left, and with his father's subsequent stroke, Vince got everything he wanted—total control of the lodge.

So what was his problem? If that was, in fact, what he had really wanted.

Nate took a long look at his brother—really looked at him—for the first time since he'd returned home. Though he was only thirty years old, his face was weathered and stress lines were already forming. A lock of hair that fell down over his forehead from underneath the baseball cap was a premature silver.

Was this what Vince wanted? Or had all this been thrust on him because Nate had left?

For the first time, he saw his actions through his brother's point of view, and he couldn't help but wonder just how much of Vince's stress and worry *he* had caused when he'd run off to join the military.

"I wasn't thinking of anyone but myself," he said aloud.

Vince quickly masked his surprise, but not before Nate had glimpsed it.

"I apologize, bro. I never realized until this moment how I completely left you in the lurch when I enlisted," Nate continued, suddenly yearning to put all his cards on the table. "Because of me, you've had the burden of running the lodge single-handedly. Maybe that's how you wanted it. Maybe not. But I sure shouldn't have left without telling you I was going."

There was a tense moment while Vince stared at him, slowly ingesting what he'd just said. The mountain, usually rife with sound—the wind rustling through the trees, the river in the distance rushing over jagged rocks, the birds and wildlife—was suddenly painfully silent.

Nate held his breath and waited.

Finally, Vince shrugged.

"What's done is done," he said, sounding lofty and philosophical in his tone. "There's no sense talking about it."

Nate swallowed hard, wondering if this might be Vince's awkward way of showing forgiveness, if it might be the first step in reconciliation between them.

Nate didn't know, but he could hope. The tension didn't leave his shoulders as he held out his hand to shake Vince's.

"I'm glad to be back home," he said huskily. To his own surprise, he realized he meant it.

Vince eyed Nate's extended hand for a moment, then raised one eyebrow and spun away, snapping his tape measure against a beam of wood and concentrating on his project as if he and Nate had never spoken at all.

As if Nate wasn't still standing there, waiting for... *something*.

Nate dropped his arm, experiencing a wave of defeat that nearly overwhelmed him. His father's happy reception had given him a false sense of hope. He should have known Vince wouldn't back down so easily.

If there was a way to get back into Vince's good graces, Nate didn't know what it was.

Back in Vince's good graces?

Ha! Who was he trying to kid?

He'd never been on Vince's good side, and at the rate he was going now, he never would be.

Maybe it was time to buck up and face the truth. He wasn't wanted here. Like he'd said to his father, coming home had done more harm than good.

But, knowing Jess was here at Morningway Lodge, a place that represented all that was bad about Nate's life, could he still consider leaving?

He snorted aloud, shook his head.

Not a chance.

His feelings for Jess were simply too strong to ignore, and his brother was just going to have to learn to deal with it, or simply ignore him the way he had done when they were kids.

Because he wasn't leaving.

Jessica hadn't bothered fussing with a big dinner for herself. Instead, she'd put a can of tomato soup on the stove and grilled a cheese sandwich, washing it down with a tall glass of milk. Usually she enjoyed cooking, even if it was just for herself, but tonight her heart hadn't been in it.

Knowing she was going to be an emotional basket case if she held it all in, she allowed herself the luxury of grieving for the past. There were times, she knew, when the best way around an obstacle was through it, and this had been one of those nights.

She'd taken out her baby album and spent the evening with the paradoxically joyful and heartbreaking memories of her daughter, Elizabeth.

No matter what, she promised herself she would not dwell on the events of the past afternoon; but try as she might, Jason's confused words echoed over and over again in her consciousness.

Such a lovely little family.

She wondered what Nate would have said about his father's observation if Vince hadn't shown up when he did, and then decided it didn't matter.

Okay, so maybe it *did* matter, but she wasn't going to think about it.

When she finally drifted off to sleep late in the evening, it wasn't into her usual stress-induced black void. Rather, her dreams were filled with a handsome marine and his baby girl.

When Jessica awoke the next morning, it was with a joyful heart and a thankful spirit. It was Sunday, and as was her usual habit, she would go to church and worship God, laying all of her burdens down at His feet.

As she suspected, the worship service was just what she'd needed. She returned home with her heart much lighter and her soul refreshed, scrubbed clean and ready for a new week, her focus on God.

Her mind was still humming a praise song as she approached her cabin and exited her SUV, so she did not, at first, notice the note taped to her front door.

When she did, she reached for the ragged piece of paper and tore it off in surprise.

Her name was written in a big, bold script on the back side of an old gas receipt.

Jess—
Gracie and I stopped by your cabin, but you weren't home. Guessing you're at church. Anyway, call me or come by when you have a chance.
—Nate

Jessica crumpled the note in her fist and held it close to her heart, trying to steady the sudden upswing in her breathing pattern. There was simply no denying the way her pulse leaped at the knowledge that Nate wanted to see her, nor the way her gut tightened painfully in response.

It was an oddly pleasant form of torture, she mused thoughtfully; and the funny part was, she was doing this to herself.

What did Nate want?

Could it be possible that he was going to tell her he was planning to stay at the lodge? Permanently?

She smiled to herself as she remembered the utter joy and relief apparent on his face after he had reconciled with his father.

Did she dare to hope?

But the past clouded her future. In her mind, she acknowledged that having had one bad relationship with a terrible outcome didn't necessarily doom her to an entire lifetime of bad relationships; but in her heart, not so much.

The truth was, she accepted silently, she was a total coward.

She was afraid to fall in love again. Because if she opened herself to loving, she would also open herself to losing.

Was that a risk she was willing to take?

Nate had just put Gracie down for the night when Jess knocked on his door. He grinned broadly as he let her in, especially when he saw the plate of delicious, still-warm-from-the-oven chocolate brownies she'd brought along with her.

He was so excited about sharing the new plan he'd worked up that he would have welcomed a phone call, but it was much better to see Jess's beautiful face in person.

"I got your note," she whispered as she entered the cabin and handed Nate the plate of brownies. "Is Gracie asleep?"

"Yes," he answered in a low voice. "As a matter of fact, I just put her down for the night."

"I'm sorry I didn't make it over before she fell asleep. Is she sleeping well for you?"

Nate smiled. "All the way through the night, most nights."

Jess returned his smile. "See? I told you it would get easier."

Nate laughed softly. "Well, I don't know about that, but the two of us are finally starting to get into a routine together, I think."

Jess peered down into the playpen where Gracie was

sleeping, tilting her head to one side as she hesitated, her smile faltering. "You know, I could come back tomorrow. I'd hate it if we accidentally disturbed the baby with our chatter."

"Oh, no, you don't," he said hastily, shifting from one foot to the other. "You're not getting away from me that easily."

Her eyes widened, but he didn't coax the smile from her he had hoped to, with his teasing words, and it made him curious.

The woman acted as if a man had never flirted with her before, and he didn't believe that for a second. He wondered, not for the first time, how such a beautiful, kind woman had ended up holed away in a mountain retreat, all by herself. Why hadn't some lucky man before now swept her off her feet?

Well, he thought wryly, their loss was definitely his gain.

And Gracie's.

If ever there was a woman meant to be a mother, it was Jessica Sabin. He was more appreciative than she would ever know for all the help she'd given him over the past few weeks.

"If you don't mind, we could go sit out on the front porch," he suggested, smiling down at the sleeping baby. He was so excited about his new idea that he wasn't sure he'd be able to keep his enthusiasm in check if they spoke indoors.

"That sounds lovely," she answered. "It's a really nice evening out, compared to how frosty the weather has been lately. Today it almost feels like an Indian summer night."

Nate slipped into his bomber jacket and then held the

screen door for Jess and waited until she'd seated herself on the porch step before sitting down beside her. He left the door open so he could hear if Gracie stirred, but he thought they would be able to talk without bothering the baby.

"So, what's up?" she asked after they'd sat a moment in silence. "You've made some decisions?"

He nodded. "In a way, yes. I've been thinking a lot about my future. And Gracie's."

She tensed up, which looked to Nate like a shiver. She was right about the night being mild, but she'd only worn a light windbreaker for a jacket. Even in the summertime, the Rocky Mountains could get cold once the sun went down—and this was not summertime.

He put his arm around her shoulders, thinking to keep her warm, and smiled to himself when she shifted, cuddling in under his arm.

"What have you decided?" She didn't look at him when she spoke, but rather at the shadows of the trees lengthening in the setting sun.

"Nothing permanent, yet." He followed her gaze, for once enjoying the mountain view. Funny how his perspective changed when Jess was around.

"Oh." She sounded a little bit taken aback, and Nate wondered why.

What was she thinking? He wished he knew, but he didn't know how to form the question to ask her about it, so he mentally dropped the subject and continued with his previous train of thought.

"Anyway," he continued, "I've been thinking about my dad."

"I thought you might be," she commented, and then sighed. "I'm glad that situation worked out for you as well as it did."

"Me, too," he agreed fervently. "I didn't realize that was going to be such a giant step for me. You have no idea how much it meant to me to be reconciled with Pop."

"Oh, I think I might," she disagreed, smiling softly and shyly.

He arched one eyebrow, questioning her without speaking.

She shrugged. "I could see it on your face when you came back from talking to him."

"That obvious, huh?"

"Oh, yes," she said with a laugh. "At least, to me, it was. But then I've always had a gift for being able to discern what someone is feeling, even when they don't say anything out loud."

He squeezed her shoulder. "I believe that. You always seem to know what Gracie needs."

"Babies are easy."

"Ha!" Nate burst out with a spontaneous laugh. "Says you."

She stared at him a moment, her lips pursed. "You're very good with her, you know."

"Do you think?"

"I know. I don't think you give yourself enough credit."

"Hmm."

"I also know, based on the expression on your face, not to mention the note you left taped to my door, that you are dying to tell me something. So just go ahead and spit it out, already."

"Once again, you've read my mind," he teased. He couldn't wipe the grin from his face if he tried. "I do have something I want to get your opinion on. It's about my pop."

Chapter 9

"I'm always happy to offer my opinion," Jessica answered in the same teasing tone. "So what's going on with your father?"

"Well, when I went to visit him, I noticed that he seemed to be cold. The central heating was working just fine, but he was shivering, even though he had a wool blanket covering him. When I asked him about it, he told me he feels like he can never get warm."

"That's too bad. He has already suffered through so much with that stroke."

"I know," Nate agreed. "I can't get him out of my mind. I want to do something to help him—to make up for the way I wounded him when I left the lodge and joined the marines."

"You don't have to do penance," Jess said softly.

"What's done is done. And your father already forgave you, you know."

"Yeah," Nate said on an exhale. "I know. But I still want to do something for him."

"What did you have in mind?"

"I want to build him a fireplace. You know, something easy on the eye, made out of stone, maybe, that will help him keep warm. I was thinking he could stoke it up as much as he needs to and have a lot more control over how warm he keeps the room."

Jess bounded to her feet, spun around and took Nate's hands in hers. "That's a wonderful idea!" she exclaimed, obviously sharing his enthusiasm.

And his vision.

He stood and hugged her, enjoying the way his heart soared at her encouragement. He was so grateful for her support.

He thought about what it would be like to have her at his side every day for the rest of his life, and he liked the mental picture he drew. How high could he reach with her love?

"You'll have to run your idea by Vince, you know. I don't see how you can get around it."

Her words popped the bubble of Nate's daydream like a stickpin.

Telling Jess had been the easy part.

He'd already known he'd have to get Vince's permission to proceed with his plan. Vince had the final say on every aspect of Morningway Lodge, and what Nate was proposing was a pretty major renovation.

He dropped his arms from Jess's waist and shrugged, hoping he'd pulled off nonchalance but knowing Jess saw right through his bravado.

"Do you think he'll go for it?"

To his relief, Jess nodded. "I think he may surprise you."

Nate snorted. "Highly unlikely. But as you said, I have to speak to him first."

"What are you going to do with Gracie while you work on the project?"

He chuckled and flashed her a goofy grin. "That's where you come in, honey."

She laughed in delight. "I'll admit I was hoping you'd say that."

"I was thinking I'd drop Gracie by the day care on weekdays while I work."

"We'd be happy to have her," she said, her tone suddenly businesslike and efficient.

"There's still an opening, then?"

Jess looked away from him, then chuckled. "For Gracie, I'd *make* an opening. But in answer to your question, yes, we have an opening available."

She had a strange look on her face when she spoke, and she still wasn't looking him in the eye. Nate knew she wasn't telling the whole story.

"What?" he queried playfully. "What are you not telling me?"

Jess glanced away for a moment, her face reddening under his scrutiny.

"I saved it for you," she mumbled under her breath, shrugging as if what she said didn't matter.

"You what?" Nate asked, though he was fairly certain he'd heard her correctly the first time. Still, he wanted to hear her say it again.

"Oh, all right. I'll fess up. You know how I feel about—" she paused as if searching for words, and if it were possible, her face flushed with even more color "—about Gracie."

Nate cocked an eyebrow, feeling certain that wasn't what she'd been about to say. She had mentally amended her statement from…?

A slow grin spread over Nate's face as he inwardly answered his own question. "Go on."

"I wasn't sure what your plans were, so I saved Gracie a spot at the day care, just in case."

His smile widened.

"So sue me, already," she snapped, looking increasingly flustered.

Sue her? He wanted to kiss her.

With effort, he restrained himself. He didn't want to scare the lady off, after all. As much as he recognized the strength of his own heart and wanted to propel their relationship into fast-forward, he coaxed himself to stay in check until he knew for certain she returned his feelings.

How he would know that, he hadn't a clue. He didn't have much experience in reading women's emotions; he gave himself a mental tug backward.

Somehow, he encouraged himself, he would instinctively know when the time was right for him to speak. And this wasn't it.

Yet.

He shoved his hands in his pockets and rocked back on his heels, mentally distancing himself from the captivating woman before him. He tried to speak, but his words came out hoarse and raspy.

He cleared his throat and tried again. "Is tomorrow too soon?"

Jess shook her head.

"I thought I would talk to Vince and then go into Boulder to order materials for the fireplace. I don't know how long it will take me."

"It doesn't matter," she assured him, her big brown eyes glowing incandescently. "Tomorrow would be just perfect."

Jessica seated herself on a rocking chair in the corner of the day care nursery, tucked Gracie onto her lap, and then coaxed the warm bottle of formula into the baby's mouth. She smiled as Gracie reached out and propped the bottle with her own little fists.

Gracie was not only pulling herself up to a standing position when she was in her crib, but she was starting to show some manual dexterity, as well.

Babies grew into little girls too quickly, Jessica thought, with a mixture of joy and downheartedness. It would not be long now before Nate was chasing Gracie all over the mountain.

If he was around that long. She had so hoped that when he'd said he'd made some decisions, that he had meant he was going to stay at Morningway Lodge.

But he hadn't said that.

As she stared down at the sweet baby who'd completely won her heart, melancholy washed over her in black waves. She wondered if she'd get to see Gracie walking and talking and growing into a busy toddler.

She hoped so. With her whole heart, she wanted them to stay.

And if she were being honest, it wasn't just Gracie she would miss when they left. There was Nate to think of, as well.

Strong, charming, honorable Sergeant Morningway.

She smiled tenderly when she thought of Nate. He'd been so convinced that he was going to run into resistance when he'd approached his brother with the fireplace idea, and had been genuinely astonished when Vince gave him—albeit grudgingly, Nate had assured her—consent to do the work.

And so for the past three weeks he had been dropping Gracie off at the day care early every weekday morning and taking off to work on his new project. He had the unfettered enthusiasm of a little boy in a toy shop. It was, Jessica mused, quite contagious. She couldn't seem to stop smiling these days, what with Nate running energetic mental circles around her.

She couldn't even really say it surprised her that he'd made it a practice to seek her out after hours as well. The fact that she visited his cabin as often as he came to hers was beside the point.

When Nate and Gracie weren't around, her life seemed conspicuously empty and quiet. While she used to consider the silence as a measure of her serenity, it was now a constant aching reminder of the past, and she found herself counting the minutes until she would see Nate and Gracie again.

They'd fallen into a comfortable routine. Nate picked her up in the morning, saying it was silly to drive two cars when he was headed in the direction of the day care anyway. Then, when he picked Gracie up in the evening, he waited around to drive Jessica home.

It only seemed fair that if he was going to ferry her about, the least she could do was cook him dinner. And then the next evening, he'd reciprocated, fixing her a killer omelet for supper. One evening led to another, and before Jessica realized it, the pattern had been set.

Much to her surprise, Nate had even accepted her invitation to accompany her to church the previous Sunday. She didn't know why she had felt compelled to ask him at all, given that he was not a religious man, and she certainly hadn't expected him to agree.

Now she wondered if he might not start attending church with her on a regular basis. And what, if anything, that meant about his relationship with God.

Speaking of Nate, she thought as she brought Gracie up to her shoulder for a burp, where was the man? She had expected him to arrive to take her home by the time she had finished feeding Gracie her bottle, but he was apparently running late.

When another half hour quietly passed and Nate still hadn't come to pick her up, Jessica started to worry in earnest.

Had something happened to him? Had there been an accident, maybe?

He'd told her that morning that he was going to be working on the roof today, building a chimney. What if he'd slipped and fallen?

She chastised herself for being a silly goose and turned her attention to Gracie.

"Hey, baby girl," she said, brushing her fingers through Gracie's soft curls, "what do you say we have a little fun with your hair?"

Gracie clearly didn't think that Jessica gathering her curls into a sprout on the top of her head and weaving a rubber band around it qualified as *fun*. She squawked and she wiggled and she even tried to slide off Jessica's lap, but Jessica just laughed and followed her movements until she'd achieved the look she desired.

How delightful Gracie looked bobbing her head with

the little ponytail in place on top. That was why little girls were so much fun, Jessica thought, at once happy and sad. It was fun to play with their hair and dress them up in plush velvet and sparkly red shoes.

There were so many things she missed about Elizabeth, and so many more she would never see.

Jessica shook herself mentally, not wanting to entertain her morose feelings any further. Gracie was here in front of her, and that was all that mattered. Time moved so quickly. She needed to grasp the moment and live for *now*.

Sitting cross-legged on the indoor-outdoor carpet that covered the day care floor, Jessica willed her mind into the present, where Gracie was merrily pounding away on a toy xylophone and singing in a language all her own.

How could Jessica not find joy as she interacted with baby Gracie?

But when yet another half hour had passed, she decided it was time for action. She didn't have her SUV with her, but the day care van, complete with a car seat, was parked behind the building and she had the keys.

Without letting herself think too much about it, she bundled Gracie up and headed for the main lodge. Nate had no doubt simply lost track of the time, but she couldn't wait another second to know for sure.

She tried to remain calm, telling herself not to panic for no good reason, but to no avail.

Despite her best efforts, she mentally worked herself into such a state as she drove that she half expected to see an ambulance in front of the lodge, or at the very least a crowd of concerned onlookers; but upon approaching, the lodge was as quiet as ever, and Nate's Jeep was parked in the front lot.

She breathed a sigh of relief, mentally chastising herself for her own stupidity. It wasn't like her to let her imagination run away with her.

With Gracie in her arms, she beelined for Jason Morningway's room.

When she knocked, it was Nate's smooth baritone that bid her to enter, and it was his beaming gaze that caught her eye the moment she stepped into the room.

Nate was sitting at the dining table with his father, a soda in his hand.

"Jess!" he exclaimed, bounding toward her and giving her an enthusiastic hug before sweeping Gracie into his arms. "What a surprise. What are you doing here? Is something the matter?"

Jessica arched an eyebrow and pointedly looked at her watch.

Nate looked at his own watch and then back at her, his expression genuinely surprised.

Jessica laughed. "So you lost track of the time, did you?"

He hung his head in mock shame, but he was still smiling. "I did. And I left you stranded and starving, no doubt. And speaking of stranded—how did you get to the lodge?"

"Compliments of the day care van," she answered, and then looked over his shoulder at the mostly finished fireplace. Nate had built it against the outside wall in gray stone. Though brand-new, it had an aged quality about it that Jessica recognized as exceptionally superior workmanship.

"Oh, Nate," she exclaimed, clapping her hands in delight. "It's gorgeous!"

"If not yet fully functional," he added with a grin. "Soon, though, Pop. I promise."

"You don't hear me complaining," Jason said, wheeling his chair around to face them. "I'm just enjoying your company. Now hand me my little granddaughter so I can give her a kiss."

Nate laughed and handed Gracie off to his father. "You got it, Pop. Hey…look at that, why don't you?"

He tapped his finger against Gracie's little sprout of a ponytail and laughed as it bounced. "Oh, man. Now that is what this little girl is missing, having to stay with a grumpy old marine. I'm never going to be able to do the hair thing with her. It's a good thing she's got you around for a female influence, Jess."

Jessica's heart welled as she watched the scene unfold and ingested Nate's compliment to her. Gracie's presence took years off Jason's features, and Nate's eyes were glowing with pride and joy.

Nate squeezed her shoulder. "How about I follow you back to the day care so you can drop off the van, and then I can take you home?"

Jessica nodded. "That sounds good to me. I'm starving."

"And I'm cooking," he assured her with a grin. "It's the least I can do to make up for the way I abandoned you like that."

Jason laughed along with Jessica.

"Okay, Pop," Nate said, scooping Gracie back into his arms. "I'll be back first thing tomorrow morning to keep working on the fireplace."

"You take good care of that baby girl. And that lovely lady," Jason teased with a wink.

Jessica blushed.

Nate chortled and swung Gracie into the air, making her squeal with delight. "You can count on it.

"C'mon," Nate said as he and Jessica exited his father's apartment. "Let's go out the side door. I have something I want to show you."

Once outside, he reached for her hand and practically dragged her to the corner of the building. His enthusiasm was absolutely contagious, Jessica thought, laughing aloud as she jogged beside him. He was definitely unlike any other man she'd ever known, a delightful cross of all man and little boy.

"I've set the pipes for the flue," he explained, pointing toward the roof. "Now I'm working on stoning off the chimney. After that, all that's left for me to do is call in the county inspector to make sure everything is up to code. Then Pop can stoke it as high as he wants and enjoy the heat."

"And the view," Jessica added. "The fireplace is just beautiful, Nate. You did a fantastic job. I know your father appreciates it."

Gracie squealed and clapped her hands together as if in agreement.

Jessica giggled and pointed to the baby. "See? Even Gracie thinks so."

Nate's eyes warmed with pride.

"My girls," he said huskily. "I don't know how I ever got along without you two."

His words had an immediate effect on Jessica, who felt heat flooding her face. Her throat constricted and burned until she was dizzy with the need for air. And it didn't help her one bit that Nate's gaze never left her face. She probably would have passed out cold right there on the spot had Gracie not distracted them both.

The baby clapped again, her little hands missing each other as often as they connected. She bounced in Nate's arms, her legs pumping in excitement.

"Da-da!" she crowed triumphantly.

Nate held the baby at arm's length, looking at her in amazement, his jaw literally dropping.

"Did you hear that?" he asked Jessica, his voice hoarse with emotion.

"Da-da," Gracie repeated, as if making certain Nate had, in fact, heard what he'd thought he'd heard. "Da-da-da-da-da-da."

Jessica knew Gracie was simply testing out her consonants, but her timing couldn't have been any better. Sure, the baby may not yet have connected the words to the person, but it was the adult response that would teach her what the words meant. And Jessica couldn't imagine anything taking the moment away from the beaming new father.

"I think she's proud of you, too, Da-da," Jessica said, excitement threading through her voice.

"Da-da," Nate repeated, wonder in his voice. "Her first word was Da-da."

"Well, of course it was, silly," she said, laughing at Nate's astonished expression. "What else would it be? You are the center of her little world, you know."

Hugging Gracie close, he whooped in delight and then reached for Jessica, fastening his arm around her waist and dragging her against him. He lifted her clear off her feet and swung her around and around.

Talk about being swept off her feet! It was Jessica's last conscious thought.

She laughed. Gracie laughed.

And Nate froze, his grip loosening enough for Jessica to find her footing. She was glad he continued to prop her up by his side, or she thought she might have melted right into the ground.

And then she looked up.

The smile on Nate's face faded and his eyes grew warm and golden. His free hand slid up her arm and splayed across her cheek.

"Jess?" His voice was husky, the word hovering somewhere between a question and a statement.

Jessica couldn't have answered him if her life had depended on it. Nor could she help her response, which was more natural even than breathing. She tipped up her chin and leaned in to him, an infinitesimal movement, but laced with meaning.

It was all the answer he needed.

Ever so slowly, he tilted his head to one side and brushed his lips over hers. It was the softest, briefest butterfly-wings of a kiss, but it sent Jessica over the moon and back again.

In that moment, she forgot all the reasons why this couldn't—and shouldn't—happen.

There was just Nate—his glowing eyes, his warm breath, his strong arms.

She wanted this. She wanted to be right here, right now, with this man. Tomorrow would be soon enough for regret.

He might have pulled back, but Jessica clutched onto his shirtfront and drew him forward.

That was all it took. He smiled, tunneled his fingers through her hair and kissed her again.

Just as their lips met for the second time, Jessica felt another hand in her hair. Gracie bunched up her little fist and pulled, and then laughed as if she understood her own joke.

Still locked warmly within their circle of three, Jessica and Nate laughed right along with her.

Chapter 10

Nate's world was in overdrive, and all because of one little kiss. Okay, so maybe technically he'd gone in for seconds, but who could blame him.

Jess certainly had him off-kilter. He was a man who liked to act, not sit around mulling over his emotions. Yet here he was, checking and rechecking his handiwork on the chimney, knowing he ought to be concentrating solely on the final test to come and on whether or not this *project* of his was actually going to work and not smoke out the entire lodge.

He knew he should be nervous.

Instead, he was thinking about how similar his current emotions, those he experienced whenever he was with Jess, were to those of when he'd first received guardianship of Gracie.

Overwhelmed.

Confused.

Was this what it felt like to be in love?

He wished Ezra were here. He would know what Nate should do, or at least he would have had his back, leaving Nate feeling less exposed and vulnerable.

He remembered back to when Ezra first met Tamyra. Up until that day, Ezra had been a committed bachelor, just as Nate was. And then suddenly his friend was out to conquer the world, and he'd had the energy and confidence to back that up.

It had come, Nate knew, from the love of a good woman. Tamyra changed Ezra's whole outlook.

Ezra would have added his renewed faith in God, which seemed to go hand in hand with Ezra and Tamyra's deepening relationship. At the time, Nate had chalked it up to a man molding his life to please a woman, but now he was not so sure.

Had there been more to Ezra's faith? Was that what his friend had been trying to tell him?

Nate ran his fingers along the edge of the dried cement all around the stones, making sure there were no cracks in his handiwork.

For his part, Nate had teased Ezra unmercifully, and he'd certainly never understood what had come over his friend, not only to give up his bachelor freedom, but to step into the heavy-duty responsibility of being an active-duty marine, a husband and, eventually, a father.

There was a good reason Nate had never pursued a serious relationship with a woman, for who would willingly want to take on the life of a military spouse? He wouldn't have wished that on any of the women he'd dated over the years, and so he'd kept things simple, and the women at arm's length.

Or at least he'd *thought* that was the reason he'd remained emotionally distant.

Until now.

Until Jess.

Maybe the honest truth was he'd just never met the right woman—a woman who not only turned his head, but his heart.

Nate climbed down the ladder, only half aware when his feet met solid ground. With a grunt, he collapsed the twelve-foot ladder and carried it to the back of the building, where lodge guests wouldn't accidentally trip over it in their comings and goings. He would have put the ladder away, but the toolshed was already full to overflowing, and he thought he'd probably need it to climb back on the roof for the county inspection.

Funny, but now that he'd been thrust into a role of responsibility for another person, an unexpected new father figure for baby Gracie, becoming a family man didn't seem so bad.

Overwhelming, to be sure.

But not bad.

He'd never imagined that having someone depending on him for his well-being would feel so—*good.*

And never, ever, in a million years would he have imagined he could love someone as much as he did that baby girl.

If only his relationship with Jess was as straightforward and uncomplicated as his relationship with Gracie. He had less trouble reading Gracie's mind than he did trying to figure out what Jess was thinking.

He let himself into his father's apartment without knocking. These days, Pop anticipated his visits, and Nate certainly enjoyed spending time with his father. If he wasn't mistaken, it seemed to him that Pop was getting stronger and healthier by the day, a fact that Nate thanked God for.

"When are you going to bring my little granddaughter around again?" his father asked as Nate fiddled with the flue to the chimney. He'd done quite a bit of construction on the lodge when he was a boy, but building this fireplace for his father had been a new kind of challenge. He wanted it to be just perfect when the inspector came.

"The county inspector comes out tomorrow," he said aloud. "I'd like to invite Jess to be here, so maybe I'll bring Gracie along as well."

Pop crowed happily. "You do that. I can't get enough of her. You know I have a God-given responsibility to spoil that baby girl."

Nate chuckled and shook his head. "I'll keep that in mind."

He turned to face his father, who cocked his right eyebrow at him. With the way the left side of his face sagged from nerve damage, it gave his pop kind of a comical look.

"What?" Nate asked.

"You," his father replied sagely. "You look different."

Nate gazed down at his jeans and olive-green T-shirt, the same as he always wore. He shrugged. "I don't know what's different."

Pop guffawed loudly. "Not your clothes, boy. Your face."

Nate instinctively ran a hand across his cheek, noting the stubble. Other than the fact that he needed to shave, he couldn't feel any difference. "What's wrong with my face?"

"How is Jessica doing?" Pop asked, ostensibly changing the subject.

"Jess? She's fine. Why?"

Pop crowed again and pointed at Nate as if in accusation. "I knew it! I *knew* it! You're walking around with your head in the clouds, boy. There's only one thing that can put such a gleam in a man's eye, and that's a good woman."

Nate spent exactly two seconds thinking about trying to talk his father out of his fanciful notion, and then decided it wasn't worth the effort. Pop was dead-on with his assumption, and anything Nate could think of to say would only confirm it and subject him to an even worse bout of teasing.

Better just to remain silent.

He turned back to the fireplace and grunted. "Shall we light her up?"

Pop chuckled. "By all means. Let's see if a bomb defuser can build something up as well as he takes things apart."

Nate stiffened, feeling that his father was talking about more than just the new fireplace. Nate had torn down his share of family relationships over the years.

But Pop was still chuckling, so Nate let it go. He placed a couple of logs he'd cut earlier in the fireplace, and then added some old newspaper for kindling, pushing the wadded-up paper into the cracks between the logs.

"Ready?" he asked, glancing over his shoulder as he fished in his pocket for a pack of matches.

Pop beamed and nodded.

Nate struck a match and lit the crumpled newsprint in several places, blowing on the small flames to add more oxygen. After a moment, the wood caught fire, and soon there was a warm, snapping blaze.

Still crouched before the fireplace, Nate leaned on his elbows and stared intently at the crackling flames, thinking how the golden warmth reflected what he was feeling in his heart.

Life was good.

Better every day, in fact. He couldn't help but send up another silent thank-you to God. He seemed to be doing a lot of that lately, he realized.

Pop wheeled his chair up next to Nate and laid a hand on his shoulder.

"It's wonderful," Pop said in a hushed tone.

"Yeah, Pop," Nate agreed in the same quiet, reverent tone of voice. "It is."

Nate bounded forward with the most adorable combination of anxiety and youthful anticipation that Jessica simply didn't have the will to resist him when he showed up at her cabin an hour before she was due at the day care and asked her to spend the day with him while the county inspector looked over his handiwork.

The day care wasn't at full capacity today, and she knew the other teachers could handle the children. Besides, Nate had coerced her with the knowledge that Jason Morningway wanted to spend some time with Gracie, and Nate would, he wryly pointed out, be too busy with the inspection to keep an eye on the baby.

She felt decidedly awkward after the kiss she'd shared with Nate, but he wasn't treating her any differently than he ever had, so she forced herself to relax and go with the flow, mentally denying the intimacy she was feeling in her heart.

Could she put the past behind her and forge her future with Nate? Her stomach clenched just thinking about it.

Eventually, she would have to face what she was walking headlong into. She would have to put a label on them. She would have to crawl off the fence she'd been straddling since the day she'd met Nate and Gracie and declare a side.

But not today.

This day belonged to Nate, and Jessica wanted to be by his side as he triumphed over the skeletons in his own closet.

She didn't protest when he took her hand to help her out of his Jeep, nor when he hitched Gracie to his other side and laced his fingers through Jessica's. He was looking for support, she reasoned; and after all, that was what she was there for.

The county inspector, who introduced himself as Michael Sheridan, was waiting for Nate in the dayroom, sitting on the sofa and consulting his clipboard.

She and Nate ushered Michael into Jason's apartment and the inspection began. Giving Jessica's hand one last squeeze, Nate slipped Gracie into her arms and turned his attention to Michael Sheridan's questions. Not wanting to be in the way, Jessica hurried to Jason's side and propped the baby in his lap.

She watched the inspection from a distance, her attention slipping back and forth between Nate and Michael, and Jason and Gracie.

To her surprise, Jason slowly lifted his left arm and crooked it to give Gracie a better seat on his lap. The strain on his face told her what kind of effort he was expending, but the results were astonishing.

"Why, sir," she exclaimed. "You're moving your left arm!"

Jason grinned widely and winked at her.

"Call me Jason, please. And yes, I'm getting limited movement back in my arm. My leg is still giving me problems, but my physical therapist is hopeful I'll regain some sensation there."

"That's wonderful news!"

"Rosemary, my physical therapist, is a real drill sergeant. She doesn't let me get away with anything, and she is constantly pushing me to work beyond what I think I can do."

"Sounds like she's doing her job," Jessica teased, punctuating her sentence with a chuckle as she slid into a chair across from Jason and leaned forward. Nate was leading Michael outside, so she turned her full attention to Jason and Gracie.

"And this little one," he continued, kissing Gracie on the forehead, "has turned the word *motivation* right on its ear."

"She does that, doesn't she?" Jessica queried softly, reaching her index finger out so the baby could clasp it. "She's turned all of our lives inside out."

Jason chuckled. "Only Gracie?"

Her gaze snapped to the old man, who was grinning at her like the cat who had eaten the proverbial canary.

Jessica felt her skin burning from the tips of her toes to the top of her head, and knew she must be blushing a frightful color of red.

"So I take it from your reaction that my son is getting to you, as well?"

Jessica rocked back in her chair as if he'd physically pushed her there. He hadn't touched her with more than his words, of course. It was a good thing, too, Jessica thought. If he so much as grazed her with his pinky finger, she would no doubt fall to the floor.

"I— He—" she stammered, but couldn't seem to get her mouth to form a single coherent word for the life of her.

And what would she say, anyway?

How could she deny what was clearly written all over her face, at least if Jason's gleeful chuckle was anything to go by.

Jason patted her knee reassuringly. "There, there, dear. I apologize. I didn't mean to embarrass you. This old man just doesn't know when to keep his opinion to himself."

"It's not that," she assured him, sweeping in a giant breath of air in order to keep herself from feeling that a noose was tightening around her neck. "I just—it's just that I'm a little confused right now."

"Of course you are," Jason agreed with a knowing nod, now laughing heartily.

Gracie stared up at her grandfather a moment with wide, startled eyes, and then flapped her arms and squealed happily, catching Jason's excitement.

Jessica stared at the baby and tried desperately to regain her equilibrium. *Confused* didn't even begin to cover what she was feeling.

Jason winked. "I still remember how completely out of my head I was when I fell in love with Nate's mother. It was a disconcerting feeling, to say the least."

Jessica dragged her gaze away from Gracie and centered it on Jason. The choking sensation had returned with reinforcements.

Fall in love?

Was that what she was doing?

There was no denying her strong attraction for Nate, or how empty her little cabin felt whenever he and Gracie weren't present.

But *love?* Did she even dare think of the word in context with Nate Morningway?

The L word, her friends in high school used to call it. *First comes love, then comes marriage, then comes the baby in the baby carriage.*

Only this time the baby had come first. But that didn't make what she felt for Nate any less real or tangible. If anything, it only added to the joy she felt whenever she was around the two of them.

And the confusion.

Because she could never forget—not for one second—that she had already been around this particular block once, and with disastrous results.

A shattered heart. A broken home.

A husband who didn't mean his wedding vows for forever.

Even with the faith in God she now held dear to her heart, there were no guarantees in life. Her destination was assured, but the road getting there could be bumpy, and she knew that better than anyone.

If she gave her heart to Nate, she risked having it broken all over again. It had taken her two years to even begin to recover from her last relationship. She might never recover from another bad experience.

"Are you okay?" Jason asked, breaking into her thoughts.

"Huh?" she asked, dazed. "Oh. Yes. Everything is fine."

Jason looked deeply into her eyes and shook his head. "I don't think so."

Jessica didn't know the words to say to put Jason's mind at ease. *Her* mind wasn't at ease. And somehow she could tell Jason knew that.

But as it happened, she didn't have the opportunity to say anything, as Nate burst back into the room, followed by Michael Sheridan, who was still scribbling notes on his clipboard.

"Light the fire," Michael said, tapping the point of his pen against the clipboard.

Nate winked at Jessica as he moved to the fireplace to do as he was bid. Jessica smiled to herself. Apparently all was well with the inspection. She was glad, for Nate's sake.

After a few more minutes, the inspector announced that he was finished, and he complimented Nate on a job well done.

Nate beamed. Jason chuckled under his breath.

Jessica wondered if Jason understood just how important it was for Nate to complete this project for his father. She thought, gazing at Jason's bright gray eyes, that he probably did.

"Jess and I will walk you out," Nate told Michael. He moved to Jessica's chair and held out a hand to her. "You'll be okay with Gracie for a few minutes, won't you, Pop?"

Jason chuckled. "Take all the time you need. My little granddaughter and I are doing just fine here all by ourselves."

Jessica accepted Nate's hand, and wasn't really surprised when he didn't let it go after she'd stood. Despite her mixed feelings, it felt *right* to be linked with Nate in such a natural way.

Together, they walked the inspector outside. Jessica heard the sound of a table saw splitting wood the moment they walked out the door, and absently wondered where it came from.

As soon as they stepped off the porch, she saw the source of the sound. Vince was at the far side of the lodge, dressed in jeans and a denim shirt that Jessica thought looked odd on a man who usually wore a suit, despite the fact that they were at a mountain retreat. A backward-facing baseball cap covered his hair.

Looming behind Vince was the project he was clearly working on. He had framed in what looked like was going to be a good-size shed and was now cutting plywood to attach to the two-by-fours.

Nate lifted his free arm and waved to Vince, who just stared back at the small group, his arms propped on his hips, his posture suggesting they'd somehow interrupted his work. Still, Jessica was proud of Nate for trying, even when Vince didn't respond positively.

Nate's movement caught the inspector's attention, and he looked to where Vince was building. His gaze narrowed as he crooked a hand over his forehead to block the glare of the sunshine so he could see better.

"Who is that?" Michael asked.

"My brother, Vince," Nate answered cordially. "He runs Morningway Lodge."

"I see," Michael muttered, tapping his pen on his clipboard for a moment before moving decisively in Vince's direction.

Nate flashed Jessica a surprised look before following the inspector to where Vince was working.

"Vince, this is county inspector Michael Sheridan. He's come to look over the fireplace I built."

Vince wiped his palms against his jeans and then held out a hand to Michael.

"I assume you have a permit to build here?" Michael asked, looking over Vince's shoulder and gesturing toward the frame of the shed.

Vince's gaze widened, and he shook his head. "No, sir. It's just a shed. My old one is full to overflowing with tools. I thought I'd better get another one up before winter hits us hard. It's not a big building project or anything."

"Even so," Michael continued, "you will need to have a permit to build."

Vince looked flustered. And frustrated. Jessica squeezed Nate's hand, wondering if he might be able to say something—anything—to diffuse the situation. She felt Nate tense, but he remained silent.

"Is this a new law?" Vince asked. "I don't recall my father getting permits to build. And this is private property."

"I realize that," Michael said, his voice a clipped, businesslike monotone. "And yes, the law is new—at least relative to the age of your property. Still, the fees must be paid in to our office before you can continue with your work here."

"I see," Vince said, not sounding happy about it at all, and Jessica couldn't blame him. He had enough to worry about without having to jump through extra hoops to complete a simple project. "In that case, I'll see to getting a permit right away."

"I'm afraid I'm going to have to insist that it be done immediately," Michael informed him, his voice and expression neutral. "If not, you will be fined for building without a permit. I warn you now, the fine is pretty steep."

"You'd fine me over one shed?" Vince snapped, then pinched his lips together and frowned.

"That's the way it works," the inspector insisted. "I don't make the rules, but I do have to enforce them."

"Yes, sir. Of course. I understand, and I'll see to it right away."

"All right, then. I'll expect to see you in my office immediately, so we can clear up this paperwork."

Vince nodded, his face still strained, but the inspector had already turned to Nate.

"Mr. Morningway," Michael said, shaking Nate's hand. "It's been a pleasure."

"Thank you, sir," Nate responded. His voice was coarse and cracking, and Jessica knew he was struggling merely to speak. She squeezed his hand again as Michael got into his vehicle and turned off down the unpaved road.

Nate immediately turned to Vince, his arm outstretched in supplication. "Hey, I'm sorry about that, bro. I didn't realize that—"

Vince whirled on him, his sizzling scowl bringing Nate's words to an instant stop.

"Well done, little brother," Vince said, his voice sharp with sarcasm. "You've really gone and done it this time, haven't you?"

Chapter 11

Though Vince hadn't moved from where he'd been standing, Nate felt as though his brother had sucker punched him right in his gut. He stiffened to keep from clutching at his midsection.

"What did *I* do?" Nate knew his question sounded defensive. It was. And it was the wrong question to ask. He already knew Vince was going to blame him for whatever inconvenience he would face.

"If they slap me with a fine because of this stupid permit business it's going to be on your head. I have to meet with suppliers in Denver this week, so I'm not going to be able to get it right away. Thanks a lot, Nate."

Nate dropped Jess's hand and took an unconscious step backward, as if reeling from a blow. He felt the overwhelming urge to come out swinging, to settle their differences the way they had as children.

He hoped he'd matured a little bit in ten years, and with effort, he unclenched his fists. Still, he couldn't let it completely go. "How is it my fault you didn't get a permit before you started building?"

Real mature, there, Morningway, he chastised himself. *Way to go.*

"I didn't know I was supposed to get a permit for a measly shed," Vince barked. "Pop never needed a permit to build."

"Look," Nate said, holding out his hands in a placating manner. "I just wanted to do this fireplace thing on the up-and-up. It's been years since I've built anything. I had to make sure it was safe, for Pop's sake. You wouldn't have wanted me accidentally burning down the lodge, now would you?"

Nate scowled, hating the feeling he had to justify his actions to his brother. Vince glowered back at him, which didn't help matters at all.

"Sure. Make me look like the bad guy."

Nate opened his mouth, then snapped it closed again. Of all the pigheaded, irrational—

He jumped, startled, when Jess placed her hand on his arm. When he'd started butting heads with his brother, he'd almost forgotten she was there. Guilt and humiliation flooded through him, raw and stinging. It was bad enough that Vince thought him every kind of fool without having Jess as an audience.

"We need to go get Gracie," she said, her voice low and even, as if she hadn't just witnessed the juvenile scene in front of her. "Despite what he said, your father isn't up to watching her for an extended period of time. He's still so weak, and you know how wiggly she gets when she has to sit still too long."

Nate sighed, the anger draining from him. Jess was right. And more than that, she was clearly giving him a way out of his latest confrontation with Vince.

Vince shrugged and waved his arm in what Nate thought was a condescending manner.

"Go get your baby," Vince snapped. "But this isn't over between us, bro. Not even close."

Nate thought it the best part of valor not to respond at all, so he turned and stalked away, hearing Jess's murmur of surprise and her quick steps after him.

In record time, he said goodbye to his father and bundled Gracie in her car seat in the back of the Jeep, all the while not speaking to Jess at all. Wisely, Nate thought, she didn't try to strike up any kind of conversation with him, either, but simply buckled herself in and waited. He was in no mood for small talk, and he *sure* didn't want to talk about the humiliating incident between he and Vince.

Jess didn't speak until he had parked the Jeep in front of her cabin. Nate clutched the steering wheel as she opened the car door, but she didn't immediately disembark as he expected. If he had been in her position, he'd be running for cover right about now, fearing an imminent explosion.

Out of the corner of his eye, he could see that she'd turned toward him and was quietly searching his expression, but he just stared straight ahead, knowing he was glowering. Though it was unfair, he couldn't seem to be able to put a lid on his anger, even for Jess's sake.

"Are you okay?" she asked at last, her voice quivering with emotion.

Nate pinched his lips together and said nothing, afraid if he did he would bark at her.

"Vince was caught off guard," she explained, hesitating, her big brown eyes widening, when Nate's gaze snapped to hers. "Give him some time to think it through, and I'm sure he'll see reason."

"Why should he? He's right and he knows it," Nate growled sharply, then squeezed his hands on the steering wheel, angry at himself for lashing out at Jess. None of this was her fault. She was trying to be supportive, and he knew it.

"He's had a lot of time to think about my coming back home," he said, softening his tone. "All I've done is cause him problems since I've been here. This is just the icing on the cake."

Jess reached out and touched his shoulder, but he shrugged it off.

"You know that's not true," she pleaded. "Whether Vince wants to admit it right now or not, you've been a great help to him—and to your father. Jason is enjoying a warm fire as we speak because of all the hard work that you've done."

Nate snorted. "Pop is going to hear about this. What is he going to think of me interfering? Morningway Lodge is his baby. His dream. And now I've gone and made things more complicated for him by not thinking things through."

"Take a deep breath, Nate," Jessica suggested softly. "It isn't your fault Vince didn't get a permit. You followed the law, which was the right thing to do. Vince will realize that, too, once he's had time to cool off. I'm sure he wasn't trying to do anything illegal, so in the long run, this can only help him."

"Not if they slap a huge fine on him," Nate grated, his forehead aching from his deepening scowl.

"That doesn't have to happen, now does it? I mean, all the inspector said was that he has to go get a permit to build. How is that so bad?"

Nate shrugged. Jess was right. It wasn't an insurmountable difficulty, just an extra hoop to jump through.

Except…

"I don't know for sure, but I get the impression Vince doesn't have a lot of working capital. Morningway Lodge was built as a ministry, not to make a lot of money."

"Then I'll pay for it," Jessica stated, nodding and smiling as she warmed to the idea. "I have some money tucked away in my savings account that we can use to get Vince his permit."

Nate's gaze widened, and he surprised himself that his jaw didn't drop. His pulse pounded in his temple. "You'd do that for Vince?"

Her gaze widening, she shook her head. "Not for Vince. For you."

Nate tried to swallow around the raw lump of emotion burning in his throat.

"I'll do it," he said. "But I don't need your money. I have some savings of my own."

"Okay," she agreed with a gentle smile. "I'm sure Vince will appreciate it."

Nate barked out a dry laugh. "I don't know about that. But I'll sure feel better."

"And now that you're finished with the fireplace, maybe you could assist Vince in building his shed. You can't depend on the weather in Colorado to stay nice in October, and he'll need all the help he can get."

"Maybe," Nate agreed, but his mind was already migrating to more pleasant thoughts than trying to work things out with Vince.

Like how wise and thoughtful Jess was.

And how beautiful.

And how he didn't know if he could ever get along without her.

He felt closer to Jess in that one instant than he'd ever felt to another human being. His mind stuttered over the words to tell her what he was thinking, but they just wouldn't come out of his mouth.

What a time to get tongue-tied, when it suddenly seemed so monumentally important for her to understand how he felt, how much she meant to him.

"Jess, I—" he started, only to stumble to a stop. The awkward silence loomed before him in the air, feeling very much like that breath-holding moment when he was about to disarm a bomb, knowing that the slightest false move would cause it to blow up in his face.

Only this time he wasn't working to save the lives of others. It was his own heart on the line.

"Nate?" she asked, her voice full of concern.

He turned as much as his large body would allow within the confines of his seat. The steering wheel bit into his side, but he didn't really care.

The only thing that mattered was this moment.

This woman.

When she reached for the door handle, Nate put out his hand to stop her. Their fingers met, and the electricity between them was palpable.

"Jess," he said again, but when no more words came, he simply took her in his arms. He might not be able to tell her how he felt, he thought as he drew her to him, so close that their breath intermingled, but he could certainly show her.

With a groan that came from deep in his chest, he slanted his head and centered his mouth over hers. Her lips were soft and pliant, and without conscious thought, he deepened the kiss.

She was so sweet and giving. He heard her murmur as she clutched her fists into the lapel of his bomber jacket, but he didn't know what it was that she said, if it had been real words at all.

Time ceased to have meaning. There was only Jess. Sweet, wonderful Jess.

"Nate."

He loved the sound of his name on her lips.

"Nate, stop."

It was only then that he realized she was no longer clutching at his jacket to pull him closer, but was pushing him away, her hands flat on his chest.

His mind was still reeling with the discovery of his feelings for Jess, but he didn't miss her troubled expression, nor the tears that welled up in her huge brown eyes, making their depth seem infinite.

He sat back, giving her the space she obviously needed. "What's wrong, honey?"

"I'm sorry, Nate," she choked out, scrubbing her palms across her eyes as if she were angry at her own tears, as if it was a show of weakness.

Nate didn't think there was anything weak about Jessica Sabin. She had a strength of character he could only hope to aspire to, and she had the kind of faith that could move mountains.

But he had clearly upset her with his actions, and he felt like a big oaf for not realizing it sooner. If she needed more time, he would certainly give it to her. He'd only wanted to express what was in his heart, not cause her any kind of distress.

"I'm sorry, Jess," he apologized, his voice low and gravelly.

"No," she replied, so softly he could barely hear the word. She had been looking down at her hands, which were clasped in her lap, but now she gazed up at him. "*I'm* the one who should apologize."

The sorrow in her gaze took his breath away. He mentally scrambled to figure out what he had done to make her react that way.

"What?" he asked at last, still clueless as to what he had done, and even more as to what he should say, only knowing he needed to do *something* to make things right between them.

"I—I'm really sorry, Nate," she stammered. "But things just cannot go on this way."

Without another word, and without giving him the opportunity to say anything—not that his cloudy mind could think of anything to say—she reached behind her for the door handle and scrambled out of the Jeep and into her cabin, slamming both the car door and the cabin door behind her as she went.

Nate didn't try to follow her, gathering himself up enough to realize he wouldn't accomplish anything by pushing her too hard. But he sat for a long time in front of her cabin, his arms crooked over the steering wheel and his head on his arm.

What was wrong?

How could he fix it?

Not knowing where else to turn, he began to pray.

"Dear God, if You are there, and Jess believes You are, please help me. Please."

Sitting in the corner easy chair with the lights off, Jessica chastised herself as every kind of fool. And the worst thing was, the only one she'd been fooling was herself.

How had she thought, after the first time Nate had kissed her, that they could continue on as friends? Something foundational had changed between them in that moment, and she had either failed to recognize it or, more likely, had simply shoved it to the back of her mind and refused to acknowledge it, hoping against hope it would go away on its own.

Like *that* was going to happen.

She was an idiot.

And now she had hurt Nate.

She'd seen the pain of her rejection in his eyes, and that was the very last thing she ever wanted to do. She remembered his expression when she'd made her escape, and it broke her heart.

Of course the man was confused by her sudden emotional turnaround. She had sent him every mixed signal in the book.

If only she was the sweet, innocent woman Nate thought her to be. If only she had half the strength Nate attributed to her.

The memory of his voice warmed her heart even now—the way he laughed, how he tenderly shortened her name to *Jess*. He was the only one who called her that, and oddly enough, it was rubbing off on her. She was beginning to think of herself by that nickname.

If only there was no past—only the present and the future.

But all the wishing in the world would not make it so. It was what it was, and it was high time she stopped ignoring the facts.

Why, oh, why had she not been honest with Nate from the beginning?

It wasn't as if she hadn't had plenty of opportunities to tell him the truth about her past. She'd just chosen *not* to, despite the fact that he had opened up to her early on in their relationship, and had trusted her with the depth of his secrets.

Yet she had remained silent. And look where that had gotten her.

All this time she'd been telling herself that she was protecting herself from heartbreak, and now she faced the truth.

No more excuses. She cared for Nate—and Gracie—very deeply. And that raised the stakes to intimidating odds.

How could she now bring her past into casual conversation? *Dinner was lovely, and by the way, I've been married before.*

No. That would never work.

What she needed to do, she realized, was to confront the whole situation head-on and tell him everything she'd been hiding. She couldn't go on living a lie.

She had to revisit her past, and take Nate along for the ride.

Yes. That was what she would do. She would talk to him.

But not now.

Nate was up to his ears with the situation with Vince. Jessica thought it was best to give him time to work that out before she sprang anything new on him. He was in enough emotional turmoil without her adding dry kindling to the flame.

She wrapped a blanket around her legs and curled into the chair. She was no longer in denial, but she would put Nate's needs before her own.

It wouldn't be easy. She knew the next time she saw him, the weight of her decision would likely cause her to blurt it all out to him. And that was the last thing he needed right now.

Perhaps the best thing, for the time being, was not to see Nate at all.

Chapter 12

Nate had never been so frustrated in all his life. He was angry at himself for pushing Jess too far, too fast. In his rush to make his feelings known to her, he had trampled all over hers. He had clipped the wrong wire on the bomb and it had exploded.

He should have known better.

What concerned him most, however, was not the sad state of his own heart. It was Jess.

She was avoiding him.

At first, it had only been a suspicion on his part. He'd brought Gracie to the day care so he could go to Boulder to pursue getting the permit for Vince, and Jess had been nowhere to be found, even though her SUV was parked in the lot.

But what had started out as mere conjecture was now, in Nate's mind, an unavoidable fact. Not only was Jess not visible at the day care, but in the following week, she hadn't once called or come over.

And that wasn't like her.

No more shared dinners. No more quiet evenings. Nate was going out of his mind.

He could have sought her out, visited her cabin in the evening like he used to do. But if Jess was avoiding him—and she clearly was—it was for a reason. He hadn't a clue what that reason might be, but he sensed the right thing to do was give her the time and space she had asked for in her actions, if not with words.

But after an entire week of not seeing her pretty face, it was killing him to stay away. He didn't know how much more of this forced isolation he could take. It was sheer torture.

And because it was Saturday, he had nothing to do except think about it. Even caring for baby Gracie's needs didn't do more than mildly distract him.

It was still early morning, Nate realized when he glanced at his watch. How was he possibly going to make it through a whole, long empty weekend?

With Gracie fed and changed and now playing quietly in her playpen, Nate found himself pacing back and forth from the kitchen to the living room and back, feeling caged in by his own tiny cabin.

On his tenth trip from the kitchen to the front door, he finally decided he couldn't stand to be cooped up inside for another moment. He was so wound up mentally, and his muscles were so tense and tight, that he couldn't think straight.

"How about you and I go for a run, baby girl?" he asked Gracie, sweeping her into his arms and tossing her into the air. Her laughter echoed in the small cabin.

"I'll take that as a yes."

It only took him a minute to bundle Gracie up and prop her in the backpack. He was getting better at this baby stuff, he realized as he took off down the mountain path nearest to his cabin.

Now, if he could only adjust his learning curve with Jess. He knew it was pointless to beat himself up about it, but he felt as if he'd somehow failed in nearly every relationship in his life. He'd failed God. He'd failed his father, and then Vince.

And somehow, he'd failed Jess.

He'd been running down a little-used path, mulling over the situation with Jess, when she suddenly materialized in front of him.

At first he didn't believe his own eyes when she burst over a hill, her thick blond ponytail swinging behind her. Had he finally lost his mind completely, conjuring her up from some messed-up part of his brain?

But as she approached and slowed before him, he knew he wasn't dreaming.

She had obviously been running hard. Her face was flushed from exertion and she pinched at a stitch in her side as she struggled to slow down her labored breathing. Sweat poured from her brow, and wisps of hair that had escaped her ponytail framed her face. She looked like someone had sent her through a tumble cycle in a clothes dryer.

And Nate thought he'd never seen her look as beautiful as she did at this moment. Relief rushed through him at finally having the opportunity to see her face-to-face, just to be able to talk to her.

"Jess," he exclaimed, not able to keep the enthusiasm he was feeling from his voice. "I wondered when I would see you."

Jess's face showed a combination of shock and panic. Her eyes were wide, and her nostrils flared. She reminded Nate of a cornered wild animal, and he thought she might bolt at any moment.

He couldn't let that happen.

His meeting with her in the woods like this was nothing short of divine intervention. Had God been listening to the prayers he'd uttered only with his heart?

"Did you get the permit?" she asked politely. Nate thought she sounded almost as if she were speaking to a stranger, not a man with whom she'd shared so much of her life, a man with whom she'd shared kisses.

"It took the better part of a week, but yeah, I did finally get it. I'm glad Vince was tied up in Denver or this never would have worked."

"I'm happy to hear it went well for you. What did Vince say when you told him?"

Nate shrugged. "I haven't told him yet."

He wanted to add that he'd waited because he'd hoped she would be with him when he told his brother the good news. She had more than a vested interest in this, after all. It had been her idea in the first place.

But she'd already flashed him a distant smile and was jogging in place.

"Good to see you," she murmured, and then pulled herself up as she started to jog by him.

Nate's hands snaked out of their own accord, blocking her way. He didn't know what to say, but he knew he had to keep her here with him, so he blurted out the prominent thought on his mind.

"Have you been avoiding me?"

It was a rhetorical question. Of course she'd been avoiding him. The question was, *why?*

As he hadn't given her room to run by him, she stopped and took two steps backward, crossing her arms in the age-old line of defense. He wanted to reach for her and erase the tension on her face, but he knew that was probably the last thing she would want him to do, so he jammed his hands in the pockets of his gray sweatpants.

Jess stared at him for a long moment without answering him.

"Does it matter?" she finally asked, her voice so low Nate could hardly hear the words.

Her question angered him. And flustered him. And frustrated him. His pulse pounded in his ears.

What did she mean, *does it matter?* Did she think he was stringing her along in some way, toying with her emotions?

"*You* matter," he replied gruffly. "Jess, what's wrong? Talk to me. Whatever is bothering you, we can work through it together. Just please don't shut me out of your life. Please."

The fight instantly went out of her, and she physically drooped before taking a seat on an old log that had fallen along the side of the path.

"Okay, Nate," she said softly. "You're right. It's time you knew the truth about me."

Jessica sighed and folded her hands in her lap. This confrontation was inevitable. She'd known that since the moment she'd walked out of Nate's embrace a week ago. But that didn't make it any easier.

How would she ever find the words to make Nate understand what she didn't really comprehend herself?

How could she tell him that she couldn't go forward without moving back?

"I think—" she started, and then stopped and cleared her throat. "That is, I—"

She stared down at her hands, unable to find the courage to look Nate straight in the eye. He crouched before her and gently lifted her chin with the crook of his knuckle.

"Know this," he whispered raggedly. "Whatever it is that you need to say to me, it won't change the way I feel about you."

Jessica wanted to exclaim in disbelief, but his warm, gold-flecked gaze stopped her. He really believed in what he was saying.

He believed in *her*.

And she trusted him. Not because she had to, or because he was pressuring her to come clean with whatever was bothering her.

She just *did*. When he smiled at her, she felt as if she could see right into his heart. And she liked what she viewed there.

"There are some things about my past I haven't told you about. Things that make me nervous about a new relationship."

Nate nodded. "I know. Go on."

"You know?"

Nate nodded again and smiled in encouragement. He brushed his thumb along her cheek. "Nothing specific, of course. But I've been around you long enough to know that something's been bothering you, and I'm glad you want to talk to me about it."

The deep end wasn't going to suddenly become shallow, no matter how much she wished it to be so.

Jessica swept in a breath to calm herself before she could speak, and then dove in. "I feel really close to you and Gracie."

"We like you, too, Jessica Sabin."

"That's just it," she muttered.

"What? I don't understand."

"Jessica Sabin is my married name."

Married? Jess was *married?*

Whatever Nate had thought she was going to tell him, this was not it. His heart dropped through his shoes and his mind struggled to catch up.

"I didn't know," he breathed raggedly.

He reached for her left hand, gently uncurling her fingers and staring down at them.

Just as he thought. No ring.

"You aren't wearing a wedding band," he pointed out softly.

"Oh, no. I'm not married *now,*" she clarified briskly. "I was married. It ended."

"I see," he said, although he wasn't really sure he did. He didn't know whether or not to be relieved at her words. "I'm sorry."

He was still struggling to mesh the mental picture he had of the Jess he knew with the woman who was sitting before him now, telling him she'd had a whole other life before him that he knew nothing about.

"I had a baby," she said, her voice cracking under the strain of emotion. "A baby girl. Her name was Elizabeth. Sweet baby Elizabeth."

Nate reached for her other hand and pressed them both to his lips, and then close to his heart. He couldn't bear to hear the agony in her voice. He wanted to erase the suffering from her countenance.

When she hurt, he hurt.

And he hadn't missed the tense she'd used in reference to her daughter. *Had* a baby. Her name *was*.

When she didn't elaborate, he slid onto the log beside her and put his arm around her shoulders. She had to know he would be there for her, no matter what.

Still secured in the backpack, Gracie hadn't hollered or squirmed, so he thought she must have fallen asleep as she usually did from the rhythmic rocking movement of his jog. He was glad for it, since at the moment, Jess required his full attention.

"Was?" he asked gently.

"Elizabeth was eight months old when she passed," she said, her breath ragged. "I put her to bed one night as always. I checked in on her before I went to sleep myself, and she was fine. When I woke up the next morning, she wasn't breathing."

"Crib death," Nate whispered. He'd heard of the horrible term, but had never known anyone who'd lost a child to it. He couldn't even begin to imagine losing Gracie that way. Even the thought of it sent sharp stabs of panic through his chest.

What kind of horror had Jess lived through?

"Oh, Jess. I'm sorry."

"SIDS." She shook her head. "It was the beginning of the end for me. Or at least that was how it felt at the time."

Nate pulled her closer, feeling that, if he let her go, she would simply disappear.

"I can't imagine what you've been through."

"And I can't even begin to describe it." She stared off

into the distance, somewhere over Nate's left shoulder. "It was as if my grief for Elizabeth sucked the life right out of my body. I went through the motions of eating and sleeping, but my mind had retreated to somewhere deep inside me, somewhere where my sweet baby girl still lived. There was a big, black pit in my stomach. I kept waiting for it to grow smaller, but it never did."

Nate tenderly brushed a wisp of hair from her forehead. "That must have been awful."

His sympathy must have touched her heart, for tears sprang to her eyes and she quickly wiped them away.

"I still grieve for Elizabeth. Every single day. I miss her so much. But life keeps happening whether you are ready for it or not."

Nate knew the feeling. Ezra's death had been really hard on him, and Ezra was just a friend. If it hadn't been for the fact that he had Gracie to care for…

The baby, he realized, had been his lifeline during one of the toughest times in his life.

"How long has it been?" he asked gently and tentatively.

She sniffled. "Elizabeth would be nearly three years old now."

No amount of time would really be enough, Nate thought. Not ever. And her wounds were obviously still fresh—too fresh to talk about. At all.

How, he wondered, had he missed this deep of a dynamic in her life when he'd spent so much time with her?

Was he blind?

"And your husband?" he asked as an afterthought. "What happened to him?"

Jess looked away from him. "Russ didn't deal with

his grief in the same way I did. I know I wasn't looking at things rationally at the time, but I just couldn't understand the way he wanted to throw himself back into normal life."

"He did that?" Anger at a man he'd never met surged through him. Jessica deserved strength and support from the man who'd vowed to cherish her, not rejection and abandonment.

"I've had a lot of time to contemplate what happened. I know now that he was grieving, just in a different way than me. But at the time it felt like he was in denial, that he had betrayed Elizabeth's memory. I thought he didn't even care that Elizabeth's life had been snuffed out so prematurely."

"I'm so sorry," Nate said again. He knew he was repeating himself, but he didn't know what else to say. He wished with all his heart he was better with words, that he could think of something to say that would bring her real comfort.

But of course he couldn't, so he simply continued to hold her while she sobbed, gently brushing away her tears with the pad of his thumb.

"Russ tried to find me in the dark space into which I'd retreated. He really did. But I was inconsolable, and he needed someone to be there for him, too.

"That person wasn't me. Couldn't be me. And so he left."

"He left you?" Nate's voice rose in pitch with every word. He tried and failed to contain the sudden surge of righteous indignation he felt toward Jess's ex-husband on her behalf.

What kind of a man would leave his wife when she had just lost a child?

"He needed someone," she explained matter-of-factly. "And I wasn't there for him. He found someone else who was."

Nate clenched his jaw. "I still don't understand how he could—"

Jess cut him off. "We were divorced by then. She got pregnant. Russ married her. Maybe out of a sense of obligation. Maybe because he fell in love with her."

Honor? That man didn't know the meaning of the word, Nate thought fiercely. An honorable man didn't abandon the woman he'd married when the going got tough. That wasn't love. "Of all the inconsiderate, stupid, selfish—"

She cut him off again, this time with a wave of her hand. "It's the past, Nate. I've set aside my anger toward him. In a way, I kind of understand why he did what he did."

"He had no right to hurt you that way. Not when you were already suffering. If he were here now, I'd give him a piece of my mind." *And my fist,* he added mentally, fuming so strongly he thought he must be having smoke come out of his ears.

"I'm over it," she snapped, her composure breaking as she broke into a new round of sobs.

No, she wasn't.

Nate couldn't see how. No wonder she'd balked at the thought of a new relationship. She must have trust issues a mile long. And rightly so.

If he could stand before Russ Sabin right now, he'd throttle the man. He'd teach him a lesson he would never forget.

But then, he realized suddenly, if Russ had responded as a real man ought to have, nurturing and protecting the woman he'd sworn to love for better or for worse, Jess wouldn't be here now with Nate.

There was a part of him that was selfishly thankful Russ had turned Jess away, though he felt guilty for having such feelings.

If Jess was his wife, he would cherish and protect her with his last breath. It was the same flare of masculine emotion he felt for Gracie; yet at the same time, what he felt for Jess was completely different.

At that moment, Gracie wailed, kicking at Nate's back with her amazingly strong little legs and fisting her hands into his hair.

"Ow!" he exclaimed when she gave an exceptionally hard yank. "Take it easy, little one."

He reached behind him to untangle the baby's fingers, wondering how she had gotten such a firm grip in his inch-long hair. It must really be getting shaggy.

"Okay, sweetheart. That's enough of that, thank you very much."

To Nate's surprise—and relief—Jess laughed. "I think she's trying to tell you she's tired of being in the backpack."

"Or maybe that I need a haircut," he suggested with a grin, shuffling the backpack off his shoulders. Jess leaned in to help shuck it off, and soon baby Gracie was wiggling on Jess's lap.

He didn't consciously decide to slide his arm around her shoulders. It was as natural a move as the breath he took, and completely in line with the cacophony of his feelings for her.

"I don't know how you did it. I don't think I could have. And then you went to work as a day care director," he mused softly, running a palm over the baby's soft, smooth curls.

"Not that you aren't the best at what you do," he hastened to add, squeezing her shoulder. "But I'd imagine that would have been hard for you to work with children, given the circumstances."

"It was. And it wasn't. I've been working in day care since I graduated from college, and there was nothing else I've ever wanted to do, career-wise."

She paused, her gaze distant. "It was tough to go back. I have my good moments and my bad moments, but all in all, it's been kind of therapeutic for me to continue working with children. It's my passion and my ministry. I can't really imagine doing anything else with my life. And Morningway Lodge has been good to me. I've found peace here."

"I'm thankful you were here when I arrived," Nate said earnestly. "I know I would have been at a complete loss with Gracie if you hadn't been here to help us."

Jess nodded and kissed Gracie's forehead, laughing when the baby squirmed in protest. "Gracie is extra-special. In many ways she reminds me of Elizabeth, but always in a good way. Maybe that's why I feel so unusually attached to her, as I have from the very first moment I laid my eyes on her that first day you came to the lodge."

Nate could see the strain on her face as she spoke. None of this had been easy on her, and he realized he had inadvertently bounded into her life and played a part in causing her pain.

"I'm sorry," he said aloud.

Jess smiled tenuously. "So am I. But God was faithful even when people weren't. When I was in the blackest part of my grief, God reached out to me and pulled me through it, put me back on my feet again. Don't get me wrong. I still struggle. I still worry." Her eyes took on a luminous quality as they met his gaze and held.

A burning lump of emotion lodged in Nate's throat and, for a moment, he could not speak. He stared at her, his heart full of longing.

"You really believe that, don't you? In spite of everything you've been through, your faith in God is strong."

He couldn't relate. He'd persistently turned away from God, using every bad thing that happened in his life, every worldly tragedy he saw, as an excuse to go his own way. And yet the sum total of all of that was nothing in comparison to the personal agony Jess had gone through.

Jess shook her head. "No, that's not quite right, I don't think."

"What?"

"Not *in spite* of everything I've been through. *Because* of what I've been through, my faith is strong," she amended thoughtfully. "But it wasn't until I looked back on my life that I could see how God had carried me through the dark times, even when I cast the blame for my circumstances squarely at His feet. It's a long road. It took me a long time to accept that God loved me unconditionally, no strings attached, but when I finally did, He gave me the courage to go on."

Nate envied her that courage. He had faced IEDs threatening to blow up in his face with less fear than he had about facing his Maker.

He shook his head. "I don't know, Jess. You're a stronger person than me."

Her gaze widened. "Why, Nathan Morningway, I

think that is the most foolish thing I've ever heard come out of your mouth," she teased.

"Well, it's true."

"No, Nate. It isn't," she replied softly. "All of us are weak. It's only when we realize our limitations that God can reach us with His strength."

Nate felt a sense of panic surge through him and he didn't know why.

She reached out a hand and laid it on his forearm. "Stop running," she encouraged him. "In our weakness, He is made strong."

Chapter 13

Jessica didn't know what to expect after she and Nate talked, so she was more than a little surprised when Nate showed up bright and early Sunday morning, offering her a ride to church.

Relieved and surprised.

She'd never known a man like Nate Morningway. Even yesterday, as the words had burst out of her mouth that wiped her past clean, she knew Nate would never judge her for it.

She trusted him. She cared for him. And heaven help her, she was starting to see a future with him and that darling baby girl he now called his own.

The notion of offering herself up to any kind of relationship, any form of commitment, still frightened the socks off her.

But Nate himself, not so much.

She felt a lot of things for Nate, but not fear. As she'd learned the hard way, no one was completely faithful and unchanging, except for God. But Nate, she knew, would always do his best not to let her down.

As she would him.

While Nate's presence at church Sunday morning was a surprise in itself, his introspective attitude was even more confounding. Usually boisterous and outgoing, Nate had acted peculiarly quiet and thoughtful after the service and all during the drive home.

She'd remembered catching his gaze several times during the service. She thought he looked as if he was wrestling with something inside himself, and by the time they'd reached the car and Nate had yet to say a word, she was sure of it.

She hoped he might reveal to her what it was he was thinking so seriously about, but he continued to be silent, and she didn't ask. He was polite, but distant, and Jessica began to doubt herself and her earlier assurance that everything was working out between them.

What if Nate *couldn't* handle all the information she'd piled on him? What if it was too much?

Over and over she thought about asking him outright what was bothering him, but she wasn't sure she really wanted to hear the answer.

"Do you want to stay for lunch?" she asked him when he pulled the Jeep up in front of her cabin. "Nothing fancy, but I have some cold cuts for sandwiches."

Nate looked at her for a long time, almost as if she had spoken to him in a foreign language and he hadn't understood what she was saying to him.

What's wrong? she wanted to scream.

But of course, she didn't. She just sat frozen in her seat, staring back at him and wringing her hands together in her lap.

She wasn't even consciously aware of her stressed movement, but Nate clearly noticed. He leaned across the seat and laid his large hand over both of hers, stilling them.

"Maybe another time," he said gruffly, and tried to smile.

She thought her own answering grin wasn't any more convincing.

Again, Nate noticed. He brushed the rough pad of his thumb across her cheek, then pushed the corner of her mouth upward.

"It's going to be fine, beautiful Jess," he murmured. "It will all be okay."

Jessica wasn't sure of that. She wasn't even certain to what Nate might be referring. But she shrugged and nodded anyway.

"I know."

He smiled again, this time soft and genuine. "Tomorrow, then?"

She started to nod again, and then cocked her head to one side. "What's tomorrow?"

"You're going with me to tell Vince about the permit." He paused and screwed his lips into a wry pout. "You will go with me to tell Vince about the permit, won't you, honey?"

How could she resist him when he looked at her that way, his golden eyes glowing with warmth?

"Yes," she replied, knowing that was the only answer Nate would accept, and the only answer she wanted to give. "Yes, of course."

* * *

Nate couldn't seem to brush off the uneasy feeling that was hovering over him like a little black rain cloud. He tried to tell himself it was just that he had to confront his brother—*again*—with who knew what kind of a result waiting for him.

But that wasn't it.

Ever since Jess had told him the story of her past, he had been haunted by her words.

Because of what I've been through, my faith is strong.

And it was. With all the horrible tragedy the woman had experienced, she was a walking, breathing testament to God's existence and love.

Nate still didn't understand how that could be. He'd thought about it day and night. He'd gone to church and felt like the worst of all hypocrites, his own unbelief pointing its finger at him in accusation.

He'd thought maybe if he gave himself some time, he could sort it all out in his mind. He'd excused himself from having lunch with Jess, knowing she would see right through any kind of facade he hoped to establish. And then he'd spent a restless night tossing and turning, despite the fact that Gracie had peaceably slept the whole night through.

He was no closer to an answer now than he'd been twenty-four hours earlier, though he was a good deal more weary. And Jess was no doubt waiting for him to pick her up this morning so they could go tell Vince the good news about the permit.

Jess. He ought to be focusing on her.

Now that he knew the whole story of her past, he

understood the oddity of her hot-and-cold moments. He got why she unconsciously sent him mixed signals.

And he knew, now more than ever, that he wanted—*needed*—to be the man in her future, the one who *didn't* leave her when the going got tough.

Gracie needed her as well—to be the soft, feminine influence every little girl needed in her life. Jess offered Gracie something he never could give.

But Nate knew that in order to have the chance to be those things to Jess, he needed to speak the words that lingered quietly in his heart. It wasn't going to be enough just to show her. She needed to hear the sentiment from his own lips.

As always, he broke into a sweat just thinking about trying to put his emotions into words. What could he say that Jess would believe?

He was still pondering the dilemma when he picked Jess up from her cabin and they dropped Gracie off at the day care center.

Not surprisingly, Jess was acting a little withdrawn this morning. He couldn't blame her. In this instance, he had been the one who'd been sending mixed signals, and he knew it.

"Well, I guess it's now or never," he commented as he pulled the Jeep in front of the main lodge, breaking into the uncomfortable silence that had hovered over them for the entire ride over from the day care.

She stared at him for a moment, then smiled shakily. "Are you ready?"

"As ready as I'll ever be," he replied with a clipped nod. "Let's do it."

Nate took her hand as they entered the lodge and walked up to the guest services counter. He half expected her to pull away, and was glad when she didn't. He needed her support more than she could possibly realize.

He rang the bell on the desk and waited, his muscles tensing as if ready to spring into a quick getaway.

His marine training, he thought. Anticipating disaster was second nature to him now, and from where he stood, he felt as if he was facing a minefield.

The sensation increased when Vince came out of the office, his expression going from polite reserve to anger the moment he saw that it was Nate standing on the other side of the desk.

"What do you want?" Vince snapped without preamble, his brow lowering over his eyes.

"We're here with good news," Jess exclaimed, giving Nate's hand a tug, as if to remind him it was time for him to step up and take control of the conversation.

"Yeah? And what would that be?" Vince asked, crossing his arms over his chest in a combination of a protective and distancing manner.

Nate leaned his forearm on the counter, closing the space between himself and Vince.

"I spent most of the week in Boulder," he began briskly.

To Nate's surprise, Vince's expression turned to that of wary concern. "Where's Gracie? Did something happen? Is she okay?"

"Gracie is fine," Nate assured him. "We dropped her off at the day care before we came up here."

"Oh. I see," said Vince, who visibly relaxed for just

a split second before drawing himself back up to his full height. "Then what's the problem?"

"I've been to see the county inspector."

Nate held up his hand when Vince would have interrupted. "I know it may look like I'm messing with your business, Vince, but that's not how it is."

"How is it, then?" Vince asked acerbically, refusing to back down from his hostile stance.

"Look," Nate said, blowing out a breath to steady a surge of anger and doing his best to placate his unreasonable older brother. Getting mad wouldn't help his case any. "This whole building permit fiasco was my fault, so I thought it was only right that I be the one to clear it up."

He dug into his pocket and laid the signed permit in front of Vince. "It's a done deal. You—*we*," he amended when Jess nudged him, "can get that shed built now, before we get socked with a bad winter storm. Oh— and as of right now, the lodge is officially in the 'no fine' zone."

Vince studied the paper for a moment, his expression unreadable. Finally, he looked up, locking his gaze with Nate's.

"We?"

Again, Jess nudged Nate with her elbow.

He *got* it, already.

"Yes, *we*," Nate answered, his gaze flitting to wink at Jess before settling back on Vince. "Two heads are better than one, and all that. I figured since I plan on staying around for a while, I might as well be doing something useful."

Jess gasped and dropped Nate's hand. He turned to find her staring up at him, wide-eyed.

His shrug was meant for both Jess and Vince. "It's no big deal."

But it *was* a big deal, and all three of them knew it. There was a tense moment of silence while each of them were lost in their own thoughts.

Unable to take the strain of the sudden quiet, Nate thrust his right hand forward, toward Vince.

His brother just looked at Nate's extended hand for a moment without moving. Then, just as Nate was about to pull away, Vince suddenly put his hand forward and shook with Nate.

"Thanks for the permit," Vince said, pocketing the piece of paper.

"And the shed?" Nate prodded. "Do you want my help with it?"

Vince shrugged as if it didn't matter one way or the other, but Nate saw a sparkle of something in Vince's blue eyes that he hadn't seen before.

Acceptance?

"Do what you want, Nate," Vince said. "I'll be out here in the morning to work on the shed. With or without you."

It was as close to a peace offering as Nate knew he was going to get from his bullheaded brother, and he couldn't help but smile—first at Vince, whose frown never wavered, and then at Jess, who beamed back at him, showing without words that she knew he'd just won this battle, and that she was celebrating the victory with him.

Nate turned back to Vince.

"Done," he said, keeping his voice a clipped, businesslike monotone that belied the elation pounding in his chest. "I'll see you tomorrow morning, then."

"Whatever," Vince said grudgingly, and Nate just laughed.

* * *

"That went well," Jessica commented shyly. They'd been sitting in the Jeep for five minutes now, and Nate had yet to say a word, much less make any kind of effort to turn the key in the ignition to take them back to the day care to pick up Gracie.

He looked at her as if he was surprised she'd spoken to him.

"It did, didn't it?" he said, bemused. "What do you know?"

"I told you Vince would act rationally once he'd had time to think things over."

Nate flashed her a twisted grin.

"And now that you've solved his problem for him, I would hope that things will be better between the two of you."

"Do you think?" He chuckled. "Don't forget that I was the one who created the problem in the first place. I'm sure Vince won't."

"It's a start," she insisted, patting her knees for emphasis. "A good start."

"I don't know, Jess. I've spent all these years resenting Vince, but lately I've realized that the real problem is with me."

"No, it's not," she denied instantly, then paused thoughtfully. She wasn't doing Nate any kind of favor by blurting out her opinion before she'd listened to what he had to say. "I'm sorry, Nate. Go on."

"I don't know. I'm struggling, but I'm not sure why." He paused, squeezing his fists against the steering wheel. "Can I ask you a question?"

"Of course." She was both curious and hopeful as to what he would say.

"The other day, when you told me about Russ and Elizabeth, you explained how God got you through the bad times."

"Yes, that's true. He carries me through the bad times and rejoices with me in the good. I'm not saying faith in God erased my pain, or made it somehow magically easy for me. It's not. I struggle every day."

"You do?" he asked, sounding genuinely perplexed. "I wouldn't have guessed that. I mean, I know you have your problems, but you seem so joyful."

"I'm only human."

Nate nodded. "I know. It's just that you have such a sense of peace about you. I want that. I've been trying to do the right things with my life, for Gracie's sake as much as my own, but nothing I do seems to help. No matter how hard I try, I just don't perceive the world the way you do, with your faith."

"Maybe you're trying too hard," she suggested softly, reaching out to stroke his biceps.

"What else can I do?"

Jessica looked at Nate for a long moment, seeing him through new eyes. Here was a man who had worked hard for every single thing he had ever received in his life. He was a self-made man in the very best sense of all of those words.

So it just made sense that he would approach God the same way he approached everything else in his life. By putting Gracie ahead of himself. By asking himself what he could *do*. By measuring himself up to some impossible standard he'd created in his own mind.

"I think maybe you're approaching the idea of faith in God all wrong," she suggested tentatively, not wanting to inadvertently hurt his feelings.

"I am? How?"

"Being in a relationship with God isn't what you do. It's who you are."

Nate blanched a sickly white color. "I'm in trouble, then."

Jessica was taken aback. Nate had always exuded self-confidence. It was one of the things she admired most about him. And now he was demeaning himself with surprising fervency.

"Why do you say that?"

He shook his head, a wild look in his eyes, as if he was being pursued by something, as if he was the prey in some crazy hunt.

Jessica squeezed his arm. "What is it? Talk to me, hon."

"You know me better than anyone, Jess. When I should have been turning to God, I shunned Him. And now that I suddenly see how foolish I've been, and how much I want Gracie to grow up in the very faith I despised as a youth, you want me to believe God will just turn a blind eye and accept me the way I am?"

He didn't sound as if he believed it could be possible, and Jessica knew exactly how he felt. The circumstances were different, but at the heart of it all, not too long ago, she had been in the same place, spiritually speaking, that Nate was in now.

"God accepts you for who you are," she explained quietly, praying for the right words to make Nate understand. "But it's not because He blinds himself to your faults. He knows everything, Nate, and He loves you anyway."

He stared at her, unspeaking.

"The Scriptures say that while we were yet sinners, Christ died for us."

His mouth compressed into a tight line and his face became even more grim.

"But how can He…" His question drifted off into silence.

"I know that's a lot to wrap your mind around," she continued. "But it's true."

Nate reached for the ignition and gunned the Jeep into motion. Jessica thought to say more, but she could see she had overwhelmed him with what she'd already said. She drew her hand away from his arm and clasped her hands together in her lap, praying silently for God to reach Nate with His love, the way He had in her heart and life.

As Nate maneuvered down the road, he kept his gaze facing forward. Jessica watched him out of her peripheral vision, noting the stony expression on his face. With the way he was reacting, she maybe ought to have been worried about him, but her soul was oddly at peace.

God was clearly at work in Nate's heart, and she was thankful for both Nate's sake and for baby Gracie's. When all was said and done, Jessica had faith that God would prevail, even with tough, stubborn, single-minded Nathan Morningway.

God had reached her stone-cold heart when she didn't think anyone or anything could. She was so thankful that God was greater than their sins, even stubbornness and disbelief.

There was no doubt about it. Nate might be fighting it, but his heart was softening.

And when that final barrier had been broken, Jessica thought she might just lose her heart to Nate, once and for all.

Chapter 14

Nate's mind was a million miles away as he tried to wrap his thoughts around what Jess had said to him. It all appeared so monumentally complicated in his mind, but Jess made it sound simple and uncomplicated. Somehow she streamlined it in his mind in a way he hadn't thought of before.

What it boiled down to, Nate realized with a start, was faith.

Even after all his time with Jess, faith wasn't an easy concept for Nate to grasp. Yet in a way he could not begin to explain, he *felt* it—God's presence—as the truth of the Scriptures made the slow migration from his head to his heart.

"What is that?" Jess asked, pointing over the ridge in the direction Nate was driving. "Look at all the smoke. Is something burning?"

"Probably just a barrel of trash," he answered, still in a hazy state of mind. Then he glanced to where she was pointing and pressed down hard on the accelerator. The Jeep leaped forward in time with Nate's heart.

This was no burning barrel of trash. The smoke billowing out over the top of the tree line was too thick and too black to be an organized burn. His gut clenched as he realized he was driving right into it.

The day care.

Gracie was there, along with at least a dozen other small children and two teachers.

"Nate?" Jess questioned uncertainly.

Nate flashed a quick, encouraging glance at her, most of his concentration on maneuvering the Jeep across the washboarded dirt road at the highest speed he dared. He hoped the shock and panic registering on Jess's expression didn't reflect his own gaze.

"The day care!" Jess exclaimed. "Oh, God help us. Nate, hurry!"

Responding to the horror in her tone, Nate gunned the engine, clasping the wheel tightly with both hands as the Jeep fishtailed around a curve. In moments, they had crested the ridge and could see into the valley where the day care was located.

At his first glimpse of the flames and smoke pouring from the burning building, the knifing pain in his belly stabbed into his chest and throat. As he drove nearer, the black, ugly clouds of smoke billowing from the front windows seemed to be blocking out the sunlight. Flames surged from the windows on the east side of the building.

The day care, like all of the other buildings on the Morningway retreat grounds, was built to resemble a rustic, old-fashioned log cabin. Nate wondered, fighting down panic, how fast a structure such as this one would burn to the ground.

Too fast.

Nate took in the whole chaotic scene at once. One of the teachers was ushering a handful of preschoolers away from the burning building. The children were surprisingly subdued, given the circumstances. They moved in an organized line. The teacher, an older woman, was scurrying back and forth between the front and back of the line, pointing toward the trees and encouraging the children to walk faster, away from the burning structure.

Nate refocused his gaze on the building itself just as the second teacher emerged from the front door, covered with soot. She carried a little girl under her arm like a football and was pulling another child, a little boy, by the hand. Scooping the boy up in her other arm, she rushed toward where the other teacher and the children now stood, hunched in small groups near the tree line.

He heard Jess praying under her breath, her fists clenching the dashboard as she leaned forward to survey the scene. "Lord, help us."

Nate sped into the parking lot and punched on the brake. The Jeep slid several feet on the loose gravel under the tires.

Jess was out the door before the Jeep had slid to a stop.

"Jess, no!" Nate cried out. He reached out to grab her, to stop her from putting herself in harm's way, as he knew instinctively she had every intention of doing. Like him, her only thought was for Gracie and the other children trapped in the inferno.

His hand met empty air. Jess was already rushing toward the burning building.

Nate looked after her for a split second that felt like a lifetime, his entire being supplicating God for help as Jess disappeared through the billow of black smoke coming through the open front door of the building. His stomach lurched and he swallowed hard, forcing down the increasing sense of fear and panic eroding his thoughts.

Focus, he ordered himself, forcing a breath into lungs that appeared to have stopped working.

He jammed his hand into the front pocket of his bomber jacket and retrieved his cell phone, while with the other hand he was putting the Jeep into Park and shutting down the ignition.

His first instinct was to run in after Jess, but he wasn't sure if either of the teachers now huddling over the children near the tree line had a cell phone with them, nor if they would have the presence of mind to make the necessary call.

It looked as if they had all they could do just to contain the gaggle of children, some of whom were staring wide-eyed at the blaze, others who were chattering up at the adults, though Nate could barely hear them through the ringing in his own ears. He felt a little dizzy, and he realized he was hyperventilating.

He had to pull it together, to remain in control, for Jess's sake now as well as Gracie's. His military training finally kicked in, slowing his pulse and his breathing so he could think.

He jumped down from the Jeep and was racing toward the front of the day care center even as he punched in the emergency number. Thankfully, a new cell tower had recently been built just north of the Morningway property, and the signal on his phone was strong. After just one ring, the emergency dispatcher picked up.

"Nine-one-one. What is the nature of your emergency?"

"This is Nathan Morningway of Morningway Lodge," he said, enunciating every word. "We need the fire department here right away. The day care center is on fire. I think there are still some little kids inside. I don't know how many."

One, for sure. His baby.

His baby!

He paused before the entrance of the building and gave the emergency dispatcher all the necessary information on the location. Fear like he'd never experienced before clutched at his chest, and he could barely think past the pain.

What if he lost Gracie—or Jess?

No!

He couldn't—wouldn't—think that way. He had to get into that building and get them out of there.

Alive.

"Please stay on the line, sir," the dispatcher said in the calm, determined manner to which Nate knew she had been trained.

"Just get them here quickly," Nate replied. "I've got to go. My daughter is in there."

Panic preceded every thought as he snapped the phone closed and took one last deep breath before plunging into the smoky room, ducking as low as he could to the floor while still at a dead run, one arm sheltering his mouth and nose.

He couldn't see a thing through the black smoke, so

he reached out his other arm in front of him, hoping to feel his way around, if it came to that.

Suddenly he felt a hand on his arm.

It was Jess. He could barely see her through the haze and the way the smoke stung his eyes, but she was there, holding a handkerchief over her mouth and nose and gesturing with her free hand, pointing back toward the front door where he'd just entered.

What was she trying to tell him?

Jessica's hand slid from Nate's upper arm and clasped to his wrist in an iron grip. She tugged in earnest, but he was so tense his arm didn't budge. She knew he couldn't see anything through the thick smoke, and the fire was roaring too loudly for him to hear her speak. Touch was her only choice in finding a means to communicate with him.

She fought down the rising surge of panic. They were running out of time, and she couldn't get Nate to move in the right direction.

She yanked harder and felt him subtly shift. Desperate for him to understand, she dragged his hand in front of her, waist-high, where several children were huddled. When his fingers connected with one young boy's silky hair, she felt him freeze as the realization of what she wanted finally hit him.

When she'd burst into the building moments earlier, she'd found five small preschoolers huddling under the art table. Her first thought had been to go for Gracie, but she couldn't abandon these tiny innocents to the elements, no matter how much her heart cried out for the baby she knew was in the next room.

The children had been terrified and afraid to move,

and she hadn't been able to reassure them with her voice. Dropping to her knees, she'd gathered them in front of her, in her arms, and then was attempting to push and prod them toward the door and safety when Nate had materialized next to her.

They needed to get these kids out, so they could get to Gracie before it was too late. The raging fire itself wasn't the only danger. Jessica was already feeling the effects of smoke inhalation despite the handkerchief over her nose and mouth. Granted, the children were smaller and therefore lower to the ground, but the thick, merciless smoke had to be affecting them, as well.

And Gracie…

Panic surged again, painful in its intensity, but she tamped it back, willing herself to focus and concentrate on what needed to be done.

Nate nodded frantically, letting Jessica know he understood what she was trying to tell him. She let go of his wrist, and a moment later, he had a mop-headed little girl in one arm and a young boy in the other. Jerking his head in the direction, he turned, he lurched toward the front door.

Jessica was right on his heels, holding one toddler in her arms and clasping the other two by the hands, dragging them forward with a momentum she hardly believed she possessed, fear and adrenaline making up for whatever strength she might have lacked.

They all burst outside at the same time. The sunshine temporarily blinded her as she choked and coughed and propelled the children forward, toward the teachers and the rest of the waiting children.

"How many?" she choked out, aiming her question at no one teacher in particular.

"Thirteen," called Miss Cathy, who was in charge when Jessica wasn't present. The sheer panic on her face, along with the older woman huddled over the children at the tree line, matched the turmoil in Jessica's own heart.

"We've got them all, Jessica, except for Gracie," Miss Cathy continued hastily. "I'm sorry. The chaos. I couldn't leave the children to—"

"Keep those children away from the building," Nate ordered, sternly staring down first one teacher, then the other, looking ominous and almost threatening with swirls of ash lining his powerful face.

He whirled and ran full-force back toward the building. Jessica was right on his heels. After a moment, he became aware she was following him and tossed a stern glare over his shoulder.

"Go back with the children," he barked in the same no-nonsense voice that had worked so well with the teachers and, Jessica imagined, dozens of marines over his years in the service.

"No way," she uttered through gritted teeth.

She was determined to continue back into the building, no matter what Nate thought, and she only balked for a moment at his harsh tone before starting forward again, resolve in every step, moving at such a quick pace she soon rushed in front of him.

"Jess," he roared, reaching out to grab her arm in a viselike grip. "Go back. I don't have time to argue with you."

"Then don't. We have to get Gracie!" Panic edged her voice, but her movements were surprisingly firm.

"I'll get Gracie," he said, pulling her backward and

stepping in front of her. "You go back. The children need you."

"Gracie needs me," she insisted, jerking her arm away from his grip and dashing into the day care, gagging as the smoke pierced her lungs, thicker even than it had been before. She ducked down, trying to avoid the worst of the smoke.

Nate burst through the door moments after Jessica, ducking down just as Jessica had, and gestured for her to go ahead of him. She knew the way better than he did, and she was glad he was no longer fighting for her to leave the scene.

She moved without hesitation into the adjoining area, the nursery, and immediately moved to the left side of the room. Cribs ran the circumference of the room, and she frantically struggled to get her bearings for what felt like hours but was probably only seconds.

The smoke was so thick she hardly knew which way was up. She prayed as she hastened toward what she hoped was the crib where she usually placed Gracie when she was working in the day care, hoping that the other teachers had placed her in the same spot.

A beam right above their heads cracked ominously, and Jessica ducked instinctively, then staggered the last few feet to the crib. She couldn't see him, but she sensed Nate was right behind her.

Her eyes and her lungs burned with the effort, but as she approached, she thought she saw movement from within the crib, though with the thick smoke, she couldn't be certain.

Panic surged through her once again.

Gracie!

She had to get to the baby.

ithout another thought, she reached for the metal
that would release the side of the crib.

Jess, no!" he tried to scream, but the heavy smoke
owed into his lungs and he gagged instead.

His warning, even if he'd been able to voice it, had
ome too late. Jess wrapped her bare hand around the
metal latch and then jolted and staggered backward,
cradling her burned skin close to her chest. Her mouth
was open, but no sound emerged.

She would have fallen, but Nate darted forward and
swept her against him, one arm wrapped firmly around
her waist and the other urging her mouth closed.

More than one beam cracked and whined above
them, and the heat was growing more intense by the
second. He was feeling woozy again, but he fought the
sensation with every fiber of his being.

As from a great distance, he heard the sound of si-
rens, but he knew he didn't have time to wait for the
firefighters to help with the rescue. He had to get his
baby girl and the woman he loved out of this building
before the whole thing came down on them.

Pulling Jess with him, he reached over the edge of
the crib, relief flooding through him when his hand
made contact with the baby's head. Gracie was sitting
up, her arms flapping in distress.

Nate reached for her, but Jess was faster.

Ignoring her own injury, Jess plucked Gracie from
the crib and tucked her as far beneath her jacket as the
material would allow, trying to protect the baby from
additional smoke inhalation. The action left Jess's own
lungs unprotected from the smoke, and put her at the
very great risk of losing consciousness.

He had to get them out *now*.

He reached out and grabbed the collar of Jess's coat, dragging her with him to the nearest window. His head was swimming from the lack of oxygen, but his mind was amazingly focused on this single task.

Get them out alive.

There was no time to work their way back to the front door, and Nate suspected the fire had made the route impassable, in any case.

Sending up a silent prayer for his actions to work, he turned sideways to the window, bent his elbow and slammed into the glass.

Pain shot through his shoulder as the glass splintered but did not break. Knowing there was no time to waste, he ignored the pain, gritted his teeth and threw his shoulder into the window again.

This time, the glass shattered under the full force of his weight. Nate gasped as oxygen poured through the window, but his relief was short-lived as the fire all around them flared to a new intensity, being fed by the burst of air.

The blaze was growing worse by the second, and Nate didn't hesitate as he pulled the sleeve of his bomber jacket over his right hand and thrust his arm around all four sides of the windowpane, jarring loose jagged edges of glass so the three of them could crawl through to safety.

Two firefighters, dressed in full regalia and face masks, reached for Nate's arms, gesturing for him to crawl through the window.

Nate balked and jerked away from their grasp. He wasn't about to go through that window until Jess and Gracie were safe.

Jess nudged Nate's side with her shoulder, then shoved the now-limp baby into his arms, gesturing wildly toward the window.

Nate wanted Jess to exit with Gracie, but he knew she wouldn't budge until the baby was safe.

He stepped forward, thrusting Gracie at the two fire-fighters. The baby had clearly lost consciousness, and terror such as Nate had never known coursed through him. He prayed with all his might that they had not arrived too late to save her.

If he lost Gracie…

No.

He couldn't think of that now. Jess was still standing behind him, and she was still in very great danger from the flames around them.

He spun on his heels and reached his arms to her, intending to catapult her through the window and into the waiting arms of the firefighters.

But this nightmare was far from over. He didn't even know for sure that they hadn't missed any little children when they had evacuated the building. He prayed the teacher's head count had been right.

He could only react to the moment and pray for the best.

Only seconds had passed, but it felt like hours. He stepped toward Jess, his arms outstretched. Jess reached back to him.

Their fingers met. Their eyes met through the smoky haze. Fear masked her face, but Nate read determination there, as well. He would have sighed in relief if he could have breathed at all.

Most people, Nate thought, would have let fear take advantage of them, freezing them immobile.

But not Jess.

Not his Jess.

They both heard the hiss and crack of the beam directly overhead before they saw it. As if in slow motion, Jess looked up, and Nate followed her gaze.

Sparks rained down on them, the only warning they had before the beam came loose and pitched downward.

Jess let go of Nate's hand and instinctively sheltered her head, but it was too late.

The heavy beam of flaming wood crashed down on top of her. She jerked, her eyes wide in surprise, and reached out for Nate. Then she fell lifeless as the beam slammed into her shoulder and crushed her beneath its weight.

"Jess!" Nate screamed, scrambling forward. He fell to his knees as a wave of dizziness overtook him, but he continued to crawl forward, fighting the looming blackness with all his might.

A dry sob racked his body as he reached Jess's unmoving form, covered horizontally by the fallen beam of wood.

He wanted to cry.

He wanted to pray.

But one thought obscured all the rest. He didn't know nor did he care whether it was just in his head, or whether he was screaming out loud.

This couldn't be happening.

Not Jess. Not Jess. Not Jess.

"No-o-o-o-o!"

Chapter 15

Nate lunged forward, his arms outstretched toward Jess, and then slammed to his hands and knees on the floor when his forward momentum was crushed by someone suddenly clasping his ankle in a firm grip.

Groaning, he glanced behind him. The two firemen who had been at the window had now entered the building. The first one, clutching Nate's ankle in a viselike grip, was now pulling him backward. The second firefighter was gesturing at Nate and pointing toward the broken window and their only means of escape.

Nate's gaze swung back to Jess. She wasn't moving. He couldn't tell if she was breathing.

He knew what the firefighters wanted him to do.

Exit. Immediately.

Leave the rescuing to the experts, the men who were well-versed in what flames and smoke could do.

They might be heroes. And they might be right. Nate could hinder them as much as he could help them, especially if they became more focused on getting him out alive than in rescuing Jess.

His heart and his mind tugged in two different directions, but only for a split second. He relaxed his leg for a moment and then yanked hard, surprising the man who was gripping his ankle and breaking away.

He scrambled forward, his heart slamming into his chest. His lungs felt as if they were going to explode, but he ignored the sensation and plunged ahead through the billowing smoke.

He was thankful his mind was military-hardwired for crisis, for otherwise he never would have been able to keep it together.

Kneeling beside Jess, he leaned forward, checking her vital signs and praying all the while.

She wasn't moving.

But she was breathing. Barely.

And that beam had to weigh a ton. It was crushing her. Thankfully, it didn't appear to be burning, though it was no doubt smoldering.

He scrambled to the side, where the end of the beam lay at an upward angle, jutting off Jess's back. He had to get that rafter off her *now*. Then he could figure out how to move her without harming her more than she already probably was.

It looked bad.

He felt worse.

He didn't know what was sensible anymore. He only knew he had to do something, and pray it was the right thing. Pulling his jacket sleeves over his hands for protection, he wrapped his arms around the rafter and pulled with all his might.

Nothing.

The beam didn't so much as budge.

Nate couldn't see if there was anything covering the other end of the rafter, but he thought it might be lodged tight in some other debris. A lot had fallen from the ceiling when the beam gave way.

He wished he could see better.

He wished he could breath at all.

He had to move that beam.

Praying with all his might, he embraced the adrenaline coursing through him and felt his fear. He knew from experience his terror would either render him useless or give him extra strength.

The first firefighter reached Jess and was assessing her condition. The other man had gone back toward the window. Nate didn't know why he was backtracking, nor did he care.

He closed his eyes, gritted his teeth and pulled, straining every muscle in his back and shoulders and legs. Sweat streamed into his eyes, stinging them with the ash covering his forehead. He coughed and gagged from the smoke and the exertion.

But the rafter moved.

Nate didn't hesitate for an instant. Bracing himself, he leaned into it, forcing the wood away from Jess's upper body and hoping the momentum created by his weight and his effort would be enough to make the rafter clear her legs and feet.

The beam came crashing down to the floor again, splintering bits of wood and plaster underneath it, and

Nate winced. If he hadn't moved it far enough, he had just added to Jess's injuries.

The same firefighter that had grabbed his ankle earlier suddenly appeared at his elbow, thumping him on the shoulder and urging him back toward the window. Ignoring him, Nate dropped to his hands and knees and scuttled forward, desperate to see if he had, in fact, pushed the rafter far enough to clear Jess's body, or if he'd merely pinned her anew.

It was difficult to see anything through the thick, black smoke, but his hand made contact with Jess's foot. The smoldering beam lay several inches past the end of her body.

She was free.

But not yet safe.

The firefighter he had repeatedly brushed off was at his elbow again, this time grasping Nate firmly by the shoulders and propelling him toward the window, brooking no argument.

This time Nate didn't fight back, but allowed himself to be pushed wherever the fireman willed. His lungs were screaming for oxygen. He wasn't going to be any help to anyone if he passed out, especially if he was still within the building.

It was time to let the firefighters do their jobs, he thought, his whole body suddenly so weak he could barely move. As he crawled through the broken window, he could see they had already placed a collar around Jess's neck and were rolling her onto a board.

Nate fell to his knees when he hit the ground on the outside of the building. Smoke and flames billowed through the window he'd just dropped from, but close to the ground, he was able to take great, sweeping breaths of outside air, which sent him into a fit of coughing that racked his aching body.

He had to move.

For Jess. For Gracie.

But he found he couldn't. His arms and legs felt impossibly heavy, and his mind was clogged and dizzy, almost as if he had been drugged. A persistent, angry headache was slamming at his temples.

He had nothing left to give, he thought miserably. No more strength left to fight with.

And he knew why. He had done everything he could, but his girls might not make it. Grief washed over him in unceasing waves. How would he go on if he lost Jess or Gracie?

Faith.

This was where the rubber met the road. He'd been wrestling with his faith in God. Now was the time to use it.

He reached deep down inside himself, searching for strength, but found none.

And then his soul stretched upward, seeking God's presence as never before.

To his very great surprise, he found it. Or rather, God found him. Strength, peace and love as Nate had never before experienced replaced his fear and set aside his panic. Though his headache persisted, his mind cleared. And though he continued to hack and cough, his soul breathed the fresh air of God's presence.

He groaned and tried to roll to his feet, but he was so shaky he couldn't make it off his hands and knees. He knew he was in the way. Firefighters were pouring out the window, leveraging the board which carried an unconscious Jess. Efficiently and quickly, they passed her through to safety, and the last firefighter crawled through the window after her.

The two paramedics on the scene were already there, rushing to Jess's side as they jogged her farther away from the building. Someone placed an oxygen mask over her face. Nate couldn't see anything else, couldn't tell if she was all right, if anything was broken. Even if he could have seen her, he had no way of knowing if she was going to survive.

Suddenly someone dropped a thick wool blanket over Nate's shoulders. Strong arms looped under his shoulders and drew him to his feet.

Hazily, Nate glanced upward.

Vince.

"Come on now, little brother," Vince said. "You're in the way, as usual."

Vince's teasing tone overlaid his more serious expression. Nate didn't know why Vince was here, but he'd never been as glad to see his brother as he was at that moment.

With Vince's assistance, Nate managed to swerve drunkenly toward the waiting ambulance, where they were already bundling Jess inside.

Behind him there was a big whoosh as the once-solid structure of the day care collapsed from the heat. Firefighters were dousing it with water, but it was far too late to save the building.

But not, Nate prayed, the human beings.

"Gracie," he choked out raggedly, his voice hoarse from the ash he had inhaled. The children huddling by the tree line were being herded into the day care van by the teachers, presumably on their way to be checked out at the hospital in Boulder.

But Nate could see no sign of Gracie.

"Where's my baby?" he rasped, grasping desperately for the collar of Vince's jacket.

"She's already on her way to the hospital," Vince informed him tightly, pulling on his sleeve and urging him to sit down by the ambulance. Nate's knees were shaky and he thought he might fall down if he didn't sit down, so he slumped to the ground.

"How is she? Is she…?" He couldn't seem to get the words out.

Vince crouched in front of Nate and clasped him on the shoulders. "Gracie is already on her way to the hospital in Boulder," he repeated. "The first ambulance took off with her several minutes ago."

A female paramedic approached and Vince stepped away as she placed a pulse-ox monitor on Nate's finger and checked his lungs with her stethoscope. Nate wanted to brush her away, but he was too fatigued to move.

"Is she…?" Nate repeated, unable to complete his thought.

"She's going to be fine," Vince said with a clipped nod. Nate wasn't so sure, from the way his brother set his jaw after he spoke.

"She was unconscious when I passed her through the window."

"I know," Vince said. "But she quickly regained consciousness after the paramedics worked on her and gave her some oxygen."

"Thank God," Nate murmured.

"Amen," Vince answered, sounding as choked up as Nate felt. He chuckled, a dry, forced sound. "It looked to me like Gracie was giving the paramedics a hard time when they bundled her into the ambulance. I think she wanted her daddy."

Nate tried to smile but couldn't.

"I've got to get there," he mumbled, as much to himself as to Nate.

"You will, brother. If I have any say in the matter, you'll be taking this ambulance with Jess."

Nate grimaced. He didn't need medical attention. Jess did. She had been so brave, not thinking of herself at all as she had burst into the blazing building. Were it not for her, there would be many grieving parents right now. Nate most of all.

"And the other kids?" he asked.

"All safe," Vince assured him. "The teachers have contacted all the parents, and they will be using the day care van to take them down to the emergency room to be checked out for smoke inhalation. But the important part is that everyone made it out alive, thanks in great part to you and Jess."

"Jess," Nate repeated, his throat stinging as he spoke, as much from raw emotion as from the smoke he had inhaled.

The female paramedic broke in to tell Nate he could ride along with Jess in the ambulance, but that they needed to go now.

"You're a hero, little brother," Vince said, supporting Nate as he rose. "Foolish, but a hero nonetheless. You saved Jess's life back there."

Nate shook his head, then ducked into the ambulance to take a seat by Jess's still form. He reached out and gently traced her forehead with his finger. He couldn't stand to see her this way, so utterly still and silent and devoid of life.

But she *was* alive, Nate reminded himself. Her chest was rising and falling with precious oxygen, and the paramedics were busy making her stable.

"I'll follow the ambulance down and meet you at the hospital," Vince told him as the paramedics made to close the doors to the rescue vehicle.

"But the day care—"

"Is a goner. There's nothing I can do here. The fire department has it under control. People before buildings, you know?"

Nate's eyes were stinging again, and he didn't think it was because of the smoke and ash. He swallowed the lump in his throat with difficulty.

"Thank you," he whispered raggedly.

Vince gave a clipped nod and his jaw tightened. "Just be well, Nate. You have a couple of very important ladies depending on you."

Not that Nate needed to be reminded of that very sobering thought, but he thrust out his hand toward Vince anyway. Vince clasped his hand forcefully, and Nate saw that his were not the only eyes watering.

For possibly the first time in his life, he knew what it felt like to have the support of family, Nate thought as the doors closed and the vehicle jerked into motion. He knew Jess would see it as a blessing rising from the ashes of tragedy and she wouldn't have hesitated a moment to tell him so.

And despite the fact that this ordeal was far from over, Nate found to his surprise that he could see the blessing through the tragedy, as well.

Nate wanted to smile, but simultaneously experienced the desire to weep. It wasn't over yet.

* * *

Vince thumped Nate on the back. Hard. "Don't scare me like that again, little brother."

"What?" Nate had been gazing down at Gracie, sleeping in a tented bassinet in the hospital neonatal intensive care unit, and his mind had been a million miles away, remembering the moment he had scribbled his signature on the papers that officially proclaimed him the baby girl's legal guardian.

Gracie had turned his life upside down, changed his whole reason for living. Raising a baby was the hardest thing he'd ever done, but it was also the most satisfying. He'd never imagined that the little lady could steal his heart away as she had.

And he'd never imagined he would also find the woman of his dreams. He'd figured his life was pretty much in a holding pattern once he'd become Gracie's guardian. Instead, he'd found Jess.

"What a little darlin'," Vince murmured, keeping one hand on Nate's back as they both leaned over the tented bassinet. "How's she doing?"

Nate breathed out on a sigh. "She's going to be fine. The doctors want to keep her overnight for observation, but they said that if all goes well, I can take her home in the morning."

Vince squeezed Nate's shoulder. "I'm glad. God is good."

"Yes," Nate whispered raggedly.

"And Jessica? Have you heard anything about her condition?"

Nate shook his head. "Not yet. They whisked her

away the moment we reached the hospital. I won't be able to see her until they admit her into a room."

"Intensive care?" Vince queried quietly and sympathetically.

He shrugged. "I don't know yet."

"Well, she's not alone. And neither are you. I'll wait with you."

"You don't have to do that. I know you must be anxious to get back to the lodge."

Vince scowled, reminiscent of old times. "You know better than to tell me what to do. I said I'm going to wait with you, and that's exactly what I intend to do. End of subject."

True to his word, Vince stayed by Nate's side as they waited for word on Jess in the emergency waiting room. Nate asked to see her, but as the doctors were working on her, he was not allowed to go in.

All he could think of was how she was alone, how he didn't want her to regain consciousness without him being by her side. If—*when* she opened her eyes, he wanted her to see him there. She had been through enough pain and abandonment in her life. Nate wanted to make sure that didn't happen again.

Ever.

He wished for the hundredth time that day that he had spoken to her earlier, told her the deepest feelings of his heart before it might be too late to tell her at all. There was so much he wanted to say, so much he needed her to know about him. About her.

About them.

But of course he couldn't have said anything to her even if he'd gotten up the nerve, for a very simple reason.

Because he wasn't right with God. And until that happened, it wouldn't be right to ask Jess for more than friendship. She deserved to have a man by her side who shared her precious faith, and Nate wasn't yet that man, though he wanted to be.

For Jess. For Gracie.

But most of all, for himself. He recognized the truth, and prayed that it would, as the Scriptures said, set him free.

A feeling Nate couldn't begin to explain washed over him as he realized God was no longer on some high, unattainable mountaintop.

The truth *had* set him free.

And it had happened when he had least expected it, in that moment when everything had changed. He had faced his worst nightmare—losing the two people who meant the most in the world to him.

And God had been there.

Nate didn't know what had changed, or why. Only that somehow, the faith he couldn't seem to wrap his mind around had wrapped itself around his heart. It was a mystery he wasn't sure he would ever understand, but he would thank God for it every day of his life.

He couldn't wait to tell Jess the good news. She would be overjoyed at Nate's newfound faith.

If he ever got to tell her.

He was as frightened as he had ever been in his life. He'd already known he'd fallen hard for Jess, but it wasn't until he'd heard the ominous cracking of the beam over her head at the day care that he had realized the true depth and breadth of his love for her.

Somehow he had to convince her his love was real,

a forever love that would carry them through the rest of their lives.

He had to tell her.

It had been two hours, and Nate hadn't heard a word. Vince still sat beside him, his head bowed and his hands clasped. Nate thought he might be praying. There was a lot about his brother that Nate didn't know.

Suddenly Nate couldn't sit still a moment longer. He stood and stretched his sore muscles, then tensed as one of the emergency room doctors strode through the double doors that led back to the emergency triage.

The doctor's scrubs looked as wrinkled as his brow. As he glanced expectantly around the waiting room, Nate strode forward.

"I'm looking for information on Jessica Sabin," he said without preamble. "Do you know anything?"

The doctor stared at Nate a moment without answering, and then nodded, his expression serious. "Are you family, sir?"

"I came in on the ambulance with her," Nate said. "She has no family."

Except for me and Gracie, he thought, his chest clenching. "Is she okay?"

The doctor hesitated as if trying to decide whether or not to disclose any information to Nate. Nate drew himself to his full height and took a step forward, grasping the doctor on his upper arm.

"Please. If you know anything…I've been waiting for hours."

Finally, the green-scrubbed doctor nodded. "She is in stable condition. Miraculously, no bones were broken, but she inhaled a lot of smoke. That is our greatest concern at the moment."

"Can I talk to her?"

"I'm sorry, but no. She hasn't yet regained consciousness."

"What?" Nate's grip tightened reflexively on the doctor's arm. Murmuring an apology, Nate took a step back and released his hold on the doctor. "That's bad, isn't it?"

The doctor's lips drew together in a firm line. "It could be."

Nate felt as if he'd been struck as his breath heaved out of his lungs. The roaring in his head intensified and all the colors of the room faded to black and white, like a television with a malfunctioning picture tube.

His knees might have given way, but suddenly Vince was there beside him, propping him up with a strong, steady arm under his.

"Take it easy, there, bro," Vince whispered, loud enough for Nate's ears alone. "Be strong."

Vince turned his attention to the doctor. "So what's the next step? Is there anything you can do to help Jessica regain consciousness?"

The doctor shook his head. "We wait."

Nate pulled back his shoulders and fought against the deafening noise in his head. "Can I see her, please? I just want to be by her side."

"We're moving her upstairs now. Room 455. You can visit her there. What is your name, sir? I'll let the nurses know you'll be coming."

"Nathan Morningway," he answered, a new wave of strength suddenly encompassing him.

Jess would wake up. She had to. And when she did, he would be there.

Chapter 16

Jessica's nose itched.

Without opening her eyes, she reached up to scratch it, but her hand felt unusually heavy, too weighty to lift. There was something lying across her cheekbones, plastic tubing of some kind, she thought drowsily.

How long had she been sleeping?

The air streaming from the tubing was what was making Jessica's nose itch so bad, she realized. She now recognized it must be oxygen tubing draped around her ears, but she couldn't immediately remember where she was or why she needed oxygen.

She tried her left hand and made contact with her nose, but the movement caused the back of her hand to prick with a sharp, needlelike sensation, and her whole body ached as if she had been on the losing end of a fistfight.

Groaning inwardly, she tried to open her eyes.

Where was she?

Light was streaming in through the half-open blinds on the window, and it took a moment for her eyesight to adjust to the brightness. She didn't recognize the room at all, though she now realized the stinging sensation on her left hand was from an IV drip, and her right hand was tightly bandaged.

And she hurt, worse than she ever thought possible. It wasn't localized pain, but more of a radiating muscle ache, everywhere at once.

Panic edged through her as her whereabouts finally struck home. It all came rushing back to her—the fire at the day care. The sting of the black, billowing smoke filling her lungs.

The children. Gracie.

She caught her breath, remembering Nate passing the baby through the window he had smashed out with his elbow, into the arms of the firefighters hovering on the other side.

Gracie was safe. Wasn't she?

What had happened then? The last thing she remembered was hearing the beam above her head hiss and crack, just before it crashed down on her.

She was in a hospital.

She was in pain.

But, she recognized suddenly as her head drifted to the right, she wasn't alone.

There was a reason she hadn't been able to move her right arm up to her face, and it wasn't just that her hand was bandaged.

Nate was here.

He was asleep, slumped in a very uncomfortable-looking chair which he had pulled by her bedside. His head rested at an awkward angle on one of his palms. His other hand gently covered her right shoulder.

Though her muscles ached with the effort, she drew herself carefully to her side. Nate didn't budge. She didn't know how long he'd been sleeping that way, but there was no way he could be comfortable. He must be truly exhausted to be sleeping so soundly in such an awkward position.

Easing her left hand over her body, she reached out and ran her fingers down Nate's stubbly jaw. His chiseled features were boyish and relaxed in sleep, and his hair had grown out enough that it was adorably disheveled and sticking at various angles from his scalp like a ruffled porcupine.

She loved this man. So much so that her heart ached worse than her bruised body.

The thought came so quickly she couldn't have quelled it if she tried—and she didn't even want to try. There was no way to deny the way her heart sang when she was around Nate.

She hadn't been looking for love, but Nate and Gracie had found her anyway. The moment the gruff marine had walked into the doorway of Morningway Lodge toting his sweet baby girl, her life had changed irrevocably.

And, she thought, smiling softly, definitely for the better.

She had been so paralyzed by her past that she couldn't see the good gifts God had given her right under her nose. How could she ever have denied the feelings that were now so prominent in her heart?

Nate gave a cute little snort and jerked awake, his eyes wide as they focused down on her.

"You're awake," he breathed, his voice laced with relief and thankfulness. "Thank God. Jess, you had me so scared."

Jessica tried to nod, but the small movement sent ripples of pain throbbing through her head and all the way down to her toes. Groaning from deep within her chest, she rolled onto her back.

"Don't try to move, sweetheart. You've been through the ringer. How are you feeling?"

"Gracie?" she croaked through parched lips, ignoring Nate's fervent question about her own health.

Nate smiled and gently brushed her hair off her forehead with his palm. "Gracie is fine, honey. Thanks to you."

She breathed a sigh of relief. "And the rest of the children?"

"Also fine," he confirmed. "Everyone got out of the building safely. In fact, no one else besides you and Gracie had to be hospitalized."

"Hospitalized?" Jessica repeated, horror returning with reinforcements. "I thought you said Gracie was okay?"

Before Nate could answer her harried question, a nurse entered the room.

"I'm glad to see you're awake," the nurse said, hovering over Jessica and wrapping a blood pressure cuff around the upper part of her right arm. She tossed a sideways glance at Nate. "I'll have to ask you to leave now while the doctor checks her out."

"Yes, of course," Nate answered, scooting out of his chair and kissing Jessica on the brow. "I'll be back soon, sweetheart."

"But—" Jessica started, and was interrupted by Nate shaking his head.

"You take it easy." He exited the room with such swiftness that Jessica could not even finish her statement before he was gone.

"And how are we feeling this morning?" the nurse asked compassionately as she jotted the numbers from the blood pressure monitor onto a clipboard.

Jessica licked her dry lips before answering. Her throat was raw and burning.

"Sore," she murmured, punctuated by a low groan as muscles she didn't know she had clenched and released, spasming painfully.

The nurse smiled and patted her arm. "I know, dear. You must feel like you've been trampled by a herd of wild elephants."

Jessica twisted her lips. "Uh-huh. Something like that."

"You just relax, dear. I can give you something for the pain. You're just lucky to be in one piece. Not a single broken bone, and no serious burns, despite being hit with that beam, except for your hand, but that should heal nicely."

The nurse hovered over Jessica again, this time thrusting a thermometer under her tongue. "You've suffered from a bit of smoke inhalation, and probably a bad concussion, but the paramedics on the scene had you quickly stabilized. Now that you are awake and alert, I think you will mend up just fine."

Jessica groaned again. She didn't feel fine. Not without Nate at her side.

The nurse just smiled in encouragement. "I know you feel pretty banged up, but believe me, it could have been a lot worse. The way I hear it, that young man who just left saved your life."

"Nate?" Jessica struggled to remember what had happened after the beam fell on her, but came up blank. The last thing she remembered was looking into Nate's panicked eyes and thinking that was the last thing she was ever going to see.

She had reached for him, and then...

Nothing.

"Do you know what happened?" she asked, her heart fluttering with more than curiosity. Had Nate risked his own life for hers?

"Well, I don't know all the details," the nurse chatted conversationally, waving her arms as she spoke. "What I heard was that your young man ignored the direction of the firefighters and wouldn't leave the building until you were safe. He pulled the beam off you single-handedly, I believe they said."

"Oh, my," Jessica breathed. "And he wasn't hurt?"

The nurse shook her head. "Not so far as I know. A real hero, that one is."

"Yes, he is," Jessica agreed around the lump growing in her throat. It wasn't smoke inhalation making her throat burn now.

The nurse continued to speak as she administered pain medication through Jessica's IV, but the medicine made her instantly groggy and she found it hard to follow the nurse's random, yet comforting chatter. She was only half aware of the doctor checking her over, and cringed only slightly when he shined a penlight directly into her eyes.

"Your pupils are reacting normally," the doctor briskly informed her.

She stared up at him, waiting for him to explain what that meant, and wondering when Nate would come back and see her again.

"That is very good news for you," the doctor continued. "I think the worst of your injuries are the burn on your hand, some bumps and bruises, and minor smoke inhalation. Your condition is no longer critical, so we'll be moving you down to the third floor. I'm going to keep you here one more night just to be certain, but if all goes well, we can release you tomorrow morning. I'll write you a prescription for some painkillers to take along with you."

Painkillers were the last thing on Jessica's mind. Her head was foggy from this latest round of meds, and now more than ever she wanted to be thinking clearly, not be in a medicated daze.

How was she going to tell Nate what was in her heart if she couldn't even form the words in her head?

She half dozed as the orderlies moved her from one room to another, but she was instantly alert when Nate came into the room.

"Are you up for some company?"

Jessica smiled until her face hurt when Nate entered the room carrying Gracie in his arms. When the baby saw Jessica, she giggled and flapped her arms.

"Take it easy, baby girl," Nate said with a laugh. "Jess can't hold you right now. She has enough bruises for one day, thank you very much."

Jessica's arms ached to hold Gracie and smell her sweet baby smell, but she knew Nate was right. She wasn't strong enough right now to keep a wiggly baby safe in her arms, no matter how much her heart wanted Gracie near.

"She's sure happy to see you," Nate commented, chuckling again. "As well she should be, since you saved her life."

Jessica knew her cheeks were stained with color from the wave of sudden shyness that overtook her. She didn't know how to handle Nate's compliments, and it unsettled her more than she cared to admit.

Nate moved to the edge of the bed and carefully propped himself on his hip, allowing Jessica to be near Gracie without having to strain herself to hold the baby.

"I admire you so much," he said, his voice low and rough and his gold-flecked green eyes glowing. "You didn't just save Gracie's life, Jess. You saved all those other little kids, too. If it weren't for you dashing headfirst into that burning building, who knows how things would have turned out."

His gaze narrowed on her. "Although, to be honest, at the moment, I wanted to throttle you for risking your own life that way."

Jessica reached for Nate's hand and squeezed it with all her remaining strength. "The way I hear it, you're the hero."

Nate immediately shook his head in denial, but Jessica pushed her point.

"Deny it all you want, Mr. Tough Guy Marine," she said, and chuckled. "I'm still going to say it. Thank you for saving my life."

He shook his head once again. "It was nothing. Really. I'm just glad you're okay. What did the doctor say?" he continued in an obvious diversion tactic, meant to take the heat off him.

"The doctor says I'll probably be able to go home tomorrow," she informed him. "And I can't wait to get back home. I hate hospitals."

"Me, too," Nate agreed. "But are you sure you'll be ready to go back home by tomorrow? How are you going to take care of yourself?"

Jessica barked out a laugh at Nate's obvious distress. "The way I always have. I've suffered more than a few bruises in my lifetime."

Nate brushed her cheek with his palm and stared deep into her eyes.

"More than your share," he whispered, his ragged voice frayed at the ends.

She shook her head, ignoring the throbbing pain. "I have no cause to complain."

"Oh, Jess," he murmured, leaning closer. "I don't know how I would have handled it if you had been seriously injured."

Her heart hammered in her head, replacing the throbbing headache with a new sensation. She tried to swallow, but her throat was too dry and scratchy. She hesitated with the question poised on the tip of her tongue, but at length she could stand it no longer.

"Why?" she inquired softly, half afraid to hear the answer but needing to know just the same.

Nate's gaze swept away from her and focused somewhere out the window, which was telling in itself. There was nothing to view except the stark windows and brick exterior of another wing of Our Lady of Mercy Hospital. He bit his bottom lip reflectively.

Jessica immediately regretted asking the question, and would have wished it away if she could have. She had obviously embarrassed him by putting him on the spot. She should have known he didn't necessarily re-ciprocate the depth of what she felt for him. She cer-tainly shouldn't have pushed him. She had no right.

Nate was enough of a gentleman not to want to hurt her when she was down, and he clearly didn't know how to answer her abrupt question. How had she not realized what she was doing to him? The medicine must have addled her brain more than she had realized.

Heat flooded to her face as she searched for some-thing to say that would effectively take Nate off the grandstand she'd placed him on. She would say any-thing if it would return the smile to his face.

After a long moment of silence, Nate's gaze returned to hers. His eyes appeared shiny and glassy, and he shrugged as if apologizing for taking his time.

She shook her head, trying to figure out a way to apologize for putting him on the spot.

"I don't know if now is the right time," he began, then cleared his throat over his rough voice. "But I have to speak."

Jessica held her breath, waiting for him to continue, expecting he would try to let her down easy, given the circumstances.

"I cannot imagine where Gracie and I would be with-out you," he said, his voice still filled with gravel. "If you hadn't shown up in our lives when you did, who knows whether or not I could have coped with becom-ing a new father."

"You would have done fine," she assured him, her throat so dry she could barely speak. Tears pricked at the backs of her eyes. "You love Gracie. You would have found a way."

"I'm not so sure about that," he replied, shaking his

head. "Either way, though, it would have been a lot rougher a ride for me without your encouragement."

"I'm glad I could help," she said, and she knew it was true. Whatever Nate was trying to get at, and even if her heart was about to be broken once again, she could never regret the time she had spent with Nate and Gracie. She would treasure those memories forever.

His gaze captured hers. "I guess you already know I'm in love with you."

Her sudden intake of breath was audible to both of them, and her hands were trembling.

"I'm sorry," he apologized immediately. "I knew I should have waited until later to say something, until you've had more time to recuperate. I'm an insensitive oaf."

"You," Jessica argued softly, "are the kindest, most patient, most wonderful man in the whole world."

Hope flamed from his eyes as he reached for her hand and held it gently. He didn't speak for a moment as he stared down at their interlocked fingers.

"When you ran into the blaze to save the children, I thought my world might end. I didn't know what I would do if I lost you."

"But you didn't."

"No. And to my great surprise, I was never alone, not even when I didn't know if you and Gracie were going to be okay."

His gaze beamed even brighter. What was he trying to tell her?

"God was there," he said simply.

She squeezed his hand, joy flooding through her at his admission. "I'm glad."

"Me, too," he agreed. "More than you know."

He paused, pursing his lips as he considered his next words.

"Jess?" he asked softly.

"Yes?" Her heart was roaring in her ears so loudly that she wasn't certain she'd be able to hear him when he spoke.

"I know you've been through a lot, both in your past, and now with the fire. You've suffered pain and loss that I've only had a glimpse of, but somehow I think that is part of what makes you the strong, vibrant woman I see before me now."

"Oh, Nate," she breathed.

"You're the kind of woman I never even dared to dream about," he continued. "I never expected to find the love of my life, especially not coming home to Morningway Lodge, which always held bad memories for me.

"But I did. I found you. I love you. And I want to make you happy."

"You do," she assured him.

He leaned in closer, so that his face was only inches from hers. Baby Gracie was still cuddled into his chest, but she didn't add distance between them; rather, she seemed to complete the little circle of their love. "Will you be my wife?"

She couldn't speak, and stared at him wide-eyed and trembling.

"I know that's asking a lot from you. I come with strings attached. Marrying me means becoming Gracie's mother. But I know Gracie loves you as much as I do. Please say you'll make our family complete. Can you see us as part of your future?"

Jessica brushed her palm across Nate's cheek. Even with her commitment phobia, she could not deny the love in his eyes, nor the answering beat of her own heart.

"You and Gracie *are* my future," she whispered raggedly. "And I can't imagine anything that would give me greater joy than to be your wife and Gracie's mama."

"Ma-ma-ma-ma-ma," Gracie squealed, patting Jessica and Nate on the head simultaneously.

They both laughed. Ignoring her body aches, the IV drip and her bandaged hand, she wrapped her arms around Nate and the baby and tipped her chin up to receive Nate's gentle, bargain-sealing kiss.

God was good, all the time. He had known the desire of Jessica's heart before she even knew herself, and had blessed her with a hope and a future that she never would have imagined.

"My family." She said the words aloud, wondering how one human being could experience as much joy as was flooding from her heart at that moment. "God has blessed me with a family."

The next day, while the doctor signed Jess's release papers, Nate stepped out of the room to call his brother to inform him of his plans.

"Vince," Nate said when his brother picked up the line. "Jess is being released from the hospital today. I was wondering if you could meet us at her cabin to help her get settled in?"

"Of course," Vince answered immediately. "How is she doing?"

"Better," Nate assured him. "But she has to rest and

recuperate for a while before she'll be all the way back to normal."

"I imagine so."

"Meet us at Jess's cabin in an hour and a half?" Nate queried.

"You got it, bro."

Nate clicked his cell phone off and stuffed it in his jacket pocket, but he didn't immediately return to Jess's room. He closed his eyes, savoring the excitement of the moment.

He and Jess hadn't yet told anyone of their engagement. Vince would be the first to know. And for some reason Nate didn't really understand, he couldn't wait to share his good news with his brother.

Up until the day of the fire, Vince would have been the last person Nate would want to share good news with. There was still a niggling of doubt in his mind of whether or not Vince would approve of the engagement, and an even bigger uncertainty as to why that mattered one way or the other.

Why did he care what Vince thought?

But he did. Something had changed between him and his brother. It was small, but it was a start to rebuilding a relationship with him.

At least, that was what Nate hoped.

It was another half an hour before Nate had Jess strapped into his Jeep for the drive back up to Morningway Lodge. The road was bumpy even before they hit the washboard dirt, and Nate worried for Jess's comfort. Out of his peripheral vision, he saw her clench her jaw a few times, but she never complained aloud.

Still, she was looking fatigued by the time they reached her cabin. Vince's SUV was parked in front, and he was leaning against the hood, waiting. As soon as Nate parked the Jeep, Vince moved to the passenger door to help Jess out of the vehicle.

"Are you sure she should be out of the hospital already?" Vince asked Nate over Jess's head.

"*She* can hear you," Jess complained playfully. "And trust me, I'm going to get a lot more rest in my own bed than I did at the hospital."

Vince scowled. "I still don't like the idea of her—you—being alone up here."

"She won't be alone," Nate assured him, swiftly unbuckling Gracie from her car seat and lifting her into his arms.

"I can check with the Rocky Mountain Rehabilitation Hospital to see if they have any nurses available. At least for the first few days."

Nate flashed his brother a wide grin. "Not necessary, bro."

"I just think that—"

Nate held up his hand to stop Vince's flow of words. "You're going to have to put up with my presence here at Morningway Lodge for a little longer, I'm afraid."

Vince looked flustered. He shook his head. "You're welcome to stay on here. The lodge is your home as much as it is mine."

Nate smiled at the unexpectedly welcome tone in Vince's voice. "I'm glad to hear it. This may be permanent."

"Yeah?" Vince asked.

"Yeah," Nate agreed. "I'll personally see to it that Jess isn't left alone, and that she rests up according to the doctor's orders. Believe me, no one is more worried about the health of my future wife than I am."

His grin widened at Jess's surprised gasp of breath and the way Vince took a literal step backward, as if someone had punched him.

"Your *what?*" Vince squawked, looking between Nate and Jess in disbelief. "Did I hear you right?"

Nate experienced one brief moment of uncertainty about Vince's reaction, but he quickly brushed it off.

Did he really care how Vince took the news? Nate was marrying the most wonderful woman in the world. Life didn't get any better than this, and Nate was going to enjoy every moment of it.

"Jess has agreed to become my wife," Nate announced, moving to Jess's other side and draping his arm across her shoulder.

Her answering smile meant everything to him.

"Seriously?" Vince asked, his voice rising to an unusually high pitch.

Jess's smile didn't change, nor did the love flowing from her eyes, but Nate felt her shoulders tense under his arm.

To his surprise, she winked at him before turning to Vince. "Seriously."

"W-well, then," Vince stammered. It was the first time Nate could remember seeing his brother lose his self-possession. He waited, holding his breath, to find out whether that was a good thing or a bad thing.

"I see," Vince continued, his expression still deadly serious. "You're sure about this? Hitching yourself up to this fellow?"

Jess beamed. "More sure than I've ever been about anything in my whole life."

"Even though he has a baby?"

"*Especially* because he has a baby," she assured him

with a laugh. "Who could resist this gruff marine when he's holding that cute little baby girl in his arms?"

Vince pressed his free hand to his hip and cocked his head to one side, sizing Nate up as if considering whether or not Jess's words were true.

Nate stared at the pair, speechless, feeling as if he were a zoo animal on display.

Suddenly, Vince's face split into a grin. "You've got a point there."

"Of course I do." She wrapped her arm around Nate's waist and squeezed him hard, then winked at Vince. "Honestly, I couldn't possibly love your brother more than I do. And I love Gracie as if she was my own daughter."

Her eyes misted, but only for a moment, and then she smiled radiantly.

Vince shrugged and chuckled. "In that case, let me be the first to welcome you to the family."

He leaned down and pressed a kiss to Jess's cheek, then reached around her to slap Nate on the back. "Well done, little brother."

"I'll say," he agreed, pulling Jess even closer against him. With Gracie in one arm and Jess in the other, he turned them all toward Jess's cabin.

"Come on, now," he murmured, his heart welling with so much love he wondered how he could bear the weight of it. "Let's go home."

* * * * *